Praise from Britain
for *The Golden Cat*

"A magical tale . . . Part feline *Watership Down* and part highly original adventure story, it shows there's more to the fantasy genre than goblins, wizards, and improbably proportioned women."
—*The Daily Mirror* (London)

"This splendid sequel to *The Wild Road* features an unforgettable cast of fur and blood characters on a globe-trotting mission of rescue—and deftly establishes author Gabriel King as new master of epic fantasy."
—Amazon.co.uk

*Please turn the page
for more reviews. . . .*

"EXHILARATING . . .

The love of language simply spills off the page—I found myself stopping constantly to savour phrases. The feline protagonists are wonderfully realized. . . . King has a painter's eye, and the scenes in New Orleans in particular are sensually and vividly described. . . . The plot climaxes with a literally earthshaking supernatural confrontation. . . . A very enjoyable read."

—*Starburst*

"Utterly engrossing. A truly magical adventure for each and every animal lover."

—*Animal Watch*

Praise for Gabriel King's previous novel, *The Wild Road*

"Most enjoyable . . . The exploits of the kitten are so easy to believe and although the story is sometimes sad, it is always intriguing, making the book difficult to put down. . . . As a fanatical cat lover and owner, I would recommend this book to everyone, and if, like me, there are people who believe in the spiritual awareness of cats, they will be moved, saddened but ultimately overjoyed at this tale."
— RICHARD ADAMS
Author of *Watership Down*

"A diverting fantasy tale."
— *USA Today*

"Unabashed, freewheeling fantasy in the great Battle of Good against Evil tradition . . . [with] a fine Dickensonian multitude of characters, cats and otherwise."
— *Realms of Fantasy*

"An adventure story filled with heroes and villains, a fantastic, perilous voyage over land and sea, a true odyssey . . . *The Wild Road* succeeds on many levels. Its characters are well drawn, and it is beautifully written and filled with suspense."
— *ASPCA Animal Watch*

By Gabriel King
Published by Del Rey Books:

THE WILD ROAD
THE GOLDEN CAT

Books published by The Ballantine Publishing Group
are available at quantity discounts on bulk purchases
for premium, educational, fund-raising, and special
sales use. For details, please call 1-800-733-3000.

THE
GOLDEN
CAT

Gabriel King

A Del Rey® Book
THE BALLANTINE PUBLISHING GROUP • NEW YORK

A Del Rey® Book
Published by The Ballantine Publishing Group
Copyright © 1999 by Gabriel King

www.randomhouse.com/delrey/

Library of Congress Catalog Card Number: 99-90789

ISBN 0-345-42305-4

Manufactured in the United States of America

First Hardcover Edition: May 1999
First Mass Market Edition: December 1999

10   9   8   7   6   5   4   3   2   1

*For all the cats that have died in the name of science.
May they rest in peace.*

CONTENTS

x   *Contents*

PART THREE: THE BRIGHT TAPESTRY

ACKNOWLEDGMENTS

With thanks to everyone who has provided inspiration and support during the writing of *The Golden Cat*; but particularly to Russ Galen, Veronica Chapman, Kuo-Yu Liang, and Eleanor Lang—and to all those who care for the feral cats of America. Thanks also to Xavier for help with the Cajun French!

Summoned or not, the god will come
From the inscription carved above the door
of Carl Gustav Jung's house

Legend tells of a Golden Cat, a creature of great and mystical power, sought by humans through the age. One desperate seeker came perilously close. His name was the Alchemist.

This man pursued the Golden Cat for three hundred years, prolonging his mortal span with magic distilled from the cats he bred and discarded in his quest, until finally he managed to procure the Queen of Cats, the beautiful Pertelot Fitzwilliam, from whom the precious kitten was destined to be born.

And thus began a terrible time for catkind: for the Alchemist was determined on his course, and with his magic and his army of alchemical cats he pursued the Queen and her consort, Ragnar Gustaffson, through the wild roads and across the land. Had it not been for the courage and resourcefulness of the friends they encountered in their flight—a silver cat known simply as Tag; a brave fox and a strutting magpie; the travelling cat, Sealink, and her heroic mate, Mousebreath; and especially for the sacrifice of the Alchemist's own cat, the wise old Majicou—the fate of all Felidae would even now hang in the balance.

But on the headland above sacred Tintagel, where the first royal cats forged the first wild roads, a momentous battle took place. At the height of that battle, the Queen's kittens were born: but even as the Alchemist strove to take them, so the Majicou struck. Together they fell; down from the cliffs, into the depths of the ocean; then up they soared into the radiant dome of the sky. Then, in a last despairing gesture, bound together by the hatred of hundreds of years, they plunged back down to Tintagel Head, where, in an eruption of dirt and vegetation, and a hot mist of vaporized rock, they drove themselves into the earth; and the earth sealed itself over them for ever; or so it seemed . . .

From The Ninth Life of Cats

PROLOGUE

A large gate tower once controlled access to the city from the east. Its excavated remains, reduced by time to seven or eight courses of pale gray stone, lie on the north bank not far upriver from the Fantastic Bridge. They are railed off so that human beings cannot fall in and hurt themselves. People are always to be seen here, whatever the weather. They walk about with that aimless human vigor, narrowing their eyes at things and talking their dull talk. They stare down into the asymmetric mass of the old tower. They boast about its walls—so sturdy and thick, packed with chalk ballast—as if they had built them only the other day. They draw one another's attention to the broken arrow slits, the rusty bolts, the chisel marks on the ancient stone, the doorstep clearly visible after all these years, polished by the passage of ten thousand feet.

The keep itself has a mossy, pebbled floor. Weeds infest its inner ledges, where the walls are streaked with moisture. Coins glint here and there: people have thrown them in for what they call in their dull, human way "luck."

The children gaze down and, a little mystified by the safety rails, ask their parents, "Mommy, are there tigers in here?"

"No dear, that's at the zoo," the parents say. "The tigers are only at the zoo."

But what do they know?

🐾

One unseasonable day at the end of spring, a cat flickered briefly into existence in the ruins. He was large and muscular and had the look of an animal who lived outdoors. His coat was pale metallic gray, tipped with black and shading to pure

1

white on his underside. It seemed to take up the dull, rainy light and give it back fourfold, so that he glowed amid the broken walls. His face, with its blunt muzzle and gently pointed ears, was decorated with patterns of a darker gray, and charcoal gray stripes broke up the outline of his forelegs. In that light his eyes were a strange, glaucous green, like old jade.

He stood alertly, with one forepaw raised, and sniffed the air. Then he vanished.

❦

When he reappeared, it was perhaps four hundred yards away in Royal Mint Courtyard, where similar ruins were exposed beneath the brutal concrete support piers of the modern building. The air was colder here, the old stone drier, sifting down like all human history into rubble and dust.

He looked around.

Something?

Nothing.

He sniffed the air again, and was gone.

❦

In this way he quartered the city.

He knew how to keep himself to himself. It was an old habit. Unless he wanted them to, people rarely knew he was there. A toddler caught sight of him from a window high up in some flats. An old woman wearing too many coats and cardigans bent to offer her hand for him to sniff. "Here puss! Puss?" He was already gone. He was already looking westward from the open bell tower of a church ten miles away, across the shiny slate rooftops of a million human houses.

Was it here?

It was not.

What a place the city is, he thought, as he flickered out of the bell tower. Bad air, worse food, dirt everywhere. And noise, noise, noise. Human beings don't care anymore. They're tired. They daren't admit to themselves what a mess they've made of things.

Now he stood in the middle of a narrow canal footbridge. From the northern bank, behind the moored barges, the sweet smell of hawthorn rolled toward him. Something moved on one of the moored barges, but it was only an ancient tabby barge cat with arthritic legs, fidgeting among the polished brass hardware under a line of damp laundry.

Was it here?

No.

He visited a burned-down warehouse in the docklands south of the river—appearing briefly at the base of a wall, nothing but a shadow, nothing but the filmy gray image of a cat caught turning away, dissolving back into the scaly old brickwork even as he arrived.

It wasn't there, either.

Finally he set himself to face the east, and an abandoned pet shop in a place called Cutting Lane.

❧

He stood uncertainly in the gloom, as he always did when he came here. A few feeble rays of light fell across the blackened wooden floors. There were faint smells of dust and mice, even fainter ones of straw and animal feed; and—there!—beneath it all, the smell of a human with a broom, long ago. If he listened, he could hear the broom scrape, scrape, scrape at the rats' nests of straw in the corners. He could smell a white sixteen-week kitten in a pen. The kitten was himself. Here he had taunted the rabbits and guinea pigs, eyed speculatively the captive finches. How they had chattered and sworn at him! He was always unsure what to feel about it all. Here his fortune had changed. Here the one-eyed black cat called Majicou had found him a home and changed his life forever. He still shivered to think of it.

"Majicou?" he whispered.

But he knew that the Majicou was long gone.

He sat down. He looked from corner to empty corner. He watched the motes dance in the rays of light. He thought hard. The color of his eyes changed slowly from jade to the lambent green of electricity.

"Something is wrong with the wild roads," he told himself, "but I don't know what it is."

His name was Tag and he was the guardian of those roads. At Cutting Lane, they stretched away from him in every direction like a vibrant, sticky web. He felt them near. He felt them call his name. He got to his feet, looked around a moment longer, and shook himself suddenly. He vanished, leaving only a slight disturbance of the dust and a trail of footprints that ended in mid-stride.

🐾

Now it was dusk, the time of water. Soft rain, hushed as mist, fell on broadloom lawns sloping down to a river. Gray willows overhung the dimpled water. The cat called Tag emerged from a hook of filmy light beside the wooden boathouse. He paused for a moment to sniff cautiously the damp air, then made his way without haste through drifts of last year's fallen leaves, across the lawns toward the great house above. It seemed to await him. He scampered across the terrace, up the broad flight of steps, halted on the worn wet flagstones to crane his neck up at the deserted iron-framed conservatories, derelict belvederes, and uncurtained windows that loomed above him, drawing his gaze all the way up to highest point of the roof, where the rain ran down a copper dome green with patina.

The great doors of the house lay open. He approached, then turned away to stare uncertainly across the twilit lawn, one paw raised. His own steps were visible as a dark meandering line in the wet glimmer of the grass. For a moment it seemed that he might retrace them, leave now, while he could . . .

It was an old house, and parts of it had been lived in until quite recently. Large high-ceilinged rooms, full of odds and ends and shrouded mirrors, opened off the gutted entrance hall. Tag fled in silence up the sweeping central staircase. His head appeared briefly between the mahogany banister rails of the mezzanine, as he looked back the way he had come. Up he went, until marble gave way to old dark wood, the stairwells narrowed to the width of a human torso, and the soft sounds of his progress were absorbed by swathes of cobweb stretched like rotten cheesecloth across every corner. He went up until he stood at the top of the house, at the entrance to the room below the copper dome. The door had jammed open two or three inches the last time it was used, but Tag knew he would not go in. He had tried and failed too many times before. In there, the copper dome brooded over a gathering night; in there, silence itself would bring an echo. Cold drafts flowed out even on a warm day, and the air was heavy with something that made his eyes water.

In there, the Alchemist had worked for centuries to make the Golden Cat.

Tag shivered.

He remembered Majicou again, and the events that had led, not so long before, to Majicou's death on Tintagel Head. Nothing could be concluded from those events. While something had ended there, Tag knew, nothing had been solved. This new mystery was a part of it. If there was an answer, much of it lay before him, for the faint, cold stink of the Alchemist was draped across the room like a shroud. One day he would be forced to go in and seek it. For now, it was sufficient to be aware of that. Equally, he knew, time was not in infinite supply.

"Something is wrong with the wild roads," he told himself again.

He turned and quickly descended all those stairs. Halfway down he thought he heard a voice calling him from a great distance. He stopped, lashed his tail, and half turned back, though he was sure the voice hadn't come from above. It was so faint he couldn't tell who it was, yet so familiar it almost spoke its own name.

It was full of urgency.

Part One

Things Fall Apart

Chapter One

A KINDLE OF KITTENS

The dog fox known to his friends as Loves a Dustbin lay in the late-afternoon shade of some gorse bushes on top of a Cornish headland, waiting for his old friend Sealink to make up her mind.

Long-backed, reddish, and brindled, he was strikingly handsome, until you saw that one of his flanks was completely gray, as if the fur there had somehow lost the will to retain its foxy hue. In another life, humans had shot him full of lead pellets; but for the support of his companions, his soul might have trickled away with the color of his coat. Now two of that gentle but determined company were no more, and the rest had begun to scatter. After such dangerous events, after a lifetime's service in another species's cause, it was strange for him to lie here in the sunshine and be an ordinary fox again, bathed in the warmth of the returning spring, the confectionary scent of the gorse. He rested his head on his paws and settled down, prepared to wait as long as necessary. Patience was a luxury his other life had not encouraged. He intended to explore it to the full.

His mate, a vixen from the suburbs by the name of Francine, very good-looking and therefore uninclined to give and take, sighed boredly and said, "Must we stay with her?"

"I promised Tag," he answered simply. "Anyway, she needs the company."

After a moment he admitted, "I know she's difficult to get on with."

At this, the vixen sniffed primly. Loves a Dustbin contemplated her out of the corner of his eye. She really was quite

9

fine. And the smell of her, along the cliff-top fields in the dusk or early morning! He would go anywhere for that smell.

"It's been a long, hard road for Sealink," he observed.

"Life's a long, hard road for all of us," said Francine, unaware perhaps that life had been rather kind to her so far, "with one thing or another all the way. Why should she make so much of it?" And, tawny eyes narrowed against the sun, she stared hard at the sturdy figure of Sealink, who was sitting perilously close to the edge of the cliff and looking vaguely but steadfastly out to sea. Every so often she blinked or her ears flexed as if calibrating the onshore breeze. Other than these small, precise movements, she showed no signs of life. Every line in her body spoke of deep preoccupation. This served to further irritate Francine, who said, "I have never understood your fondness for felines. Foxes have plenty to contend with in this world without having to bother themselves with cats, too." Then she added so quietly that Loves a Dustbin thought he might have misheard her, "These cats make such a meal of it all."

"Have a heart, Francine," he appealed. "She's sad, that's all."

And she was.

🐾

A wind-rinsed sky full of wheeling gulls, sunlight glittering far out on the water, sea shooshing inexorably back and forth: the day itself seemed to be urging Sealink to forget the things she had seen and done, the things she blamed herself for and couldn't change.

Time had passed since the battle with the Alchemist had left the grass of the cliff tops west of here scarred and scorched. More time, still, since her mate, that old bruiser, Mousebreath, had lost his own fight for life in some nameless part of the English countryside, borne down by a score of alchemical cats. Most of them had been among the deluded creatures who subsequently hurled themselves off the headland to fuel their master's unnatural powers. But Sealink had felt no satisfaction in that—not even when days later she had looked over the cliff and seen them there, a sodden mass of fur lining the shore as the tides pressed them gently but purposefully into the shingle. She had only been able to think, Where was I when he needed my help? Somewhere out at sea, bobbing up and down on a boat with Pengelly and Old Smoky the fisherman. Fulfilling some damn ancient prophecy. Helping a foreign queen get to Tintagel Head and give safe and timely birth to the very kittens who were the cause of all this tragedy.

It had been difficult for her to mask her pain over these last weeks; but most of the time none of her companions had been watching her, anyway. They were all bursting with relief and optimism. They had, after all, defeated the Alchemist. A few domestic cats and a dog fox had prevailed against appalling odds. They were still alive! They had new lives to make! Tag and Cy, reunited, chased and bit each other like youngsters. Ragnar Gustaffson, King of Cats, cornered whoever would listen and described in considerable detail his adventures on the wild road. Francine the vixen rubbed her head against Loves a Dustbin and promised him a life filled with Chinese take-away and sunlit parkland.

And as for the foreign queen's kittens . . .

One of them was the Golden Cat; one of them, when it grew up, would heal the whole hurt world. But who knew which of the three it was? No matter how hard she had stared at them, she hadn't been able to tell one from another. Tiny and blind looking, they had pushed and suckled and mewed and struggled. They had all looked the same. Like any kittens she'd ever seen . . .

Like her own litter, in that other existence of hers, in another country, another world. I'm still alive, she thought. Perhaps they are, too. Her own kittens! In that moment, she knew that there was only one journey she could make now. The world could never be whole again; but she would damned well recover from it what she was owed. *We* make our lives, she thought. There ain't no magic: just teeth-gritting, head-down, eye-watering determination. She stood up slowly, but with a new resolve, stretched her neck, her back, each leg in turn. She felt the warmth of the sun penetrate her coat.

"Okay," she said quietly.

She turned to the two foxes.

"Let's move on, you guys," she said. "No use waitin' around here. Places to go, things to do. I'm goin' home and find my kittens!"

They stared at her.

❧

Some way down the coast, another cat sat drowsing on a warm rock while her brood played on a sunlit headland above the sea.

Her fur was a pale rosy color. Her eyes were as deep as Nile water. Faint dapples and stripes made on her forehead a forgotten symbol. She was the Mau—a name that, in a language no longer used, means not just "cat" but "the Great Cat, or wellspring, that from which all else issues." Only months before, she had been the pivot around which the whole world moved. Even now, when she blinked out at sea, it was as if the world was somehow peculiarly hers. The Mau's blood was half as old as time, but she was newly a mother; and her husband, who was less in awe of her than he had been in those hectic days, called her Pertelot.

Pertelot's kittens were named Isis, Odin, and Leonora Whitstand Merril—"Leo" for short—and after some encouragement they had run a mouse to earth in a patch of gorse that smelled like honey and cinnamon. The mouse—which, she reflected, had so far shown more acumen than all her children put together—had quietly retreated into the dense tangled stems and prepared to wait them out.

"Leonora," advised the Mau quietly, "it would help if you kept still and didn't keep rushing in like that."

"I want to eat the mouse," said Leonora.

"I know, dear. But you must remember that the mouse does not want to be eaten. She will not come out if she knows you are there."

"I told you not to push in," said Odin. "Remember what the rat told Tag: 'It's your dog that chases. Your cat lies in wait.' " Then, to his mother, "Tell her she's no good at this."

"None of you is very good at it yet."

"She just wanted to get in first."

"I did not."

"You did."

"I did not," said Leonora. "I'm bored with the mouse now," she decided. "It's rather small, isn't it?"

"You're just no good at hunting."

Leonora looked hurt. "I am."

"You're not."

"I bite your head," said Leonora.

The kitten Isis stood a little apart and watched her brother and sister squabble, making sure to keep one eye on the place where the mouse had disappeared. Isis had her mother's eyes, dreamy and shrewd at the same time.

She suggested, "Perhaps if we went 'round the back?"

The Mau blinked patiently in the sunlight. Her kittens perplexed her. They were already getting tall and leggy, quite fluid in their movements. They had no trace of their father's Nordic boxiness; and, if the truth were told, they didn't look much like Pertelot either. They had short dense fur a mysterious, tawny color. Every afternoon, in the long golden hours before sunset, the light seemed to concentrate in it, as if they were able to absorb the sunshine and thrive on it. "What sort of cats are they?" she asked herself. And, unconsciously echoing her old friend Sealink, "Which of them will be the Golden Cat?" As they grew, the mystery, much like their color, only deepened. Paradoxically, though, it was their less mysterious qualities that perplexed her most. The very moment of their birth had been so fraught with danger. The world had hung by a thread around them. Yet now . . .

Well, just look at them, thought Pertelot a shade complacently: you couldn't ask for a healthier, more ordinary litter. Leonora, suiting actions to words, had got quite a lot of Odin's head in her mouth. Odin, though giving as good as he received, had a chewed appearance and was losing his temper. Claws would be out soon. The Mau shook herself.

"Stop that at once," she ordered.

She said, "Isis has had a very sensible idea."

Leo and her brother jumped to their feet and rushed off around the gorse bush, shouting, "My mouse!"

"No, my mouse!"

Isis followed more carefully. The Mau listened to them arguing for a few seconds, then yawned and looked out to sea.

In a minute or two, if she thought they had worked hard enough, she might go and catch the mouse for them. For now it was nice to rest in the warm sun. She lay down, gave a cursory lick at her left flank, and fell asleep. She dreamed as she often did, of a country she had never seen, where soft moony darkness filled the air between the palm trees along a river's glimmering banks. At dawn, white doves flew up like handkerchiefs around the minarets; a white dove struggled in her mouth. Then suddenly it was dark again, and the bird had escaped, and she was alone. "Rags?" she called anxiously, but there was no answer. All around her whirled an indistinct violence, the darkness spinning and churning chaotically, as if the very world were tearing itself apart.

"Rags!" she called, and woke to the warm air enameled with late afternoon, to the sound of a voice not her own, also crying for help. Rounding the gorse bushes, she found the two female kittens distraught. There was no sign of the male. On one side short upland turf, luminous in the declining sun, fell gently away to the cliff at the edge of Tintagel Head. On the other, the dark mass of gorse smoked away inland, aromatic, mysterious with flowers. "Quickly now," she ordered the kittens, "tell me what has happened!"

They stared helplessly at her. Then Isis began to run back and forth in a panic, crying, "Our brother is gone! Our brother is gone!"

Pertelot thrust her head into the gorse. "Odin!" she called into the dusty recessive twilight between the stems. "Come out at once. It's very wrong of you to tease your sisters like this." No answer. Nothing moved. She ran to the cliff and looked down. "Odin? Odin!" Had he tumbled over the edge? Could she see something down there? Only the water stretching away like planished silver into the declining sun. Only the sound of the waves on the rocks below.

"Our brother is gone!"

❧

If you had been in Tintagel town that early summer evening, you might have seen a large black cat half-asleep in a back street in a bar of sun. He was a wild-looking animal, robust and muscular, who weighed seventeen pounds in his winter coat, which had just now molted enough to reveal stout, cobby legs and devastating paws. His nose was long and wide, and in profile resembled the noseguard of a Norman helmet. His eyes were electric, his battle scars various.

He was Ragnar Gustaffson Coeur de Lion: not merely a king among cats but the King of Cats. No one went against him. His name was a legend along the wild roads for mad feats and dour persistence in the face of odds. But he was a great-hearted creature if a dangerous one. He exacted no tribute from his subjects. He gave more than he received. He was known to deal fairly and honestly with everyone he met, though his accent was a little strange.

Kittens loved him especially, and he loved them, pedigree or feral, sickly or well-set. He never allowed them to be sickly for long. One sweep of his great tongue was enough. He could heal as easily as he could maim. Toms and queens fetched their ailing children to him from all over town. There were no runts in Tintagel litters. There was barely a runny eye.

Everywhere Ragnar went, kittens followed him about with joy, imitating his rolling fighter's walk. Dignified sixteen-week-olds led the way. Tiny excited balls of fluff, barely able to toddle, came tumbling along behind. Slowly, like a huge ship, he would come to rest, then turn and study them and muse with Scandinavian irony, "They all can learn how to be kings from Ragnar Gustaffson—even the females!"

This evening, though, he dozed alone, huge paws twitching occasionally as in his dreams he toured the wild roads, bit a dog, retraced some epic journey in the face of serious winter conditions. Suddenly, his head went up. He had heard something on the ghost roads, something Over There. Seconds later, a highway opened three feet up in the bland Tintagel air, and Pertelot Fitzwilliam of Hi-Fashion jumped out of nowhere followed closely by what remained of the royal family.

"Rags! Rags!" she was calling.

While Isis cried, "Our brother, Odin, is gone!"

And Leo complained darkly, "It wasn't my fault. He just *had* to go in there after the stupid mouse—"

🐾

For Sealink, Francine, and Loves a Dustbin, the next day started innocuously enough. They awoke to the sound of wood pigeons and the cawing of crows as the first light rose over the hill to shine through the trees like a great, splintered prism.

With a yawn, Sealink uncoiled herself from the depths of her feathery tail, and, shaking each leg out in turn, went off to find some breakfast. She was filled with a sense of anticipation, the prospect of new life, a new journey. Sealink was a traveling cat. But previously she had traveled without a goal, letting her watchword be "the journey is the life," and going with the flow from America to Amsterdam, from Prague—which she pronounced to rhyme with *vague*—to Budapest, Constantinople, and the mystic East. But returning to New Orleans, place of her birth, to look for her kittens—well, that was altogether another kind of venture. It was a whole new experience, and *that* was just what a calico cat liked best.

Sniffing lazily around among fern and nettle, dog's mercury and sorrel, she found herself daydreaming about Cajun shrimp and chicken gumbo, and thus it was more by luck than by judgment that she stumbled on a sleeping vole. She was just about to deliver the killing blow, when Francine the vixen woke up, saw that something nasty was going on, and raised her voice in disapproval.

The vole sat bolt upright, took one look at the hungry cat looming above it, and legged it down a convenient hole.

"Hot *damn*," said Sealink.

Francine had grown up in the suburbs, where food came neither on the hoof nor out of trash cans but was reverently placed on trimmed lawns at owl light, at close of day, by children. In that well-planned zone between the wild and the tame, no one wanted to kill foxes. Where Francine had tumbled and played as a cub, the risk was less death than photography. Even though the badgers, those untamed civil engineers, were threatening it all by undermining people's gardens and getting themselves a bad name, human beings were still out there every night with long lenses and photo-multipliers. In cubs this bred a certain sense of security, on the heels of which often followed a demanding temperament and, paradoxically, a less-than-satisfactory life. Francine knew what she wanted, and though she was aware of death, her idea of nature had never given it much room. Nature was trimmed once a week. It featured fresh rinds of bacon, orange-flavored yogurt, a little spicy sausage. It had neither the addictive jungly glitter of the city, nor the *darkness* of the wild. Darkness never fell in the suburbs; and everything that was there one day was there the next day, too. You had to face things, of course, but nothing could be gained by dwelling on them. A steely will gave you the illusion of control.

As a result, Francine divided the world into the wild—nasty—and the tame—nice. Wild food—live prey, the sort you caught yourself—was nasty. The scraps left out for you on lawns were nice. The people who prepared food like that were nice. People were, on the whole, Francine believed, nice. They were civilized. On the other hand, the animal roads—being wild by definition—were uncivilized and nasty. The primal state was not something Francine aspired to. What she did aspire to, Sealink suspected, was matriarchy. Francine wanted Loves a Dustbin back on familiar ground, where she could encourage him to "settle down." She seemed an unlikely mate for him, given his dark history and adventurous life.

"I reckon he didn't have too much choice in the matter" was Sealink's assessment. "And once she's given him the cubs, he'll have even less. No more adventuring with cats."

Particularly with cats like herself. Sealink had a distinct intuition that—as an attractive, intrepid, and unencumbered female, albeit of an entirely different species—she was herself encompassed by Francine's definition of "nasty," too, with plenty of room to spare.

This morning, she wasn't disposed to be patient. She was hungry. Worse, she could hear the vole, safe underground, incapable with laughter as it boasted to its friends about her incompetence.

"Honey," she told Francine, "I'm gonna try one more time here. Read my lips: *You are frightening the damn food away.*"

She lowered her voice.

"Okay?" she said sweetly.

"You call that *food*, do you?" said Francine unpleasantly.

"Suburbanite."

"Trollop."

At which point, the dog fox intervened.

"Come on," he said. "Bickering isn't going to get you to Ponders End," he told the vixen, "or you," he said to Sealink, "back to your kittens. There's a highway entrance here, and we'd better take it."

Behind his back, Francine made a face.

🐾

Bitter and icy, the winds of the highways blew their fur the wrong way no matter in which direction they faced. All around, as far as the eye could see, ashen and inimical, stretched a landscape as old as time and just as forbidding. Sealink watched as Loves a Dustbin raised his long, intelligent head into the worst of the blast and listened intently. Beside him, Francine trembled, unable to accept the descent into the wild life. One moment she was an elongated, russet-coated thing with pointed muzzle and fennec ears; the next just an ordinary vixen again, full of fear, her eyes closed tight against the wind. After a moment, though, the road took her, and she gave herself up to it. She was running.

They were all running!

Powdered snow whirled and eddied around them, lit by a preternatural moon. Outside the wild roads, glimpsed briefly through the flurries, Sealink could see fragments of countryside skim past, sunlit and fragrant, the pulse of nature as slow as the heartbeat of a hibernating dormouse. Inside, shades of gray whirled and flowed, shadows upon shadows, as their muscles bunched and stretched, bunched and stretched, and they ate the ancient ground away stride by giant stride.

Sometime later—it seemed like hours, but how could you count time in a landscape without day and night, a world in which the sun shone through a haze, and the moon, shrouded by mist, hung always overhead?—Sealink could tell that they had covered a considerable distance. It was not just a sense of things shifting at speed but also a feeling of enervation, of weariness achieved by long effort. And just as she had recognized the leading edge of this fatigue, a debilitating exhaustion crashed down upon her, sweeping through her like a cold, dark wave.

The calico shook herself. She could never remember having felt so tired, particularly on the Old Changing Way, which channeled all the energy of the world. It was as if a hand had reached up through the earth and squeezed her heart. She could hardly breathe. The foxes had stopped, too.

There was a voice, too, distant yet powerful, then the stench of something fetid. The voice seemed for a moment closer, and Sealink thought she heard the words, "Got you!" Then the fabric of the wild road started to tear. Light from the ordinary world poured in like sand. The highway gave a great, galvanic convulsion, as if attempting to vomit, and suddenly Sealink and the foxes found themselves spun out of cold winds and icy plains into English woodland dappled with warm shade.

Sealink picked herself up and looked around.

"Damn! Ain't never been spit out like *that* before."

Twenty yards away the foxes stood, blinking bemusedly in the sunlight, looking down at something that appeared to have fallen out of the wild road with them.

It lay on its side at the foot of a beech tree, and it was bigger, even in death, than Sealink in life. Despite experience with the wildlife of fourteen countries, she had never before encountered its shaggy gray coat or striped face. She thought briefly of the raccoons of her native land. "Your raccoons, though," she reminded herself, "don't bulk up anywhere near so big. Anyhows, this thing ain't got no tail." Powerful claws lay drawn up under its body. Its face was a mask of terror, black lips drawn back defiantly from yellowed teeth. Its eyes were glazed. There was no sign of how it had come by its sudden demise. Black flies buzzed in lazy spirals in the air, and the exposed roots of the beech seemed to close loosely around the corpse like a human hand.

"Looks like it was good at life, this one," Sealink said to Loves a Dustbin, who was sitting by the corpse as if he might deduce something from the angle of its head, the slack gape of its jaw.

"Yes," he said.

"So what exactly is it?"

The fox looked up at her, but before he could speak, Francine interrupted. "It's a badger," she told Sealink. "Haven't you seen one before?"

"Nope."

"Personally I never liked a badger. They've ruined it for everyone where I come from. I am surprised you've never seen one before, dear, you having traveled so far and wide—"

"Well, I'll know him again," Sealink promised—thinking to herself, I bet you love this. You know somethin' I don't— oh, I bet you *love* that.

"A *badger*, huh?"

"Just a dirty old badger," Francine agreed complacently.

Loves a Dustbin gave her an odd look, then said, "We must have seen a dozen deaths like this since we left Tintagel."

They had lain in the unlikeliest places, always at the outlet of their customary highways, among the trees of a peaceful copse, beside benign moorland streams—the inexplicable dead.

"What do you make of it, hon?" asked the cat.

The dog fox shook his head.

"It's the wild roads," he said simply. "There's something the matter with them. I smell the hand of the Alchemist in this."

"But the Alchemist is dead. I saw him die. Him and the Majicou, both."

The fox shrugged. "There was always the chance that his magic would dominate the highways for a while. They'll be cleansed by use." But he seemed unconvinced by this explanation. He had a fox's nose and an understanding of the Old Changing Way second only to that of his original master. Old evil has a thin, faded reek; evil newly done smells as pungent as dung. If anyone knew the difference between the two, it was Loves a Dustbin. "Perhaps it's just some disease," he said.

This caused Francine to step smartly away from the corpse.

"Oh, dear! Come along now," she advised. "It's only something dead. We know these things happen, after all. We don't have to rub our noses in them every day."

The next morning promised better things. Sunlight crept down through the ghostly breaths of mist in the river valley and burned them away to a sheen on the grass. Birds called in the ash trees. The light was pale and bright, so that everything looked brand-new, as if someone had come by in the night and retouched the reeds and butterbur, the broom and the jack-in-the-green, the golden celandines and wild thyme from a fresh palette of watercolors.

They came out onto heathland among lazy bees and rabbits that bolted at the first scent of them, white scuts bobbing away over the close-bitten turf. Thwarted by the rabbits but fueled by the warmth of the sun, the foxes took to play, ambushing each other from behind trees, chasing and biting each other's brushes.

After a while, Loves a Dustbin trotted back to the calico, his long red tongue lolling humorously out of his mouth.

"What a life, eh, Sealink? What a life!" He laughed wryly. "Bet you never expected to see me acting like this. I never expected it myself. I thought my death was waiting for me behind every tree, watching in every shadow." He chuckled. "Ironic, isn't it? You think your life's over, and it's only just beginning."

Sealink was unprepared for the misery this evoked. A protective inner shutter slammed down. Too late. Suddenly, all she could see was the gleam of a pair of mismatched eyes—one an honest speedwell blue, one a wicked sodium orange. All she could smell was dusty tortoiseshell fur, aromatic, peppery.

The fox saw what was happening.

"I'm sorry," he said. "I—"

Sealink stared past him, her face lit with memory and pain. She swallowed hard and opened her mouth to speak. Nothing came out. Eventually she reassured him, "It's okay, it's okay, I—"

Suddenly, there was a high-pitched shriek from the rabbit runs behind them.

"Francine!" called Loves a Dustbin. "Francine!"

🐾

They found her lying on her back, her head thrashing from side to side. Wild with panic, her limbs waved in the air, and something appeared to be attached to her front foot. As she thrashed, this something glinted in the sun, and she wheezed with distress, tail thumping the ground in hard, rhythmic thuds. Blood oozed from a barely visible line above the ankle joint. A metallic line stretched away from the vixen's foot to a peg hammered into the ground some distance away beneath a twist of bramble.

Sealink stared at it puzzledly.

"What's happening here, hon?" she asked Loves a Dustbin.

"A rabbit snare," he said angrily.

He bent to lick at Francine's face, making strange, chirruping noises in the back of his throat.

Sealink inspected the snare. It looked far too simple to be a problem. She bent her head to it and bit down experimentally. It tasted cold and steely in her mouth. She applied her back teeth to it, an awkward maneuver, since cats have few molars, and rarely chew. Even after some minutes of concentrated biting, the wire remained unchanged except for a slightly more silvery sheen. She pulled at it until it came taut. At once, Francine emitted a thin, high wail that crawled under the skin and along the spine. Sealink leapt away from the wire in alarm.

"You do it!" she called to the dog fox. "You can dig, honey. You're damn near a dog, after all."

Clouds of earth flew up from the fox's paws until at last the peg came free and the wire went slack. Francine opened pain-dulled eyes. Twitching the stricken leg, she found at last that she could flex the foot without the wire's terrible pulling. She sat up and started to lick at the hurt place, but even though the peg was out the snare was still biting deep into her flesh, invisible beneath fur and welling blood. They stared at the wound.

"Try and stand, babe," Sealink urged, at the same time as Loves a Dustbin suggested, "Now just lie there, and be still."

They scowled at each other. The fox nosed at the snare. He touched it tentatively, but his nails were too big and blunt to get behind the wire. Sealink shouldered him out of the way.

"Leave this to Momma: she's got the proper equipment," she asserted, and, bending her head to the wound, worked on it with a single razored claw until she had loosened it enough to get her teeth behind it. After that, it was like nipping a tangle out of fur: nip and lick, nip and lick, until her muzzle was a mask of red.

"I got to say, hon," she told Francine, looking up with a ferocious grin, "that I never expected fox blood to taste so *nasty.*"

❦

The wire, released at last from its bed of flesh, lay like a coiled snake on the turf, a jeweled circle of red and silver, studded with little tufts of russet fur. Once the snare was off, Francine would let neither her mate nor the calico near her or it. She snarled at them indiscriminately.

"I don't understand," Loves a Dustbin said tiredly. "She just won't part with it."

"That ain't healthy, hon."

It wasn't.

❦

The wheezing of the vixen's breath through the night reminded Sealink of the sea breaking on a distant shingle beach. She drifted into sleep herself on this thought and dreamed of dark clouds racing across a stormy sky, the cries of seabirds like those of a cat mourning a lost child.

The next day, the flesh around the wound had swelled and Francine found it impossible to touch the foot to the ground. Loves a Dustbin made mournful figures-of-eight around her, murmuring encouragement; but it was clear that the vixen would not be traveling for some time.

Sealink sat at a distance from them and wondered what to do. It seemed disloyal to leave the foxes to their plight; but the pull of her vanished kittens grew stronger by the day. She heard them at night, though she could barely remember their voices. In her dreams she was on the old boardwalk again, dancing under a phosphor moon, when she heard them mewing like Pertelot's litter. Whenever she thought she had found them, they were calling from somewhere else! Everything was entangled, past and present, pride and hurt and abiding loss. She had never acknowledged her real reasons for leaving New Orleans. In the middle of reveries of Mouse-breath, huge chunks of her early life had begun to come back to her, as if all that was part of one thing. Sealink had lost more than a mate: she had lost her sense of who she was. New Orleans, that Mother of Cats, might tell her. Would the foxes understand?

She sat for some time, feeling the cool breeze riffling her fur, watching clouds scud high up in the sky. In the reeds at the bottom of the hill she could hear moorhens calling, and when she stood up she could see that they were shepherding errant chicks with impossibly large feet. She looked down at her own substantial paws.

"These feet was made for walkin'," she said, to no one in particular, "and that's just what they'll do . . . Lord knows what will have become of those youngsters of mine without their great big momma to take care of 'em."

Not that they'd had much choice in the matter. But then, neither had she.

Ten minutes later, Loves a Dustbin looked up from his wounded mate to see the silhouette of a large-furred cat staring down on him from the hillside above, its tail tip curled and its ears flicking minutely. He could read the signs.

"Good-bye, Sealink," he said softly. "I hope you find what you're looking for out there."

Francine whimpered at his feet. He bent his head to console her, and when he looked up again, Sealink was gone.

Chapter Two

MYSTERIES OF TINTAGEL

*D*arkness fell in a little seaside town a few miles along the coast from Tintagel. A yellow moon hung low over the maze of fishermen's cottages on the hill above the harbor. There were thin clouds high up and wrinkles of light on the sea. It was the hour of fish teas, coal fires. Somewhere in the mazy cobbled streets, which smelled of seaweed and orange peel, in a corona of light high up where an old wall met an older roof, a cat flickered into existence out of nowhere. One quick glance around him and he was off again, trotting up against the pitch of the roof to vanish around a chimney pot. Moments later he could be seen leaping confidently from one roof to the next, lowering himself down an old metal drainpipe, scampering across the salt-damp setts and around a corner.

Though they watched him covertly from gutter and doorway, the local toms issued no challenge. Only a few short months before, this hard-boiled toff had stumbled half-blind into the village accompanied by a mad tabby female with a spark plug in her head, and turned their lives into a long weekend of battle, disruption, and disorder. They were still trying to work out what had happened down the coast. They knew him as Mercurius Realtime DeNeuve and were careful not to catch his eye. He knew himself as Tag and he was wondering what was for tea.

He and the tabby kept no fixed abode. They loved the coast and they loved each other. They loved the windy illuminated breadth of the beach, the smells of food, the jangling music from the tourist shops and amusement arcades. They had quarters in a bus shelter or under an upturned boat. They liked

25

it that way. They were friends to visitors and lost children. Sometimes they would spend some time with a fisherman's family or in the steamy, scented fug of the Beach-O-Mat Laundrette, where the tabby would watch the clothes go around all day with a dreamy expression on her face. Her real name was Cy. Down at the quay, where she shamelessly courted the fishermen, they called her "Trixie." At this hour, Tag knew, she would be waiting for him in one of her favorite spots—a round granite building near the top of the hill.

Before these two adventurers turned up, no cat had entered that place. Not that they weren't curious—a cat is a cat, after all. Throughout the summer it was packed with human beings. They stood in lines, then shuffled in. They shuffled around inside, then shuffled out again, blinking and chattering in the sun. "What do they do in there?" the village matrons would ask each other, giving their kittens a good spruce-up. "With human beings it's so hard to tell, my love. Don't you find?" All a cat could say for sure was that it was a taller building than the chapel, more spacious than the lifeboat station. Its roof was home to some fat-looking gulls. Above the faded green doors an old enamel sign announced to the reading public:

OCEANARIUM.

Tag ran up the steps and slipped in through a gap low down between the two doors.

🐾

A single octagonal glass tank filled the echoing space inside. Whole shoals of mackerel scintillated there in millions of gallons of seawater, lorded over by thornback rays and spiny sharks. The sharks were powerful, streamlined, slim, less than two feet long. They circled endlessly. They pushed their clever noses out of the water and into the hot glare of the electric lamp that hung above their domain. All the creatures of the sea were represented. There were octopuses and squids. Lobsters made their homes in the detritus on the floor of the tank. Though the room itself was kept dark, a kind of ocean light—filtered through the seawater until it became a cool pale glow—illuminated the concrete floor between the tank and the walls, where just enough room had been left for two human beings to loiter along abreast. Torn fishing nets sagged in the shadows above. The air was still, not quite warm. At night there was complete silence.

The tabby loved it. She had pushed her sturdy little head through the gap in the doors one day while Tag was out walking the wild roads, and there they were—fish, fish, fish! What cat could resist them? But here was the strange thing: even if the water had been empty, Tag believed, she would have been drawn back by the tranquil and yet penetrating quality of the aquarium light. If you looked long enough, its lucent interior depths began to seem more real than the world outside. This calmed her. Relieved of her madness by their friend the New Black King, she retained a hair-trigger awareness of unseen things. At night she whispered to the empty dark and could still be seen accompanied by a cloud of little motes like moths. She was still a puzzle to Tag. Of that, oddly enough, he was glad. Every day they met all over again, and they felt brand-new to each other.

This evening she was sitting up tall, eyes bright with reflected tank light, gazing at a large ray. Its wing tips curled and curved in lazy arcs, its eyes like jet beads as it hovered in the water so close to the glass you could see its gill slits curl and palpitate, the ray was staring back out at her. Tag shivered a little. They seemed so intent upon each other. What did they know? What could they have to say to each other? But he loved the way the light caught the set of the tabby's head and the shape of her white bib. So he sat in the shadows and watched them, cat and fish, for a long moment before he said quietly, "You'll never catch it."

"Ace," she answered patiently, "I don't want to catch this fish. He stays in the water, I stay on the land."

"I can see the sense of that," agreed Tag, "given how well you swim."

She looked at him oddly.

"But can you see the perfection of it?" she demanded.

She spun around twice, reared up, and banged her neat white front paws on the glass in front of her. Taking this to mean that their encounter was at an end, the ray pivoted slowly on its vertical axis and banked away into the depths of the tank, trailing a few bright motes and strings of matter. Cy watched it go, then turned and cuffed Tag's ears in delight. She rubbed her head against his. She purred.

"I got you a special dinner," she said.

His heart sank.

From a niche at the base of the tank she withdrew one condensed milk can—empty—one plastic clothes-peg, and two small fragile white shells. After some thought she added dry-roasted peanuts from the floor of an arcade, bread crusts she had won off a herring gull, and a square of milk chocolate still wrapped in blue foil. Tag thought he could probably eat the chocolate. He sorted through the rest with one paw and not much hope.

"Come on, Jack," she encouraged. "Don't play with it. Get it down you!"

Then, before he could answer: "If you liked that, you'll love this."

With some ceremony she brought out her chef d'oeuvre and dropped it in front of him. It was a cigarette butt.

"Very nice," he said as enthusiastically as he could. "I think I'll leave that for after."

The tabby pretended to groom herself. Then she sat back, eyes sparkling, head to one side. He realized she had been laughing at him all along.

"All right then," he said. "Where is it?"

She wriggled into the gap between the tank and the concrete floor until only her bottom showed; then, after some excited scrabbling about, backed out carefully and brought forth two pilchards. Their scales glittered. Their eyes goggled in the dim wash of light. They were plump and perfect, apart from the odd toothmark. They might still have been alive.

"Tag," she said, "we got star-gazey pie!"

Though he loved her, Tag was suddenly a little tired. All the way home from the house by the river, he had felt he was being followed. In the tank a fish caught the light suddenly like sunshine on a coin, then vanished. An octopus hung high up against the glass as if pasted there, motionless but

pulsing gently, waiting—even more patient and alien than
the sharks—for the change in the nature of things that would
permit it to take up its rightful place.

"Let's eat at the bus shelter," he said. "It's nice out tonight,
and sometimes this place makes me shiver."

"I want to talk to my fish."

"Come on," Tag said gruffly. "You can see it again tomorrow."

After some thought, she was willing to concede this.

"I can," she said. "Can't I?"

She said, "I'd forgotten that."

Outside, she added, "Oh, Ace, that fish is one old soul. It's
almost as beautiful as you. That fish is just, well, my friend."

🐾

The weather was turning.

The moon went down in a greenish glow on the horizon. A
glutinous swell lapped the cement piles down by the lifeboat
station. Out on the esplanade, rag-mop palms leant on the
wind like old ladies surprised by a Sunday squall.

But the bus shelter was warm, and soon decorated with two
perfect ichthyoid skeletons, sockets jolly with mortality, wiry
bones like cat's whiskers in the live fluorescent darkness of
the oncoming storm. The tabby licked her lips, gave her paws
a cursory wash, scratched busily beneath her chin. There was
an odor of pilchard oil and electricity.

"Nice here," she said. "Curl up tight now."

"I hope you're happy," Tag said anxiously, as he watched
the tide steal in, a wave at a time, across the dark beach.
"Living here, I mean."

She stared at him.

"It's a fall-on-your-feet life, Tiger," she replied. "It's sunshine every morning. It's boats and cream and, I mean, there's
even mice here. I seen this life in dreams. How can you ask?
Oh, Tag, I like it fine!" She flexed her claws and purred luxu-
riously. "Sleep now," she advised; so, reassured, he did. Only
to dream of shoal after shoal of feathery pilchard skeletons
swinging as restless as compass needles beneath the waves
and to be woken unceremoniously by a single clang of
thunder.

He sat bolt upright and craned his neck. Nothing landward.

Then, as he turned toward the sea, there was a silent explosion over the beach, a split-second flare that faded instantly through all the colors of the spectrum to a black that was a kind of light in itself. Tag jumped to his feet. In the moment of illumination, he had seen the palms, the roiling surf, the wind whipping spray off the chop, and then a monstrous cat that burst out of the naked air and began to forge its way in a kind of eerie slow motion across the beach toward him. Sand sprayed up from pads the size of dinner plates. Heat haze boiled around it. It came spilling the fire and anger of its life, waves of silent lightning, the ungrudging broadcast of substance into some space not quite the world we know. Its eyes were yellow. Its ears were flattened. Its great teeth gleamed white against a red mouth. Decreasing in size and speeding up as it approached, this fierce apparition hurtled up the three concrete steps from the beach. By the time it burst into the bus shelter, it was an ordinary cat, if you could ever use the word "ordinary" of Ragnar Gustaffson Coeur de Lion, the New Black King.

"Ragnar!"

"Tag! Tag, my friend!"

Drenched and wild looking, his fine coat disordered and dirty, Ragnar stood head down, sides heaving, filling the bus shelter with a kind of regal dejection. He was so exhausted he could barely stand. He was so anxious he could hardly speak.

"My friend! I— Tag, quick!"

"Ragnar, what is it?"

"Tag, something awful has happened!"

🐾

Tag left Cy in the bus shelter.

"I don't want you lost, too," he told her. She gave him a look, but he knew she would stay.

"Now run!" he said to Ragnar.

The tabby watched as they pounded over the sand and sprang one after the other into the ghost-ridden spaces of the wild road. Ten minutes later, Tag and Ragnar were stumbling around in the howling Tintagel dark.

"Odin!" they called as they went. "Odin!"

Nothing.

Shortly after the kitten's disappearance the bottom had dropped out of the weather. A bank of cloud had slunk in from the sea on the steadily sharpening wind. Visibility had shrunk to a few yards. Now the gorse bushes thrashed as if trying to uproot themselves. Torrents of rain blustered in, huge cold silver drops suspended roiling for an instant in the turbulent air at the edge of the cliff before they were sucked away inland. Tag ducked and winced into the storm, his eyes fixed grimly on the black cat in front of him. Tintagel Head, so peaceful on a sunny day, now reminded him of the first time he had seen it—arriving, as he had done, wild-eyed and winter-boned at the end of a long and sometimes bitter journey. Today as then, Pertelot Fitzwilliam, Queen of Cats, awaited him.

This time she was huddled in the lee of some rocks at the cliff edge with her two remaining kittens. Her face was hard and puzzled. Her eyes were dull with fatigue. Tracks like human tears blackened the taupe fur either side of her sharp, ancient muzzle. She looked like a stone sculpture, obdurate and defeated both at once. She looked like an ax head. Nothing could be seen of the happiness she had found at Tintagel, nothing remembered of the long summer evenings in which ocher sunlight thickened the flowers of tormentil amid the sheep-cropped turf, and the golden kittens tumbled and played in safety at the court of the King, under the watchful eye of its Queen.

"Pertelot," said Tag.

She could not make herself respond. When he tried to comfort her, she would only say, "Mercury, you must find him. If you call he'll come to you. You know he will!"

"Pertelot, I—"

"He loves you so. They all do."

From inside that pocket of quiet still air, she stared at him with hope already turning into a sort of soft reproach. Overborne by the intensity of her need, he could only look away, gutter into silence.

"I'll try," he said.

"No!"

"Pertelot—"

"It's not to try, Mercury. It's to find him. Do you see? You must, or how can I ever forgive myself?"

"We'll find him," Tag promised.

What else could he say?

The two male cats quartered the headland, while the night battered them senseless with its cold wings. Merciless and unassuaged in the exposed corridors between the stands of gorse, the wind picked them up and threw them bodily about. Out there, they couldn't even be sure of each other's voices. Listen to that! A cat? A gull? The wind? Who knew? Worse, they often thought they could hear each other calling out, "Tag! He's here!" Or, "Ragnar, Odin's safe!" Ghost voices, night voices, voices in the surf far below. A momentary trap for the heart, then disappointment. By sunrise they had to admit they'd found no sign—not a footprint, not a scuff mark or a faint smell—of the missing kitten. They had combed rocks and ruins, they had teetered about on the cliff above the raging tide. They were soaked and shattered and their feet were sore.

Odin was gone.

The storm blew itself out with the dawn. The headland looked washed and emptied, all primrosey yellows and faint tawny browns. A single gull planed over the rocks at the edge of the cliff. Apologetic gusts of wind crept among the gorse stems. Later the sky would be very blue; for now, gray light like watered silk found out Pertelot Fitzwilliam, keening beneath her rock. Huge-eyed, Leo and Isis huddled close to her, but she was too distraught to comfort them. Tag and Ragnar, too tired to stand, told her what they now knew.

"We can't find him."

"Go out again, then," she said.

"When the light is better," said Tag, "we'll widen the search. When it's properly light I'll fetch some others."

The Queen hissed at him.

"We have to rest now," he said.

"I cannot rest," said Ragnar.

"You're so strong," said Pertelot, mad with loss. She was trembling. "You big strong toms can't find a kitten."

Ragnar said, "I can never rest again."

"Go out and look, then," said Pertelot.

She stumbled to her feet and fell down on Leo and Isis.

"I'll go myself," she said.

🐾

In the days that followed, the search was continued and broadened.

Sense returned to Pertelot, but she lost her interest in things, turned vague and forgetful, was preyed upon by sudden angers in the afternoon. Cy came down the coast to help Ragnar look after the remaining kittens. No one was sure how they were taking it. Throughout, they had stuck to their story, which was this: as their brother laid siege to the mouse in the gorse bush, a human hand had reached out suddenly and dragged him in. Quizzed by Tag, they couldn't remember exactly how it looked.

"It was a big dull human hand, that's all," explained Leonora.

And Isis said, "There was dirt under those blunt nails they have. As if it had been digging like a dog."

Tag shook his head.

"I'll have to think about this," he said.

"You'd better believe us," Leo warned.

Then she said cautiously, as if introducing a subject to which she had given more thought than she wanted to admit, "Do you think the Alchemist ever would come back? When I was a very young kitten I used to believe I could still hear both of them down there underneath the headland. But now I think Odin was right—it was only the sound of the sea."

"Perhaps," said Tag. "Does something so important, so violent, end so suddenly like that and never trouble the world again? We don't know enough to know."

Leo said, "You're the new Majicou. You know everything."

"We'll see about that," said Tag.

Young animals often wander off, and are found again quite quickly. With this firmly in mind, an air of activity and cautious optimism descended on the headland.

The community there not being comprised solely of the King and his family, there was plenty of help to be had. Among the ruins of the ancient castle, on the soil-creep terraces along the cliffs, in holes and under banks, lived many animals who had stayed behind after their part in the battle against the Alchemist. Foxes, badgers, urban feral cats settling down to find mates and found dynasties, even a pair of mink so angry no one had yet dared talk to them, now occupied the rising land eastward of the head or lived cheerfully in a muddle of warrens, fallen-down chicken coops, and allotments at the edge of Tintagel town.

"Come and help," Tag appealed.

"It took you long enough to ask," they said.

Prey made peace—at least for the duration—with predator. Species that would only be seen dead with one another were spotted working the headland in teams—a rook with four young herring gulls, the two mink with an old gray squirrel who called himself Broadsword. Cats cooperated with foxes to comb the town in case Odin had somehow made his way there and gotten lost. A very old racehorse named Smithfield went over the paddock fence every night just after dark and quartered the territory for twenty miles in every direction.

Nothing.

Two weeks passed, and then a third. Depression filled them all. Even the climate collaborated in this: a heat wave set in suddenly and burned the grass brown. June brought a sudden upsurge of human visitors to the ruins of the castle. They came from thousands of miles away, to wave their arms; blink in the sun; and talk, talk, talk. They trudged along the complex contours on the northern flank of the peninsula, charmed and exhilarated by the way the land fell away in huge windy chamfers to the tide. Talk, talk, talk.

(The Felidae come here, of course, but more quietly. It is a place of pilgrimage for them, too. They remember how, in the fourth age of cats, Atum-Ra and his Queen—who was also called Isis—arrived here from Egypt armed only with unborn kittens and the magic of warm countries, to reopen the old wild roads.)

You had to keep out of their way. Their feet polished the stone. They wore the earthen paths to trenches. The gorse, that most desiccated of shrubs, seemed to dry up further, and dust whirled about in the spaces between its gnarled stems. Meanwhile, the King exhausted himself with worry. His wife stared dully ahead of her and would not be consoled. In less than a month, Tintagel had gone from a place of promise to a wasteland.

🐾

Around full moon, unable to think clearly amid all this misery—and needing, besides, to attend to certain of his responsibilities as the new Majicou—Tag sent himself to the city, where he spent a night at the abandoned pet shop in Cutting Lane. There he received the usual trickle of odd visitors, gnarled old animals for the most part, who spoke in low voices, kept their eyes on the door, and remembered favorably the old Majicou. He dispatched a message or two. He watched the spiders making their webs in corners.

The web quivers, the spider lives along the line. That is how knowledge comes to you when you have eight legs. "The wild roads are in this," Tag told himself. "They always are." The wild roads are in everything. But how does a cat find out what they know?

He was loath to leave his friends alone with their great sorrow.

And yet— he thought.

You know what the wild roads know by traveling them.

He thought, All this is one thing. The lost kitten, the highways out of joint, a voice I'm not even sure I heard.

He sat all night. Vapor light penetrated the dusty windows, fell in concise bars across the bare floorboards. Later, the moon sent in its own agents, long yellow fingers to scratch bonily from corner to corner. The spiders worked busily. Tag watched. Filmier than spiderweb, filmier than moonlight, the wild roads pulsed around him.

Tag thought, I wish Loves a Dustbin was still here. That fox always knew what to do!

🐾

Nothing had changed when he returned some while later, to find Cy alone on the cliff top watching the sun go down under some long black clouds.

"Hello," he said.

He licked the side of her face, where each short hair was tipped and ticked with tabby gold. All cats inhabit the tabby—or anyway they have hung up their coats there at some time or another. She tasted of wine. Flowers. Yolk of egg. She tasted of Cy.

"You're nice," he said.

She seemed distracted.

"Hi, Sky-pilot," she said after a moment. "Good day at the office?"

"I looked at spiders."

"Fine. But see this?" she said. "This is the story so far. I nearly died here, Jack. Remember? It was nip and tuck. I was spread-eagled on the Wheel of Flame. The Alchemist had burned me to the ground, you know?" She shivered. "There was fire all 'round. But for the big Norwegian, I was going to cash in my chips." She shook her head. "Oh, Tag, he seems so down now, that New Black King. I want to help him. And the kittens—I tell 'em things, but they don't stay to listen."

"They hardly know where to turn," said Tag. "They miss their brother."

They did miss him. But while Leo was clearly downcast, she knew what she wanted, and already had the air of a cat who could make decisions—though she kept them to herself, which did not help later. Isis found it harder to live with loss.

In many ways, Isis was the most puzzling of the three kittens—quiet, clever, obedient, neat in her movements, but at the same time as unknowable as air. She evaded your understanding. The moon was her planet. She was drawn to water, to twilight, to all things that changed and shifted. The circumstances of her birth had been no stranger than that of her siblings, but Isis was open to the shadows. She had a drive to the invisible. She felt, she said, the strong dead awaiting their resurrection. They were curled up in every leaf. As a tiny kitten, she could already be found sitting and blinking and staring at unseen things—for her, every object in the world seemed to have an extension or counterpart somewhere else. At four weeks old, she began to sing to them. Pertelot and Ragnar woke to inexplicable caterwauls in the night. Investigating, they found Isis, alone on the windy rocks, yowling and fluting to the reflection of the moon in the sea. "I was trying to make it feel better," she explained. Who knew what the moon thought of her song? To everyone else it seemed tortured and raucous. "Not even a cat could find music in a voice like that," was her father's opinion. But the Mau was not so sure. Such music reminded her of her own dreams, Egypt dreams pregnant and unresolved. When Isis sang, unformed things seemed to gather in the air near her, and a shiver went down your spine.

Sometimes the Mau would assert, "If any of my children is the Golden Cat, it's this one. She could sing life into a stone."

Ragnar agreed. "A stone would get up and run away," he said, "when it heard that daughter sing."

"Ragnar!"

In the absence of Odin, Isis grieved more openly than her sister, becoming rawboned and nervous. Her coat lost tone. She closed up. She ranged alone over the parched headland, talking quietly to herself or to Odin, who in some way still walked beside her. She acted as if she was no longer quite sure what had happened. She sniffed at the gorse stems and the scattered stones, following the mystery down into her own heart. She was like her mother in that respect, the other cats said: too much of a puzzle herself to be happy with one. A strange, ululating wail sometimes issued from the cliff top on the offshore wind. It was Isis, singing to her vanished brother. One night she went to look for him in the little church on the headland, and disappeared in her turn.

She was seen several times that night—sitting alertly in the moonlight, flitting among the castle ruins, cautiously approaching some piece of human litter at the side of a path. But no animal had sight of her after midnight, when Leonora Whitstand Merril, who was energetically washing her bib at the base of the war memorial, watched her sister enter St. Madryn's by its primitive northern doorway. A wind had got up by then. The whole length of the graveyard stretched between them.

"Isis?" called Leo.

Isis looked around once. Her eyes flashed blank and empty. Then she was gone.

"Isis? Wait for me!"

Three hours later, just before dawn, Tag, Ragnar, and Leo stood just inside St. Madryn's—known to humans, who understand less of their own history than they think, as St. Materiana's—looking down toward the east window, which had begun to harbor a faint but growing light. The white-washed walls were tinged with pink and gold. Above, the complex roof beams stretched away in the echoing silence; below, it was glossy pews. The air seemed to coil on itself, as if something had just that minute left the church.

Tag raised his head and sniffed. Polished wood. Flowers. Cold old stone.

Was there something else?

"Keep an eye open for rats," he warned. "This is just the sort of place you find them."

"Show me a rat," bragged Leo. "That's all."

She laughed.

"I won't treat it well," she promised.

"Isis!" she called.

"Hush," said Tag.

"Isis, I know you're in here!"

Her name was written on the air; they could listen to it with their noses. But why had she come here, and where was she now? The two adult cats stood shifting their paws uncomfortably on the tiled floor of the nave. They eyed the artifacts hanging on the walls. A kind of diffidence, an embarrassment on behalf of humankind, caused them to look away from the emblems carved into the reredos—spears and nails and whipping posts. Leo, who felt no need to understand the things human beings do, marched about, bellowing, "Isis!"

Nothing.

Suddenly, dawn was upon them, in a soundless, unusual flash of light. The undersides of the clouds flared with pinks and greens, the whole sky seemed touched with gold. Ragnar Gustaffson looked up for a moment. He blinked. "We haven't so long to search, I think," he said. "In an hour or two the tourists will—"

"Aha!" interrupted his remaining daughter loudly.

"—be here."

"Look!" ordered Leonora.

Behind the altar, down at floor level in the angle between the walls, not too far from the east window itself, she had found a hole in the masonry. It was irregularly shaped, large enough to squeeze through. When you put your face to it, a draft of damp salty air stirred your whiskers. Two or three long feline guard hairs were caught on its edges. They glinted in the light. They were gold.

Leo stuck her head in.

"Leave it to Leonora," she announced, already sounding distant, "as usual."

"Leo, wait!" said Tag.

Before he could move, she was gone.

"These children." Ragnar sighed. "I think they are more impossible than their mother."

"You love them anyway," said Tag.

"Leo?" he called.

No reply. When he listened at the hole he thought he could hear something breathing far away.

"Let's go," he said.

"It is a very small hole."

"Come on, Rags."

"Many cats would balk at a small hole like that."

"Not cats like us. We're too determined."

"I feared as much."

A line of slippage, an ancient fault between two folds of rock—filled by the ages with their sediment, then scoured even longer by water and moving air—ran like the pipe of some secret ear down into Tintagel Head. At first it was very narrow. Rats had polished that part of it and gone, leaving a lively, bitter stink and littered nests in chambers. As it penetrated the head, the pipe widened and fell away suddenly into a series of polished steps and ledges as rounded and complex as wax from a burning candle. It was a committing descent. Some of the steps were eight or ten feet high. How will we climb back up? Tag thought. He decided not to ask Ragnar, who looked less than happy to be under the ground. Eventually, the going eased off. They found themselves in a wide, low passage, floored with crushed shells and tiny fibrous flakes of slate. A salt wind blew into their faces. A pale radiance seemed to spring from the damp, smooth walls. Leonora ran ahead, tail up, in little fits and starts, halting every so often to look back.

"That daughter," grunted Ragnar. "Where does she get the energy?"

"At least she's quiet now," said Tag.

They listened appreciatively. Into the silence came a long, shooshing sound. Then another, like a breath.

"The sea," said Ragnar.

"I imagine so."

Ragnar looked apprehensive.

"Do you think the tide comes all the way in?"

"No," said Tag decisively.

But he did.

The passage ended abruptly, on a ledge fifteen feet up the back of a huge domed cave. Tag stared out. A smell of iodine and rot. Huge boulders, draped with fluorescent green weed that made them resemble velvet cushions in a sitting room. They were surrounded by pools of old tidewater. On the other side of the cave, so bright he could barely look into it, a slot of blue-white daylight, split into long beams by the intervening rocks. Against that light, he could just make out the lonely figure of Leonora, sitting at the entrance looking out. Her mouth was open, but all he could hear was the tide, crashing against the rocks at the base of the head.

"How did she get down there?"

"Jumped, I should say."

Tag looked at the nearest boulder. It was a long way down, and if you missed . . .

"I suppose she did." He sighed.

"Never mind, Tag. We are some very determined cats here."

"I suppose we are."

"You first."

Down they jumped.

❦

The cave opened on to raw ocean.

Glitter and dazzle. Gray-green swell far out. Bright blue sky. A rising tide among the massive zinc-colored boulders just outside the cave mouth, rendered too real by sunshine so intense the eye could only wince away. The cliffs soared up on either side, the great waves roared and smashed against them, breaking into ferocious white plumes! It was a big place for a small animal. Tag was dazzled and deafened and elated all at once. Then something tiny shifted his focus and his field of view, and he saw, suddenly and quite clearly, how the spiders had strung their morning webs between the rocks, just a foot or two above the tide line. Though they trembled and were sometimes spangled with saltwater dewdrops flashing in the sun, each web remained taut and unbroken. He was filled with a sense of the triumphant frailty of life.

You've got to give it to those spiders, he thought. They're a very determined lot.

Then he heard Leonora.

Sitting upright, her eyes narrowed, staring in anguish at the spray as it exploded up in front of her, she was calling out over and over again, as if her brother and sister had just that moment vanished.

"Isis! Odin!"

Tag jumped up beside her.

"They were brought this way!" she cried. "Human beings brought them this way!"

"We'll find them, Leonora, don't fret."

Even as he spoke, she was gone.

With a despairing cry of "Isis!" she had launched herself into the sea.

❦

Tag stared. No kitten, not even the iron-willed Leonora Whitstand Merril, could survive that tide. He knew he could never face the Queen again or bear the expression on Ragnar Gustaffson's careworn face if his friends lost their surviving child. Besides, he had always loved and admired Leo for a confidence he did not remember in himself at that age.

"Stay here!" he warned Ragnar.

He drew himself together. His head dipped once, twice, as he marked the place in all that fury he'd last seen Leonora. His hindquarters fidgeted and were still. A heartbeat pause. Then he unbent himself in an arc as bright as a rainbow.

The ocean boomed and coughed upon the rocks. It rose up to meet him. It was all around him, and there was no more Tag, only struggle and chaos and fear. He thought his heart would stop from the cold. The tide dragged him into its salty recesses, where it battered him, then flung him up, up, up again and out into the air. He was up in the air in a mist of spray! He felt the sun on him, he felt himself turn slowly over. He saw rocks, blue sky, a cliff with a puff of cloud above it, then sky and green brine again. He was sucked down to where the deep stones rolled around in the draw and backlash of the water—he heard their voices grind and growl against the fixed land—and there he found Leonora. A glimpse of her in a stinging salt-gray fog—bubbles came out her gaping mouth—then they were whirled together like two rags in a washing machine. He got her by the scruff, then lost her again. He clutched at her with his teeth, his front legs, his heart. "Let me up now!" he told the water. But it only drew him further down between the stones. He felt them roll around him in blackness, huge slow grinding forms. He thought of the spiders in their frail webs. Hold on, Leonora! he thought. His breath was a stone in him. He held on to her. He held on. He told the water, "Let us up now!" But the water had them. One of Leonora's legs was caught between the rocks. The salt tide pulled at her. Nothing. Tag pulled at her. Nothing. Bubbles came out of her mouth. "Leonora!" There was a dull booming all around. They were in the water for good; things were going from gray to black. Then a strange furled shadow fell across them. Half-conscious now, Tag looked up and saw, through the gray prism of the salt, a great ocean ray like a live blanket, hovering and banking over his head. Its gill slits were cut like metal, its strange sail furled and unfurled, its tiny black eyes regarded him with unreadable emotion. The ray's shadow descended on them. There was a great wrenching, some pain, and Leonora was free. They rushed to the surface like bubbles, exploding up in light and spray; and the tide—full of power and a joy of its own, because to dice with life is the joy of the tide—flung them up onto the rocks again.

♟

"That was a very stupid thing to do, Leonora," Ragnar Gustaffson told her a few minutes later, as she and Tag—looking less like cats than bottle brushes—sat in the sunshine, frantically washing themselves to get dry and get warm.

"I know," said Leo. "But they went that way. I'm sure of it. They were taken away on the water."

Ragnar considered this.

"I can only comment, 'That is no reason to jump in,' " he decided after a moment. "You should remember: cats and water are not best of companions." He became lost in thought. Finally he added, "Your mother, who fell in a canal last year, has told me as much, many times."

Tag laughed.

Then he shivered and said, "We weren't alone out there. Something helped us. Did you feel that, Leo?"

But Leo only answered, "This tastes foul. Doesn't it?" And, "I didn't like it in the sea."

As soon as they felt better, Ragnar led them across the rocks at the cave mouth to show them something he had found. Not far in, there were paint scrapes on the rocks, as if something had recently been dragged ashore there. There were strong complex smells of burnt chemicals, wet wool, and human beings and their rubber boots. Even more interesting was this: on one of the larger rocks, a curious symbol had been constructed. An arrangement of pebbles, barnacle shells, and bits of seaweed, it looked at first like an accident of the tide. Then you saw what it was meant to represent:

"Ha," said Leo, who had regained her confidence. "I thought as much." She stood up on a boulder, stretched to her full length against the wall, and, failing to quite reach the symbol with her nose, dabbed at it with one paw. She fell off the boulder, jumped back up, and tried again.

Ragnar gave her a look.

"There are times," he told Tag, "when a daughter—how can I say this?—is less of a blessing than I have imagined. But she is right."

Tag pushed Leo out of the way and examined the symbol.

"The kittens may have been taken away by human agency" was his opinion. "But no human being made this. It smells of something else. It smells of—" He shook his head, wishing for the nose of Loves a Dustbin, that organ so educated it could detect life in the dead. "I don't know what it smells of," he concluded, "but humans didn't make it."

"In which case," Ragnar said, "we should enquire, 'If not humans, who?' "

"Who indeed?" the new Majicou asked himself darkly.

"They were taken by sea," Leonora insisted, in a determined effort to regain the attention of her elders.

She dropped to all fours, raised her head, and opened her mouth to allow damp, salty air across the exotic sensory organ—not quite smell, not quite taste—cats keep there. Suddenly, she was off again, this time toward the cave's landward entrance. The back wall barely gave her pause, though it slowed the two adult cats. They shrugged, exchanged a glance of reluctance, and did their best to follow. She scampered along the slate-floored passage, turned the "staircase" by a series of deft leaps to intermediate ledges, and jammed herself into the pipe that led back to St. Madryn's. There she stopped, opened her mouth again for a moment to taste the air, then, with some energetic if disconnected scraping and paddling of the back legs, compressed herself into a niche which stank of rats. Out of that, a second pipe led, via sudden constrictions and changes of direction, to the surface.

Ragnar followed his daughter, grumbling.

Tag followed Ragnar, wondering what it all meant.

Human beings, he thought.

He thought, Human beings in a boat.

Dust rained down and got into his eyes. It was the dry powdery granite earth of the headland, he knew it by its smell.

Pale light appeared ahead, then suddenly the bright glare of day. When he hauled himself out, he found himself in the middle of a gorse bush. Through the stems he could see sunshine crackling off the sea. It was going to be a fine day. A little way off, the King of Cats was shoving his way out onto the turf with cheerful oaths he imagined to be Viking in origin. Bits of gorse had already embedded themselves deep in his ruff. Leonora Whitstand Merril sat waiting for Tag, smugly licking her paws.

"I told you you'd better believe us," she said. "This is where the hand came up. This is the bush they took my brother from."

🐾

"Here's what I think you should do," Tag told the King and Queen a little later that morning.

They were assembled in the warm sun on the cliff top—Tag and Cy, Pertelot and Leo and Ragnar. A warm breeze ruffled their fur. Behind them, huge white clouds sailed landward over the sea, on the streaked ultramarine surface of which could be seen the flecks of little waves and, distantly, a fishing boat with a jaunty red hull chugging its way slowly northward. If human beings could have seen them there, five cats sitting in a circle on the edge of a cliff under a bright blue sky, what would they have thought?

"I am going to look for Isis and Odin," Tag went on grimly. "I am the Majicou now. It is my responsibility. I will be back and forth, here and there. We may not see each other so often. To be safe, you should go north and live with Cy, and be looked after by our friends the fishermen."

"We won't leave here."

"But Pertelot—"

She gave him a look of reproach.

"And we will never live with human beings again. Mercury, how could you ask that?"

"Easily. Whoever took Odin and Isis will return for the third kitten. You know that. We are up to the tips of our ears in something here—I feel it."

"Even so."

Tag had always found her difficult to convince. He might

be the Majicou, but she was the Mau. Though she had visited it only in dreams, another land spoke through her. Ancient responsibilities ran hot and mysterious in her veins. Also, he loved her too much to argue. When she sat up straight and powerful like that, and stared at him with her eyes half closed, he could only look away. He watched the fishing boat as, bobbing like a silly painted cork, it rounded a distant dove-gray point, a headland barring its way as lazily as a human arm outflung across the water. Suddenly he had an idea.

"Then at least go to the oceanarium," he said. "It's empty at night. In the day you can—" He paused. What could they do? Then he had it. "In the day you can have a holiday," he said.

"What's a holiday?" demanded Leonora.

"I'm not entirely sure," said Tag. "Human beings are doing it all the time."

"Are there fish on a holiday?"

"More than you saw in your recent visit to the sea," said her father. "Don't interrupt when your mother is thinking."

After a moment, the Queen blinked once.

"Very well," she said.

Cy the tabby stood up, stretched briefly, then turned around and around in a delighted circle, tail up, rubbing her head against their heads in turn. A purr like the clatter of a broken lawn mower filled the headland.

"Ace to base," she said. "I'd love to have you. At my place there's all kinds of real stuff to see." She paused shyly. "I got this fish for a friend," she admitted, aside, to Leonora.

Tag felt relieved.

"Then that's settled," he said.

"But what will you do?" the King asked him. "Where will you start?"

"I am going to do what I should have done a month ago," said Tag. He stared out to sea. The red boat had turned the point at last and vanished.

"I am going to do what the spider does."

🐾

He was the Majicou.

He went to the heart of his web.

From there called in his proxies. They were reluctant, but

they could not resist. Outlines shifting and warping under the pressures of magic, they came bounding, shuffling, galloping down the Old Changing Way toward him. Heat smoked up from their feet. At night, in Cutting Lane, pale lights could be seen coming and going behind the grimy windows of the old pet shop. If you had had business along that street in the early hours, you might have stopped—puzzled and a little anxious, perhaps—for a moment or two to listen to the subdued cacophony of animal noises, to catch the sudden circus reek of large creatures in a confined space, before you shivered suddenly and passed on. The black shadows of antlers moved on the walls. There was a coughing grunt. There were sudden uneasy movements in corners.

The new Majicou regarded his servants.

They shifted their feet and tried not to meet his glittering green eyes.

"Two golden kittens," he said. "Find them."

He said, "Use every strategy you know." He said, "The Alchemist may be back. You know what that would mean to all of us." He said, "If I am not here you will know where to find me. You will know by the signs. Come to me wherever I am. Come to me with news."

He paused. His gaze rested on them one by one, uncomfortable, intense.

He said again, "Find me the golden kittens."

The proxies fled. Tag followed them into the night, on a search of his own. He burned like a meteor in long flat arcs down the Old Changing Way. He was looking for Loves a Dustbin, who, as the original Majicou's lieutenant, had lived through more of the secret war against the Alchemist than anyone now alive. As he traveled, proxies came to him with their reports of nothing. Nothing to be heard. Nothing to be seen. Nothing to be found. "If you can't do anything else, at least find me the dustbin fox," he told them. "Send him to me." But the fox, it seemed, had gone to earth. Was that significant in itself? Toward dawn, Tag stumbled across a *vagus*, a scrap of the Old Life, in upland oak woods somewhere north of the city, and after two hours of mutual stalking, ambush and debate, dispatched it back into the deep communal consciousness where it belonged. Finally, he returned to Cutting Lane. There, he dozed for a while with his eyes open.

Suddenly, he thought, Unless it is Leonora, we have already lost the Golden Cat.

Chapter Three

THE BIG EASY

$\mathcal{S}$ealink watched the last of the passengers and cabin crew trailing away into the airport haze, then slipped silently down the gangway onto the baking tarmac. Balmy southern sunshine struck off her brilliant harlequin coat of orange, black, and white. A tail like an ostrich feather curled over her back. In her lifetime, this feature had won her many admirers. For herself she called it "an animal all its own, and a damn nuisance," but never without a certain pride. Her paws were large to match the rest of her frame, and she carried herself with considerable ease for a cat that had just hitched a ride across the Atlantic Ocean, right over the water to the town they used to call the Big Easy—they had called Sealink the Big Easy, too, but rarely to her face—the air of which was like a gentle steam bath freighted with the heavy scents of better times.

New Orleans! She drew in a deep breath and looked around. Crescent City, city of cats, city of food. She had set out from here to eat the world. If she was returning with a little less appetite, well that might be corrected, as soon as she had found her kittens.

In a manner of speaking, they had already found her. She had spent the Atlantic crossing imagining that they were close but unseen—trapped in the overhead lockers, zipped into carry-on bags, mewling from under every tourist-class seat. They were behind every closed door. Thirty thousand feet up and two hundred miles out from Heathrow, the cabin crew had found her scrabbling at a pressurized exit door under the impression that she heard kittens crying in the whistling blue emptiness outside the plane.

"But how'd she get here?" they'd asked each other, answering, "Just swanned right in during the stopover. A proper English lady." And when Sealink wriggled out of their arms and applied herself to the door again: "She's cute, but a real nervous flyer."

She was a hit with the passengers.

"Guess you can't throw her off now," they told the cabin crew. "Guess she got her free ride." They said, "Just make sure she doesn't open that damn door!" That had them all laughing.

Sealink, meanwhile, worked obsessively at the door, even though another voice in her head urged, Get a grip, hon. She shredded the airline carpet. All the way over the gray ocean, she was a haunted cat; but curiously enough, the sense of them faded directly as the airplane touched its wheels to the Moisant International runway. Was that a good sign? Was it a bad one? She had no idea. She was on brand-new territory here with nothing to go on but instinct. Ghost kittens, memories of kittens: they frazzled her when they were there; she missed them when they weren't. She wasn't used to this. What if none of it worked out?

"You'll find 'em."

And, setting her chin high, she resolutely made her way across the tarmac, ignoring the trucks and carts, the aircraft groaning and complaining as they taxied from place to place, the human beings distracted and panicky as they dragged their baggage about. She was careful never to run. *A running cat catches the eye* was a saying she recalled from her own kittenhood, though since she had no more recollection of her mother than her name—Leonora Whitstand Merril—she guessed the advice came from one of the many scarred old tomcats she had once hung out with on the Moon Walk, the wooden boardwalk that ran along the banks of the great Mississippi River.

The Moon Walk! That promenade of soft airs and gently riven dreams, whose denizens, though luckless and self-defeatingly individual, had always known how to live—how to eat, how to love, how to improve the midnight hour!

"I'm back," she told them in her heart, as she skirted the glass-walled buildings of the terminal.

"I'm back."

❧

If you are a cat, travel in New Orleans begins with the Grand Highway, which issues from a huge cemetery in the lakeside area of the city and sweeps down from there to the levee on which Sealink had been raised. If you are looking for something, there is no better place to start.

From the Grand Highway, paths branch, then branch again in all directions, to Greenwood and West End Park, Audubon and Armstrong, through the grounds of Loyola University, into the elegant, sunlit courtyards of the Garden District and out to the Fairgrounds Race Track. The wild roads—busiest wherever human inhabitation is at its most dense yet always beyond human view—run through the river to the suburbs of Jefferson and Gretna and Algiers and out into the bayou wilderness. Around Metairie they run in localized tangles branching off the greater highways; but south and west, toward the Garden District and the Vieux Carré, they are as bunched and knotted as rats' tails, mapped onto the city by cats heading en masse for their favorite haunts, where they cool themselves in shady courtyards or beneath the camellias of an elegant town house or beg for scraps from the tourists at the markets, the street cafés, and hot dog stands around Jackson Square. They cross and recross the Pontchartrain Expressway, occupying the same space in a manner no human being can possibly comprehend—though some have tried. Glimpsed through the swirling, dense light of the highways, car headlights on the interstate flash past in blurry streaks, occupying another dimension entirely. Centuries before men built their raw, literalistic imitations, the wild roads were here, laid down as patiently as a geological sediment by the Louisiana panthers, the bobcats, and swamp cats. When the humans have gone and their poor artifacts have fallen into decay, the cat roads will remain. They are less a road than a way: a way of life. Give yourself to the highways and they return your investment a thousandfold.

They give you back a larger self.

Thus Sealink as a kitten, years before. Jazzed, jangled, and pixillated, joined up with other runny-eyed disobedient brats—driven by the same mix of hormones and nosiness, all zest and gall and natural bristle, elated to find themselves out there unsupervised among all the scary grown-up cats—she had tumbled hourly down the curves and re-entries to burst out at some unplanned destination with a puzzled "Wha—?" and a prompt collapse into group hysteria, play-fighting, and general bad behavior.

"How'd we get here?"

"This here a church, Octave! You brung us here to pray?"

"No, I brung you here to *prey*."

Young queens, propelled into the flux by drives they barely comprehend, glory in its sustaining power, which—comprising partly as it does the souls of a million queens down the ages, all glorying in their newfound power—is primal and shared. To begin with, it had delighted Sealink to make the gift of her own individuality. It was fine to be feline! To walk out, tail up and boardwalk bold, a cat among other cats, was enough. It had filled her with pride. Later she was not so sure. As her sense of self developed, her enjoyment of shared experience had declined. Was she some ordinary cat? Honey, she was not! She was the Delta Queen, good-looking, strong, daring, and—above all—unmistakable. Tomcats pursued her. Other queens were jealous; their eyes hardened when she hove into view, hips rolling like a whole shipful of sex. She laughed in their faces and passed on by.

That was how she had made an adventure of travel on the more visible surfaces of the world. Cars, boats, and planes, invited or not; on her own four feet if she had to, grinding out the miles to the next ride. How many human drivers, tired at the end of a long day, had rubbed their eyes at that ostrich feather of a tail and motored on, dismissing it as a hallucination? How many more—by truck stop and diner, not having an atom of shared language—had understood its message nevertheless: "Say, babe, you goin' to Topeka?" Crushed-shell lots, juke joints, sleep snatched in the back of some redneck pickup rusted out to orange lace, so you woke up two hundred miles away from where you started, puzzled and hungry: it was a hard, slow road.

But what freedom! To be a cat and live in the human world! It went without saying that human beings loved her, too.

After that, what could it have been but good-bye to the Moon Walk, good-bye to the Delta? That was the paradox of Sealink's early life, she guessed. Easy travel had kept her tied to the Deep South; hard travel had made the world her oyster. Dizzy with a sense of her own self, she had gulped it down, juice and all, the whole delicious, salty works of it.

But such freedom can be illusory. The wild roads wait—patient and real, like parents—for you to return. Still travel them suckers when you need 'em, thought Sealink, sniffing around behind the Moriarty tomb. "Now let me see. I recall a entryway not too far from here—"

Grand white mausoleums towered up among grass passages, luxuriant trees, and shrubs. Above her the statues known as Faith, Hope, and Charity guarded the base of a sixty-foot tunnel. Faith, Hope, and Charity sinking down into a long, dark hole in the ground. Sealink tilted her head consideringly.

"Seems kinda apt," she had to concede.

She pushed her face into the highway. She was tempted to withdraw, but it was too late. Her will to remain separate collapsed into itself. Her senses were engulfed. The world rushed away in a gray blur. As soon as she entered the flux again, she saw how damaged it was, how things had deteriorated even as she crossed the Atlantic. "This ain't good," she told herself. The roads were cold and wrong, difficult to navigate. Her kittens began to call out for her again, loud and accusing down the years. "I'm coming," she told them. "Momma's coming." She shivered and pushed on.

🐾

An unknowable time later, she was back in the Old Square. The highway debouched behind the Farmer's Market, amid a chaos of boxes and crates, corn husks and garbage bags. As the buzz of the old road faded, Sealink's nose was assailed by a thousand different smells: liquefying produce; fish in various stages of decay; the dry, musty scent of diseased pigeons; engine oil; human sweat; roasting pecans. Somewhere close by someone was deep-frying shrimp popcorn. Oddly disoriented, Sealink closed her eyes, inhaling deeply. It smelled as much like home as anything could. And yet—

Familiar ground, brand-new territory.

There was a sudden eruption from among the crates. A big white cat, his face marked by long, gummy runnels down the nose, burst from the debris, scattering chewed corn husks, sad crusts of bread, and bits of rotting tomato. His shoulders were wide and muscled, his haunches bunched ready to spring. A new pink scar showed raw against the fur of his lower belly. An onion skin hung out of his mouth. Why was he eating this crap? Sealink stared at him with a kind of puzzled distaste. On the other hand, you had to begin somewhere.

"I was looking for some kittens," she said.

She might not have spoken. The white cat hissed. His ears—such as they were—went flat against his skull. Unsavory curses spilled out of his mouth.

"This is my food," he said.

Sealink was disgusted. It was not what she had expected. It was not your hometown welcome back. It was not the voice of the Big Easy. "This ain't food," she said, treating their surroundings to a look of contempt. "It ain't even consumer-quality garbage." She decided on a change of tack. "Look, babe," she went on, in the drawling contralto that had served her well in fourteen countries—a voice that had charmed *camels*, let alone tomcats, whose knees it had been known to turn to jelly, "let's take it easy here—"

"This is all mine," said the white cat. He put his head down and began to advance on her.

Okay, she told herself, so the voice didn't work.

She thought, Time for Plan B.

Unsheathing her claws, which she kept impeccably honed, she hurled herself at the white cat. He was some pounds heavier, and his muzzle was scarred with the marks of many previous encounters. But as he lunged to meet her, Sealink leapt high in the air. With an acrobatic twist surprising to see in a cat of her size, she turned herself through 180 degrees and landed on top of him. The white cat looked appalled. His eyes rolled up in his head, trying to pinpoint this unconventional aggressor. Sealink seized the initiative. Opening her jaws as wide as they would part, she sank her teeth into the thick skin at the back of his neck. Curiously, for all his bulk, it felt flabby and wasted. Suddenly she found herself swinging around in front of him, still with his flesh clamped firmly in her mouth. Alarmed at this unexpectedly close head-on view, Sealink let go. The white cat stared at her, sparks flaring in his puzzled blue eyes. Then he turned tail and bolted.

Sealink sat down heavily, gazing after him.

Some homecoming.

"*T'es culloté.* You sure got a nerve. You done dusted Blanco *bien.*"

A neat little tortoiseshell-and-white had appeared as if from nowhere. Now she seated herself carefully among the rotting greens and, balancing with precision, began to clean between the spread toes of an elegantly extended hind leg.

Sealink turned in surprise.

"You a stranger around here, *cher*?"

"Kind of beginning to feel that way." Sealink fluffed out her not inconsiderable coat. She was already three times the size of the little tortie, yet the smaller cat appeared unperturbed.

"I ain't seen y'all before."

"I ain't seen you, neither."

The little tortoiseshell cat narrowed her eyes. Her tail flicked on the ground once, twice, with irritation.

"Kiki know you here, *cher ami*?"

So Kiki la Doucette still maintained her position as high queen of the boardwalk cats. Sealink did not have fond memories of that yellow-coated madam, with her cold stare and seraglio of attendant males. She'd been less than tolerant of other females, especially uppity young calico queens with a roving eye. Constantly in heat, Kiki had mothered litter after litter of scrawny kittens, extending her court from the Riverwalk to Esplanade. When the moon was high over the Mississippi, the levee had echoed to her ear-splitting yowls. Toms had traipsed from far and wide to visit the famous Kiki, then left the next day, scratched and sore, with a tale to tell of a wild Creole queen with a misleading name and insatiable appetite.

This was probably yet another of her myriad offspring.

"Since when does any cat need Kiki la Doucette's permission to come down the Grand Highway?"

"You not bowed your head to la Mère, you better *vamos*."

Sealink was infuriated. So much for shared heritage! She'd traveled half the world for this? To be set upon by a flea-bitten tom with the manners of a hound dog was bad enough; but to be expected to pander to some raddled old yellow queen who'd once tried to scratch her eyes out? Not likely. She turned her back with calculated disdain upon the tortie-and-white, stuck her tail straight up in the air like a standard-bearer marching to war, and sway-hipped it down the alley. Without looking back, she called, "I don't bow my head to anyone, sweetie; you go tell your mama her old friend the Delta Queen is back in town."

🐾

The little tortoiseshell cat watched Sealink turn the corner left toward the streetcar tracks and the river. There was a strange light in her eye. When the calico had disappeared from view she stood up, shook out each leg in turn, muttered something in a singsong voice, and slipped into a tributary highway. Three or four large blue flies rose as if out of the ground to buzz lazily around the fruit crates.

🐾

Everybody who is looking for something in New Orleans is bound to end up on the boardwalk. Down there, at least, everything was much as Sealink remembered. The Mississippi stretched away gray and leaden to the distant greenery on the opposite bank. Over at the Algiers docks, cranes towered above the water like huge predatory birds. She crossed the wooden planking and jumped down onto the beach, hoping to meet a cat she knew, someone whose unbroken link to the past would enable her to start the search in earnest. All she found was a rocky shoreline littered with driftwood and indefinable bits of plastic. Mooching along this murderous strand, she passed the hollow where she had once dallied with a salty ginger-and-white fresh off a foreign cargo ship. He'd spoken oddly and his fur had smelled of oil and spice. It had been her first time. He had bitten her hard in the back of her neck, and, being a feisty youngster as yet unaware of the appropriate etiquette, she had bitten him in return. He had leapt up in affront and rushed off down the boardwalk to groom himself obsessively and attempt to regain his composure. And then there had been Ambroise and Zephirain, Bill and Trophy and Spid. Sealink smiled to herself in recollection.

So many since then. All gone and all—but one—forgotten, cast aside with the brutal negligence of youth: always somewhere new to move along to, some new temptation. And if they didn't want to come down that road with her? Well, hell, she was Sealink, and the journey was the life. Except that the road had led her back to its beginning, another spin of the great big wheel of the world.

Everything seemed so much smaller now.

And so quiet.

Where was everybody?

There wasn't a cat in sight. And, curiously, no humans either. In her youth it had been a wonderful place to cadge titbits off tourists: a slice of sausage here, some little delicacy from a bursting po'boy sandwich there, maybe even a piece of soft-shell crab, if you'd hooked a real sucker.

But best of all was the old wooden bench, third from the steps. For the cats of the Moon Walk it was a favorite gathering spot. Every evening just as the light began to fade from the sky, as constant and inexorable as the Mississippi tide, the old man known as Henry had come down to the boardwalk. He'd moved slowly and stiffly, and his face was seamed with lines; but every night he would miraculously produce bags full of food: fish heads and chicken skins, shrimp and crab and mudbugs. As if from nowhere cats would appear in droves, a purring, mewing entourage who would wind themselves adoringly around his feet until all the food was gone, when they would slip away in selfish bliss among the shadows or drift along the weedy shoreline to groom and doze. To Sealink, Henry had seemed perfect. He smelled wonderful—fishy and catty and hardly human at all. Other people avoided him. He never tried to pick cats up; never

forced his will upon them; but arrived, uncomplaining and
punctual every night to smile upon their impersonal and mer-
cenary greed.

She rubbed her cheek against the bench. It smelled disused. There were crumbs under the seat, gone hard and stale.
Not even the pigeons were hanging out here anymore.

🐾

She moved south toward the Toulouse Street Wharf, still on
the lookout for the denizens of the levee, until struck by a
scent that made her nose twitch. The farther down the boardwalk, the stronger the smell became. Sealink sniffed appreciatively. An enormous sense of well-being swept over her.
There is little in life quite so fine as those moments a hungry
cat experiences immediately in advance of satisfying its appetite. Her nose led her to a trash can at the end of the boardwalk. It was an undignified squeeze for a cat of her size, but
was dignity at issue? It was not. Sealink squirmed her way
into the trash like a furry bulldozer and emerged some seconds later with her jaws clamped around a chicken carcass
that was still transmitting its irresistible signals into the
humid Louisiana air. To Sealink, these were signals of love.
She slipped with a grace born of many years of patient scav-
enging back onto the boardwalk. There, she wedged the de-
ceased fowl against a fence post and after some awkward
maneuvering, managed to insert her entire head inside it.
There were bits of gizzard left!

Thus engaged, she did not notice the large ginger cat,
who had been sitting silently for some time on top of the
fence, slip soft footed to the ground behind her. The tabby
markings of his coat swirled like a great, furry magnetic
field in gorgeous, complex patterns from shoulder to tail—
storms of ocher and orange and cream, marmalade and si-
enna converging as if drawn by some powerful force to a
nexus at his neck.

The calico's hindquarters swayed provocatively as she pursued the last remnants of meat deep inside the chicken. Her
glorious tail waved in the air.

The ginger cat made himself comfortable on the warm
planking and watched this show with considerable pleasure.

"Well, well," he mused aloud. "My afternoon has brought me a number of blessings: a gentle breeze on a humid day, half a boudin sausage down at the park, the remnants of a fine chili dog just by the tram stop. And now—just as my contemplations reach the conclusion that I am a sorry no-good vagabond with whom no self-respectin' female is ever likely to spend her time—I come down here and what do I find?" He fanned his whiskers appreciatively. "Why, a calico cat with the most entrancin' rump that I ever did see. My day sure is lookin' up. Tell me, honey, what brings a beautiful lady like yourself down to this sad shore?"

Deeply entrenched in the chicken, Sealink heard his words as a hollow blur. "Hold up, honey. My attention is engaged elsewhere right now," she muttered. She got hold of a last strand of meat and wrestled to extract it. Her considerable haunches swayed and jounced. This was too much for the ginger cat. With a growl of desire he launched himself upon her, burying his teeth where the back of her neck should have been—only to meet two-day-old chicken bone and slippery sinew. Feeling his unsolicited weight and plain intentions, Sealink howled in outrage. She backed out of the carcass, and, whirling like a dervish, fastened herself to his throat. He shot skyward until gravity intervened and Sealink was detached, spitting with fury.

Down on the boardwalk again, he backed carefully away from her, a shocked expression on his strangely marked face. Sealink noted how an irregular black patch spread itself across one ear and eye, lending him a distinctly untrustworthy air.

"What d'you think you're playing at?"

The marmalade cat stretched out his neck, cleared his bitten throat, looked shifty.

"Well, honey, it sure looked like a invitation to me."

Sealink growled.

"How could any red-blooded male resist? What could be more alluring than the sight of such a fine, mature queen offerin' herself like that?"

Sealink gave him a hard stare. He looked back at her, and the lazy eye in the middle of the black spot drooped so that for a moment Sealink thought he had winked. She felt the short fur on the top of her head bristle.

Suddenly she thought, Why, he ain't but a boy, and laughed.

"Honey, I was eatin'! I wasn't offerin' myself—to you or any male. And I don't take too kindly to bein' called old, either."

The tomcat, embarrassed, set about an elaborate toilette, starting with his face and front paws.

"So what's your name?" she asked at last.

"Red."

"Figures." A pause. "And where do you call home, babe?" she enquired.

"This burg is where I first seen the light of day," Red explained, "but foreign places have not been foreign to me, I confess. Though I return here every so often, home is just 'bout anywhere I lay my head." And indeed, despite his Southern drawl, he had a smell the calico recognized. It was the smell of docks and truck stops, cardinal points on the long, genial road to nowhere. "My story's easy told. I've been places where the nights are sweet with lilac, and places not so sweet. I'm a cat you don't meet every day, a cat of no fixed abode—" He gave her a look that had already shattered a heart or two along the road. "And I like it like that."

Sealink smiled into her fur at this callow Delta spiel, culled from the monologues of the traveling toms Red had met on his journey: it was one she had rehearsed a time or two. She warmed toward him in consequence, and found herself saying, "I know that feelin'. I'm from just about anyplace myself."

She deliberated for a moment, then, deciding that she might trust him with her difficulties, went on. "I come back here looking for kittens."

Red treated her to his sensual, lopsided stare.

"Might still be able to help with that," he offered.

"In your dreams, sonny. I come back looking for some kittens I already had." Sealink appraised the territory. "I have to say I find things changed. Soon's I leave the market highway, I get set upon by some old white mog with his skin hanging off him like a secondhand coat. Jeez, did he smell! Then this little scrawny female tells me I gotta check in with Madam Kiki 'fore I walk the boards of this town. Now I come down here, a place known to swarm with cats, and all I find is you."

"Guess you just got lucky, babe," said Red. Then he shrugged. "Cats don't pass their time here no more. Folks ain't so friendly as they were."

"Honey, this is the city of cats. There are darn near a million of us here—every one fed, directly or indirectly, by human bein's. What are you tellin' me?"

The marmalade cat regarded her askance.

"You been away too long," he said.

Chapter Four

THE LABORATORY

The cat known only as Animal X passed his time with four other cats in a five-chambered metal cabinet that left only their heads free to move. There were other cabinets nearby—though Animal X couldn't see them—and other cats in those cabinets. Some of them had been afraid when they were first brought here. Some of them had been angry. Now they accepted their situation. The only thing they couldn't get used to was not having enough mobility to groom themselves. The strain of this left them dull-eyed. Their necks were chafed into sores by the enameled edge of the cabinet. In an attempt to relieve the irritation this caused, they stared outward away from one another all day while human beings came and went around them, treating them as if they weren't there and saying things like "Hanson wants the workups as of yesterday, but he won't say why." Or "We can do the blood now, on its own, but it won't show anything. Doesn't he know that?" These people never touched the cats in the cabinets. They didn't need to.

"Doesn't he know that?"

Of all the things the human beings said this interested Animal X the most, because he knew so little.

He had no idea who he was. He certainly didn't know himself by the label Animal X. The life he lived did not require anyone to call him anything. It only required him—so he supposed—to feel pain. He woke up and he was in pain; he was in pain and then he slept. Something had been done to him. He felt a fool at having to stand there in one place all day; he felt as if it was his own fault. "Somehow I got caught," he would tell himself. He smelled his own smell suddenly, and a kind of shame went through him. He was dirty. Worse, there was a soft place in his field of vision where whatever it was had been done to him. He didn't remember it—that was the odd thing. Sometimes he kept very still in case it was done to him again. I want to avoid that, he thought. Thinking was difficult for Animal X. Thinking had been taken away from him with everything else. The soft place in his visual field was matched, somewhere deep in his head where thinking should have been carried on, by a kind of lesion. Some days everything was sucked into that gap or black wound and he was hardly there at all; others, at least he knew he was alive. On his best days he thought of himself, in his confused way, as a voice in a vacuum, a monologue held with the facts of a dull life. He didn't know who he was. He barely knew he was a cat. But his body remembered, and at night, in the cabinet, where no one could see them, his weak, withered legs kicked and trembled as, in dreams of their own, they tried to run him away from his prison.

🐾

A window was set high up in the room somewhere behind Animal X's head. He had never seen it, but he knew it was there by the parallelogram of sunlight projected onto the white-painted wall in front of him. He knew that shifting, flattened lozenge by heart. He had watched as it changed shape stealthily, hour by hour, across more days than he could count. At the end of the long afternoons the light from the window warmed each object it found, making everything, even in that place, seem friendly and familiar. The air became a rich, creamy-golden substance, less like air than pure color. You forgot the ammoniacal smell of the trapped cats around you. Light fell through the air in a single slanting bar; dust motes fell gently through the light like dandelion seeds.

Animal X thought, Dandelion seeds!

He thought, I wonder if—

He thought, No.

He had forgotten what a dandelion seed was, if indeed he had ever known. But he enjoyed the words as they drifted up out of the soft place in his head, then back down again, slowly losing their shape and coherence. And whatever else he thought, he had no doubt that the words, and the light—

especially the light—reminded him of some other life he had once lived. Things stirred and flickered just out of sight at the back of his mind. He couldn't remember what he was remembering; but whatever it was had been part of a more comfortable existence—at any rate, a more interesting one. These fragments of memory made him both happy and inexpressibly sad.

🐾

On a good day Animal X could just see, out of the very corner of his eye, the heads of the nearest cats to him in the cabinet. (A better view could be had by turning his head, but if he did that he was given a sharp reminder of the sore that went around his neck like a collar.) Next to him on his right was a cat so depressed it never spoke. This cat had replaced a very lively female, dimly but fondly remembered by Animal X as "Dancey." (Dancey—Animal D—had never stopped talking. Everything she said began with the announcement, "As soon as I get out of here—") On his left was Stilton, Animal B. He liked Stilton and the silent cat. Living so close, they were important to him. If they smelled a bit strongly, it was a smell to wake up to, a dependable smell. If there was something odd about the shape of their heads, well, something had been done to all the cats here, and perhaps there was something wrong with the shape of Animal X's head, too.

Stilton had been in the cabinet longer than any of the others. He predated both Dancey, whose departure Animal X had witnessed, and "the Longhair," a cat Dancey herself had often remembered fondly. Stilton had got his name because he always talked about Stilton. He would stare into space for a bit and then say, as if he was continuing a conversation that had already started, "Now, what you can get if you go to the factory shop—well, what my owners used to get anyway—is seconds. A bit overripe perhaps, you see. A bit runny. So for seventy pence you can get this great wheel, this whole cheese. It's a lot, but they'd split it with their friends. I'd see them eat it after their supper, lumps as big as your head. Lumps that big." But however much Stilton liked his favorite cheese, he couldn't finish the imaginary piece he always had with him. "Look at that!" he would say in astonishment, and then offer some to Animal X. "I love Stilton, but this is just too much." His voice was full of the regretful awe of the truly great eaters when they are forced to acknowledge defeat. "Can you imagine eating this much Stilton? It's not often I'm stumped. I'll say that."

Animal X could never think how to respond to this.

"It is big," he would try. Or "It's certainly big."

But what he said didn't seem to matter anyway, and after a moment or two Stilton would go on, "Never mind. The old girl'll come by; she'll be along soon enough." He nodded to himself in a satisfied way. He was always waiting for the "old girl," who seemed to be his mate—or perhaps one of his owners. The old girl liked Stilton almost as much as he did. "She's bound to come by. She'll help us polish it off."

Silence would descend for a moment before he added reminiscently, "Oh yes, I love Stilton."

"I hate it," said Animal X.

This exchange took place daily. Sometimes, to vary things, and so that his friend shouldn't feel too hurt, Animal X would reply not with "I hate it," but with "I suppose I quite like it sometimes. For a treat."

He wondered if—in the days before his own arrival in the cabinet, in the golden days of Dancey and the Longhair, perhaps—Stilton had ever talked about anything else. He wondered if he should admit that he had no idea what Stilton was, no idea what "pence" were. He wasn't even sure about cheese, though he thought he remembered something like it.

🐾

The two cats on the far side of the cabinet rarely joined in. That was the nature of this kind of captivity: in the cabinet, two animals were always behind you. But Animal X knew they held their own conversations. He heard them talking in the night. They asked each other the same question all the cats asked: "Can you remember who you were? I mean, before the cabinet? Can you?" Neither of them could, although they tried hard enough. After all, they were cats: they knew how to persevere. They tried so hard that, in the end, they were making up stories about themselves. They tried out memories the way a human being tries on clothes, picking them up and then putting them down apparently at random.

"I was a town cat, me. Oh, yes. It was backyards every night, backyards and singing and bad sisters, out on top of the wall where everyone could see. It was one long party for us, and no regrets!" Then, after a pause: "I've got a bit of a funny neck now, but I've got no regrets." Next night, the same cat would be claiming, "Sometimes I think I must have lived on a farm. You know? Because I remember the smell of straw and the warm breath of the cows."

"You remember that, do you?"

"I do. Sometimes I think I do remember that."

So their bemused dialogue droned on into the night, thoughtless and obsessive, broken by longer and longer pauses, until near dawn it petered out.

"Can you see what color I am? I've got this feeling I was a tortoiseshell."

By then, though, Animal X was asleep.

Sometimes he believed he had had another life than this one, sometimes not. One thing was clear: when he tried to remember the things that happened to him before he came here, his head hurt even more. Generally, he accepted that his life now would always be pain.

🐾

Plenty went on in the room, even if you could only see directly forward from your cabinet. There was a white door with a small square of glass in it, and people came in and out through that at most times of the day, though rarely at night. They were always talking. With a sigh and a shake of the head: "Figures that simply don't mean anything unless they're backed by observation." And then: "I know he said that. But look at his track record." They all had the same white coat on, but each one had a different smell, and their shoes creaked on the polished wooden floor. Animal X knew every dip in the shiny, pitted surface where it stretched between him and the door. He had even seen into the corridor outside; that was like a country in itself. And what a day when an insect got in, and you could follow its long, puzzled, looping passes across the room! He knew by heart the objects in front of him. An examination table on which were arranged a clipboard, a thermometer, and a powerful long-necked lamp; two white metal cupboards with glass fronts through which he could make out cardboard cartons, brown glass bottles, complex, sharp-edged shapes; the white door with its scuffed kickplate and satin-finish handle; then on the wall itself, a corkboard covered with pieces of paper that lifted and rustled in the draft when the door was opened or closed.

❧

One day the door opened and a human being in a white coat came in from the corridor carrying a wire cage. It walked across Animal X's field of vision from left to right, called something to one of its colleagues, and passed out of sight. Animal X heard it talking behind him, then another door opened and closed, and it was gone. The whole transaction took place in a minute, but remained sharp and clear in the watching cat's mind. The human had backed awkwardly in through the door, banging the cage against the doorframe. It crossed the room, its gait made awkward and lopsided by the weight and size of its burden. It exchanged a few words, then dropped the cage and left. It seemed relieved. That was that; but in those few moments, Animal X's life had begun to change again, although he couldn't know that.

In the cage was a creature of some kind. He caught a brief glimpse of it. It had glorious red-gold fur. Its eyes glittered a kind of hot jade color, with unlikely specks of silver. It was very agitated, turning ceaselessly back and forth in its own length, spitting and hissing, often throwing itself against the wire so hard that the man carrying it staggered sideways suddenly and swore. Animal X's immediate thought was, It doesn't belong in here, not with us. It's too good to be in with us. After that his impressions were confused and contradictory. Was it a cat at all? If so, it was clearly a kitten. Yet despite its leggy, slightly unformed lines and immaturity of face, it was bigger than many a full-grown tom. He had never seen a kitten so big. Before he could decide anything, it had vanished. But he was to see more of it, almost immediately. They had difficulty getting it out of its cage. And then, while they were trying to transfer it to a cabinet, it escaped.

Much of this took place behind Animal X's head. All he heard was shouts from the human beings. "Look out, just pull it out of there, can't you?" "I've got it, I've got it, it's okay." "Bugger!"—and a bubbling, ululating wail that rose suddenly into the fine mad high-pitched shriek of outrage all those confined cats remembered so well. Then the new animal streaked into view, low to the ground, ears flat, eyes bulging. It stopped for an instant in front of Animal X's cabinet to gaze back over its shoulder at the pursuit. It was a male kitten, all anger and beauty, piss and vinegar, but Animal X could see how much fear was mingled with its rage. "Hide now," he heard himself advise quietly. "You can get out later, when one of them opens the door." He was immediately aware what a counsel of despair that was. Sides heaving, hindquarters dropped protectively, every muscle bunched and hard under the short, velvety coat, body rocking to the beat of its own heart, the kitten stared up at him with a kind of empty defiance. For a moment he thought it would acknowledge him, tell him contemptuously, "I'll never be trapped like you." Instead it spun around and rushed away, to be followed an instant later by three or four human beings, all hands and shoes and spectacles. Their huge dull faces red and sweating, they grunted and stumbled after the escapee; while, unknown to them, the cabinet cats cheered it on. "Go on," they called. "Go on!"

That kitten had come into their lives from nowhere, and passed in half a minute from a zero to a legend. Hopes they never knew they had were invested in him. When he hid, they looked away, in case his pursuers should follow their line of sight. When he upped and ran, their feet scrabbled and scratched uselessly in the cabinet. They were trying to run on his behalf, and at the same time catch for themselves a little of his wild speed and freedom. The were filled with elation and a kind of savage pride. The kitten was undauntable. He was all energy. No cat in there had ever put up such a fight. If it looked as if the pursuit had its hands upon him, he could always find another ounce of pace. He stretched himself and ran and ran. He leaned into the corners. He was under the examination table in the blink of an eye. He was behind the cabinets. He was up and down the aisles between them in blurred figures-of-eight with his claws scraping for purchase on the slick and shiny floor. When nothing else would do, he seemed to be able to run around the very walls in defiance of gravity itself. It was then that the silent cat on Animal X's left spoke the only words anyone in that place had ever heard him say.

"Did you see that?" he asked, in a quiet but clear voice. "He went 'round there like the Wall of Death." And then, much louder, to the kitten itself, "Go on, my son! Give 'em the bloody Wall of Death!" None of the cabinet cats had any idea what he meant by this; but they took up his call—"Wall of Death! Wall of Death!"—and in the aftermath of these events, for a few days at least, Wall of Death became the nickname of the silent cat.

If the kitten heard any of this, he gave no sign. Favorite son or no, he had his own motives. He had his own life to live. Even as they egged him on, he was losing it. Animal X saw with dismay how tired he had become. He had burned himself up, and there was nowhere left to hide. His efforts became increasingly desperate. Eyes rimmed white with panic, he threw himself repeatedly against the closed door. He tried to get under the cupboard, but the gap was too small. Toward the end, trapped among the feet of the human beings, whining and bubbling angrily, he made them pay. He rocked back on his haunches. His claws shot out, his teeth flashed, drops of blood hung in the air like a spray of scarlet fuchsia. "Christ! It got me!" they shouted, backing away with nervous skips and jumps, shaking their fingers, staring at one another in astonishment. But eventually one of them went and fetched a pair of scarred leather gloves and a needle full of sleep, and after that it was soon over. The glorious savage, brought to bay in a corner by the cupboard, suddenly became silent and passive and was taken away dangling at arm's length like the empty pelt of a cat, out of Animal X's sight.

There was a shocked and empty pause in the cabinets.

Then someone whispered, "Did you see the eyes on him? Weird!" And someone added, "He was something to catch, that one." And someone else said, "It's a shame."

Suddenly, full of excitement, they all began to talk at once, shouting from cabinet to cabinet across the white room of their captivity, brought together in a way they had never been before. Animal X said nothing. He was saddened by this proof that life is, indeed, only capture, silence, and the cage: only pain.

✿

For some days afterward the laboratory was quiet. Things went back to normal. The sunshine moved across the white wall, beginning a little earlier every day, lasting a fraction longer. No one seemed to know which cabinet the gallant kitten had ended up in, if it had ended up in a cabinet at all. There were those that whispered it had not; they hinted at worse. As this rumor spread, conversation between the cabinets died out. Their occupants shrugged to themselves and went back to the long haul. Wall of Death—who had said nothing more anyway—became again the Silent Cat and stared ahead of himself all day. The human beings, perhaps, had received a reminder. They were a little more wary of their charges; but there was no more or less dried food in the stainless steel feeders than usual. The cats were fed last thing, just before the staff left, so that every evening the room was full of a sound like stones being sorted in a tin. Animal X regarded listlessly this manufactured stuff, with its strong but somehow unappetizing smell of fish products, and then, as usual, ate half of it.

"Sometimes," Stilton told him as they ate, "we'd have a nice bit of blue. That's a mold of course—they get the cheese like that by encouraging a mold to grow in it."

"I think they've encouraged a mold to grow in this," said Animal X.

"A bit of blue can make a nice change."

✿

Animal X often woke up before the other cats in the laboratory. Despite himself he loved the dawn. He loved the deepened silence around the first chirp of a bird, the edge of silver on things. He liked to be awake then, and know that everyone else was asleep. It made him feel warm toward them. Sometimes dawn dressed the room with pinks and golds; sometimes it stole in feathery gray, and a faint prickle of rain could be heard falling on the vegetation outside the unseen window: but good weather or bad it was filled with promise. No matter how ill he was, he couldn't stop himself from feeling optimistic. He thought he had probably loved dawns in his previous life, too.

Four or five days after the arrival of the kitten, he opened his eyes and looked around puzzledly. The room was too warm. There was a kind of hush. He shook his head. Things felt wrenched; barely awake, he already knew the day was out of shape. It had broken the wrong color, yellow on the edge of gold, increasingly tinged with a strange, hot, transparent green, like light falling through thick foliage.

"Well now," he asked himself, "what's this?"

The light intensified as he watched. It fizzed and crackled silently, like a burning fuse. The laboratory warmed under its touch. It was like high summer, like the light, he found himself thinking, though he had no idea where the thought came from, in some foreign land.

It was hot now. It was very hot. All around him now, the sleeping cats were bathed in light. It thawed their strained, uncomfortable attitudes. They sighed without knowing it, and relaxed, and did not wake, but for the first time in many months rested as if they had forgotten where they were. The light flickered about them, full of the power and humor of itself. Here and there it seemed to gather and spark. It glittered and crackled. It drew itself away for a heartbeat, during which Animal X held his breath. "I've never seen anything like this," he told himself. "Never. I know I would have remembered anything like this." Outside, every bird in the world began to sing suddenly. The fuse of the dawn burned and burned, then ignited in a great soft roar. A green flame exploded beneath the ceiling, spread rapidly, roiled down and across the laboratory floor. Everything in its path caught fire. Everything it touched was engulfed. Everything in the room began to fly apart, in complete silence. The cabinets were pulled to pieces and thrown about; equipment toppled through the burning air; the very walls tumbled outward and away, pulled and twisted as they went, into dust and detritus and falling bricks.

Animal X heard a voice say, "Even this." All the air was sucked out of him and he, too, was whirled away. He went end over end through the sky—forelegs splayed in front of him, feet spread, claws out as if they could find purchase on the air to slow him down—and landed in a vague, unending dream of kittenhood. He was very young. His mother was close. His brothers and sisters tottered and fought around her. They bounced and sprang. They were so safe! surrounded by something that stretched away in all directions and yet cupped them like a hand. He could feel it. Was it love? What was it? It cupped Animal X too tight, and everything he knew was taken away.

🐾

When he woke again, he was chilled right through. His fur was wet. The light was gray. He opened his eyes and the first thing he saw was the laboratory door. Something was wrong with it. It was hanging off one hinge, leaning into the room like a drunken man into an alley. He stared for a moment, then, not yet able to understand quite what he was seeing, let his gaze be drawn away. The laboratory had been opened up in a dozen other places. The windows had blown out; the ceiling had sagged and split. Loops of cable hung down. The floor was thick with splinters of wood and shards of glass, the air with plaster dust through which fell a fine cold rain. The examination table, site of so many indignities and so much pain, lay buckled and barely recognizable at the foot of a wall. It looked as if it had been thrown there by some enormous angry hand, which had gone on without a pause to dissect every cabinet into its component panels. Barely damaged, these lay distributed across the floor in curious, eddying patterns, like hundreds of playing cards scattered on a tabletop.

In the aftermath of the explosion, it was clear, many of the captive cats had taken their chance and fled the laboratory; but many others, too far gone to move, had been released by death. Animal X stood shivering in the wreckage. He gazed out dully over the windrows of silent animals, cats of all colors, coats clotted with neglect, patchy with eczema, sodden with the falling rain. Damp air moved over them and brought Animal X the sour simple smell of mortality. He felt an awful cry of misery and rage well up inside him, then fade away unexpressed. What would be the point? Intervention had been welcome to all these animals made old and miserable before their time. They lay in relaxed postures among the tangled wires and detached implants of their captivity, happy to accept the embrace of the green fire. Many of them had stretched out their forelegs in welcome, the way cats sometimes do when they are rolling in the sunshine.

Without the cabinet around him, Animal X felt alone and exposed. He stood shivering dully in the wreckage—his spine a bony, uncomfortable curve, his tail tucked tightly into his hindquarters—trying to make sense of it. He had been there as long as any of them. He had seen it all come and go. Why was he alive? What was he to make of that secret dawn and jungle light?

"I don't know what's happened," he kept telling himself. "I don't know what's happened."

Suddenly he said it out loud.

At that there was a stealthy movement in the remains of the cabinet. With considerable struggle and disconnected effort, the cat called Stilton hauled himself into view. He was coated in grayish dust. He looked down at himself in horror, made three staggering steps forward, and fell over.

"Are we dead?" he whispered.

"I don't know," said Animal X. "All these others are."

"Come and sit here," said Stilton.

They curled themselves as tightly as they could around each other. Shaking fits passed through them. They tried to lick each other clean, but their bodies were so relieved to feel the touch of another cat again that they fell asleep immediately. They stayed that way for much of the morning, unwilling to leave the site of their old cabinet—though they kept a distance between themselves and the bodies of the cats they had shared it with. Animal X found himself remembering those three with more affection and less discomfort than he had expected. The Silent Cat had given up speaking because he didn't have anything left to say about life, he thought. Death must have been a release for him. Then he reminded himself, I never knew the others, though I heard them talk. They might have been interesting cats. He thought, I would have known them better if they'd been next to me in the cabinet. His memory was already garbled and confused, so that some repeated phrase of theirs had become mixed up with the luminous dawns, the rattle of hard food in a tin tray, the flutter of paper on the corkboard by the door. It all seemed one, and surprisingly like a life.

🐾

The rain stopped. The sun came out. Mid-afternoon saw the two survivors poking about independently in the ruins.

Cabinet life had so wasted them that they had to teach themselves to walk again. Animal X's progress was punctuated by unexpected skips and jumps, sudden shies and spasms of his depleted nervous system as it readjusted to the proper life of a cat. At first he felt rather excited by these sensations; but it was a vigor that proved illusory. He hadn't eaten since the previous evening. Despite his excitement, despite the optimism the watery sunshine had brought with it, he had no stamina, no condition, no muscles worth speaking of. Stilton was worse. He limped. His fur, draggled into hard, crusted little curls, tasted of blood when you tried to groom him. There was something pushed-in about his ribs. Sometimes he forgot where he was and stood swaying and blinking and repeating quietly, "Now, my owners, you see—"

Once he called over to Animal X, "Aren't we a pair, eh? What a pair!"

Whenever they met, they backed off and stared at each other, surprised all over again, trembling with fear of the future.

"You're a tabby then," said Animal X.

"I'm starving."

"There isn't any food left. I've looked and looked."

"What are we going to do?"

"It can't hurt to try again."

They were wobbling stiff-leggedly about in the dust when the golden kitten appeared. It walked up quietly out of nowhere and stood patiently in front of Animal X. Though it was clearly distressed, it couldn't or wouldn't speak. Oh, it was still all beauty and thuggishness, a kind of glowing, raging overstatement of itself. A week in the laboratory had done nothing to change that. The muscle still bunched and shifted beneath its sandy, luminous coat. It still moved with the kind of fluid absent-mindedness common to young animals. One eye still flickered with lights like specks of gold in jade. It had lost the other in the explosion.

"You'll be all right," said Animal X.

He couldn't think of anything better to say. Despite a sticky discharge at the inner corner, he thought the wound looked clean. "What do I know?" he asked himself. "You'll be all right with us," he tried to reassure the kitten. It stared silently ahead. The lids were already drawing closed across the insulted eye socket to seal it off. When Animal X looked closer, he saw that they had been sewn together some days before. Humans had taken the eye. The explosion wasn't to blame at all.

"Can you remember who you are?"

The kitten looked away from him. It trembled a little, then stood closer and, still looking away, began to purr loudly.

"Come on," Animal X said tiredly. "We'd better get you out of here."

Chapter Five

LEAVE IT TO LEONORA

*T*ag the cat sat on a shelf in the abandoned pet shop at Cutting Lane.

It was the end of a wet afternoon, and the light was fading to brown on the other side of the dirty, rain-streaked windows. Soon the street outside would echo briefly to the sound of hundreds of human feet. The sodium lamps would turn it orange. Then the noise would die away, and the pavements would belong to cats again. "The night," his old mentor had once advised him, "is always the best time for doing the work of the Majicou." So—though he could have done that kind of work at any time from Cutting Lane, so central was it in the web of the wild roads—Tag sat on his shelf to wait.

Come on, night, he thought.

As soon as he had finished here, he planned to visit a pie stall three streets away and eat battered scallops, white pudding. In the meantime he got up, shook himself, and was just turning around to find a more comfortable position when he heard a noise at the back of the shop.

Scrape.

It was like claws on bare wood. He heard it once and then again. What's this? he thought. Scrape. Click. Scrape. Like a lame animal circling quietly in the back room.

Something had come along the wilds roads to him, something that owed allegiance to the original master of Cutting Lane. Tag got to his feet and backed carefully along the shelf until he was hidden behind some thick spiderwebs. With no one to teach him how to be the Majicou, he had learned caution early. Most of the proxies were harmless. Some weren't. He never showed himself until he was sure.

Out loud, he said, "No one asked you here, but you won't be hurt."

Scrape.

"Come into the light," he said.

A thick voice answered, "I saw something the Majicou would pay to see."

"There are no payments here."

"Then there is no news."

"Come further into the light."

Click. Scrape.

Perhaps it had once been a dog. Perhaps it had wandered onto the Old Changing Way and something had happened to it there, and it could no longer go back to whatever life it had once enjoyed. It was very old now, as if the wild roads had kept it alive too long. It was large and shapeless, and it had a large, shapeless smell. Coarse brown and black hair with an oily look. A misshapen head that nodded up and down as it walked on its three legs. Eyes milky with cataracts. There was something indeterminate about all these things. Its voice was like a voice strained through kapok. Tag had dealt with it before.

"I know you," he said.

"You are not the Majicou."

"Yes I am."

"Then come with me."

"Why should I?"

"What do you know about death?"

"Less than I could."

"Then come with me and learn."

Limping and pausing, panting and dragging, it led him into the back room, where it promptly vanished into the air. Tag followed. They debouched in an alley between two buildings. There was no talk between them. In a little while they came to the river. There, as the day packed itself away into the west, the Dog showed him what it had found. At low tide here, a small but well-used highway had its entrance in a filmy gray twist of light between two rotting piles. It was popular with the animals of both banks as a way across the river and had comprehensive links to much larger roads. Tag stood in the smell of mud and stared at the heap of corpses the Dog had brought him to see. There were ten or fifteen of them. They were all cats. Their fur was sodden. Their limbs were entangled as if they had fought in panic with one another at the last. Their eyes bulged so hard that the whites showed. They had died with their ears back.

"How did this happen?" said Tag.

The Dog looked at him dully.

"The life has been drained out of them," it said. "Something is wrong with the Old Changing Way. I don't know what."

"Go away and learn more."

"You are not the Majicou," grumbled the Dog.

"I am the new Majicou. Always come to me when you find something."

"Yet there is no reward."

"Find me two golden kittens and we'll see."

The Dog turned away with a sigh and dragged itself up the shingle toward the buildings. Something made it stop and say, "I am a dog. A dog has a sense of smell. If I did not know better I would say I smelled the Alchemist on that road. I would not use it if I were you."

Too late.

The new Majicou had gingerly negotiated the heap of dead cats and stuck his head in the highway.

🐾

What he found there was not unusual. How can a road go in all directions at once? No one knows the answer to that. The Old Changing Way, which will take you anywhere in hardly any time at all, is full of ghosts. Nothing more can be said. Unless you know what you are doing it is a dangerous place to be. Even at the best of times.

Hmm, thought Tag.

He thought, Nothing here.

But as soon as he pushed his way inside he knew that the old dog had been right. It was like moving through glue. He was exhausted suddenly, and his bones felt hollow. Worse, something was waiting for him. He couldn't say how he knew. Only that when the strange, tinny echoes of that place fled away from his feet, something moved among them. It was following him. He stopped. He raised his head, and let the wind talk to his whiskers. As Leo had done in the sea cave, he opened his mouth to taste the air.

Nothing. And yet—

I'll just go to the other end, he thought, and see what things are like there.

It was a longer walk than he had anticipated, and with more twists and turns than was proper. He couldn't shake his lethargy: he felt as if he had been walking all day. By the time he admitted, "I could have swum the river quicker than this," he knew that he had made a mistake. The inside of the old road was like an accordion-pleated tube of plastic, full of a brown fog you couldn't smell, only see. It seemed to flex and shift. When you turned, you thought you felt it turn with you. Tag kept calm. "I've made a mistake," he told himself. "But I've made mistakes before. Things always came out right in the end." He closed his eyes and got himself facing back the way he had come. His energy was returning, but he knew he had better not try to run. He knew what might happen to you if you panicked in there.

I can get out of this, he thought.

Then he heard the follower again.

"Who's there?" he called.

When he walked, it walked. When he stopped, it stopped. It was hiding quietly and patiently in his footsteps.

"I can get out of this," he told himself.

He set his ears back and ran until he thought he would burst.

In a moment, he had reached his start point and popped back out onto the bank of the river, where he tumbled end over end among the dead cats, spitting and hissing with fear and disgust. The fur bristled along his spine. His teeth bared themselves with no help from him. He got to his feet and turned to face his pursuer, a shriek of rage building up in his throat—

It was Leonora Whitstand Merril.

"Hello, Tag," she said shyly. Then she caught sight of the corpses.

He took her home immediately, and without a word spoken, so that her parents could scold her roundly in the dim green light of the oceanarium.

"What were you thinking of?" demanded the Mau. "What could you have been thinking of?" While Ragnar Gustaffson shook his head and—conveniently forgetting his own first acquaintance with the Old Changing Way—said that in his opinion it was a very irresponsible thing to travel wild roads as a kitten without protection or preparation.

"A very irresponsible thing, Leonora."

Leo looked abashed for a moment. Then her confidence returned. "I want my brother and sister back," she said.

"We all want that," said the Mau tiredly. "You could help by not being taken in your turn." With a kind of puzzled distaste she looked up at the great tank, where the sharks circled relentlessly in the illuminated water. "We live here with these—" for a moment, she seemed lost for words "—these fishes, to keep you safe."

This only made Leo angry. "I don't want to be safe," she said. She said, "No one is doing anything!"

"I'm doing what I can, Leo," said Tag. Now that his fur had settled down, he felt mainly relief that he hadn't hurt her. Nor could he forget her expression when she saw the grotesque and pathetic heap of fur at the end of the highway. It was hard to stay angry, though Leo seemed to have no difficulty with that. "I might have killed you by the river," he added quietly. "I had no idea who you were."

She looked away. "I'm sorry," she said.

He could see that she was, but that it wouldn't change things for now. He felt uncomfortable on her behalf—though he knew she wouldn't thank him for that either—as she turned and stalked off toward the door.

"Where are you going?" demanded the Mau.

"All these fish make me hungry," said Leonora. "I'm going to find Cy and get chips from the tourists."

"Leonora!"

"It's quite safe."

When she returned in a better mood about two hours later, licking her chops and smelling strongly of hot lard and vinegar, she found Tag waiting for her on the oceanarium doorstep.

"You've hurt their feelings, Leo," he said

"I know," she said. "I'll go in and apologize."

"Wait," said Tag. "Sit here for a moment."

She sat.

"You look tired," she said. She began to groom herself absently, then turned her attentions to him. "And you've let your ears get dirty."

"Leonora, that wasn't the first time you'd followed me, was it?"

She stopped licking him and looked away.

"I'm sorry," she said quietly. "I knew you'd guess in the end. I wanted to learn about the wild roads. They're such a part of your life—and Ragnar's and Pertelot's. I feel left out. I'm only a kitten, but I want to know things."

"I wish you'd asked me," he said.

"Are you angry?"

"No," he said. "In fact I'm rather relieved that it was you. Still," he chided her gently, "you should never take an adult cat by surprise like that. Your mother and father and I, we fought the Alchemist—" How could he explain? "We've seen some awful things. We—we were toughened by it, whether we wanted to be or not. You shouldn't surprise us. And especially not the Majicou. The Majicou can be a more dangerous animal than you imagine."

Leonora laughed. "You didn't look so dangerous when you fell over," she said. "Oh dear, now your feelings are hurt, too."

Tag blinked.

"If you really want to learn things," he said, as offhandedly as he could, "you'd better start coming out with me."

❀

His main argument to Ragnar and Pertelot had been simple: "If you forbid her she'll just keep doing it anyway." They had seen the force of this. They had expected him to make promises, of course. Leonora must agree to do what she was told. She must always stay by him. Once all that was sorted out, he had tried to calm their fears further by adding, "She'll soon get bored when she sees how humdrum it all is."

"Don't misjudge Leonora," the Queen had advised him grimly. Hurt feelings or not—and who could use such a phrase to describe the wells of sorrow and anger, the Egyptian deeps of the Mau's affections?—she loved her daughter. "She's an untapped soul."

In a way, both of them turned out to be right.

❈

Leonora was soon bored.

"Love the world, Leo," Tag would advise her. "That's the secret of success. Love the world and follow your nose." This axiom gave rise less to a search of the wild roads than a communion with them, less an interrogation of their denizens than a conversation. It hardly suited the leonine temperament. True, she enjoyed learning how to find and navigate her chosen highway, how to recognize a safe or a difficult entrance, how to watch the ever-changing smoky light. It was an adventure. "Quick now, Leonora!" Tag would urge. "Follow close!" Or "Wait! Wait here and make no sound!" She soon learned to listen for that edge in his voice, that promise of excitement and danger. And she soon fell in love with the bizarre and eccentric animals he knew—the "creatures of Majicou" who had acted as agents, informants, proxies to the original guardian of the wild roads. She loved the marginal places they lived in and the odd relationships they seemed to have with one another or with human beings. All this was rather exciting. But it was broken up by long periods at Cutting Lane, during which her teacher sat among the spiderwebs and seemed to do nothing at all.

Instead of changing his plan when it produced no discernible results, Tag only became thoughtful. On their third day along the Old Changing Way, he took her to some city gardens. There, he spent an afternoon in the sunshine on the lawn in front of a house with weatherbeaten blue paintwork. He lay sprawled out on the warm grass, all creamy white and silver, watching amiably the huge bees that zizzed and

bumbled in long arcs through the summery air. He was silent
for so long she thought he had gone to sleep.

"Tag," she said, after some time, "why have we come
here?"

"I often come here to think."

There was another long pause.

"The thing is," he said eventually, "I used to live here. Or
somewhere like it. Two rather dull but very generous human
beings bought me from a pet shop, and I lived a good life."
He laughed. "I ate some things!" he said. "Tuna fish may-
onnaise. Meat-and-liver dinner. Chicken-and-game casserole. Chicken-and-game casserole was my downfall, in the
end. I don't suppose you've had any of those?"

"No," said Leo.

"Or mackerel pâté, which is like a whole shoal of fish in a
tin. Silver fish in a tin: that's something!"

"Now you're just teasing me," Leo said primly, and added,
having perhaps forgotten her passion for chips, "Pertelot says
convenience food is bad for us anyway. And if you were
having such a good time, why did you leave?"

"Well," Tag said, "I can't say I went of my own accord. But
I did leave. The Majicou saw to that. He and his magpie, they
gave me no rest until I did. One thing led to another, and we
sorted things out, and here I am. It was a big fight, the day you
were born and the Majicou died."

"Was he wonderful?"

"He was big. I never saw a bigger cat, or heard a more con-
vincing one."

"You were his apprentice."

"I suppose I was."

"And did you love him?"

Tag looked puzzled.

"I don't know if love's the word," he said. "He was full of
anger and good advice. One of the last things he told me was
this: 'The wonderful place is inside you, and it goes wherever
you go. Homes are made.' But you know, even though he was
right, and I've made a new life for myself, sometimes I still
miss the home I had. So I come here, or go to one of the other
gardens I remember, and scout about for it. I would recognize

the voices of those dulls, I'm sure. Although what I'd do if I found them I've no idea. Does that seem odd to you?"

"I think I'm too young to have an opinion."

"Ah," said Tag. "Of course."

He turned his attention back to the house. After a while he raised his left hind foot and scratched vigorously beneath the ear on that side. Leo, meanwhile, launched herself after a passing cabbage butterfly, missed comprehensively, and turned the leap into a grave, complex little dance—a series of enchained steps, a spring, a turn. She loved to dance. I'll never learn to hunt if I keep doing this, she thought. She thought, Odin is the hunter. I wonder where he is now?

"Anyway," said Tag suddenly, "that was how it was explained to me. Home is what you make."

Leo, who had already suspected this, continued her dance.

"Am I your apprentice?" she asked lightly, so that he shouldn't see how important is was to her.

Tag yawned.

"Time to get you home again," he said.

Then he added, in rather a surprised way, "Do you want to be?"

"Oh, only if you would like it, too."

"There is one thing more we could try," Tag told her, "before we go home. We could visit the domain of Uroum Bashou, the cat they call the Elephant."

Leo shivered.

"Is he called Elephant because he's very big?"

Tag stared at her.

"To be frank, I'm not entirely sure what an elephant is," he said. "I only know—"

"It's something very big," Leo told him. "Don't you know anything?" She added matter-of-factly, "Mother dreams of them sometimes. She dreams almost every night." She thought for a moment. "One day," she said with a kind of careless hauteur, "I shall dream of elephants, too."

Tag continued to stare at her. He wondered if he had been as impenetrable at her age. "I only know that he can read," he finished. "Would you call someone Elephant because he can read?"

"What's reading?"

Tag wasn't entirely certain about that, either.

"Wait and see," he said.

He only knew what Uroum Bashou had told him: that human beings kept what they called "books," and that the Reading Cat was able to sense the meaning of the "words" these books contained by passing his paw quickly along each line of the text, or sometimes by licking it, and even by using his whiskers to sense faint changes in pressure caused by the movement of the air across the print. Uroum Bashou rarely used his eyes now that he had grown older—although of course that was how he had learned to read as a kitten, sitting on his owner's shoulder as his owner turned the pages of some interesting volume—*Birds of the Green Forest* or *Small Rodents of the Northern World: Their Habits.*

"I'm tired of waiting and seeing," said Leonora, "actually."

For a moment, Tag looked amused.

"Oh, you actually are, are you?" he said. He jumped to his feet with an empty-eyed suddenness that startled her, snapped at a passing bee, and went bounding across the lawn, scattering last year's leaves as he went. "Then try and follow me if you can!" he called over his shoulder and with that, vanished.

She caught a twist of light in the corner of her eye, dived into the highway before it closed after him. The world tipped sideways, righted itself, ghosts streamed past, the compass wind howled around her. She could see Tag in the middle distance, running tirelessly along in a kind of slow motion. Echoes flew up from his pads in the shape of small brown birds. "Call yourself a cat?" he taunted. And without warning he turned at right angles into the wall of the world and vanished again.

Leonora stood among the echoes, panting. What now? she thought. "What now?" the echoes said, as they fluttered around her muzzle. "Oh, go away!" she told them. Off she went again, and this time caught up with him a little sooner. "I do call myself a cat!" she said.

But he answered, "Do you indeed? Then you already know the way. Such a clever animal doesn't need my lessons," and disappeared again. So it went, from the huge ancient high-ways laid down by saber-toothed cats after the ice receded to the little local mazes made by domestic cats, Tag always ahead, always allowing her to catch up, until she was thoroughly out of breath and out of temper, and they stood in the cluttered yard of an abandoned redbrick house somewhere in the Midlands, where early-evening light lay in slanting gold bars against the boarded-up windows, the scuffed and sun-bleached back door.

Into the door was set an old-fashioned wooden cat flap, scratched and battered and grubby with the passage of many cats. Above that, a smaller hole had been gouged in the door itself, perhaps so that the occupants could look out without themselves being seen. Behind the door, the air was disturbed by a stealthy movement, and a rank smell. One amber eye appeared in the hole and stared out at Tag and Leo. Its surface had an oily iridescence. Its pupil was dilated.

Leo rubbed her head nervously along the side of Tag's head. "Is it Uroum Bashou?" she whispered.

"Go away," said the animal behind the door.

"No," said Tag to Leo. "It is his guardian, Kater Murr."

"Go away," said Kater Murr again. Its voice was reasonable and dangerous. Its breath was bad.

"I am the Majicou," Tag said. "You know me, Kater Murr."

"I know no one."

The amber eye was removed suddenly. Leo had a sense of something ponderous and ill-favored shifting its weight in the gloom.

"Kater Murr, let us in," said Tag patiently.

A contemptuous laugh came from behind the door.

"He is not seeing anyone today."

"Stand away from the entrance."

There was a pause. Then the voice said, "Very well. I will not harm you if you come in."

But Tag answered, "Empty speech, Kater Murr. Empty promises. A cat like you can't hurt the Majicou." Then, quietly, to Leonora, "Don't follow too closely, just in case." The cat flap opened—a thick, sour smell poured out, like old food and ammonia—and closed again behind him.

Silence.

Leonora waited as long as she dared, looked fearfully around the yard in case Kater Murr had associates hidden among the buddleia bushes, then pushed her way inside. It was a kitchen, almost dark, with a few lines of gray light falling across a worn tile floor and a shallow stone sink full of green mold. Human beings had stopped using it years ago. That sour, disturbing smell hung over everything; but the kitchen was empty except for Tag, licking himself unconcernedly in a dim corner. Leonora felt let down.

"Where is he?" she said.

"He won't bother us now until we leave. He is the gatekeeper of this place."

She didn't like the way he stressed "this place."

"It looks like a house to me," she said, in an attempt to appear unconcerned.

Tag raised the paw he had just washed. He eyed it with approval. "Then come this way," he invited, "and I'll show you the Great Library of Uroum Bashou."

The empty house murmured with traffic noises, as if a decade of passing cars lived in its peeling wainscots and half-open cupboards. Leo followed Tag up narrow flights of uncarpeted wooden stairs varnished years ago a sticky brown color. Each landing was lit by a small dirty window. Off the landings, doors opened into rooms empty and broken looking: rooms with stale charred grates like open mouths, rooms that looked as if birds had taken up residence in them.

"What is that smell?" asked Leonora, wrinkling her nose.

When Tag advised, "You shouldn't ask 'what?' but 'who?' " she stared over her shoulder as if the walls had quietly sprung to life behind her as she passed.

She was unprepared for the top of the house—where everything had been knocked into one huge room, now lighted by the dull gold-and-orange wash of a setting sun, which ran like hot metal through a series of skylights and onto the scene below—or for the animal who greeted them there.

Uroum Bashou had once danced and scampered in the alleys of Morocco—or so he claimed. Now he lived in some state, albeit in the cold north; and books surrounded him. Books large and small, books bound with green and brown leather or orange paper, books in drifts, books in rafts. Closed books, open books, books swooning into piles, books whose wings and backs seemed broken. Books had slipped from the walls and slithered across the floors like the moraines left behind by some strange retreating glacier from a vanished age of print. Among them, like a pasha on a cushion in a souk, sprawled the Reading Cat, a browny-black, short-haired, skinny, long-legged old thing, who nevertheless exuded the dignity of the expert, the confidence of the emeritus professor. The fur around his ears was threadbare, as if he were a toy from which someone had thoughtlessly rubbed the velvet of his little sharp head. His eyes, a dim amber, were flecked with the many things he knew. When he spoke, though, his voice was light and fluting, the voice of the eunuch like a musical instrument in the closed courtyard; and he often spoke of himself in the third person.

When he saw Leonora, he began to purr.

"Uroum Bashou," he greeted her, "welcomes you, my dear. How can he help?"

"We are looking for two kittens—" Tag began.

Uroum Bashou ignored him.

"I see," he said to Leonora, "that you are admiring the Tail of Uroum Bashou."

She was indeed looking at it, but not perhaps with admiration. It was as skinny as he was, and there was something wrong with the tip of it.

"Come closer. This is the story. In brief, a cat is born, a cat with a knot of tangled vertebrae at the end of its tail. Do you see? This is not a malformation but rather the world trying to remember something. All well and good, you might think, and it is. But now things go immediately awry: because when a human hand is run lovingly down this tail and catches in the knot instead of sliding smoothly off the end, well then, many things come to mind, and the owner thinks, 'I must buy dates, or have dates bought for me.' Or it remembers, 'I must have someone's hands chopped off in the market today for thievery.' As a consequence, that cat's first name, his given, or kitten name, is Handkerchief."

Uroum Bashou's laugh was reedy and contemptuous.

"To put it shortly, I was that kitten, and you see him before you, not much aged. That was before I learned to read, and understood my task. I am the Great Aide-Mémoire. Through me the world remembers. But what? What am I here to signify? I do not know."

He shrugged a little.

"That is my tragedy," he said.

Leo, who thought he had finished, opened her mouth to speak.

"Oh, I know," he interrupted her. "You think me obsessed. I am. I will probably remain so." He brooded. "They called me Handkerchief, but what is that? Only the name of a kitten. So I learned to read. I read this: 'Imagine a prince, handsome, gentle, black haired; in his hand he holds the stripped and polished skull of a cat;' And this: 'weasels.' I read: 'smoke,' 'sensuality,' 'meringue,' 'mystery'! I read everything I could find, and when I came into my power I called myself Uroum Bashou, the Elephant. The Elephant never forgets—I have read that."

Leo stared at him. This time, she realized, he really had finished and was waiting for her to say something. All she could think of was "Have you seen my brother?"

At this he seemed to lose interest in her immediately, and turned to Tag.

"What does the Majicou know?" he asked.

"Nothing that Uroum Bashou does not," Tag said. "The world turns—"

"As ever."

"As ever. But the wild roads . . . The wild roads are uncomfortable, Uroum Bashou. They have begun to take where they should give. One day they are reliable; the next day they are not. Something is out of joint."

Uroum Bashou nodded his little threadbare head.

"You walk wild roads," he acknowledged, "while the Elephant stays among his books. That is good. What does the Elephant know? This: there is more than one prophecy that speaks of a Golden Cat. This: the Golden Cat may not be what it seems. This: the Golden Cat may not be all of it, or the end of it. Do you see? I see that you don't. And yet, there is a fuse burning in the world today. I do not know who lit it, or how. But something quite new is coming, and not just to us cats."

Leonora inspected one of her front paws modestly.

"I have often thought *I* might be the Golden Cat," she suggested.

Their heads went up, and they stared at her for a moment or two; then they went back to their talk.

"Don't mind me, I'm sure," said Leonora.

She reminded Uroum Bashou, "It must be one of us, you know."

But he only said, "I believe all this began in Egypt, where we began the fatal relationship with men. Whatever happens will be one end of a great arc across the history of cats and human beings." And he urged Tag, "Don't let yourself be diverted, as I believe your predecessor to have been, by simple oppositions. If the world is to be made new, the Golden Cat must be more than some simple piece of magic. To heal the world it must do more than cure the ills of cats or settle their old scores." It was advice he had given before.

They spoke of such generalities for a moment, then Tag said, "This is no longer a matter of theory, Uroum Bashou. Now that kittens are missing, it is vital that you make the books reveal what they know."

"Missing kittens are never a good thing."

"A cat must take note of that," Tag suggested, "where he might ignore other things."

Uroum Bashou inclined his head to show that he agreed. "I will interrogate the books," he promised, "on behalf of the new Majicou."

After that there was a silence.

"Your caretaker becomes more and more self-willed," said Tag eventually. In a corner of the room, away from the fierce gold light of the evening, he had noticed a pile of books that looked as if someone had recently tried to pull them to pieces. Pages were scattered about like mauled doves; there were toothmarks on some of the board covers. "Did he do that? You should have a care, Uroum Bashou."

A light laugh. "Kater Murr? There are days when his jealousy of my work is so great that he runs amok among the volumes, compelled to earn his name. He tears them with his great yellow nails. He does not understand them, so they are his rivals. He is barely feline. But he will never leave me."

"Don't underestimate him, my friend."

"I am quite tranquil about the whole thing," said Uroum Bashou.

🐾

Even as they spoke, Leonora Whitstand Merril was prowling the Reading Cat's house alone. At first she felt quite bold. She heard the murmur of conversation from above, and was both reassured and irritated by it. Leo had a great appetite for the particular: for things in themselves. She liked to get her nose into them. "You can't get your nose into a generality," she told herself, poking it instead around an open door on the floor below the library. Nothing. In another room, strips of wallpaper hung damply off the wall. Beneath them a mummified pigeon flopped, beak wide, eyes gone, one long wing extended in the fireplace. She dashed in and had a look, dashed out again. She hung off the lip of an empty drawer: newspapers; two coins with a dull, brassy smell; a bit of string. Really, it was all quite fun; but then, lower down, the stairwells darkened and seemed too narrow, and were further narrowed by the pervasive odor of ammonia, spoilt food, pheromones, as if she were continually having to brush past some other animal. By the time she reached the stairs to the ground floor the air was rank and solid, a substance rather than a smell. Leo hesitated and lifted her head to listen. The mutter of conversation from the library had grown faint and comfortless; three more steps down and it faded altogether. She was alone in a brown gloom, in some sort of stone-floored hallway. When she ran she could hear the shush and patter of her own paws. She stopped. She half turned back. She listened. Something touched her foot. She stiffened. She leapt away. It was the head of a discarded broom, as big as a cat, its bristles chewed off by time. She crept back, neck extended, to make sure it was dead. Other objects loomed in the hall: a bag of cement, half-empty; some broken floorboards; a dusty bicycle wheel propped up against the wall. An old coat on a hook looked like a human being.

Eventually she came to the kitchen. There she wandered about for some minutes, nosing into corners, pushing her head into a chipped enamel bread bin to inhale its ghosts of mice, jumping up to teeter along the rim of the old sink. She skirted a pile of old leather shoes. Until she was satisfied it was unoccupied, she kept to the margins of the room. Then she trotted into the middle of it to have a look at the kitchen table, with its ancient checkered-plastic tablecloth. The rank odor was thick and solid there. Leo looked up and saw her mistake. Oh no, she thought. The hair went up on her back. Staring away from the table as hard as she could, she began to inch out of the room. No decision of hers was involved. She directed her eyes down and away; and very stiffly, and slowly, and carefully, her legs began to take her toward the door. Ever since she came into the kitchen, the guardian of that place had been sitting on the tabletop in the soup of his own smell, watching her.

"And what are you?" he said quietly. "What are you, I wonder?"

He was an enormous, dirty, half-maimed old marmalade tomcat, with a broad flat head and ears chewed to mere frills of flesh a dirty pink color. One cheek had collapsed, bashed in perhaps by some hurrying car or angry human foot. Snaggle teeth protruded on that side and, viewed front-on, gave his expression a left-hand grin, widened, cannibalistic, matching in ferocity the yellow claws that would no longer retract into his huge, cobby paws. His front legs were as bowed as bulldog's, as if with the effort of supporting his hard-packed, muscular front end. His orange fur had once been on fire with complex, beautiful patterns—flames and bars and stripes that had curled and curved all down his flanks. As a kitten, on fire with life, he had been justifiably proud of those signatures. Now they were caked and matted, patched with black where the fur had fallen out. His eyebrows, wrecked in fights, were running sores. His ears crawled with mites. His voice was a battered growl, his laughter like gravel shaken in a tin; his scent was a nickname sprayed upon a wall.

"Hello," said Kater Murr.

And he jumped down off the table, his eyes a blazing, potent yellow in the gloom.

Leo backed away.

"I'm not here alone," she said.

Kater Murr put his head on one side.

"You might as well be," he said.

Then he said, "A question you might ask yourself is, 'Does he care? Does Kater Murr care I'm not alone?' " He sat down suddenly and scratched one of his ears until it bled. "Kater Murr lives in a house," he said to himself in quite a different voice. "His ears hurt, but he welcomes that. His bones ache, but he welcomes that. Kater Murr cares about nothing." Leo continued to inch away from him, only to find that on the word "nothing" Kater Murr had somehow slipped to his feet, gone around behind her, and placed himself smoothly between her and the door. "The gatekeeper," he explained, "though powerful, is a cat of considerable subtlety. You come here," he went on, "as you say, not alone, a kitten of a barely credible color, with no credentials—"

Leonora drew herself up. "I'm a princess, actually," she began to inform him; but then thought better of it.

"You're what?" said Kater Murr. "Speak up."

"Nothing," said Leonora.

The gatekeeper sat down and scratched himself again. "His skin itches, but he welcomes that," he mused. "His ears grow deaf, but he welcomes that. Kater Murr is a cat in a million." Waves of bad smell issued from him.

He studied Leo and concluded, "Come to Kater Murr, my dear. You're enough to make anyone wonder."

Leo turned her head away from him.

Somehow she had got herself against a wall.

"Come to the gatekeeper."

"Empty speech, Kater Murr," said a voice from the hallway behind him.

"Tag!" called Leonora.

At that exact moment there was a flurry of violence in the kitchen: a savage hiss, a scratch and shuffle of claws on tile. Paws were splayed, teeth were bared in the gloom, aggressive postures struck then suddenly folded. Light flickered off the points and edges of things. Everything seemed confused, too quick, too real; and Leo thought she was trapped in the kitchen with two much larger animals, one made of brass and the other of silver. It was only for an instant. Kater Murr's smell flooded sickeningly over everything, then another smell—of musk and winter, powder snow on an icy wind—washed it away. There was a distant, fading roar. Then the Majicou was standing amiably beside her and saying, "I think we can go now, Leonora."

She stared at him.

"Did you see that?" she said.

"See what?"

"In here. I— Never mind. You couldn't have seen anything from the hall."

Tag shook himself to settle his fur.

"Not from out there," he agreed.

In the yard, somewhat recovered, she asked him, "So— what have we learned?"

Tag considered this gravely.

"I don't know about you," he said, "but I've learned that Uroum Bashou has a more unruly servant than I imagined."

Leonora shivered.

"Why doesn't he just leave?"

"Where would he go? Who would look after him? They are locked together, those two. Without Kater Murr, the Reading Cat would have starved to death long ago. At the same time, Kater Murr is bound to Uroum Bashou by some emotional bond that drives him mad with frustration. They were kittens together. He loves the Reading Cat and hates him in one and the same breath."

He looked sidelong at Leo. "That might be hard for you to understand."

"It's not hard," she said; but she was quiet for a moment, and when she next spoke it was to change the subject.

"How did the Reading Cat get all his books?" she asked.

Tag considered this.

"His memories are confused, and sometimes he will admit that he has rearranged them to his own liking. I don't think he came from Morocco—wherever that is. Some human being brought them here long ago, books and cats together. Here the books stay. And Uroum Bashou stays with them: but not for much longer, I think. He is getting old. And Kater Murr won't hold back forever. One day we will come to this place and find the Reading Cat dead. Kater Murr will snuff him out in a moment of rage, and spend the rest of his life regretting it."

"Well, I can't say I liked either of them," said Leo. "What's the next plan?" Then, before Tag could answer, "I know, I know—'Love the world and follow your nose.' " She sighed. "There must be something quicker than that."

"Let's go home now."

🐾

That night the wild roads were difficult to navigate, even for a cat of the Majicou's experience. For some reason winter had come to them in full summer. It would be gone by tomorrow; but now it was like walking in a cold deserted house, down long, twisted corridors howling with ghosts. You had to have your wits about you. On the way back, Tag lost his apprentice. He couldn't be sure when or how. When he arrived at the oceanarium, glad to be home in the warm seaside night again, Leonora wasn't there.

After he had waited two hours for her, he had to admit she wasn't coming. By then, he had other problems.

Everyone else had vanished, too.

He prowled the oceanarium or sat outside on its doorstep. He searched the lanes and rooftops 'round about, calling, "Cy! Rags! Pertelot!" but he didn't dare go far in case they arrived while he was gone.

"Leonora!" he called. "You bad kitten!"

While he thought: It was wrong of me to tease her like that in the house of Uroum Bashou. I was just showing off.

In the shadows by the oceanarium door, a spiral iron stairway led to the lip of the fish tank. From there you could look down on the water, itself bathed in the greenish light of the powerful aquarium lamp. Tag climbed it and looked down on the little sharks, turning and weaving in the hallucinating light and silent tranquility. They reminded him of dogs, unassuagable and muscular dogs—though they had a quality of patience no land animal could ever possess.

He hated them.

Chapter Six

A CHANGED WORLD

The sun limned the tiles of the turrets of the cathedral with silver light, throwing its whitewashed façade into dusky relief, so that the columned portico grew complex with shadows. Pigeons sheltered from the punishing afternoon sun in the shade of the cornices like randomly grouped mantelpiece ornaments. Among the gigantic magnolias and the banana palms, tourists sat and ate sandwiches, each family or pair facing away from the next to make their own separate space. Beyond the imposing black gates, with their twin lampposts and spiked railings, the statue of a rearing horse and rider appeared to be emerging in a heat haze from the midst of an ornate urn.

Sealink gazed around her. It all looked as benign as ever. How often had she inveigled tidbits out of the unwary in such places? She was such a bad girl when it came to food.

Farther up the sidewalk she found the Café du Monde packed with a mixture of locals and tourists consuming café au lait and beignets. Not much for a hungry cat there. The sparrows that frequented the café, picking their way between the tables for fallen crumbs, were on a permanent high. Hooked on confectioners' sugar by a diet of sweet doughnuts, they bobbed around like manic toys. With barely a gram of fat on them, they weren't worth eating; and catching them, in their oddly distracted state, was too easy for sport—a quick paw among the chrome chair legs, a swat across the old brick tiles, and it was all over. They went down with their scaly legs pointing skyward, the reflection of the ceiling fans dying slowly with the light in their eyes.

Sealink loved the Café du Monde for reasons of nostalgia,

but it was in Jackson Square her real targets lay: the hot dog stands, the bars, and the trash cans from which an enterprising cat—a cat like herself—could con a meal for one . . . with luck, for two. This would mean crossing Decatur Street. Sealink and Red sat on the edge of the curb and stared up and down. The four-lane street was busy with traffic: a bizarre mixture of modern automobiles and mule-drawn carts, gaily painted in bright pastel colors for the tourist trade, one of which hove into view.

"I'm Joey, and this here's my mule, Shine," they heard the elderly carter explain to his passengers, a pair of thin Japanese youngsters, clutching cameras and guidebooks, and a large couple in matching warm-up suits they had bought in Biloxi. "Eats like a elephant and pulls like a ox, when she ain't standing still, which is what she most prefers. She knows I don't carry no whip, and sometimes she likes to take advantage."

Shine stared patiently between her blinders at the ground beneath her feet. Complicated harness lines and traces looped across her back, and a bright red human's hat was perched on top of her head. Someone had cut rough holes in the fabric, through which the mule's ears sprouted indignantly. A curious fellow feeling stole over the calico. Other animals she'd never had much time for—there were always so many cat things to do—but something about the mule's trammeled patience took her attention.

"Hey, hon," Sealink said softly, walking up under Shine's nose. "Don't be so downcast. Sun's out and all. Least there's only five of them to haul."

The mule turned its velvet muzzle to her, sniffed cautiously. "*You* say that."

"I do."

A wicked light came into the mule's dark eyes. "Do you know how I got my name?" she asked obliquely.

"No."

"Jes' take care that you watch when I gets down the street a little ways."

By now, the carter was in the driving seat and was well into his customary spiel: "And when you go into Old Louie's, you tell him Joey sent you and he'll give you a whole ten percent offa your check . . ." The customers were nodding sagely; another piece of inside information to note carefully for future use. It was the usual old scam. The next moment, the lights had changed, the carter flicked the reins with a theatrical "Ho up, Shine!", and the gig was off with a mighty creak and shudder.

Choosing their space between traffic, the calico and marmalade cats nipped neatly across to the opposite side and watched the cart roll ponderously down the road. Just as it reached the old brewery, there was a lurch and a shout. The carriage skewed sharply to one side and one of the tourists dropped its camera over the edge with a shriek of outrage. Within moments there were only two passengers in the cart, and Joey was handing back money and bobbing his head and apologizing for the poor behavior of his mule.

Red grinned from ear to ear. "See, she's reduced her load again."

Sealink thought for a moment. "Do you know how she got her name?"

Red grinned even more widely. "Poor old Joey. I only been here a coupla days, and already I know! How come humans are so slow? Heard he got her from some old guy quit the carts last year. She kept losin' him custom. Called her 'a shyin' fool'—Shine for short. Figures if she keeps it up they'll have to retire her. She says there's a real nice place called the Elysian Fields where the old mules get to go for a rest. She reckons she keeps on misbehavin' she'll get there quicker."

"From what I've seen of how humans treat animals they no longer find useful to them, that ain't likely to be the way of things," Sealink said darkly.

A flickering, split-second vision: hundreds upon hundreds of cats pouring over a darkened cliff top, down toward a booming, sucking sea . . .

Now where the hell had that come from? Sealink had been trying very hard not to think about any of that stuff. Hurriedly, she replaced the bad memory with a good one. Food. Of course, food. Spicy food. Boudin with chili sauce . . .

McIlhenny's Tabasco. Sauce of the devil. Nothing like it in all the world. Its arsonous memory licked across her tongue, to sear dark thoughts away.

"You hungry or something?"

The big marmalade was watching her with interest. Feeling his gaze upon her, Sealink shook herself out of her reverie.

"Why you starin' at me like that?"

"You're droolin'."

"Then I guess it's time to eat."

"Thank the Lord."

The two cats snaked between human feet, slipped through the traffic on Decatur, and headed down St. Louis Street, past the French Market Inn toward the Napoleon House. At the junction with Chartres Street, a mule cart was stationary by the side of the road. Joey the carter was sitting on the sidewalk with his head in his hands. Shine tossed her head gently from side to side to make her bit rings jingle. She had no passengers left at all.

The two cats turned right and ran down the sidewalk, keeping close to the shadows: beneath balconies of curlicued ironwork and windows blinded by peeling shutters in the pastel colors of faded silk flowers, under cars and pickups, from one point of cover to the next.

Sealink strode out in front, trotting backward to communicate her enthusiasm face-to-face. "Babe, you're going to love this place, I swear. Finest damned shrimp this side of the Gulf, and I should know, 'cause I've been around the whole darn world and I've ate the best of the best. *Hmm-mmm.* Been eating here since you was a twinkle in your momma's eye."

"Sure don't look older than a twinkle yourself."

"Why that's real poetic, hon," Sealink told him. "You-all make that up yourself?"

Red pretended to study something at the end of the street.

Sealink snorted. "Aw, honey, I ain't hurt your feelin's, have I?"

She was developing a soft spot for him. Doubtless he reminded her of all those mistakes of her youth, with their free-and-easy swagger and sweet lying eyes. "That's too bad."

A hundred yards or so down the street she stopped at a restaurant doorway. Enticing smells wafted out from beneath a black-and-white rectangular sign; but the door was firmly shut, and the squares of glass in the upper part of the door bore a closed sign. Taking no notice of such hindrances, Sealink stood tall on her hind legs and raked at the woodwork until little flakes of white paint eddied to the ground. All around the brass doorplate, the frame showed gouges and scratches that bore witness to years of such abuse, though someone had recently repainted with white gloss paint, so that the marks showed ghostly beneath the sheen. The door rattled, but no one came. Sealink looked annoyed.

"Are you sure this is such a good idea?" Rcd looked anxiously up and down the street.

"You kidding? I'd kill for this guy's blackened shrimp."

"Sure, but folks have got kind of inhospitable to cats 'round here."

"Not with me, honey." Sealink stood up on her hind legs again and peered between the window squares, then threw her head back and gave out an earsplitting yowl. "I always had an understanding with the chef, y'know?"

She pounded at the door again.

A few seconds later the locks rattled and a large, bearded man stuck his head out. The calico gazed upward. Blackened catfish. Chicken gumbo. She could smell it all over him. My, could he cook! A huge purr came rumbling up from the depths of her throat at all the good old memories.

The man, who had been staring vaguely across the street, looked down suddenly at his feet and found that a large black, white, and orange cat was applying herself to his ankles, purring her head off and twisting sinuously around and around in blatant sycophancy. Not far off, another cat, a marmalade with an odd eye, was staring nervously at them both.

"Hey!" said the chef. "You can't come around here, baby."

Sealink turned the purr up a notch, to a volume that would clean rust off a boiler.

"This gentleman and I go way, way back," she told Red. "Pecan-coated drumfish a specialty. Oh, yes."

So saying, she raised her head to give the bearded man the

benefit of her most adoring gaze. That gaze promised volumes. It promised deep rewards for the right contender. From Ankara to Zeebrugge, that gaze had divorced humans from their cooking. It had not failed her yet.

Red looked on, somewhat at a loss.

"Now come on, honey," the big man said again, as she fawned around his ankles one more time. "You tryin' to bring me trouble?"

Sealink, meanwhile, was giving Red the hard stare.

"So," she said. "You're my pimp or something? Are you gonna *earn* your dinner? Or am I the only one to have to humiliate myself today?"

Red returned her gaze for a moment longer than was necessary for mere politeness, then abruptly looked away. Dipping his head, he started to bump it somewhat shamefacedly against the chef's trousers, purring as best he might.

The chef looked pained.

"Come on, Red," he protested. "Two against one ain't fair."

Red was delighted.

"Hey, he knows my name!"

Sealink sighed.

"Look at yourself a moment, babe. Was he going to call you Blackie?"

The big man glanced warily up and down the street and seemed to come to a decision.

"Hell, I can't have you starve. Though—" he regarded Sealink askance "—it don't look like you're in much danger of that to me."

He disappeared inside and returned a moment later bearing a large dish of orangey-pink shells, which smelled briny and tart. The sight of boiled crawfish so close at hand had both cats salivating furiously. Little mewing noises escaped from Sealink's mouth. She couldn't help herself. Suddenly she was so hungry. Crawfish! She felt like *rolling* in them! The man put the dish down on the sidewalk a little way from the restaurant's doors then hurried back inside. At once two furry heads were butting at one another in their eagerness to feed.

"Where's your etiquette, boy? Don't you know you should let your elders and betters eat first?"

Red said something unintelligible. Spiky orange legs waved out of his mouth. Sealink shouldered him out of the way with gargantuan ease and applied herself to encouraging the soft parts out of the shells. A paw pressing here and the quick twist of a claw there, and out popped the succulent meat. They were so engrossed that neither of them noticed the tide that swept upon them out of the shadows.

Sealink felt cool shade fall across her back. For a second she thought nothing of it; then it was followed by a rancid smell, as of infection and sickness, that permeated even the food she was eating.

She looked up sharply.

The sidewalk was full of cats. Maybe two dozen had crept out of the alleys, the parking lots, and the construction debris around the Wildlife and Fisheries Building. Sealink blinked. Adrenaline shot her through like white light, like power in a circuit. For a moment, the newcomers reminded her so clearly of the alchemical cats that she was back in that other time, trapped in a warehouse with the Alchemist himself, while his proxies advanced on her like a tide. "Tag! Tag!" she heard herself call. "What you got us into here?" Shadows danced across nonexistent walls. Then she was back in New Orleans again, a little embarrassed, because they were only runny-eyed ferals with scabs on their faces. Fur that had once been of all different colors—tabby and tortoiseshell, black-and-white—had become so dry and dusty as to appear a uniformly faded gray. They were silent. Their eyes were dull. None of them was looking at Sealink or Red; instead their attention was fixed with horrible avidity upon the dish of crawfish.

Red had got close to the bottom of the bowl and was doggedly chasing the remaining food around with his mouth. Impatience made him clumsy. Bits of shell were pushed over the edge, where they fell with a papery whisper to the ground. There, propelled by a breath of wind, one drifted past Sealink and was at once seized upon by three of the silent cats. Ignoring the calico completely, they ragged feebly backward and forward at the shell, snarling and hissing between locked teeth.

Red looked up, saw the newcomers, and jumped backward

in horror. With a howl and a huge leap he hurled himself clear into the road and ran off.

"Thanks a bunch, hero," Sealink muttered.

Rarely averse to a fight, the calico nevertheless considered with some anxiety the situation confronting her. She was to all intents and purposes alone: since the only thing that could now be seen of Red was the bob of an orange tail tip disappearing around the corner of Conti Street, while all around her were twenty deranged-looking cats. Not the best of odds. She'd already had one scrap since arriving back in the city of her birth. It was becoming tedious.

They crept closer, drawn by the smell from the dish. Sealink's eyes glinted. They were in a tight bunch now, too compact a group to charge through, too many to leap over. Instead, she inserted a paw under the dish and flipped it skyward, where it spun and wobbled for a moment, showering down scraps as it went. As above, so below. Beside themselves with panic and voracity, the ferals scattered in twenty different directions, fanning out across the ground in eerie mirror image of the flying crawfish. Flakes of shell and meat rained down upon the sidewalk. In the havoc that ensued, Sealink picked her moment and wove with statuesque grace through the squabbling, empty-eyed cats out into the road.

For a moment, she looked back, puzzled, still hearing something in her head, still catching the faded echo of that other fight. "Just what is going on in this town?" she asked herself.

Then she was out of there.

🐾

"You want to tell me what you playin' at?" she demanded once she'd caught up with the big marmalade tom. "Your actions have put me in a dangerous mood, hon."

Red's lazy eye regarded her sheepishly. "Sorry about that. Instinct, I guess—why fight when you can run? And there were a lot of them. 'Sides which, why hurt 'em more than they already been hurt? They're starvin'."

"I seen hungry cats before. Hell, I *been* a hungry cat before. But I ain't never seen anyone *that* desperate for food. 'Specially not here."

"Well, I figure a lot's changed since you been in the Big Easy—"

"It ain't good enough to say that. It ain't even the shadow of an explanation."

"And as for me, I been on the road a long time, and I ain't used to company. Anyhows, seems that everyone I hook up with comes to grief."

"What a surprise, when you run off like that. And bein' on the road ain't nothin' to do with it. I been on the road since before you was born and I ain't never ratted on a friend. Where I come from, friends stick together, no matter what the odds."

Red bristled. "Well, I ain't yet your friend, and I ain't going to be responsible for you."

"Sure and I don't *need* any *male* to be responsible for me, sonny. I seen things in my time'd make your whiskers curl and your dandy orange fur turn white, babe."

Red laughed.

"Tough enough," he said. "You're fun when you're angry. I like a queen with a raspin' tongue. Get sick of them board-walk babes, make you run your errands for 'em, lick 'em here and there where they can't reach. 'Hey, Red—' " His voice took on a wheedling tone. " 'Whyn't you fetch me some nice shrimp? Would you just clean that little spot on the back of my head? The big ol' black cat over there keeps on lookin' at me and lickin' his black ol' lips, and it ain't nice. Would you go ask him to stop?' "

Sealink grinned despite herself.

"I see," she said, "that you have et some of that particular catfish in your time."

He acknowledged this to be true.

"So what's happened to your sad sorry-ass tale of a vaga-bond no self-respectin' female would want to be seen with?"

"Where's the self-respect in rolling on your back for any traveler comes along?" countered Red. He struck a pose. "They were as cheap as trash. I had my way with them and said *bonsoir*. I ate them up because they did not capture my heart."

Sealink narrowed her eyes and regarded him with interest.

If times had changed since she was one of those little board-walk queens herself, male attitudes sure hadn't.

"So, babe," she said, allowing a little of the honey-dripping South onto her tongue. "Tell me a little about yourself, and these females got you into such trouble. 'Cause you sure got a way with you, and I expect there is a number of tales to tell of their feckless behavior and lack of moral inhibition . . ."

Warm and luxuriant as her coat, her voice could twine around a receptive tomcat like a sweet Louisiana vine. Had her considerable conquests agreed to pool their experience, many would have admitted to not listening attentively to the content of her conversation, bathed as they were in the lilt of those soft Southern vowels, lulled into what might well soon prove to be a false sense of security; for who knew how an independent calico cat with a powerful will and determined ways might deal with a dreamy tomcat off his guard?

Red's eyes had become vague and unfocused. He forgot, for a moment, what he had been about to say. "Hey!" he said. "I—"

He shook himself suddenly and looked around.

But Sealink had stalked on ahead, tail up and haunches swaying provocatively. Let the famous love-'em-and-leave-'em Lothario see what he was missing.

🐾

By now they had arrived in a quieter sector of the old town, where the tourist quarter ran out and the shops and bars dwindled, leaving the street deserted but for a row of sleeping vehicles and the cats in sole possession of their surroundings. Here, the houses were silent and full of shadow, hidden behind veils of lacy wrought iron and shrouds of vine. Secret courtyards promised steamy shade amid the heady aroma of bougainvillea and mimosa.

Sealink, ambushed suddenly by those ghostly kittens of hers, ducked under some spiked black gates into a leafy courtyard and stared upward.

It was a tall house, painted as pink as freshly boiled shrimp. The windows were closed, and in some places so were the dark green shutters. Two stories of slatted balcony rose above her, supported by iron stilts and brackets fashioned like quarter wheels. From pots all along the balconies, trailing plants had festooned themselves over the railings and curlicues like party streamers left over from Mardi Gras. In among the pots, chasing dead leaves, tangled up in plants, great lambent eyes and tiny paws, the kittens tumbled. They knew she was there. They rested in their play and looked down at her seriously. She could *feel* them. Then one by one they faded away and she didn't see them again in that life.

The place looked prosperous and well kept: the house of professional people who cared about their surroundings and made sure their success in the world was apparent to all those whom they expected to gaze through the forbidding gates into this not entirely secret domain. Sealink knew this to be true. She had been here before.

Red stared incuriously over her shoulder.

"Nice house," he said ironically, as if he should care.

"It is. Shame about the people who live in it."

"You know them?"

Sealink nodded uncomfortably.

She had been an easy mark: one whiff of Louisiana crab cake and a minute or two of gentle fingers under the chin and she'd literally fallen at the woman's feet.

"Would you believe," she told Red, "that she thought I was a pedigree Maine Coon? Her and her husband, they took me in, put a diamanté collar 'round my neck, and called me 'Minouche.' "

Red snorted. "Ain't people ridiculous?"

"They sure can be self-deceiving," she agreed, "in their vanity and greed."

And this was the story she told him.

"They fed me, and I grew. It was tinned food, hon, and gourmet scraps. I musta gained a good five pounds." Sealink smoothed the fur over her belly contemplatively. Actually, she wasn't too sure she hadn't put that weight back on again . . . "But they deluded themselves about that the same as they'd deluded themselves about my ancestry. Plain truth is, I was carryin', hon. Their beautiful 'pedigree Maine Coon' had been knocked up a week or so before by some mangy boardwalk tomcat just like you, babe. So it was with considerable horror that the female opened the linen closet one morning to discover that 'Minouche' had spawned five tiny little Minouches, all over her best Egyptian cotton sheets.

"It was a messy business, hon, but surely no excuse for what followed—"

"I ain't listenin' to this," said Red. But he was.

"They took those kittens offa me that same morning. For days I quartered the apartment, searching for my babies."

On the fifth day, at the corner of the open bedroom door, she'd stopped stone still, sure she'd heard a distant whimper. It ceased. She'd stood there for some time, her ears rotating and all her will bent on locating the sound. When she had started to search again, the heartrending whimper returned at the outer edges of her senses. Whatever she did, she could not place it. Some minutes later she'd realized that it was her own voice she was hearing, a constant, mechanical lament.

"The next day, they took me in a wicker cage to a building downtown."

It stank of fear and pain and disinfectant. Inside were animals crouching in boxes and baskets. Those that could see out had turned to stare at her.

"What you in for, honey?" asked a large Siamese with a bandaged leg.

This straightforward enquiry had at the time struck Sealink as such a compassionate and motherly concern that she had at once poured out the tale of the loss of her kittens and the inexplicable behavior of the humans who had brought her here.

"That old Siamese—" Sealink fixed Red with misery-glazed eyes "—she just stared at me in silence for a few seconds. Then she said, 'Those'll be your last, honey. Remember them well.' "

Red looked hard at the ground.

"All I could remember for a long time was the smell. Whatever I did, I couldn't seem to dislodge it."

She'd licked and licked until fur had littered the apartment and the new scar on her belly was raw and red. Then, one hot summer evening, the humans had left a shutter ajar and she'd broken three claws and bruised her head as she fought her way out.

"The next day I searched for my babies. I asked everyone I knew, and a lot I didn't. I asked friends—hell, I asked *enemies*! No one knew a thing. I looked for days: I knew in my heart they were still alive—a mother knows these things, y'understand? Then one day I couldn't bear it no more. I hitched a ride on a truck and left New Orleans forever. Swore I'd never return. Since then I've traveled the world, always on the move: no ties, no commitments. Take a companion here, a friend there, and carry on my way. That old Siamese was right, but it's worse than that. They botched the operation somehow, and though I can't never have no more kittens I ain't yet neuter—as I seen you well understand, Red. Back then I tol' myself, what the hell? Life's a journey, and I like to travel light. But since those days a few things happened that kind of shook my viewpoint, if you know what I mean."

Sealink thrust out her jaw.

"So here I am, back in this cruel city to find those babies, and I ain't leaving till I do."

🐾

Twilight saw the two cats back at the deserted Moon Walk. They had, by a stroke of fantastic luck, stumbled upon some redfish heads in an alley yet to be discovered by the starving ferals, choking down flesh and eyes and scales as if they might never eat again. Above them, the sky had darkened to ultramarine, and the air took on a sultry, tangible feel, as if someone had upturned a bowl over the city, trapping inside it all the old air everyone had breathed that day. All along the river's edge, the insects had come to life: a million tiny chain saws whining and buzzing. Mosquitoes darted about the shoreline, seeking blood to suck. Dragonflies—hawks of the insect world—whirred after them, their neon glinting green and blue. All around, invisible to even a cat's eye, the crickets set up their nightly chirring.

Shamed by the calico's tale of sorrow into a confessionary frame of mind, Red had started to tell Sealink something of his own life.

"I'm not proud of some of the things I done. Treated a few

ladies badly in my time; but, hell, I been treated bad enough myself. Fell for a little queen down near the square a couple of years back. Téophine, she was called. Thought that was a real pretty name at the time. She was all black-and-white and neat—made me feel like a lumberin' fool. She was always ready for a chase. She'd nip me and run off, pretend to be alarmed when I followed; then when I caught up, all out of breath, she'd throw herself down on the ground at my feet, roll on her back, and twist all around. Then as soon as I got up the nerve to approach her, she'd be all teeth and claws and a flash of white feet. Next thing I knew, she'd be up on a fence, laughing down at me. Never knew where I was with her. I guess I was just kinda naive, didn't realize what it was she wanted from me. Wouldn't make the same mistake now . . .

"Two days later she's rolling around under the bushes in the park with some old stripy tomcat with frills instead of ears. Thought my heart would stop right there and then. She wouldn't even look at me after that.

"From then on, I guess I didn't care much for anyone. Scattered my favors around. Made a few of those little boardwalk queens squirm with pleasure down on the beach when the moon was high and the night was steamy. Left them wanting more and moved along. Probably left a few kittens of my own littered 'round this city."

"Don't you know?"

"They never seem to bear no resemblance." Red grinned so that the rising moon was reflected off the lazy eye. "Lucky for them, many'd say."

"And what happened to Téophine?"

"Guess she's gone, like most of the rest," Red answered mournfully. "I looked high and low for her when I got back. Thought we were both a bit older now; might see things a bit different. But there ain't no one around."

"I guess we all got to take our share of sadness in this life." Sealink mused for a moment. "Sure is a changed town from the one I left, though. A lot less friendly."

As if to punctuate this remark, a stranger appeared at the far end of the boardwalk. The figure swayed as he walked, as if the world was moving in ways mysterious to all its other inhabitants. The swaying was accompanied by a rhythmic mumbling, which grew louder and more distinct as he approached.

"Dey tink I don't hear them. But I hear okay. My ears may be old, but I ain't deaf yet. Dey tink I don't hear what dey call de Baron behind he back. Young varmints. Tink dey know it all. Dey all call me Baron Raticide in de old days. I kilt dem rats. I kilt 'em all dead. I was a nightmare; dey tell their chirren, watch out for de Baron or he get you in de night! Baron Raticide. Good mornin', Baron, dey all say, and dey bow and scrape and offer me their finest queens. Now dey call me Ratty. Dey got no respec'. It's a terrible ting to grow old. Old but not deaf. I hear what dey say. Dey tink I don't hear 'em. But I hear okay . . ."

The stranger's monologue continued like a hermetic tape loop, unaffected by all external factors. He was an old black cat, fur gone a dusty chocolate color from constant exposure to the elements. He shambled past Sealink and Red without acknowledging their presence, watching each step with concentration, as if he wasn't quite sure where his foot might end up if left unattended.

Sealink grinned. "Hey, Baron! Baron Raticide!"

The old cat's head wobbled for a moment as if registering some distant sound. Then he swayed on, borne along by his own weird internal rhythms.

Sealink ran to catch up with him. She bounded in front of him, pushed her face into his. His cataract-filmed eyes flickered with life at her scent for a second, then he shuffled around her and continued his walk, still muttering.

"Come on, Baron. It's me!"

"Another of your 'friends'?" Red asked the calico sardonically, keeping pace with the old cat.

Ignoring the marmalade, Sealink ran suddenly ahead up the boardwalk and started to—Red could think of no other word for it—dance. She lifted first one front paw, then the other, then her hind feet in the same way; then she started to spin like a kitten trying to catch its tail, all the time howling:

> *"In the heat of the night*
> *When the time is right*
> *And the moon hangs over the river*
> *Queens make their cry*
> *And blood runs high*
> *Hearts start to quiver and shiver . . ."*

The Baron lumbered over to the dancing calico. Suddenly he was matching her step for step; and as he danced his movements became fluid and powerful, age and madness lost in another form of lunacy altogether. At last the two cats were whirling together, the Baron's black shape a shadow to the harlequin patterns of Sealink's leaping form. Red felt his own feet start to move of their own accord, as the familiar rhythms crawled under his skin, and he began to make his own dance down among the boulders on the strand. Meanwhile, Baron Raticide's cracked old voice rose to join with the calico's wail for the final verse:

> *"On midsummer night*
> *The tomcats fight*
> *And their howls rise as high as the moon.*
> *Queens make their choice*
> *Of the fighting boys*
> *And kittens are coming soon, soon,*
> *The kittens are coming soon!"*

At last they stopped. Sealink was grinning from ear to ear, her flanks heaving with the exertion. The black cat looked changed beyond recognition. A new shine had come into his eyes, and there was now a cheerful, indeed, rakish, set to his ragged old head.

"Ai, ai ai! It's the Delta Queen! *Laisse les bon temps roulez!* I see you remember de old Baron from de good days, eh, *cher*?"

Sealink started to purr, a rumble from deep within the throat, bone-vibrating in its intensity. Red felt it shiver in his sternum and sat down, his head spinning. Why had he done that? He'd never danced before, was sure he'd never even heard the song; had certainly not been involved in the long-gone midsummer rituals on the Moon Walk.

"It's good to see you, Baron. 'Cause I sure ain't seen anyone else I know. Where are they, Baron? Where the hell are the Moon Walk cats?"

"All gone. Dey all gone. Only de Baron left. Dey disappear one by one. The kittens go first. Den one day I come back after one of my li'l wanders, and de whole place deserted. A sad city now. All gone away."

"I've come to look for my family, Baron. They took my kittens from me and I never seen them again. How'm I gonna find them if there's no one left to ask?"

"You better talk to the Creole Queen, honeychile. She de only one left from de ol' days. Hightailing it around de Vieux Carré as if she ain't got a care in de world. Got herself a li'l group of courtiers—dey don't seem to have no trouble gettin' fed. Don't leave none for de poor ol Baron. Not like de ol' days. Dey call me Ratty. Dey tink I don't hear 'em. Dey got no respec'. It's a terrible ting to grow old. Old but not deaf. I hear what dey say . . ."

And he was off again, the dull light back in his eye, the sway back in his step. Sealink watched him shamble off into the night: Baron Raticide—a big black cat once lord of the boardwalk, high priest of the midsummer ritual, a proud, valiant tom who had ruled his roost and fathered kittens on every fertile queen from Algiers to Armstrong Park—now reduced to a mad old vagrant. Looking at his retreating figure, hope withered anew and Sealink felt as if all the world had grown old and tarnished.

A light breeze was starting to raise peaks and troughs on the oily surface of the river. Red shivered. Despite the redfish heads and the crawfish it had been an odd sort of day. Instead of finding Téophine, he'd been bitten by an antsy calico cat and had danced with an old tramp. What was the world coming to?

Little swirls of dust and bits of rubbish started to blow around the boardwalk. A yellowing piece of newspaper fluttered past and lodged itself against the legs of the nearest bench. Red didn't even feel like chasing it.

"Come on, babe," he called softly to the distracted calico. "Let's go find that old Creole Queen, see what she can tell us."

He wandered over and nudged Sealink out of her grim stupor. She blinked once or twice, then turned and butted her forehead against his cheek. Surprised at this sudden rough affection, Red took a step back. "You don't have to knock me out, you know."

"Seems you just ain't up to my weight, honey."

Dodging in and out of the streetlights on the Moon Walk, the two cats disappeared into the night.

✺

The yellowing sheet of paper that Red had dismissed as a page from an old *Times-Picayune* was something far more relevant and more sinister than he could have guessed.

It was a city ordinance.

Framed in formal language, it was addressed to the human inhabitants of New Orleans:

BY ORDER OF THE PARISH OF ORLEANS
UNDER NO CIRCUMSTANCES ARE FERAL CATS TO BE FED OR
ENCOURAGED IN ANY WAY WHATSOEVER ANYWHERE WITHIN
THE BOUNDARIES OF THIS CITY IN ORDER TO PREVENT THE
SPREAD OF DISEASE.
TRANSGRESSIONS OF THIS ORDINANCE CARRY AN ON-THE-
SPOT FINE OF $50.
ALL STRAY CATS SIGHTED MUST BE REPORTED TO THE
RELEVANT AUTHORITIES WHO WILL ARRANGE FOR THEM TO
BE ROUNDED UP AND TAKEN TO THE CITY POUND, WHERE
THEY WILL BE DISPOSED OF WITHIN 10 DAYS UNLESS CLAIMED
BY AN OWNER.

Part Two

Messages from the Dead

Chapter Seven

THE WISDOM OF FISHES

*T*ag sat alone in the oceanarium.

Outside it was deep night, the sea under cloud, the rooftops of the village tumbling away downhill in shadowed disorder. Inside, the light fell across the side of his face; the fishes slipped and turned, or hung motionless, surrounded by tiny glittering motes.

I don't know what to do, he thought.

He had looked for Cy in all her favorite places. Nothing. The Beach-O-Mat was empty. The amusement arcades were closed. The docks were deserted, the fishing boats at sea. Rag-mop palms shook themselves uneasily in the onshore wind in the moonless dark, and the fish-and-chip papers that blew up and down the seafront were empty and cold. He had combed the steep lanes between the cottages on Mount Syon and Tinnery, to find only empty doorsteps and household cats who made off hastily when they realized who he was. In the end, driven by anxieties he could barely express, he had taken the wild road to the windy spaces of Tintagel, where he found himself patrolling the headland crying, "Ragnar! Pertelot!" until his voice cracked. Nothing. Nothing but the wild gorse, the empty church.

Cy had vanished.

The King and Queen were nowhere to be found.

Worst of all, Leo was still out there somewhere on the Old Changing Way, lost, puzzled, in need of help.

He remembered how, in the days of his own apprenticeship, he had run off by himself and got lost. That's the trouble with being the Majicou, he thought. Your trainee is always going missing.

Even as he was thinking, something happened to the light above the aquarium. It faltered and went out, and when it came back on it had shifted from its customary pale green color to a kind of metallic blue-gray. It began to flicker on and off rapidly with a dreary buzzing noise that seemed to get inside Tag's bones. Then he saw something quite huge hurtling toward him inside the fish tank—something so big he couldn't understand why it hadn't displaced every drop of water, so big that, if it continued to loom into the world like that, it must simply burst the glass and wash him away among all the wriggling, struggling fish that had lived such calm lives there. He hissed and jumped back quickly and banged his head on the oceanarium wall. In the tank the light roiled like disturbed pelagic ooze. A line of gill slits the size of dustbins seemed to brush against the glass. A single dull black eye stared emptily out at the air-breathing world. In a moment it was gone.

By then, so was Tag. He arrived in the street outside, crouched and wary, tail lashing, heart pounding, without much idea how he had got there. A few drops of rain fell on him. The night wind ruffled his fur the wrong way. His skin twitched. OCEANARIUM said the electric sign above the door. It blinked and fizzed. Intense hyacinthine light flared from the windows, dying across the spectrum to wine red and then black. After nothing had happened for some time, Tag gathered his courage into his paws, crept back up the steps, and stuck his nose into the gap beneath the door. Everything was back to normal inside, though the floor seemed a little damp. In a dry patch at the bottom of the spiral stair, grooming themselves unconcernedly, sat the King and Queen of Cats. The King's eyes were bright with excitement. Loosely tied around his neck like a royal sash was a bit of dirty blue cloth that glinted with silver and smelled strongly of petrol, fish, and nutmeg. There was sand in Pertelot Fitzwilliam's rose-gray fur. As she occupied herself about her toilette, it sifted down silently and grew into a little yellow pile on the floor around them both.

"Tag, my friend!" exclaimed Ragnar. "Amazing things! Things you will never believe!"

While the Queen murmured, "Oh, do come in, Mercury. Nothing can harm you here."

He crept forward cautiously and sniffed his friends. Suddenly they seemed strange to him. A curious, baked warmth clung to them, as if they had brought back not just the smells but the climate of another country. They were rich with adventures he had not shared.

"Hush," they reassured him. "Tag, we're the same cats you knew. But listen."

And this is what they told him.

That evening, while Tag and Leonora were still traveling the wild roads, the King and the Queen had eaten a fish supper with Cy outside the amusement arcade. Afterward, the three of them had strolled along the seafront in the dark so Pertelot could stare at the lights of the fishing boats on the edge of the bay and whisper, "Oh, Rags, what a perfect night!" To please the tabby, the Queen had even put her perfect nose around the door of the Beach-O-Mat though to Cy's disappointment she could not be persuaded to go in and watch the human washing spin around. Back at the oceanarium she and the King had slept soundly, only to be woken by a disturbance. The light had changed. There were noises above. Behind the glass, shoals of frightened mackerel waved good-bye like a thousand human fingers.

"It was as if something had broken the surface of the water in the tank," Pertelot Fitzwilliam told Tag. "My first thought was that something had arrived there. That was how I put it to myself, Mercury: that something had arrived there." She shivered. "I always hated that water."

"Her second thought," said Ragnar, "was of Cy." He paused for effect. "I am afraid to say, my friend, that she was gone."

"I woke Rags. Together we searched the building." The Queen looked around ironically. "It didn't take long. Cy was nowhere to be found. Had she fallen in the tank? We had to know!"

Step by step, their bodies elongated by caution, each paw placed in a furious silence, they had crept up the spiral stairs to look down into the water in its blaze of electric light.

Nothing.

"She was here, I'm sure."

"Has she fallen in?"

"Those sharks. Oh, Rags, the sharks!"

The iron platform at the top of the stair seemed to be suspended in emptiness. Beyond the light it felt like black space stretching away to nowhere. Suddenly the water became opaque as milk and lurched toward them, as if something huge were displacing it. Tottering and disoriented, they peered down at the object that had almost surfaced.

"Look!"

"Eyes! Look at its eyes!"

"Rags, what is it?"

They turned to flee, but it was too late. The light died to blue, flared white again. The world twisted and flickered. Though it remained quite level, the little platform seemed to tilt beneath them. They scrabbled momentarily at the lip. They tumbled through the hot bright air onto the back of the creature that filled the tank. There they found Cy the tabby waiting for them.

"Hi!" she said, purring and kneading happily. "This is my *friend*. I call him Ray, but I think his own guys have another name for him. These fish," she added in an aside to the Queen, "who knows what they call each other?"

Generally, though, she seemed rather proud of him. Ray was less a fish than a place. It was a mystery how he fitted in the oceanarium tank at all. "Some days, you know, he looks so small." Yet you might stand on his sinewy, shifting back and never know he had edges—until perhaps you caught a quick glimpse of them, furling and unfurling in the distance, out of the corner of your eye. He was the color of a whitewashed wall in bright seaside sunshine. His spine stretched away in electrifying perspective, like a curb at the side of some road, until suddenly it was a spine no longer but a narrow white tail. His elegant triangular fins curved away right and left, neither sails nor wings but something that antedated both. If you listened hard, claimed Cy, you could hear the ancient Silurian thoughts pursuing their slow, sure passage through his fish consciousness.

"Whatever that is," said Cy. "He tells me stuff about that, but I just don't pay attention. Listen, it's lucky I fell in, because today this fish comes with a message for you. Around and about in the ocean by Tintagel Head he's met some guys. They aren't fish, he says. They don't breathe water. They shouldn't even *be* down there! But he's been told to fetch you and take you to some old place he knows. Maybe you'll find Odin and Isis there, Ray's not clear on that. Anyway, you got to go with him."

She lowered her voice.

"Under the water," she said.

"Never," said Pertelot. "Let me up!"

But even as she spoke, the great fish began to sink. His passengers were submerged instantly.

"Ragnar Gustaffson!" called the Queen, darting this way and that in panic. "How dare you let this happen!" There was no escape. All she could do was stand and tremble. "Rags," she whispered in despair. "Oh, Rags." But Ragnar stood as straight and tall as he could beside her, and that reminded her who she was. And they soon found to their astonishment that they were still dry. They could breathe. They were beneath the water but somehow not in it. The oceanarium was already gone, replaced by a huge, dim, ribbed architecture. They were in something like an infinite gloomy hallway under the sea. Endless lugubrious echoes rolled away down it. Shoals of tiny fish souls ran everywhere, like two-dimensional silver streams. Vast shadowy forms boomed and groaned past, fish so large they made Ray seem like a mote settling in a glass of water.

Ragnar laughed suddenly.

"This is what I call an adventure," he said.

"I can't believe this," said Pertelot. "I'm dreaming this."

"See?" said Cy excitedly. "What I'm trying to say: fishes have their secrets in this wide world, too! They got things we don't know about, such as that tank is an entrance to some long-ago fish road of their choice!"

Those roads are as difficult as any. They are traveled on a notion, an idea inside. For what seemed like hours, the ray maneuvered and sideslipped through the enormous space as he sought clues to the cold salt currents that would guide him to his destination. He banked and turned restlessly. He fell like a leaf. He hung in a huge cathedral silence like a compass needle; and then, at last, finding the answer in his own fishy heart, shot forward and down. Eyes wild and bright, fur rippling back in the slipstream, his passengers fastened their claws unashamedly into his leathery skin and hung on tight.

🐾

"And so," the Queen told Tag, "we whirled away along the fish road—"

"To be carried at last to Egypt," Tag finished for her.

Love knows everything. The Queen turned her carved little head toward him and stared. He looked away shyly. It was like being studied by some stone goddess. Her eyes were lambent, full of life and death and the cycles and mysteries of the stars.

"I was carried at last to Egypt," she agreed.

🐾

Dawn in the Nile Valley, one morning some weeks after *Shamm an-Nasim*. A tender gray light suffused the mist that curled along the riverbanks. Egrets picked about in the reedy shallows like fastidious girls. A single felucca, recently re-painted pure white with a red and gold eye at the bow, drifted upon its own reflection in the glassy water. What trade this little boat might be engaged in was not clear. Its sail remained tightly furled in the dead-still air. Behind it, the village of Qebar lay, still asleep amid its palmeries, against a sky washed with lilac. Immediately above the village, on the raw stony terraces at the base of hills whose almond-colored flanks were still furrowed with night, loomed a complex of tombs and temples of the Missing Dynasty. The buildings glowed like a softly illuminated model from a centuries-old chaos of spoil and eroded rock, their blank rose-gray walls softened for once by the morning light.

The day seemed suspended, unable to develop. Everything hung as if it were in a dream. A smell of onions and kerosene rose from the drifting felucca. The young man yawning in its stern—he was barely more than a boy—wore the turban of a barge captain, to which he seemed entitled only by ambition. He was half asleep when the ray called Ray, monstrous with journeys and still moving at the speed of the fish road, erupted from the water off his starboard bow; cut a steep, whistling, iridescent arc north to south against the sky; and plunged back into the river again. The felucca rocked and staggered. Displaced water raced outward in huge ripples that, rebounding elastically from bank to bank, churned the surface of the river into spray. Egrets burst up from the reeds; doves panicked into the sky from the whitewashed dove castle in the village, their wings clapping urgently. The young man leapt to his feet and clung to the mast of his boat for support, rubbing his eyes in astonishment. Perched like a pilot on the back of the giant fish, just behind its strange flat head, he had glimpsed a small tabby cat with white bib and paws.

More cats, turning over and over, fell out of the air into the roiling water a few yards distant. This was too much for him. He shrugged.

"It can only be the will of God," he said.

🐾

Green water closed over the Mau and she sank, all bubbles and frantic legs, and the splendor and mystery of her ride on the great fish evaporated to nothing. Water is water, wherever you try to breathe it. The Nile was warmer than the canal at Piper's Quay, but no easier to negotiate with. Soon, she couldn't even remember when she was drowning—then or now. There was a high, singing noise inside her head. Oh, Rags, she thought. I do hate this. And I can't even see you. Once, she thought she could feel him near, locked in his own lonely struggle, and she tried to move toward him. Then that feeling was gone, and anyway there was nothing much left of Pertelot Fitzwilliam to feel it. For a while she was just a grim argument, carried on in the clutch of the Nile—whose meaning, partially glimpsed in her dreams of Egypt, she now saw clear and stark: the gift of water is not security but constant transformation, not rest but movement, not victory over the desert but fecundity in spite of it—between her life and her death. The kittens! she thought in despair. The kittens! But she had closed herself instinctively around the last of her breath; and in its own time, as breath will, it carried her into the light. Up out of the ancient river she burst, choking and hissing, and found chaos everywhere. The horizon lurched. The riverbanks were collapsing into the river in a slurry of mud and gravel. Something was bearing down on her through agitated water and prismatic spray. Then human hands gathered her in, and before she could sink again she was suspended by her scruff, as dripping and undignified as only a wet cat can be, against the Egyptian sky. The day had begun. The sun was already hot. There was warm human breath on her face, warm human laughter in her ears. Its eyes were dark and amused, and its skin was like polished rosewood in the sun. It smelled of nutmeg and laundered cotton and the pure generosity of the young. It made an inviting noise with its tongue like "Tch, tch, tch."

It said, "The Nile is not for you, little mother! Up you come!"

It said, "Let Nagib take care of you now."

"Never!" swore Pertelot.

She hissed and spat. She twisted and squirmed. She fastened herself onto the boy's forearm with all four legs and sank her teeth into the soft part between its thumb and first finger. When it only laughed and said, "*Maleesh, maleesh*, little mother," and patiently detached her, she bit it again. She was angry with her rescuer, she was angry with the river, she was angry with herself. She was angry with Cy and the fish for going off like that. She was angry, for no reason at all, with Ragnar. At the same time she was so confused she had begun to purr. With the whole of her heart she begged the boy to understand: "Now Rags! Help Rags now! Put me down and help Rags!"

She had never asked a human being for anything before.

❧

In the event, Ragnar Gustaffson, seventeen pounds of Nordic tomcat and ten pounds of waterlogged fur coat, arranged his own rescue. "I am not, how would you put it, impressed by the taste of this Nile," he told anyone who would listen as he thugged his way up over the stern of the felucca. "It is some rank stuff, as Tag would say." He shook himself like a dog, squinted up into the sunlight, and, discovering his beloved Mau in the grip of Nagib the boatman, nipped forward smartly and bit the boy in the ankle. At exactly the same moment, the felucca, accelerating in the current and unguided except by God, ran heavily into the east bank. Nagib fell over. Pertelot cried, "Ragnar Gustaffson, don't you dare let anything like this happen to me again!" Tearing out further gravel and mud, which fell softly into the Nile like wet brown sugar in a saucer of tea, the boat ground along the bank.

As soon as it came to rest, the two cats jumped nimbly ashore.

🐾

They fled through the palm and lemon groves, where insects were already droning in pools of hot greenish light, along the beaten paths, up toward the village that, partly shadowed by the dark terraces above it, still lay asleep. Cool air moved in the narrow crooked lanes between the houses, whose lower walls remained in a lavender shade even as the sun struck like running gold across their roofs. Goats chewed thoughtfully in a rising side street, where the earth was cracked and dry and strewn with dung. Pertelot hurried, apparently unremarked, between their delicate hooves, while Ragnar begged her to slow down and think. "There's no need to run now!" But when she stopped, she only caught the smell of the human being on her coat and panicked again. Toward the edge of the village, the desert wind blew feathery skeins of sand across the lanes. Suddenly, the damp river airs had evaporated, the ground rose steeply away from the houses. It was the end of vegetation. Terrace succeeded stony terrace. Entering the ancient quarries of the tomb builders, Pertelot began to call, "Isis! Odin!" She disappeared suddenly against heaps of spoil the exact color of her coat. "Wait!" called Rags when he next saw her, rose-gray against the shadows. She looked back at him for a second, her tail agitated with nerves or impatience, and vanished again. Rags found her delicate trail in the dust, and was soon less concerned. He didn't need to see her. He could follow her paw prints. He could follow her smell. Cinnamon. Aniseed. Raisins! "I would know that smell anywhere," he congratulated himself. He emerged onto the upper terrace to find the sun scouring it unmercifully. His coat dried out in an instant. The light made him blink and sneeze. He paused briefly to study the Nile, curving away in the valley far beneath. Then he looked across the rosy stone apron of the site, toward the tombs and rock temples of the Missing Dynasty.

It was baking hot, and the dry wind had swept it of dust. There were no footprints to be seen. The Mau was gone.

🐾

Silence.

Faint echoes of paws on stone.

The floor sloped gently downward. A massive internal architecture began to make itself felt—ramps and stairways and rooms higher than any human being could use. Pertelot Fitzwilliam of Hi-Fashion, a slip of life in the place of the dead, scampered beneath rows of vast red sandstone kings carved into high relief along the walls.

"Isis!" she called. "Odin! Isis!"

Her shadow, long and oblique, preceded her, until the light that had fallen so brightly into the outer hall faded first to a kind of orange twilight, then to gray, then to pitch black. Not even a cat can see in the dark. Afterimages fluttered before her mind's eye like soft white doves, the wounded memories of some old dream. She turned confusedly on her haunches for a moment, then followed the temperature gradient with her nose and whiskers. Each tiny cold air current urged her: "This way down."

Eventually the darkness seemed to reverse itself, and a kind of faint silvery luminescence filled the tombs, limning the edge of objects, revealing, in the silence of the huge empty stone biers and caskets, the hulks of standing sarcophagi. There were faint smells of bitumen and canopic salts. There were drifts of human dust in corners. Down here the walls were covered with painted figures, their bodies glowing softly off the cold stone in ochers and terra-cotta reds, Nile earths, desert earths, the black-and-white details as sharp as the day they were painted. They were, the Mau thought, just what you would expect from human beings: animal-headed gods whose expressions, sidelong and uneasy despite their arrogance, soon revealed them to be men in masks; gods who feared other gods; gods who gathered meaningless objects to them; gods desperate for life yet so clearly in love with death. Their postures were stiff with denial; but however they had tried to halt it, time had parted around them and rushed on.

Out of their failure, with a secret smile and kohl-blackened eyes full of delight in the world, danced a single goddess. She wore sandals, a white tunic, necklaces of garnet and lapis lazuli. Her limbs were sensual and long, her name as forgotten as the pictographic language of the Missing Dynasty itself. In the pictures she was often shown accompanying some long-buried king, her slim hand upon his shoulder, his arm about her waist. She had gathered her followers to her—musicians and dancers and celebrants—and, all around her delicate feet, cats! The cats were dancing, too, or so it seemed. Suddenly, in the next picture, the goddess was a cat, too! Huge and tawny, her eyes the deep, fecund green of the desert oases, she danced among them. They were lithe and ancient looking. They were purring and rubbing their sleek heads against her ankles or against each other. And two of them were depicted separately, in a sequence of cartouches that, the Mau was quick to see, told a story.

She sat down.

She thought, Well!

The cats seemed almost to move before her eyes. She was soon so caught up in their lives she forgot her own.

A minute passed, and then another. After a third, the light in the tomb was faintly disturbed, and there was a sound like a single drop of water falling into a pool.

The cats on the wall were a male and a female, with all the simplicity and grace of the goddess herself. She was shown smiling down on them with a special favor, while they looked up at her as an equal. They played and tumbled; perhaps for her, more likely for each other. Would they accept a great task? They would. They mated, took ship, were seen crossing a flat blue sea: on deck, a beautiful boy sailor knelt before them, eyes kohled, slim hand outstretched. A white sail, a white bird, sped them north. A high tide, a cold country. A sail like a white wing.

"But I know that coast!" Pertelot told herself.

Behind her in the tomb, as if in response to her excitement, the light shifted again. In one dark corner the air seemed to flex suddenly like a lens refocusing. Then it was still.

The cats debarked on a rocky shore. White birds wheeled and screamed overhead. A northern king, blond-haired, tired of face, leaned down to welcome them. He was young, dressed in black. Ghosts were seen riding the roof of his hall, from whence, in all directions, great abandoned animal highways sang and roared across the empty land. The king begged. The king implored. The cats listened, heads on one side. They debated with him. Were they not a King and Queen, too?

"She's pregnant, of course," said Pertelot. "That's obvious to anyone."

Disturbed, the mass of shadows in the tomb behind her fell into a new equilibrium. The air temperature dropped suddenly. Pertelot shivered. She turned from the painted wall to look around. Nothing could be seen. She sniffed. She shrugged. She felt relaxed, rational yet vague, as if the fears of the day had less receded than somehow clarified themselves within her. How silly to be afraid of a boy! Water, of course, was another thing. She gave her attention to the last cartouche, in which the cats had themselves brought to an upper chamber in the king's house.

❧

Ragnar found her there some time later. "I had been lost in many passages," he would explain when he told the story to Tag. "I will say only that the world has many directions in it, and sometimes there are more to choose from than would seem sensible." By then, anxiety had made him dangerous—but not perhaps as dangerous as the thing in the corner of the tomb.

"Pertelot!" Rags cried.

She was creeping toward it on her belly, her eyes quite blank and empty, while it bowed and wobbled over her like a top about to fall: a dense eccentric whirligig of human debris— the black loess of ancient organs, bits of bone, flakes of bandage and parchment—a dust storm of mummia and old death six or seven feet broad at its top, balanced on a tiny shifting base and reaching from floor to ceiling. It was aware. It seemed to be arguing with itself. From it issued bad smells; intermittent, disconnected voices; blasts of hot and cold air; and a strange, thready music. As the Mau got closer, it sensed her presence. A shudder passed through it. Lights flickered deep inside. Suddenly it bellied toward her like smoke in the wind, breaking up into dusty smuts and cinders. There was a deep groan. Then chanting began. Someone was chanting in there. At this, Pertelot went rigid. All along her spine the fur was up on end. Stiff-legged, a pace at a time, she moved toward it. She hated the vortex, but it was like a magnet to her. In response it pulsed and roared and shot up to the ceiling.

"I think we have had enough of this," announced the King of Cats.

He sprang forward, got a good grip of his wife's tail with his mouth, and yanked her backward. Pertelot yowled and spat. He closed his eyes and, offering up a silent apology, pulled harder. It was a grim struggle. Ragnar splayed his cobby legs and backed away, losing most of every inch he gained. While Pertelot, her signals crossed, fought both sides at once with a dour, indiscriminate passion. The whole world stank of cinders. The whirlwind staggered and wobbled over the two of them like a drunk with raised hands. We're for it now! thought Ragnar. But even as it fell upon them it was breaking up. There was a faint *pop!*, a puff of foul wind. Dust pattered on the floor of the tomb like a sudden shower of rain.

Ragnar sat down heavily as Pertelot stopped pulling away from him. The Mau shook herself, looked around puzzledly at the empty tomb, reared up on her hind legs, and thoroughly boxed his ears.

"Ragnar Gustaffson, how could you?"

"I'm sorry, I'm sure."

They stood off and observed each other, rocking backward and forward and breathing angrily. There was ruffled fur between them, no denying it, especially with no common adversary in sight. After a moment, Ragnar looked away and began to ferret bits of papyrus out of his mane. The Queen sat down and tried to unkink her tail by licking it. "Undignified," she repeated several times, until Ragnar got up in a lumbering, long-suffering way and sat down facing away from her. "Undignified!" After a minute or two she admitted, "I know you meant well."

Ragnar Gustaffson looked at the wall paintings.

"I know you meant to rescue me."

No answer.

She went and sat beside him. "Rags, I'm sorry."

He hadn't heard a word. He said excitedly, "Look! It's us!"

"Ragnar Gustaffson," she told him, "you are the most insensitive cat in the world, and I will never apologize to you again."

About to present him with her back, she saw how his thoughts turned over and across themselves, bent by wonder into an endless Viking knot. She forgave him instantly. She rubbed the side of her face against his, thinking that he was simple in some old, lost, worthwhile sense, and you had to love it; while he gave his attention to the pictures, every so often murmuring, "But this is astonishing," or "How incredible!" Or "How do we come to be here, on a wall?"

The Queen explained. "This is not us," she said. "It's the story of Atum-Ra and Isis, a version of which the Majicou told to Tag in his apprentice dreams. Atum-Ra and Isis are the ancestors, the cats—blessed of the Great Cat, known to humans as Hathur goddess of Love—who brought the wild roads back to Tintagel. Look! Here they are in the king's chamber, Discerning Invisible Things. Afterward, imprinted in the bright tapestry of their eyes the king sees and is able to identify the ghosts that disturb his sleep. He can have peace at last! In return, he grants the cats—and their kittens, and their kittens' kittens in perpetuity—the freedom of the land."

"They are us," Ragnar insisted. "We are them."

"Oh, Rags," she said.

"They are doing that quite well," he went on with satisfaction, after he had had another look at the picture that showed the ancestors mating, "but not as well as us."

"Rags!"

"He is not as black as me."

She laughed.

"His fur is not so long."

"You child," she said.

A cold wind curled around them suddenly, lifting the dust into their eyes. Electricity unzipped the air, filled it with the taste of metal. There were stealthy sounds. A cough. A rising hum, as of a child's top. They jumped to their feet, fur on end. Rubbish was being drawn up from all over the tomb, whirled about, sucked into a corner.

"Run!" called Ragnar.

Too late. The whirlwind had assembled itself again. Pace by pace, shaking with delirium, her eyes lit up from within like lamps, Pertelot was tugged toward it. For a moment its rotation seemed to slow. It wobbled. Toppled. Turned a startling Nile green, then back to black. There was music from within—bells, a reed flute, small drums arrhythmic and perverse. There were movements, as of a dance or struggle. A figure, perhaps human, became dimly visible within the swirling rubbish and mummia dust. It was as simple as the painted figures on the wall. It leaned forward. It spoke.

"I have two of your kittens," it said. "Give me the third and I will spare your lives." Suddenly a second figure seemed to curdle out of the dust. It dragged the first one, struggling, out of sight.

A friendlier voice said, "The Golden Cat is not what it seems."

Rags darted forward.

Soon she will have no tail left, he thought. I loved her tail.

But before he could act, the vortex collapsed with a vague sneeze and a bad smell.

"Look!" cried Pertelot.

A shift in the light had revealed the wall on the far side of the chamber, rearing up between two monolithic human figures into the indistinct shadows fifty or sixty feet above: a slab of rose-pink granite cracked by time and covered with one huge image:

Pertelot stared upward.

"The eye," she breathed. "Look at the great eye." She

began to dart about helplessly at the base of the wall, as if looking for a door. "We were brought here to be shown this," she said. She stopped, craned her neck to examine the image again, stood up with one front paw resting on the wall. "And that *thing*," she added, dropping to all fours again, "was talking to itself." She shivered. "Is there a reason for any of this? Oh, Rags, we have come all this way for nothing. Where shall we find our children?"

Ragnar gave his attention to the shadows in the corner.

"I think it is time to leave now," he suggested.

Pertelot blinked at him, and for once did as he asked. They were out of the chamber in a second, into the cold passage-ways, avenues of gigantic kings, and mazes where every turning was the wrong turning and every door opened on more stone. Behind them, their nemesis reassembled itself, roared up to the ceiling, and hurtled in pursuit. It was much bigger than it had been. Hot desert air, freighted with sand like a gale at a beach, was sucked past the two cats and into its maw. The floor trembled beneath it. Broken stone pattered down out of the ceiling joints. There were deep, surprised groaning sounds somewhere in the depths, where pieces of sculpture a hundred feet high had begun to lean against one another like very old men. The whirlwind raged and howled. It grew.

"Hurry!"

Stark shapes of darkness and light. Squinting into the gale, Rags and Pertelot teetered on the edge of a steep black ramp above a drop they could not measure. Dust boiled up and streamed off into the vortex behind them.

"This way! Into the wind!"

They flitted across a pillared anteroom and out into the forecourt of the temple. The light was so strong they could feel it scrape the surface of their eyes. Midday. The stone sang with it. The Nile below was lost in heat shimmer. Down through the quarries they fled to the edge of the village, where the goats, rooting senselessly among stones, sought shade at the base of the houses. Here, where heat had emptied the lanes and even the dove castle seemed empty, Ragnar halted suddenly.

"Look!" he said.

"Rags, come on!"

"It isn't following us anymore," he said. "Look!"

Through the heat haze, the tomb entrances could be seen like low black slots against the yellowish, crumbling slopes of the hills above. From each of them there now issued a thick, slow, sulfurous gout of dust. A low rumble reached the ears of the cats. The earth shook, as if something had settled. The dust clouds rose lazily into the hot air, a dozen coiling roseate smudges against a sky like heated brass. There was a long pause, in which Pertelot and Ragnar eyed each other uneasily. Then, with a renewed rumbling and shaking of the earth, as of gigantic forces in conflict, dust began to rise again—this time from the hills themselves. The tombs and temples of the Missing Dynasty were falling in one by one, taking an entire range of hills with them like collapsing paper bags.

❦

"After that," the Queen told Tag in the oceanarium, "it was like a long dream."

They had made their way down through the lemon groves to the river, where the boy Nagib, having brought his felucca into the shore, invited the "sky cats" aboard with grave politeness. "I was too tired and disappointed to resist a kind word, Tag. Besides, how else were we to get home? We had no idea where we were!" She stared absently across the oceanarium. "And yet," she said softly, "that was the most beautiful journey of my life. We seemed to be days upon the river going north. We slept or watched the banks. After two days, we changed ships. Nagib, with tears in his eyes, gave Ragnar his neckerchief, with its silver charm. He called us Atum-Ra and Isis, his little mother and father. He seemed to think he was in a story. Our new pilot spoke less. He was an older man, who made a sign with his hands if I came near."

In the river villages, in the hot afternoons or after dark, they searched for a highway to take them home. "But something was wrong with all those Egyptian roads. All I remember is the dead cats piled up at the entrances, perfect little cats who had done no one any harm—oh, horrible, Mercury, horrible!—and a Sohag street tom called Akhenaten, with deep brown fur and a tongue like pink suede, who advised us, 'Close your eyes as you go by. The dead do not wish to be seen. Something has come into the world that has no right to be here.' We took his advice and passed on down the river."

Boat gave way to boat, dawn to dawn in the soft river air. The two cats stood at the bow, their noses lifted for new smells, or lay in a hot sleep in the shadow of the sail, their dreams full of the creaking of the boat. As they drew closer to the river delta, with its blunt soft airs, the Queen's coat took on Nile colors: the dove gray of the banks at dawn, the lilac of the distant hills. Isis and Odin were never far from her mind. Were they in the vortex? Is that what the first voice had meant? If so, how would she ever bring them out again? Her eyes looked into some other distance than the distance of the river. When this mood came over her she drove the King away if he tried to sleep beside her in the night. "The children seemed to visit me in the long afternoons. I heard Isis sing, I saw Odin leap. I heard their voices but I could not help them. My mind was full of Nile dreams.

"Finally we reached the sea."

The boat lay all morning not far outside the eastern harbor bar at Alexandria, its sail tightly furled in the dead-still air. Behind it, against a sky darkened with clouds, the fifteenth-century fortress of Qa'it Bey stood on its low headland like an illuminated model, yellow walls soaking up the hot and stormy light. That morning, before making the inexplicable decision to take two cats out to sea and wait there for whatever happened to him, its captain had put on a freshly laundered white djellaba. It was his birthday. He was exactly thirty-five years old when the biggest ray he had ever seen surfaced from the Mediterranean fifty yards to seaward and began to make its way toward him. It was too late to flee. Besides, perched on the back of the fish, its fur steaming in the hot sun, was a small tabby cat. Within moments the other two cats had leapt delicately off the bow of the felucca and joined her there, the great fish submerged, the sea was flat and calm again.

The captain rubbed his eyes.

"*Inshallah*," he said, and turned toward the shore.

Chapter Eight

AT THE SIGN OF THE
GOLDEN SCARAB

*U*nder a shady wall in a courtyard behind the tourist shops of the French Market sprawled an enormously fat yellow cat, a pile of uneaten delicacies spread before her, staring out across the café in a self-satisfied trance. Every eleventh second, she gave a languorous blink. Like some great planet, her gravitational field had attracted a large and motley collection of hangers-on, less-well-fed creatures who radiated out from the yellow queen in complex little groups and huddles. Striped and spotted and parti-colored, all they had in common was the focus of their attention. That and their shiny new collars, collars that threw into harsh relief barely healed scabs and wounds and the signs of recent malnutrition.

Kiki la Doucette was holding court.

Sealink had known her, four or five years ago down on the Mississippi boardwalk, as a largish cat of indeterminate age, grown a little thick and loose around the midriff from too many litters carried to term. She had walked with a light, aggressive step, and her glance had been as sharp as knives. Females had fled from her; even males had cowered. She had ruled the Moon Walk with claws of steel, and even Baron Raticide had deferred to her volcanic temper.

The apparition which now confronted her was barely recognizable as that tempestuous high queen. Sealink had never seen any cat so vast. Rolls of fat flowed down her jowls, her neck, her shoulders; fat rippled and bunched across her flanks and belly; it cascaded over her gigantic rear like a gelid sea. Her coat was intensely, preternaturally glossy, as if, in addition to the tribute they brought, the courtiers had licked melted butter all over her. In peculiar contrast to the shambles of flesh that comprised her great body, Kiki's limbs, protruding stiffly beneath her as if they had simply collapsed there and then under her weight, were stick-thin, her tail hairless as a nutria's.

Sealink shivered with sudden, instinctive repulsion.

Red hung back, uncertain.

As the calico moved into her line of sight, the yellow queen blinked faster. She squinted, blinked again. A tiny flame of recognition sparked in the depths of those cold amber eyes. Then she yawned, displaying teeth orange with decay, a white-coated tongue.

A strange tension now overcame the courtiers. Their dullness sharpened into anticipation. As one they swiveled to regard the newcomer.

"*Eh bien,* it is the Delta Queen. I'd heard you were back. It's been a while, *cher.* You've gotten *plus grosse*."

Sealink felt the fur on the back of her neck rearrange itself.

"I could say the same, and more."

The yellow queen laughed—the sound of a hacksaw on damp wood. "Time has treated me better than you, *cher.* You look—how can I put this without making *le faux pas*? A little worn, perhaps, a little longer of tooth and claw, ha? Maybe learned a lesson or two and come back to your hometown sadder and wiser and in need of some help from la Mère?"

"I'm here to find my kittens."

A wave of reaction seemed to pass through the yellow queen and on through her courtiers. It was nothing so definite as surprise—rather an acknowledgment, a shared understanding, but there was no warmth in the response. Kiki la Doucette straightened, heaved herself upright. She smiled, so that an evil orange slit opened beneath her wide pink muzzle.

"Oho, we all want the *kittens, cher.*"

Sealink stared at her. "Do you know where they are?" she persisted.

Kiki's eyes glittered.

"Kittens are like stones on the beach, *cher.* How should I know which are your brood?"

"I thought you might know what had happened to them.

You know everything that happens in this town." Sealink watched as the high-yellow swelled with self-satisfaction.

"So the Delta Queen is a little less insolent now, eh? Well, I might know a thing or two, *ça depend* . . . You come to Kiki for a favor, *cher*? So—I shall expect something in return. What have you brought me?"

Sealink bridled, but the image of her lost kittens veiled her pride. "A calico cat travels light, y'know? I don't believe I have anything for you."

"You cannot expect a high queen to give you something for nothing."

Sealink considered briefly. "I seen the Baron, down on the Moon Walk."

"That old muskrat! You think I'm interested in *him*? He is nothing to me, less than nothing! You are *fou*. Mad!" Saliva flew from her mouth. The old temper seemed to flare for a moment, then subsided like a squall at sea.

"I know some good restaurants . . ."

"Ha! You think you can tell me anything I don't know about this town? Besides, what would I want with more food?" She gestured at the untouched pile before her.

Sealink blinked. She started to salivate. Food going to waste, while others starved. Something was out of balance in this town. And anything the size of Kiki la Doucette would certainly weigh down those scales . . .

Kiki stared past the calico, her eyes narrowing. Then she grinned. "But maybe I am feeling charitable, *cher*. Yes, I am in an excellent mood. A small *betise* has amused me. A private joke, *bébé*. I think you'd enjoy it if I were to share it with you. But no, that would spoil it entirely. I tell you what. You are a strong cat, eh? And your teeth are good, *non*?"

Sealink stared at her suspiciously.

"And your *petit ami*, too? Come out of the shadows, *cher*. Yes, you, with the coat like a fall sunset."

Red made a cautious approach from beneath the banana palm where he'd taken refuge. The calico had seemed rather an intimidating proposition, but this female was a monster! The courtiers parted before him like a sea.

"I think I seen you before, ha? Ah yes, I remember you

well. Kiki la Doucette is renowned for her remarkable memory. I know every cat on my boardwalk better than their own mothers. Hell, I am la Mère—I *am* the mother of most of those cats! Not you, though, *mon ange*, not with that ugly visage, that black stain like the devil's mark! *These* are my babies—"

She spread a paw wide to indicate her courtiers. A curiously rapacious tenderness informed her features as she surveyed this motley crew. Red followed her gaze. All different sizes they were, with fur of every color and type that the Great Cat had created. Something was wrong, though. He couldn't quite hold the thought in his head, but he felt it deep inside. Something was lost here. Something was odd. A mangled tomcat returned Red's stare, then split lazily from the pack.

"What you lookin' at, boy?"

"You're wearing a collar."

"It's an honor you gotta earn."

"Where I come from, it's thought kinda demeaning. Only house cats wear collars; no self-respectin' feral would dream of it."

"Well, boy, you can dream on, 'cause you ain't one of the queen's own, and without you ain't one of us, you don't got no collar and no food neither. Hell, boy, you don't got no *life*!"

All around, the courtiers wheezed and spluttered with laughter, rheumy eyes screwed up in derision. The tom strutted back to the group, bony rump swaying.

"Ferme ta gueule!" The laughter withered to silence. "So," she addressed herself to Sealink again. "You do one little thing for me, and I'll tell you something you'll like. A bargain, ha?"

"What is it?"

"You go down to the Golden Scarab, *cher*, and there you find two young ladies who call theyselves Venus and Sappho—" a distant wheeze from the retinue "—yeah, they got some real airs and graces, given their parentage. You know the Golden Scarab, eh?"

"The old bookshop on Orleans?"

"Go there and tell them to give you what they have for la

Mère. They will know what you mean. You do this one thing for me, I do you a favor, *bien*?"

Sealink considered. It seemed a simple enough request. Kiki was clearly too fat to shift for herself, her courtiers too degenerate. She came to a decision. It was an indignity she could bear if it meant finding her kittens again.

❧

The Golden Scarab lay in faded splendor near the junction with Bourbon Street. Dusty antiquarian books were piled one upon another, spines outward to the window browser, offering such titles as *The Soul of Central Africa*; *The Killing of the Khazar Kings*; *Sympathetic Magic: A Practical Reader*; *The Chase, the Turf and the Road*; *The Seven Sleepers*; *The Festival of St. John: Ancient Traditions Revisited*.

Some little soapstone figurines, squat and intense, were balanced on top of the largest pile, and a box of ornate silver jewelry was propped up farther back in the display.

Sealink and Red peered through this collection of artifacts into the dimly lit shop beyond. Two or three human beings moved slowly through the interior, big and dull and shadowy. Stopping at precarious piles of books they stood stock-still, heads tilted at an awkward angle like great cranes looking through water for prey.

The door was shut.

"Now what?" Red looked anxiously up and down the street. "I don't know what I'm doing here anyway."

"You gonna tell me you got something more pressing to do?"

"I still don't understand why you let that fat old queen diss you like that."

"Honey, you ain't ever been a mother—"

"That's for sure—"

"—So you don't know what it feels like to lose one of your own, let alone five. And if there's anything I can do to find them and make up for leaving them to the mercy of this town, I aim to do it."

Red's mouth opened, then a thought slid into the patched eye, and he promptly shut it again. At that moment another human being appeared, turning the corner by the bar at the end of the street and proceeding toward the Golden Scarab: a tall, gawky man in an ill-fitting linen jacket with creases that looked too random and ingrained to be deliberately casual. Without a glance at the two cats, he pushed at the bookshop door. It strained open on its stiff hinges, and at once the calico was inside, between his feet and straight under a dusty shelf. When Sealink stared back out, she could see Red faintly through the grime on the door, pressing his nose to the pane. His breath flowered and died on the glass.

The humans shuffled out to the back of the shop and disappeared. Sealink glanced cautiously around, then emerged from her hiding place. She sniffed the air. Cats! At least two distinct scents, and another smell, too, that she could not quite place. Just as she was digesting this information, she caught sight of a plumed tail, switching away high above her. Backing off for a better view, she stared upward. On the top shelf, stationed between two bookends in the form of Anubis the jackal-headed god, was a large-furred tabby whose golden eyes shone brightly in the dingy interior. She had been dozing, but now all her attention was fixed on Sealink.

Calico and tabby stared at one another. The tabby bristled. Sealink felt her fur stand on end. Maintaining intense eye contact while staring upward was something of a strain, Sealink found. After a while, she realized that she could feel the blood draining from her head, leaving it light and empty. Narrowing her eyes, she tried to focus on the cat above her. Black specks began to float in her vision. She felt hot, then cold. The world started to spin. Shadows twisted then fell apart; and all at once her nose was assailed with a complex and familiar scent: civet and attar of roses! Burnt spices! When she stared again into the gloom of the top shelf, the russet tabby had gone. Sitting in its place between the Egyptian bookends was a creature with the sleek elegance of a completely different kind of cat, a cat with a face as fine and accurate as the head of an ax. Rose-gray fur lay on her bones like velvet. The mark of the scarab was on her forehead; and when she opened her eyes, they were not gold, but the green of the oldest river in the world.

It was a Mau.

It was Pertelot Fitzwilliam, Queen of Cats.

And her eyes were a well of sorrow.

Sealink felt the Mau's loss as a raw, hollow place in the pit of her own stomach. She opened her mouth to address her old friend, and as she did so, there was a brief burst of green light, and then the Queen was gone.

Blinking hard, the calico gazed up into the shadows again. But all she found was the large tabby staring bemusedly back at her.

"Who are you and what do you think you're doing in here?"

Sealink shook her head to clear it of the scent of attar.

"My name is my own, but I'm here on Madame Kiki's business."

The tabby hissed. She leapt neatly off the shelf, landed delicately on a tottering pile of books—which swayed as her weight hit, then righted itself once more—and onto the floor in front of the intruder. The bell on her collar tinkled as she landed. There was not much to choose between the two of them for size.

The tabby stared at her curiously. "You're not the sort of cat she usually sends," it said accusingly. Then it turned imperiously, flicking its tail under Sealink's nose. "This way."

Between the shelves the tabby wove, with Sealink behind. At the back of the shop was a thick, tapestried curtain. Beyond it, Sealink could hear hushed human voices. Cats have a curious nature, but the calico prided herself on being plain nosy.

A few words of conversation emerged distinctly.

"Need more traps . . ."

"After the full moon . . . They'll say it's pest control—"

A laugh from all three men, then the sound of something heavy being dragged across the floor. A door opened and the voices retreated, dull, self-satisfied, full of the smugness of conspiracy.

"To the Elysian Fields . . ."

"For the Alchemist . . ."

"Faubourg Marigny . . . kittens . . ."

Out of this empty mutter, Sealink's brain picked first "Alchemist" and then "kittens." The world lurched. She stared at the tapestry curtain and a shudder passed through her great frame. What to depend upon among so many dreams and omens, so many uncertain signs? Lost kittens, old friends, past and future intermingled in these Crescent City blues of hers.

"Hey! You deaf or something?"

She jumped. Another cat had joined the tabby. It was equally large and well furred and brindled all over with patches of orange and black, like some randomly marked tigress. The two were clearly sisters.

"So, I ask again, you have come for la Mère's *petit cadeau*— you come to collect her gift, eh, *cher*?"

The newcomer's tone was hard but cultivated. Were they both daughters of Kiki la Doucette? Their father must have been some vast tomcat, Sealink thought, to have produced two such strapping offspring from a female who had once been so skinny as the high queen of the boardwalk.

Sealink looked the brindled cat up and down. Like the tabby, she wore a collar. Little charms and bells hung from it so that each motion produced a faint jingling. House cats, she thought derisively. Nothing more than pampered pets.

"Ain't no call to *cher* me, honey. I ain't running errands out of politeness."

The brindled cat blinked superciliously at her. The tabby sniffed. "There's no call for rudeness, either, especially from some renegade."

"Who are you calling renegade?" Sealink's tone was dangerous.

"*Cher*, you don't have no owner, you don't have no protector. You wear no collar, you not one of the saved. You not going last long in this town. What's the matter—you new around here or something?" The brindled cat—Sappho, as her name tag proclaimed her—regarded Sealink with undisguised contempt.

Sealink returned the look in spades. "Honey, I was born in this town. I've roamed free as a cat should and I know every rooftop, every café, every boneyard. I been all around the world. All you been is here, which ain't much."

The tabby made a howl of protest, but the calico went right on: "And what's all this with kittens?"

The two sisters regarded her with narrowed eyes.

"Don't know what you talking about—" said one.

"None of your business—" said the other, at exactly the same time.

Sealink curled her lip. "Hell, they humans sure got you by the short 'n' curlies—"

The tabby stared at her in mock amazement. "Humans—they're wonderful. How else you going to come by poached fish and velvet cushions?"

"Won't hear a word against them," declared Sappho with finality.

The calico fixed them with a steady, contemptuous gaze. "May as well give me the damn *'cadeau'* and let me get on with life out in the free world, then."

The brindled cat returned Sealink's stare coolly. "Come with me."

A little book-lined corridor ran past the tapestried doorway and into a storeroom. Out here it was cooler, the air damp and musty. Spiders had colonized the upper reaches of the room so that great swags of web hung from the rafters like Spanish moss. Layer upon layer of dust covered stacks of cartons and boxes; dust that spiraled lazily into the air as they passed. In the center of the room sat a great wooden chest in an ornate African style—twirls of carved leaves and birds making a complex fretwork of dark wood into which was inlaid gleaming ivory and mother-of-pearl. Despite the intricacy of the decoration the chest looked massive and dense: a mighty catafalque. Sealink walked around the object, sniffing curiously. She stood up on her hind legs and examined the lid. Of all the objects in the storeroom, its surface alone was free of dust. Light falling from some obscure source had formed a golden pattern upon it, a tall triangle with a round head, somewhat like an old-fashioned keyhole or the sun rising over a pyramid.

Sappho elbowed past her and started to lever at the heavy lid. The pattern of light dispersed into the general gloom. "Lend a paw, Venus," she hissed.

The tabby looked startled and immediately leapt to her sister's aid. After some puffing and genteel swearing, the lid fell back with a creak and sat upright in the air, supported by two heavy leather hinges. Two furry rumps heaved at something within the chest, then emerged backward, dragging some amorphous package with their teeth. Out in the uncertain light of the storeroom it looked like a badly wrapped package—layers of creased brown paper coming away in flakes, girded around with lengths of chewed string. Sealink nosed at it. The object emitted a strange smell, rather like old carpet. Overlying this fustiness was a dense perfume that made her cough and sneeze. It was heavy and felt hard to the touch.

"Take this to la Mère. And be very careful with it."

The two sisters exchanged a glance, the dull light flicking off their golden eyes. They turned to stare at the calico, their expression identically opaque.

"If you meddle with it you will be sorry."

"La Mère will make it so."

Sealink met their stare unblinking.

"She don't scare me. This is just a job of work, means to an end."

She bent her head to the knot of string. The problem with maneuvering the object was not just weight but its awkward size. There was no dignified way to proceed. Following the two sisters to the back door of the storeroom, Sealink put her back into the task, dragging the parcel until her teeth ached.

☙

"Let's open it."

Red snuffed at the thing he and Sealink had half carried, half dragged the length of Orleans. Behind the St. Louis Cathedral, they had ducked into the cool, shady gardens of St. Anthony, out of sight of human passers-by. The package lay between them, stubbornly enigmatic. Red pulled experimentally at the chewed string that bound the parcel, but it refused to budge. Bending his head lower, he started to tear at the ripped outer layer.

"No!" Sealink's howl was outraged. She launched herself at him, knocking him away.

Red hissed at her, hurt and puzzled.

"Oh, come on! You know you're just as curious as I am. We're cats, ain't we?"

Sealink fixed him with a savage scowl. "Get your god-damned teeth off it. Mess with this here box thing and I'll never find my kittens. You fancy explaining to the bitch-queen of New Orleans why her precious *cadeau* had arrived all in bits? You recall her inviting us to open it up, help our-selves? Huh? Do you?"

Red fiddled with a strand of string that had become stuck between his teeth and said nothing. He looked belligerent.

"Besides, it smells wrong: I wouldn't even *want* to know what's in here."

"We could just take a peek. Wrap it up again . . ."

Sealink bit him.

"Ow."

🐾

Kiki regarded her *cadeau* avidly. She drooled. Having deliv-ered the package she had resolutely and single-handedly dragged all the way from the garden behind the cathedral, Sealink stepped away, feeling light-headed and nauseous. Little black stars flared and died in her vision.

"So." She tried to sound casual. "My kittens. What do you know about them? Where are they?"

The yellow queen could barely tear her eyes away from the parcel. She smiled. It was not a pleasant sight. When she lifted her head, her pupils were black pits of desire. "Closer than you think."

"Where?"

"*Cher*, you performed a task for me and now I owe you a little bit of truth; but sometimes truth can be a painful thing. Maybe you not want to know what I know."

Sealink sensed a double cross. "And why would that be?"

The yellow queen rearranged her vast bulk, as if settling into some long tale. "Not all litters care to acknowledge their *maman*. Believe me, kittens can be mighty ungrateful, *cher*, their hearts as bitter as wormwood." She wiped what ap-peared to be a completely dry eye with her paw. "It can be most hurtful, when your very own kittens will not show you the love and respect you deserve. *Soixante jours*. Sixty days you carry them inside you. Sixty days of discomfort and anguish. You feed them; you give and give and give—oh, they suck so hard, it make you sore!"

She screwed her eyes tight shut, and when she opened them again she had somehow contrived to make them shine with tears. Sealink looked on, unmoved and impatient.

"Cut the crap. Where can I find them?"

"Be polite!" the old queen admonished. "You want them, you hear me out." Her eyes flashed dangerously. "And sometimes those who call you mother are not your own; and these are often the most grateful of all.

"You had five babies, *hein*? They were taken away very young. Taken and cast aside. After they had dealt with you, the humans who took you home left your babies *avec le docteur*, to be disposed of in, as they say, 'a humane fashion'; but the vet's *assistant*, he is a greedy man. He save the money on the drugs that give them peaceful sleep. He leave them, just a few days old, out on the levee, wait for the tide to take them. That's where I found them. Two were almost dead, gasping out their last breaths. I watched, watched them die. Yes: I was their last sight, *les pauvres bébés*. For the other three, I was their mother, *cher: pas toi*. Three babies, and all so fine they become. Fine and big like the mother who ran away."

A thought started to form in Sealink's head. It was unbearable. Kittens. When she thought of her kittens, it was as tiny scraps of fur; little balls of fluff no bigger than her paws, the way she had last seen them. Not as great big grown cats—cats with tails like plumes, hugely furred tabby cats with an offensive manner . . .

La Mère watched Sealink's dawning realization with satisfaction.

"*Mais oui, cher.* You already met your *daughters*." The evil orange grin split her face. "*Très* nose-in-the-air for a pair of bastards!" She wheezed. "I called 'em *Puce et Guêpe*—Flea and Wasp—for they was covered with fleas most they lives, and when they was tiny they was striped; but they never liked that much! They started to call theyselves Venus and Sappho—very grand names for such a trashy heritage! Moved

up-market, soon's they could. Got theyselves adopted at the
Golden Scarab. Got they collars, had the op—" she made a
vulgar gesture "—but they still has a healthy respect for la
Mère. Very trustworthy, those two, I find. Very useful little
princesses."

Sealink's heart felt like a lead weight, cold and gravid.
"And what about my third kitten?"

Kiki la Doucette regarded her with slit eyes. She shrugged.
"Two's enough pain for now, ain't it?"

The calico nodded dumbly. She turned to leave. Her eyes
felt hot, and there was a terrible constriction in her throat.
When she turned back to ask another question, the yellow
queen was standing over the parcel like a predator with its
kill. She sawed at the string with her appalling orange teeth;
and the brown paper wrappings started to fall away like a
sloughed skin only to reveal glorious gold within: a box
shaped like a figurine. La Mère scraped at the box. Gold paint
flaked into the air. When she squinted, the calico could see
that someone had punched apparently random holes in the
sides of the box. From her vantage point, they looked almost
like a face. As she stared, her curiosity for a moment getting
the better of her pain, the box moved. Kiki la Doucette's court
drew around it. Their eyes were as empty as a moonlit sky,
and they were waiting for something . . .

That was enough for Sealink. Ears back, head low, she fled.

🐾

Later that night the calico lay curled in an old favorite hollow
beneath the boardwalk, dozing peaceably. When she opened
her eyes just a slit, so that the world was comfortably blurred,
she could see the moonlight on the Mississippi, a silver sheen
like a secret wild road across the river. Kittens. What need did
a cat of her age have of kittens? Let alone vast, snooty, tabby
ones? Her trek from the Old World to the New had been no
more than a wild-goose chase, a flurry of fuss and feathers.
Well, she was still Sealink, and she would come to terms with
this new disappointment. She shifted position, tucking her
nose under her tail for added warmth, and was just starting to
drift weightless among the stars, when she became aware of

another cat. Before she had time to register the scent, it had joined her in the hollow.

"Hey, gorgeous," it said, its face obscured by the dark. "Move over, make room for a cold and lonely boy."

The calico grinned into the night.

Red felt her grin like the tiniest change in air pressure against his whiskers and rolled against her back. And in that position they fell asleep, head on each other's haunch, two cats alone against the world.

Chapter Nine

THE WALKERS

*A*nimal X stood blinking in the sunshine.

At first, he couldn't make much of what he saw. The ruined laboratory and the small tidy new road that ran away from it in a straight line, were held in a quiet fold of land away from which broad, gently sloping pastures rolled in every direction to skylines crowned with thickets and oak-hangers. The sun was hot. The sky was very blue and tranquil, except where, above one of the distant coppices, a lot of tiny black specks were wheeling and diving, calling out to one another in a kind of raucous, cheerful creak.

Animal X watched them for some time. That would be bedlam if you were close to it, he thought. For some reason the idea made him shiver.

The word *crows* came unbidden into his mind. He examined it, then, nothing occurring to him, let it slip away. Immediately, it became available to him as a description. He looked up at the crows in the sky. "I've seen them somewhere before," he told himself, "but I can't think where." That was the next step with everything, he supposed: to remember it. "You can call a thing a crow," he reflected, "but it's no comfort if you can't recall the last time you saw one." Over the next few days, many little pieces of his past would come into focus like this; while, however hard he tried to recover it, the past itself remained resolutely locked away from him.

A faint, pleasant breeze moved in his fur.

He had no idea where to go.

I suppose I'd better just start walking, he thought, and that's what he did. The first thing he passed was a sign that said, if you could read:

150

⊙ LABORATORIES
Winfield Farm Site

After that, the little tarmac road gave way to a lane heavily shaded by trees. The lane wasn't so neat. There was a narrow verge of vetches and couch grass; dog rose and nightshade, threaded through with old-man's beard, made tangled screens through which the glitter of water could sometimes be seen where it ran shallow and clear in the sandy bottom of a ditch. Insects launched themselves clumsily out of the flowers and blundered past, scattering pollen from their feet and wings. The thick, drugged scent of meadowsweet came and went. I like this, thought Animal X. A minute or two later, he remembered Stilton and the kitten. He turned around and found they were walking a few yards behind him. Stilton looked frail and tired already, but he was talking excitedly to the kitten. The kitten seemed puzzled. It was less distraught, though; and there seemed to be less anger in its silence. When he listened, Animal X could hear Stilton say, "What you can get, you see, from the factory shop—"

They walked like this for some time. New sights waited around every corner. They saw human beings off in the distance across the fields. They saw a lake, green water that looked solid enough to stand on, with lily pads and a heron on a post. They saw how the heat shimmered and danced above the land in the middle distance.

Toward midday the lane led them up to a broad black road down which huge energetic shapes roared and rushed. Wastepaper blew up into the air, settled, blew up again. It was a very human place. There was a smell. Animal X and Stilton stood for a minute or two at the junction, wrinkling their noses, rocked dangerously by the passing airstream. Then they averted their faces in embarrassment—because they had forgotten, if they had ever known, what all this meant—and turned away. The kitten confronted things more stoically, as if it was determined to understand only the worst about the human world. It blinked its single eye.

"Come on," said Animal X. "This is no good. We'll find some other way to go."

"I'm hungry," Stilton said to the kitten. "Aren't you?"

The kitten didn't answer, only stood up straighter in the rushing dirty air; so they left without it. A moment later it shook itself violently and ran after them. Thereafter they kept to the lanes, where the world seemed safer and less dirty. They were thirsty as well as hungry, but still pleased to be out on their own. Dusk brought them to the outskirts of a village: chestnut trees, a gray church, a handful of redbrick cottages between which the lane dipped gently until it encountered a stream. For a few yards the shallowest of water flowed over the road, glittering busily in the fading light. Two or three quarrelsome mallards were splashing about in it, saying things like, "My water."

"No. All this water's mine."

"Well, it's never the same water anyway."

"So what?"

"I'm just saying, that's all. How can it be yours if it's not the same water?"

Warmth hung in the air in the soft gray shadows beneath the chestnut trees.

By this time, Stilton was very tired. The bottoms of his feet had developed blisters, and the blisters had burst. He limped, and his head nodded up and down in time with his limp. He had been sick twice because he kept trying to eat things he found in the road. Every so often his back legs would fail him, he would sit down suddenly and say, "I think I've got heat stroke." Now he added, "I've got to stop. I really have."

Animal X was staring at the stream. For some reason, despite the tranquil look of it, he was reluctant to cross. He had no idea why. Insects bobbed and hovered above the surface. He watched the mallards stamp off to deeper water, sit down, fold their ruffled dignity, and float off with the current, still arguing drowsily with one another.

He said, "We'll stop here then, Stilton. We'll sleep if we can't eat."

Lupins filled the gardens like candles. There was a scent of roses, of lavender. Everything was drowsy with summer air: the pony dreamed in its paddock, the dogs in their kennels dozed, the human beings murmured contentedly from their kitchens. The golden kitten stared into the twilight after the vanished ducks with a kind of absentminded irritability, then followed Animal X and Stilton back up the hill, every so often shaking its head. Eventually they stood, the three of them, in front of a small clapboard shed. White paint blistered, tarred roof entangled in honeysuckle, less a home improvement than an afterthought, this construction leaned amiably up against one of the cottages. From its partly open door—like beckoning human fingers, like tendrils of weed waving in deep water—issued smells both inviting and dangerous. Stilton raised his nose in the air. He drooled a little.

"Who's going first?" he said.

"We should think before we do anything," said Animal X.

Stilton sat down.

"I'm afraid anyway," he said.

The kitten shouldered past them both.

"Wait," recommended Animal X. "We—"

Too late.

There was a scuffling sound inside, followed almost immediately by an outbreak of fierce yowling from the kitten. Behind that could be heard a deeper, more guttural complaint— the angry speech of some large unidentified animal. Stilton ran away down the garden. Animal X ran after him. When they stopped to look back, Stilton was still ahead but not by very much. Animal X felt ashamed of himself.

"We shouldn't let the kitten face whatever's in there on his own," he said.

"No," agreed Stilton.

"At least one of us should help."

"You," said Stilton. "You go."

The noise continued unabated, then rose to a crescendo. Animal X had crept halfway back down the garden path, and was crouching in a border of overgrown mint, when the door of the shed creaked and shifted and something black forced its way out into the gathering dusk. He couldn't tell what it was. It smelled strongly, even from that distance, and its white-rimmed eyes were the color of liquid chocolate. It might have been a dog. If its outline had been less fluid—if it had been more clearly formed—Animal X would definitely have described it as a dog. It paused momentarily, half turned, as if it might return to the argument, then, hearing the bubbling yowl of the golden kitten inside, clearly had second thoughts. It shook itself and limped out into the lane. If it was a dog, it only had three legs.

A minute or two later Animal X poked his nose cautiously around the shed door. It was almost dark inside. Strong smells rose from the litter of human stuff spilling out of the corners and across the floor—sawdust, straw, empty sacks, garden tools, a smear of burnt oil from some machine—but they could not disguise the pervasive odor of its previous occupant. The kitten stood awkwardly in the middle of everything, lips peeled back off white teeth, fur still bristling along its spine, the arch of its body still presented to a vanished enemy.

"It's me," Animal X said placatingly. For good measure he added, "I don't want to fight."

The kitten stared at him.

"You don't know what to do next, do you?" said Animal X gently. "Look," he went on, "there are two dishes in that corner. We should taste what's in them. In case it's food."

The kitten growled faintly.

"Aren't you hungry?"

Nothing.

"Well, I'm going to try," said Animal X.

Very carefully, footstep by footstep, his head turned aside so that he represented no threat, he picked his way through the junk toward the corner. There was a moment of anxiety as he brushed the kitten's flank. But at his touch he felt its taut muscles quiver and relax suddenly. "There, you see?" he said, more loudly than he had intended. "We're all right now, you and me." He ran the last few steps out of sheer relief, pushed his face into the nearest of the bowls, and began eating. He had no idea what the stuff was, but his mouth didn't care. After a moment or two he became aware of the kitten standing next to him. He moved over.

"I don't know what cats eat when they're out on their own," he said. "But we can eat this. Go on, try some."

The kitten tried. It ate slowly, and then faster. It raised its head and purred suddenly.

"You've got it all over your mouth," said Animal X.

A little later, they both made room for Stilton.

"I like this," Stilton said. "It's almost as good as—"

"Shut up, Stilton."

❧

Outside, the Dog—if indeed it was a dog, or had ever been one—stood completely still in the middle of the village. It was as large and as shapeless as it had ever been. It stood there, and it was the Dog. Its shapeless smell filled the summer air, overpowering for a moment the odors of honeysuckle and night-scented stock; and to anyone walking past, its outline would have seemed to waver a little in the dusk.

It was thinking, I was comfortable in there.

After a moment it thought, I would have eaten that stuff in the bowls. It thought, Now those cats will eat it instead. Finally it thought, The new Majicou—who is not the old Majicou—asked for news of two golden kittens. There is one in that shed now. I know that. But one golden kitten is not two. The Dog mulled this over. There is no reward, it concluded, for one golden kitten.

But it decided to sleep the night quite near, so that it could follow them in the morning.

A dog follows, it thought comfortably.

It thought, That's what a dog does.

❧

The shed was filled with a curious rhythmic clanking sound. Every shred of food was gone. Undeterred, the golden kitten had continued licking one of the empty metal dishes until it fetched up in the corner, where each powerful stroke of his tongue now banged it against the wall. Animal X, meanwhile, gave himself a thorough wash, remarking contentedly how the sound of *his* tongue in the fur on his chest sounded much like the rasp of the kitten's in the empty bowl. "Tongues are useful to have," meditated Animal X, "when you're a cat."

Stilton was almost asleep. He had tucked his paws up

under him and let his head fall forward until his nose was almost resting on the floor. But each time he dropped off, the same thought woke him with a start, compelling him to ask anxiously, "Will it come back, that thing?"

"I think the kitten was too much for it," said Animal X. He added, more to himself than Stilton, "I think the kitten would be too much for anyone."

"We took its food," Stilton said guiltily.

Eating had worked on him the magic it always works on a cat; but there was still a trembling in all his limbs, and the milky third lid had drawn itself almost halfway across both eyes. You don't look good, Animal X thought. Of course it's hard to know how you looked when you were well. While out loud, confident in his answer, he said, "I don't believe it had any more right to be here than we do. If it had, it would have fought harder."

"What *was* it?"

This question left him on less dependable ground.

"It was a traveler like us," he said in the end.

"Sit near me," invited Stilton, "just in case."

Then he said, "Isn't it marvelous to be out?"

Animal X curled up around him, licked his ears once or twice, and settled down.

"Sleep now," he said.

Observing their preparations from the other side of the shed, the golden kitten abandoned its pursuit of the dish, licked its chops massively, yawned even more massively, then came over. It stood near them for a moment or two as if awaiting instructions or trying to decide how to lie down, then with a sigh fell heavily on its side on Animal X's tail and began to purr.

"Make yourself comfortable," invited Animal X.

His sleep was deep, with long, sensible dreams; next morning he woke as early as ever. Stilton lay beside him in a bar of pearly light. The kitten had already gone out. Animal X went to the door and looked into the garden, which was full of white mist and pale yellow sunshine.

"I always liked the dawn," he decided quietly to himself, "but today I like it more."

The kitten had left a trail in the dewy grass to the bottom of the garden, then had plowed through the hedge into the pasture beyond, where it had sat grooming itself for a few minutes before making its way down to the little stream, to sniff around among the duck droppings, then wander off in the same direction as the current.

After a few hundred yards the stream entered a spacious water meadow—low-lying, grayed with dewy spiderwebs, buttered with kingcups, and dotted here and there by single tall thistles— on which the mist seemed to linger despite the growing warmth of the day. There it joined a broader, deeper stream—green, thick with weeds, and apparently unmoving except where it plunged over a weir with a kind of mumbling roar. Above and beside the weir the air brightened in an arc of color, as if the falling water had laundered the mist out of it. Everything was in sharp focus. Blue dragonflies hung and darted above the water. On the bank beside this theater of light, its head cocked attentively to one side, sat the golden kitten, captivated by the fall and rush of the water, the broad silver weight of it as it poured over the weir, the creamy white standing wave from which broke suds of foam that were tossed up into the shiny air. Animal X went and sat companionably in the close-cropped turf nearby.

"What do you see?" he asked.

The kitten turned its face toward him. In its remaining eye gleamed a joy so quiet and pure it made him feel shy. An adult cat could only wince away from a look like that. When he was able to face it again, the kitten had forgotten he was there. It was too busy following the roar and plunge of the water across the weir, pausing to wonder how it folded itself over and danced into foam, then tilting its head a fraction to watch the process through again—unable, indeed uninclined, to release itself from that perpetual event. After a moment, Animal X asked, "What do you see?"

Silence.

"I'm not so keen on water myself. I don't know why."

The kitten watched the weir.

"It really is beautiful," said Animal X.

The kitten hunched its shoulders.

Animal X tried another tack. "Do you remember something like this, then?" he said. The water collapsed in thunder, the spray refreshed the air, the light split apart in delight and shimmered prismatically above it all. "I mean, from before they caught you?"

The kitten turned its head and hissed at him. Its ears went back, and a low, ululating yowl proceeded from its throat. Its one eye burned.

"No!" said Animal X. "Listen," he said. "I only—"

He gave way. He gave way again. Step by slow, threatening step, the golden kitten drove him away from the water. This is ridiculous, thought Animal X. What have I done? He put his haunches to the ground. He felt his own ears go back. He felt the angry yowl build in his own throat. Then the kitten lifted its head as if it had heard the weir for the first time. With a single despairing glare toward the dancing foam, as if it were giving something up for ever, it rushed off across the meadows.

"No!" called Animal X, too late. He had remembered the ducks, bickering in the shallows the night before. "It's your water," he whispered. "It's your water."

He was about to run after the kitten and talk to it when he heard a voice call, "Wait! What's going on?"

Stilton, waking up alone in the shed, had run his heart out to catch up with his friends.

"Why were you fighting? Don't leave me!"

Animal X sighed.

He waited.

He thought, The kitten will calm down soon. And we might as well go in this direction as any.

So once Stilton had caught up, and Animal X had assured him that they would stay together, the two of them waded off into the dew in the kitten's footsteps, unaware of the shadow that followed them across the meadows like a small cloud crossing the sun.

❧

The kitten did calm down—though it took all day, and the day after that, and even then it seemed to keep a wary eye on Animal X and Stilton and to walk a little apart from them. I don't know what I did, thought Animal X, but I'd better be careful in future. To Stilton, he said, "That kitten wants friends, but it is too angry to let anyone near."

"I would be angry, too," said Stilton.

Animal X stared at him. "What do you mean?" he said.

But Stilton couldn't explain.

🐾

They walked for some days without anything happening, their course bounded by the water Animal X was reluctant to cross. The stream thickened and flexed its muscles. It wound through pastureland or along the bases of gentle chalk hills, sometimes sharing the valley with a road. The three cats were never far from human beings—there was hardly a point in their journey when they were out of sight of the gray spire of a village church—but they kept to themselves. At midday they slept beneath a hedge; as dusk gathered, they found themselves wading through chilly layers of mist as high as themselves, dammed into small fields like millponds. They froze at the call of an owl, the bark of a dog from a house in the moonlight; they caught the stark reek of a vixen and heard her cry later from the ridge for a mate. They ate what they could find, which was never enough, and they were glad of the hot afternoons.

While the golden kitten seemed to thrive on these hardships, Stilton grew increasingly ill and tired. His fur fell off in patches to reveal—smelly, yellowish, and unhealed—the burns he had come by in the explosion. The burns frightened him, and he stopped cleaning himself rather than admit they were there. He rarely complained but crouched listlessly in the open at night, his head turned away from the other cats, talking to himself as if he were back in the cabinet. You woke, and you were immediately in the middle of his monologue, which flowed past like a stream—*"Oh, my owners ate some stuff, all right. They got through some stuff. But it was blue they liked the best. And none of that barely ripe supermarket stuff, either. 'Plastic cheese wrapped in plastic!' I often heard him say to her. 'None of that supermarket stuff here!' They were pretty choosy about their Stilton, those two"*—and then you slept again. It was comforting in a way. It went on for a night or two; then the sick cat seemed to grow so depressed he stopped talking at all. Trying to cheer him up one evening, Animal X said, "That's a nice piece of Stilton you've got there."

They were sitting at the base of the wire fence at the edge of a conifer plantation. Midges danced in ghostly pagoda shapes above their heads. It was almost dark, but the birds were still singing competitively from their pulpits high in the tops of the trees. Warmth seemed to spill out of the woods, where the trees had stored it up in secret all day, warmth and shadows and a smell of resin so strong it made the cats blink.

After a moment or two, Animal X prompted, "It's rather a lot for one cat, though, isn't it?"

"I haven't got any Stilton."

This came out with such quiet matter-of-factness Animal X was unable to think of a reply.

After more silence, Stilton added, "I've never had any." He looked across at Animal X. He seemed to be forcing his eyes to open so that his friend could see all the way into them to the pain inside. He said, "I never had owners or a family or a mate called Tabs. I'm just an old cat who lived in a pen. I never had any of those things." He let his eyes close and looked away again. "I don't even know what Stilton tastes like," he admitted, "any more than you do."

"But to talk about it like that—" said Animal X.

"Oh, I learned it all from a cat in the cabinets," whispered Stilton. "He'd come from the outside, just like you, long before you or Dancey or any of the others arrived." He shuddered, then gave a frail laugh. "Maybe he made it up, too."

"I don't understand why."

"To give myself a life," said Stilton. "I was born in that place. I was bred to go in the cabinets. I had no other purpose, and I've had no life but that until now, *but I don't mind.*" He said, "I don't even mind if I die now. Do you want to know why?"

"Yes," said Animal X.

Stilton looked up at the dark wall of trees behind them, the midges dancing above his head.

"Because I've been here and seen all this," he said. "And I've had a friend who took care of me." His head drooped and he stared at the ground. "I'm tired," he said. "You don't have to talk about cheese anymore." Then he said, "Everyone minds dying. I don't know why I said that."

Throughout this exchange, the golden kitten sat upright, gazing with a kind of ancient impassiveness out across the thistly pasture, the *tapetus lucidum* of its single eye blank and reflectant in the last eggshell-green light above the river. Who knew what it was thinking, or if it was thinking at all? Silently, it rose to its feet, stretched, and looked down at the sick cat. In that light it seemed bigger than itself. It stood over Stilton and began to lick him gently. Stilton offered up his tired face to the long, slow, careful passes of its tongue. He closed his eyes, and the kitten licked the mucus from them before it passed on to his ears, across the top of his head, and down his withered little sides and the burns that hurt him so much. After a moment, he sighed, and began to relax. The kitten gave a single, grunting purr that seemed to echo away across the fields. The stars appeared, one by one. A car whirred along some nearby lane. Suddenly it was pitch-dark and off in the woods a brock was coughing. Stilton, who had begun to doze, woke up and shivered anxiously. But he was soon asleep again, and all that could be heard was the quiet rasp of the golden kitten's tongue.

You were listening then, thought Animal X. I knew you were.

Chapter Ten

THE KIND AND THE CRUEL

*I*n the middle of the night, as the moon crept toward the horizon and the constellation cats know as the Leopard faded into the beginning of a new dawn, Red came awake, bolt upright.

Red had never regarded himself as a cat with much imagination. He didn't share the resident ferals' love of superstition or ritual; hell, he never even thought about his own future. But something had just entered his dreams with such force that it had propelled him out of a deep sleep. He remembered the elusive thought that had occurred to him that afternoon, a curious sense of distortion and loss. He had dismissed it at the time, unable to trace its origin. But now he knew exactly what had triggered it.

Kittens.

Every feral community fizzes with them: little bundles of fur tumbling and chewing, mock-fighting and mewing.

Where were the kittens?

In Kiki la Doucette's feral court there was not a single kitten to be seen. Not one. Every cat there had been adult—skinny, sure—but full grown.

Where the hell were the kittens?

"Sealink." He nudged her urgently. The calico seemed the most down-to-earth, no-nonsense female he'd ever encountered. Perhaps she'd be able to provide a sensible explanation. "The kittens! Sealink, wake up!"

The calico was fast asleep, and Red could do nothing to wake her. Even as he watched, her ears twitched; then smooth black lips drew back from sharp teeth in a snarl. For a moment he thought he had her attention, but when her eyes blinked open, the third lid was closed tight across the pupil so that moonlight struck eerily off the milky-white membrane.

Her paws jerked.

Sealink was running. It was dark and icy cold. She was nowhere she recognized, nowhere she had even been, and certainly nowhere she wished to be again. The landscape through which she ran was featureless—the highway to end all highways—a black plain scoured by howling winds, winds that seemed designed to strip fur from skin and flesh from bone.

She had no clear idea why she ran, for the compulsion that drove her lay deeper than thought. Something lay ahead of her, giving off a dull green light. No matter how hard she ran, this glow remained elusive, always the same distance away as it had been when she first sighted it, although her lungs burned from her exertions. At the same time, she sensed something behind her, and she knew by the way her spine prickled with heat that this something was gaining on her, inch by inexorable inch. She felt her lips draw back from her teeth with the effort, felt the desperate fluidity of her limbs as they gathered and flexed, gathered and flexed.

And then the voice was closer.

In the teeth of the wind, Sealink heard it.

It had a double tone, the first low and booming, like the drone of a pipe organ, so deep that it shuddered in her bowels; the other was a voice she had heard before, vaguely familiar, but somehow distorted. It said, "I am one who became two; I am two who become four; I am four who become eight; I am one more after that." In and around the echo of these words, the demonic wind roared and subsided, roared and subsided. "One more after that. After that. After that."

But you can't help us anymore, Sealink thought. I saw you die.

Ahead, the glow deepened and spread. It rose from the dusky horizon like smoke from a bonfire and billowed toward the calico, who now stood rooted like a tree, her heart thumping in her chest. It twisted and twined for a moment above her head, a hieroglyph of greeny-gold light. Sealink stared at its incomprehensible shape, which was like that of a keyhole drawn on empty air, a keyhole without key or door. As she did so, a hot wind blasted past her—so that her fur felt as if it had been scorched—and ripped into the symbol like a dark hand, dashing it down so that it trembled apart and spilled away like mist. The great voice reverberated through the darkness.

"No Golden Cat. No kittens. If I die, all die!"

Then it was gone into the distance like spent thunder and the calico was left alone and shaking.

"Sealink!"

"No!"

The calico thrashed and came to her feet in a sudden, galvanic motion, fur on end. Red backed away. She looked completely mad, and the bite she had given him earlier still twinged.

"Sealink, I'm sorry for waking you—"

She stared at him, wild-eyed, her flanks heaving.

"The kittens—" The dream rumbled on through her head.

"I know—"

The calico blinked. "What?"

"Kittens. I haven't seen a single one, not even with Kiki. Sealink, something very strange is going on around here. I mean—kittens—they're everywhere usually." He gestured widely. "I remember this place, teeming with kittens; you couldn't move without falling over one of 'em. Feral cats have tons of kittens. We're known for it. Where the hell are they all?"

Gradually the focus came back into the amber eyes. The dream faded with cold finality. "Damned if I know, honey—came back here to look for my own, and received a real cruel answer; so don't ask me to give you any more answers about kittens."

A shaft of red struck the water in front of the hollow. It blazed across the mighty river and lit the warehouses on the Algiers bank so that for some seconds they appeared to be on fire. On the near shore, every rock and blade of grass was touched with the unearthly light of dawn.

"Red sky in the morning, Great Cat's warning—"

Sealink stretched and yawned. She bent her head to groom

her copious ruff, and at that moment a cry shattered the still air.

Red sped out of the hollow and leapt onto a fence post. Every muscle taut with concentration, he stared into the distance, his tail lashing in agitation.

Sealink listened intently. The delay in the reception of the sound between one ear and the other enabled her to pinpoint the source of the cry with remarkable exactitude. She was on her feet at once, full of pent vigor.

"That's a cat in trouble, hon. Boneyard, north of Rampart."

Red turned to stare in amazement. "That's some pair of ears you got on you, sister."

But Sealink was already running.

🐾

New Orleans, City of Good Times, City of Lost Care, city of cats is also the city of the dead. There are boneyards everywhere, each a miniature township dedicated to perpetual sleep. It might appear that these cemeteries are the true residential zones of the city. Grimly enduring, elaborate and monumental, this is where the masons of Louisiana have lavished their craft; these are the areas that will outlast the charmingly distressed clapboard houses of the French Quarter and the shining modern towers of the Central Business District. Built above ground to defy the mighty river and the sucking drainage of the swamp, row upon row of windowless mausoleums line dusty, weed-strewn paths. Winged stone women hover massively among the tombs, suspended forever in watchful stasis. Cold white men, crowned with thorns, spread-eagled on crosses, appear suddenly at the intersections. Many gravesites are fenced around with iron stakes, fantastic and ornate, perhaps to ward the eye from their very functionality; but whether this gesture is designed to keep the dead in, or the living out, it is hard to determine. Walkers in these boneyards may sense they are being watched, not by the blind scrutiny of marble but by quick, lambent eyes—little bundles of anima with sharp faces and slitted pupils.

And when the last of the breathing human visitors leave, the feral cats come out. This has become their domain.

❧

In the old St. Louis Cemetery there were many such cats. Sick and scared, they cowered in the shadows behind the palmettos; hid in the dark recesses of the disused oven tombs where the brickwork had collapsed under the weight of years; or lay still, all energy gone, among the curious offerings people had left for long-departed relatives—dried roses and ferns, crayon drawings of the dead and strings of plastic beads, even, bizarrely, a construction flag in yellow and black, proclaiming the legend SAFETY ALWAYS.

❧

Sealink and Red leapt the crumbling wall just opposite the plaster statue of St. Jude (patron saint of lost causes). The originator of the desperate wail was a small bicolor female who was running in tight, mournful circles in the far corner of the boneyard, all the while issuing heartbreaking whimpers. The other cats had formed a wide, ragged circle around her and were watching her antics with a sort of tired resignation.

"Hey, honey—"

Like a great ship breasting a wave, Sealink breached the circle, which immediately broke and scattered. Those ferals that could run, ran. Those that couldn't crawled into the shadows. From their hiding places they stared suspiciously as the calico reached out a paw to the distressed female.

"Honey, tell Momma your troubles."

The bicolor stared up and, taking in Sealink's great and well-fed bulk, cowered away in terror. Teeth chattering and ears flat, she struggled to speak.

"Wh-what m-more do you want?"

At this point Red intervened. "Take it easy, babe. It's okay."

She backed away distrustfully. "You'll get nothing from me—"

"We ain't here to do you harm."

The bicolor looked from Red to Sealink and back again. She quivered. "You ain't here to take me away?"

Red shook his head.

Out of the corner of her eye, Sealink saw movement around the boneyard. The other ferals had started to creep out again, curiosity having got the better of their fear. They were painfully thin, like the cats outside the restaurant, gaunt and hollow eyed. Their ribs showed through slack, dull coats like the staves of an old wooden boat. Underfed kittens huddled in unnatural silence in the long grass, the early morning sun shining off their great round eyes.

Sealink whistled through her teeth. "My, my. You guys all look sicker'n a dead dog."

One of the ferals was bolder than the rest. He shouldered his way out into the open and stood there, his eyes watering in the light. "What's it to you?"

"We heard this lady—" Red turned to the little bicolor. "Hey, honey—what's your name?"

"Azelle."

"We heard Azelle cry out—came to see if we could help."

He turned to the bicolor, who was now keening wordlessly again and, reaching up, licked her head in the most soothing way he knew.

At once, there was a movement beneath the palmettos. A little black-and-white cat with bright green eyes and a confident manner stepped out between the fronds and looked Red up and down appraisingly.

As if in reaction to this scrutiny, Red was all attention, his whiskers fanning the air. He dropped his forefeet back to the ground and stood there, his coat glowing in the ruddy light. Then he leaned forward. His features sharpened with sudden recognition.

"Téophine? Is that you?"

The little black-and-white smiled shyly. Then she opened her pink mouth wide and yelled, "Hey, girls! He's a live one. Still got his *cojones*!"

At once there was a flurry of activity. From all over the boneyard, emaciated females emerged into the light, popping their heads out of broken tombs, stretching scrawny necks over their neighbors.

"Really? You ain't kiddin', Téophine?"

"He still entire?"

"Wow! Let me at him!"

"I can't see. Let me see!"

"Hey, Azelle, this un'll sort you out—"

"Give you a whole new litter—"

Red's moment of glory turned to flustered desperation. If you could see a cat blush through his fur, Sealink decided that under Red's fine ginger coat his skin would be as red as a beet. As it was, he backed away from the mob of curious females, sat down heavily with his back to a gravestone, and covered his private parts with his paws.

"Now, ladies, please—"

The leader of the harpies pushed forward.

"One at a time, *s'il te plaît*. And I seen him first."

"Téophine, it *is* you."

Sealink regarded her with interest. So this was the little minx who had been the cause of Red's heartache, the reason he had left the Big Easy in the first place. It looked as if she had always been small framed, but now her legs were emaciated, the skin above her eyes showed pink where the fur had thinned and fallen out, and dark runnels of watery matter ran down the sides of her nose. Yet she retained a kind of waifish prettiness; and a certain scent in the air left no doubt as to the fact that she, too, was still entire. The calico felt a sudden painful stab of jealousy.

"Why, if it ain't ol' Rumby-Pumby." Téophine started to purr.

Red bristled. "They call me Red, now. Just plain Red," he growled. "It's been a long time."

Despite everything, Sealink felt her spirits rise. "Rumby-Pumby?"

Red glared at her. "So I was a little chubby in those days. It's kind of a nickname they gave me, okay?"

Sealink sauntered out in front of Red, fluffed out her gorgeous ruff and tail, and addressed herself to the little black-and-white. "Now, honey, you'll just have to hold fire with ol'—" she looked around, grinned evilly over her shoulder at Red "—Rumby-Pumby here for a moment or two, 'cause there's something weird going on and whatever it is disturbed my morning; so I mean to find out exactly what caused Azelle here to howl so loud."

The bicolor had stopped her melancholy circling and now sat, head down in exhausted defeat.

"They stole my kittens."

Kittens. It all came back to kittens, again. Something dark and forbidding rose in her soul.

"Who stole your kittens?"

The bicolor mumbled something.

Sealink stared at her, aghast. "You let other cats steal away your kittens?"

Azelle nodded. "Weren't nothing I could do 'bout it." She lifted mortified eyes. "There were so many of them . . ."

Sealink was appalled. Furious, she turned to face the group. "You let them take her kittens? You didn't try to help? What kind of cowards are you? Look at yourselves. Ain't you got no self-respect, to let yourselves get like this? I ain't ever seen so many filthy, starving cats, certainly not in the Big Easy. I seen a few on my travels—dying of cat flu in the slums of Calcutta, begging for scraps in the tourist joints of Skiathos, lining up for filthy leftovers in the arches of Coldheath—but you're the sorriest-looking bunch I ever did encounter . . . pardon my directness."

This seemed to unleash a tide of explanation.

"They bin stealin' our kittens for weeks now—"

"These few are all that are left—"

An old gray cat bobbed its head out of an oven tomb. "Takin' them in broad daylight—"

Red stared around him. "And y'all just let this happen?"

The old gray wheezed. It took a while for Red to realize it was laughing at him. "Take a look at us, sonny. Y'all t'ink we any good for fightin'?"

Another voice. "We all sick, boy."

"Hell, we ain't just sick, we's dying."

"Ain't got the strength we was born with."

"Cain't barely stand up."

A cacophony of voices.

"Ain't ate in a week—"

"People don't feed us no more."

"Ain't no rats to eat, neither."

"They aren't putting the garbage out like they used to."

"I heard there's a price on all our heads—"

"Kiki la Doucette—"

A silence fell suddenly and everyone turned to look at the last speaker—a large stripy feral who had once been a fine tom, to judge by his big bony frame and frilled ears.

"Hey, you, Mouth of the South! You ain't got no balls now, so don't act like you do!" Téophine squared up to him. The striped cat rose up menacingly as if to clout her. Half his size, nevertheless, she was undeterred. "*Tais-toi!* Kiki hear you mention her name around this, you get us all killed."

The stripy male subsided shamefacedly.

"Sorry, Téo."

Sealink stared at the black-and-white. Little pieces of information were starting to fit together in her head, but not in any way that made sense. "Why should Kiki la Doucette give a damn what a load of mangy ferals have to say about her?"

Téophine squared her bony shoulders and regarded the calico with a hauteur remarkable for one so frail. The white star on her nose seemed to blaze with indignation. "You are very rude, for a newcomer. But since you ask, you should know that we—this small and ragged group you see before you—are the last free cats of the French Quarter of New Orleans." Her voice dropped to a barely audible hiss. "For weeks now we have been under siege. Our kittens have disappeared one by one. The few that you can see here are all that are left. Sometimes other cats; sometimes the Pestmen. The hand of every human—*tout d'un coup*—is suddenly and inexplicably raised against us; and we have done nothing, *rien*, to deserve such treatment. And all because we will not join a certain queen's court of murderers and fools. So here we are, *déguenillés* and ill-used, shabby and dying of a sickness we do not understand, our kittens *ont disparus*; while all the time the yellow queen grows fatter and fatter and her court strut around showing off their pretty new collars like they own the city. We may be sad and oppressed; but we are our own cats, still holding out in whatever way we can. There is no need to insult us in our last remaining domain."

Sealink looked at her feet, for once in her life lost for words. Red stepped forward and bowed his head politely.

"Téophine—honey—I'm real sorry if we've given offense. Sealink here ain't exactly diplomatic—"

The calico opened her mouth to object, thought better of it, and closed it again.

"We only came here to help whoever was in trouble, but it looks to me as if that means all of you. We'd sure like to help in any way we can, but I have to say I'm findin' it kinda hard to take it all in. Perhaps we could sit down somewhere quiet and you could take us through things nice and slow?"

Téophine regarded him thoughtfully. "Well, you're the only two able-bodied cats I seen in a long while, so I guess you could be useful—"

"Wait!"

A spindly-legged Siamese had pushed through the throng. Its little triangular head bobbed on its neck like a flower heavy with dew.

"I seen her yesterday." The Siamese fixed Sealink with bright blue crossed eyes. "I seen her dragging some great package up the street behind the French Market—"

"That's where the bitch queen hangs out—"

"Seen her go right on in there, and come out again, unscathed."

Someone hissed.

"Spy!"

Another growled; others showed their teeth, yellow with rot. Even in their diseased state, they gave off an air of considerable menace.

Téophine put her head on one side. "So. Why you hangin' out wit' Kiki la Doucette? What you bring her? What you got to say?"

The other ferals crowded around.

The calico drew herself up to her full, impressive height. "I don't have to defend my actions to you. I was trading claw marks with that old yellow queen before you was even born—"

There was a gasp from the crowd.

"That's right: I was one of the Moon Walk cats in my time. Back then I was known as—"

"The Delta Queen—"

The old gray cat scrambled inelegantly out of the broken tomb and came sniffing at Sealink. "It is. It's the Delta Queen. Hey, chile, remember me? Not so old in those days. I remember you." He leered at her. "I remember you well."

Sealink stared at him with dawning horror. The last time she'd seen him he'd been a sixteen-pound tomcat with a retinue of female followers. Tulane—a slick-talking, quick-stepping street fighter. Moreover, a slick-talking, quick-stepping street fighter that she'd mated with more than once . . .

"Jeez, honey, you don't look so good."

Tulane cackled. "Comes to us all in time. Come to you, too, if you stick around here for much longer."

Téophine regarded Sealink with a glint in her eye. "So, *cher*, you got roots here, huh? That still don't explain what you were doing at Madame Kiki's."

Sealink sighed. "Honey, I don't want to get caught up in all this covert-action stuff. I ain't got no allegiances here no more, but I always hated that old yellow, and recent events sure ain't changed my attitude. Came back lookin' for my lost kittens; found two of 'em, thanks to the bitch queen; big disappointment; no idea what was in the parcel—what else can I say?"

"It ain't enough." The little black-and-white withdrew into the crowd. There was a lot of muttering, some sharp glances at the two newcomers. Eventually, Téophine reemerged. "Okay, come with me."

❧

As the sun rose in an empty cobalt sky, the cats of the boneyard took refuge in the shady places, away from curious eyes. Sealink and Red followed Téophine and a group of other ferals into a large collapsed tomb on the east wall of the cemetery. Here it was cool and comfortable, while outside temperatures soared into the high nineties and an enervating humidity drained the life from all who moved in the stifling air.

As Sealink's eyes adjusted to the twilight of the tomb, she scrutinized the other occupants. Besides the little black-and-white, there were two other female cats—a scruffy tortoiseshell and a little colorpoint with a flattened face and matted coat—and the big striped male with the frilled ears. His masculine beauty was certainly marred now not only by the fact that he'd been neutered but also by a tail that hung at a curious angle and the effects of the wasting sickness, which made his skin hang slack on dwindled muscles. All at once Sealink remembered her encounter with Blanco, the big white male outside the Farmer's Market whose skin had slipped away under her gripping teeth in such a disconcerting manner. She shuddered. Whatever it was these cats were suffering from, she sure didn't want to catch it.

Red was ensconced with Téophine in the far corner of the tomb, and the neutered male was watching possessively out of the corners of his eyes. They had their heads down and were talking in low voices. Clearly catching up on old times, the calico thought waspishly. To distract herself from uncharitable thoughts, she turned to the striped cat. "So tell me, honey: what the hell's been going on in this town?"

This animal, who had awarded himself the simple but grandiose title of the Hog, after the motorbike that had damaged his appendage, was obviously flattered by Sealink's interest. He dragged his eyes from the little black-and-white, and with his fur puffed up and his ears pricked, started to talk.

"It bin happenin' for months now, lady. First of all people took grown cats, give 'em the operation, then let 'em go. Then when they take the ladies, they put 'em in a box and let 'em cry out till the little kitties come runnin' to find out why they momma's cryin'. Then they takes the kitties. To start wit' they just put a needle in the kitties, then bring 'em back, give 'em food, too. The next thing we knows, the Pestmen comes wit' they boxes and kitties started to disappear in they ones and twos. Then it was whole litters, out playin' in the street—next t'ing, they gone—*shoom*—like they was never there."

The colorpoint piped up, "And then it was the chirren, y'know—"

"Chirren?"

"*Oui,* the chirren. The human chirren. The little uns. They start to lure the kits away. *C'est l'argent.* That's what they say. Take 'em to the Pestmen. They get money for kittens. It not right. *C'est mauvais . . .* And then the other cats, other ferals, they start to steal our babies, too. Now *that*, that ain't for *l'argent*, you know? Somet'ing very evil is happenin' here."

Sealink wrinkled her brow. What was it old Baron Raticide had said? The kittens go first. But go where? She struggled with her thoughts for a while. Then she asked, "Who on earth are the Pestmen?"

The striped cat shrugged. "Bad angels. That's how I t'ink of 'em. Human bein's, they split down the middle, y'know—the kind and the cruel. I call the cruel ones bad angels; the kind ones, good—and used to be they mostly in the second category till quite recent. Now a cat in mortal danger if it walk the streets wit' no collar. The Pestmen they drives up in their big vans, grab you up, you ain't never seen again—'cept in bits, y'know?"

"Bits?"

"They sell cat bones to the voodoo shops," the tortoise-shell offered helpfully. "And if you got black fur, they'll mummify your feet for lucky charms, boil your brains for magic."

Sealink grimaced. "Humans sure can be strangely super-stitious—but they used to sell this stuff in my time, and it was only ever chickens."

"They bin gettin' real weird." Hog shook his head. "It bin like a freak tide: one day cats is good, the next we all some sort of danger to 'em and they crossing themselves in the street if you pass. The next day they stop feedin' you; and the day after that there's this great big wave of hatred and they want to kill you and your kitties and sell you all for voodoo."

Sealink fell silent. Why would any cat steal another's kitten? She thought about events at Tintagel, when cat had fought against cat . . . "Has anyone," she asked, her voice raised, her face like stone, "mentioned some guy called the Alchemist?"

At the other end of the tomb, Téophine's head shot up. "I heard that name, but not for some time."

"How about the Majicou?"

"We heard the Majicou was dead."

Sealink considered for a moment, decided against ven-turing the details. "That's what I heard, too."

"Do you know the Mammy?"

Sealink wrinkled her brows. "I remember the name."

"She used to be the guardian 'round these parts," offered the tortoiseshell.

"Can't she help? Seems to me you guys could do with some guardianship."

Téophine shook her head. "She ain't here no more—she's way out in the old swamps—in the bayous."

"So?"

"It's a long way, and it ain't safe."

Sealink sensed an adventure, a new kind of journey, one with a clear goal and simple motives; a journey, moreover, that would take her out of a city she had once loved and that now seemed irrevocably poisoned. "Tell me where to find her and I'll go talk to the Mammy. Someone's got to do something 'round here before the whole thing goes to hell in a handcart."

❧

Téophine's knowledge of the whereabouts of the Mammy amounted to little more than an awareness of a little-used wild road that supposedly led out to the Bayou Gros Bon Ange from the seedy end of Iberville, but she and Red insisted on accompanying the calico at least that far. Red had offered to journey with her into the ancient backwaters, but Sealink could tell from the looks he and the little black-and-white exchanged that his heart was not in it. For a second she felt desperately jealous.

"Still," she muttered, as they trotted down Dauphine Street, "*ménage à trois* just ain't my scene."

Toward the corner of Bienville Street they found a little ginger-and-white cat with a pink velour collar wandering disconsolately up and down.

Sealink approached it.

"Hey, honey, you okay?"

"Hello! My name's Candy. I'm a bit lost."

"Lost is lost, honey. Sayin' you're a bit lost is kinda like sayin' you're a bit pregnant, y'know?"

The ginger cat looked shocked, then decided to ignore the big cat's vulgarity. "I think I live quite close to here, but I've never been outside before, so I can't quite figure out which house is mine. My owners took me out in a plastic box last night when it was dark and left me here. I think it must be some kind of test. Do you think it's a test?" She regarded the calico optimistically.

"Maybe—"

Candy tossed her head so that the little gold bell on her collar tinkled. "I'll figure it out soon. I've always been intelligent— very good at tricks. I can juggle with a ball of paper; catch a catnip mouse, even if it's thrown from the end of the room; and open every cupboard door in the kitchen." She thought about this for a moment. "You don't have any food about you, do you?"

Sealink shook her head. The ginger-and-white looked disappointed.

"Ah well, never mind. Good-bye, then."

And off she went, tail in the air, sniffing each stoop and sill along the street. The three of them watched her go in silence. Then Red said, "Do you think we should tell her?"

"Tell her what, that her humans have got rid of her? That if she even does find her way back, they'll do it again?"

"I'll tell her how to get to the boneyard," Téophine said with quiet decisiveness, and set off up the street after Candy.

She had almost caught up with the little ginger-and-white when a large, dark-colored truck pulled up in front of them and two men in black overalls jumped out. Candy looked up hopefully. The first reached down and picked her up. She hung unresisting between his big gloves while he called something to the second man, his large fingers clumsy on her neck. With a jangle, the pink collar fell to the ground. Téophine, her back against the wall, was doing her best to slide away unnoticed, but the second human had seen her. He unraveled a wide-meshed net and with some expertise cast it out into the shadow where she cowered. At once there was pandemonium. Téophine shrieked and fought the net, but the more she struggled, the more the net tangled her limbs.

"Téo, no!"

Spitting and howling, Red sped up the road toward her, a

streak of orange fury. He launched himself at the net man, fangs bared.

Sealink stared, horrified. Then she, too, fled up the street—in the opposite direction.

♣

She ran and ran. She ran until her lungs burned and the pads of her paws felt raw and bruised. And as she ran, the blood roared in her ears, roared and thundered like a great, dark storm until she could almost feel the fingers of a gigantic black hand reaching out to break the gold of a symbol that hung before her like the promise of hope. And she knew that she would have to run forever to evade it and that even if she ran from it forever the world would eventually be eaten away around her so that she would exist in a terrible void, alone save for the hand and the words that had reverberated through her dream. At last she stopped, her chest heaving, her eyes watering with fear, shame and horror washing hot and heavy through her veins.

What had she done? She had deserted a cat she had come to think of as more than a friend and a brave, sick feral who needed all the help she could get. She had run and left them to whatever fate awaited them in the hands of the men in black overalls, men who could only be the Pestmen the boneyard cats had spoken of in hushed tones. Another betrayal.

The image of the pink velour collar on the ground returned sharply to her mind's eye: a terrible image of innocence traduced.

What was happening in this city? What was happening to her? Had she, too, caught the wasting sickness the feral cats suffered from? Had it perhaps attacked not her flesh but her very soul? Not for the first time in recent history, Sealink felt nauseated by herself.

Panting, she pressed her throbbing forehead against a windowsill, so that the cool glass soothed her fevered skin. When her breathing had returned to something approaching its normal speed, she opened her eyes and stared about her. She didn't recognize the alley she now stood in. It was dingy and narrow, and the shopfronts were dusty and ill lit. She turned to examine the window she had pressed herself against.

It was an odd shop, that was for sure. The window display comprised an extraordinary clutter of unlikely objects: dolls in grass skirts and beads and exaggerated black eye makeup; bottles and vials of all different colors; alligator teeth in great long swags and ropes; books and cards and candles; silver jewelry; boxes and packets and powders; bones and totems and chickens' feet; and in the center of the display, something that made her heart clench as though it had been clamped in a vise. Something—someone—she recognized.

In the very center of all the arcane paraphernalia of a traditional tourist voodoo shop, on a rotating black velvet stand, sat the head of an animal. The head had been partially flayed on the right-hand side with the greatest care and precision to demonstrate, as if for anatomical discussion by interested veterinarians, the major muscle groups and bone structure surrounding the orbital socket of the species *Felis cattus*. The preserved red flesh stretched tightly upward from a ghastly rictus to an empty eye cavern. The brain had been removed. On the left-hand side of the head, eye, skin, flesh, and fur were all intact.

Sealink sat heavily upon the ground, all breath gone from her lungs.

The macabre carousel rotated gaily once more.

She stared at it with her mouth open and her eyes streaming.

It was the head of an old black cat.

It was the head of Baron Raticide.

Chapter Eleven

THE SYMBOL

*T*he Queen licked her paws for a moment.

"It was the water again after that," she said. "Cold currents. The bony, hollow halls of the ocean."

She sighed.

"I did not find my children," she said softly. "But if nothing else, I have seen the Nile."

It was so quiet in the oceanarium that Tag could hear waves falling on the beach half a mile away. For a moment, he imagined them as the breakers of another, gentler, sea. A dreamy warmth stole over him, full of the life and bustle of strange cities, smells of spices, the taste of things he had never eaten. He shook himself.

"But what about *Cy*?" he said. "If the Great Ray brought all three of you home, where is she?"

The King and Queen looked at each other.

"Tag, we don't know," admitted Ragnar.

"Good-bye for now," the tabby had said, looking up at the King and Queen in the hard actinic glare of the aquarium lamp. "It's Thousand Island fever for us, now you guys are safe back from the Egypt package. It's activity holidays and all and, you know, reckless navigation. We got more stuff to do, me and this Ray guy." With that, tabby and fish had vanished in a lazy swirl of black water, leaving the amazed royal couple to stare down into the tank, which now seemed shadowy and unbounded, bigger inside than out. For a long time afterward, the Queen had thought she could still hear Cy's voice, saying in a kind of receding echoic whisper, "We got more things to see!"

Tag was quiet for a long time when he heard this.

"She's very much her own cat, of course," he said eventually. "But I don't like to think of her in the care of a fish." He blinked. "I shall worry about her," he told the Queen.

"Oh, Mercury, don't be sad. She'll come home again, I'm sure."

Tag stared into the fish tank.

"The worst thing is," he said, "that I don't feel as if we are any further forward for it all."

"Oh, but don't you see?" said Pertelot. "We are!"

Then she made Ragnar display the silver symbol—the pyramid, or open triangle, surmounted by a circle—hanging from the blue sash the fisherman had given him. "This is at the heart of things. We were shown it deep in the earth," she said, "by some ambivalent force, something that helps us with one hand and hinders with the other, something powerful enough to visit the depths of the ocean and there engage a giant fish for us to travel on. Perhaps if we can understand the symbol, we will find Odin and Isis. Look: it seems pleased with its own mystery. Can an object be pleased? It has an oily sheen, like moonlight on a wave at night.

"The Great Ray took us to Egypt," she went on, after a pause. "The boats and boatmen helped us home. I have no idea why, except to make sure we understand this sign. Mercury, it is the key."

In the silence that followed, Tag stared at the symbol. Ragnar, proud of his sash but a little embarrassed to be the center of attention, scratched behind one ear. The Queen finished grooming herself, stretched, and looked around the oceanarium.

"Where's Leo?" she asked Tag in a lighter voice. "I hope she's been behaving herself."

"Ah, yes," said Ragnar. "Leonora!"

And they looked at Tag expectantly.

He didn't know what to say. He had been so captivated by their story he had forgotten his own. The apprentice was still out there somewhere, roaming the wild roads alone. Before he could stop himself he blurted out, "I've lost her."

Ragnar chuckled.

"Gone out for chips," he suggested. "It will be tomcats

next," he predicted placidly. The Queen gave him an old-fashioned look. "Oh, that is one bad daughter," he said.

"I wonder where she learns it?" Pertelot inquired.

She said to Tag, "Don't worry so, Mercury. You can't look after her all the time."

"You don't understand," said Tag. "I mean, I really have—" Appalled by their faith in him, he found he couldn't continue. "Look," he said, "she's probably down at the Beach-O-Mat now. I'll go and fetch her. No, no, you stay here." And he went off, thinking miserably, Now I've lied to them, too.

Out on the cobbles in the quiet night, he turned right instead of left, and soon stood on a wooden bench on the cliff top above the village. He welcomed the chilly onshore breeze, with its odors of iodine and salt. The cottages fell away from him among flights of steps, narrow alleys, stone-cropped walls. The big sky was planished with moonlight, the ocean a litter of small waves breaking Chinese white on charcoal. Far out on the horizon, the inshore fishing boats were at work in a scatter of lights. He imagined the fishermen drawing in the nets; water pouring over the decks; then the slithering silver haul spilling out, mixed with shells, starfish, weeds, and bits of plastic rubbish. But that only made him think of Cy, eyeing him with her head on one side and saying: "Tag, we got *star-gazey pie!*" She loved fish, and now she had gone off with one. Suddenly, he couldn't bear to have lost two cats in one night. He jumped off the bench and ran down the hill to Cy's bus shelter of choice, where he encountered two or three hard-favored village toms, boasting away the mid-section of the night as they waited for the fishing boats to return. When they saw who he was they quietly took themselves elsewhere. He was rather hurt by this; nevertheless he watched them intently as they backed away, as if to catch something unaware in their blank, reflectant eyes. He sat there for some time. After an hour or so, mist formed in the bay and sent cold fingers the color of poached egg white up across the water and into the town. Tag got up and walked about to get warm. Mist loom made the palms, the chip shops and amusement arcades, and the lifeboat station look bigger than they were—they thrust themselves upon him suddenly, in a space full not of echoes but the opposite of echoes. Then out of the cold, just after dawn, walking down the long, empty esplanade in the hallucinatory light, he saw a young cat coming toward him. Its gait was limping and tired. Its sandy fur was matted with pigeon dung and worse. It was Leonora Whitstand Merril.

She stood in front of him.

"If you don't tell them I was lost," she offered, "I won't tell them you lost me."

"We'll see" was all he could promise.

"It's the best deal you're going to get."

He stared at her with unusual severity. He said, "Just tell me what happened to you, Leonora."

She stared back. "I'm freezing," she said.

He took her to the twenty-four-hour Beach-O-Mat, with its neat yellow benches, black-and-white linoleum, and shiny machines. Cats love clean linen, even when there is no chance to sit on it. They love warmth even more, and as a place to get warm the Beach-O-Mat was a byword in the town. It was, as Cy had once told Tag, "a must-have, Jack: a major item in everyone's wardrobe." And when he'd stared at her in puzzlement, "Hey! So what did I say?" Even after a long empty night it retained much of the previous day's steamy atmosphere. So there they sat, in the drum of an open dryer while, sneezing fastidiously, Tag applied his tongue to the kitten's dirty coat, and Leo stared thoughtfully ahead of herself as if she had learned rather more than she wanted to about the world. After a minute or two she said, "You aren't going to like this—"

"Get on with it now, Leo."

"—not this first bit, anyway. After you abandoned me on the Old Changing Way—"

"Leonora!"

"After I got lost, something really strange happened. I mean, stranger than it usually is over there. It was cold and damp where I was, like a lot of empty passageways going off in all directions. Water was dripping all around me, but I knew it was a kind night out in the real world—the sky clear, the fields giving up the heat of the day. I could almost hear the mice, cupped in nests of warm grass; yet there I stood, with this raw damp cold in the bones. Tag—" she stared intently at him, as if she would recognize an answer whether he spoke or not "—have you ever felt as if your life was draining out of you? As if you were poisoned, or—" she thought for a moment "—*fading out* somehow?" She shivered with the memory of it. "I'll tell you, I was a scared kitten at that point. I was lost. I was cold. I was going to sleep without wanting to. If you had turned up to show me the way home at that moment I just wouldn't have had the energy to take it."

She eyed him shrewdly.

"Of course, you didn't," she reminded him. "Turn up, I mean."

Tag decided to ignore this.

"Lassitude," he said, "feelings of vagueness. I've never heard of anything like it. But there were many things I never had a chance to learn. And then again, perhaps it is something quite new."

"Nice to get the views of an expert," said Leonora. "Everything you say makes me feel a lot better."

"No one can know everything," Tag said.

"I'm finding that out. Have I hurt your feelings again?"

"A little. What did you do next?"

"Everything had gone gray. All the life, the beauty, the worth had gone out of everything," said Leonora. "I don't want that!" she said. "I'm young—I want the world to be worth having! So I danced. I made a dance for myself, and I was in it. Look." She jumped down out of the dryer and danced on the floor, less, Tag thought, to show him than to remind herself. "Very slowly at first. Point one toe, place one foot. Very slow, very measured steps—no jumps or pounces. Then faster, faster, until I felt strong." She laughed. "You see?" she said. "Like this. I danced my way into that space, Tag, until it belonged to me again. Then I danced down the wild roads, and made them go where I wanted, just like you. I could *choose*."

She stopped dancing and sat looking up at him.

"Well?" she said.

"Choice is good."

"It is, isn't it?"

"But there's more to this story. Or have you already explained how you came to be covered in pigeon dung?"

It was Leo's turn to look hurt.

"Choice *is* good," she insisted.

"So. What did you choose to do?"

"I chose to go back to the house of Uroum Bashou."

🐾

By the time she got there, it was dark, and a thick yellow rind of moon hung above the dormered roof of the Reading Cat's domain, spilling its light across the littered garden but leaving the boarded-up windows in the dark. Leonora made herself comfortable in a tangle of rusty bicycle frames and their shadows, as far away from the back door as she could get. There she waited. The moon rose higher. The house was quiet but did not seem quite empty. After a time there was a stealthy but assertive thud from the cat flap, and the verminous Kater Murr stuck his head out into the night.

His yellow eyes moved from side to side like the eyes of a mechanical cat in a funfair, empty of intelligence and yet at the same time full of it. He did not push his way out of the cat flap onto the doorstep: he bunched up his evil hindquarters and sprang out on a wave of his own smell, ready for any kind of violence. He sat there scratching for a minute or two and murmuring to himself. "His paws are split but he welcomes that. His bollocks itch but he welcomes that. Kater Murr is no humdrum tom." After a while he scraped up some of the moonlit dirt beneath the old kitchen window and excreted copiously. "Kater Murr is in love with his own paradox," he congratulated himself, turning around to sniff what he had produced. Then he raised his disfigured muzzle. The moon glinted off rictus grin and snaggle teeth. A low, penetrating yowl issued forth, to curl over the spoiled lawn, briefly lick Leonora's bones, then float away across the surrounding streets. Almost at once, three or four brutalized-looking tomcats appeared on the rotten board fence at the bottom of the garden. After a brief conference, they jumped down as one and swept off into the Midland night with Kater Murr at their head.

Looking for any kind of trouble, thought Leonora; and her sympathy went out to the innocents they met.

As soon as she was sure they weren't coming back she scampered over and popped her head through the cat flap. The house rang with Kater Murr's smell, suspended like a foul bell in the latent heat of the stairs. By fits and starts, in the jangling moonlight and dark, she made her way up to the ramshackle gallery at the very top of the house. She peered around the door of each empty room on the way. On the second floor landing an open window banged to and fro. She froze. She ran. "Take care, Leonora," she told herself, just to hear a familiar voice. "Now this way. Quick now! Make no sound!"

Moonlight filled the library of Uroum Bashou, pouring in so brightly that she could make out the black lines of print on the pages of the opened books. There were dark bars and smudges of shadow across the dusty floor, the dry, faded wainscoting, the otiose velvet cushions. The darkest of them was the librarian himself, a skinny black comma—as he himself would have said—in the Great Text of Life. Spread out in front of him on the dusty floor—as if he could read them, too—the remains of a pigeon made a scribble of bones and feathers. The room was full of a strange, thready humming. Broken quarter tones rose and fell. Leonora cocked her head and laughed softly. Uroum Bashou had recently finished his dinner and was purring to himself as he washed in the moonlight.

"This was all very ill-advised," said Tag.

"I know," said Leonora. "And don't think I wasn't nervous. I was. But you know, he's not such a bad old cat. He wants to boast, that's all, and tell you things you don't know; and just be sure you're listening. Not much different than my father, if you ask me."

"Leo!"

"Well, of course, Father is rather better looking. But the Reading Cat was kind. He made me sit down and offered me what was left of his pigeon—which I didn't much fancy since Kater Murr must have killed it—and showed me where to get water from the tap that still drips into the broken basin at the far end of the room, and told me stories about his own cleverness until I could get his attention. That took a moment or two, I must say."

"Hm," said Tag, who recognized the difficulty.

"Anyway," said Leonora, "you have to imagine this—"

Uroum Bashou had emptied himself out. She had heard the stories of his kittenhood in Morocco—muezzin call at dawn, an education in reading, how he had been given to chase the little twist of light focused by a lens on a white courtyard wall; how it tasted to eat small birds glazed in spices; how the scents of the bazaar stole over a household with an intensity no kitten could disdain—and, for a second time, the story of how he came by his name. She had encouraged his opinions on date palms and drains, anchovies, mice, and the proper care of the kidneys in the older animal. She had heard his versions of the biographies of notorious human beings, among whom only Catherine the Great interested her. Now, they sat facing each other in companionable silence across a strip of dusty floorboards, and she judged it the moment to ask, "Uroum Bashou, then, can read anything?"

The Great Aide-Mémoire inclined his head in acknowledgment. Moonlight glimmered on the hairless patches above his eyes.

"He can."

"Will he read something for me?"

He sprang to his feet.

"Show me which book," he ordered.

"It's not in a book."

He made an impatient motion. "Then there is nothing to read," he concluded.

"Wait," she told him.

And with considerable concentration, because cats do not often try to do this, she used her front left paw to trace in the dust the symbol she had seen in the sea cave below Tintagel Head:

As soon as Uroum Bashou saw what she was trying to do, he became violently excited. "It is a book of the floor!" he cried, his reedy voice full of delight. "It is a book of dust!" His dignity fled him, to reveal the kitten beneath. All the young Handkerchief's intellectual delight, his raging curiosity, escaped for a moment the ponderous academic skin of the Elephant. He purred and chirupped. He jumped back up onto his pillows and stood with his knotted tail quivering in the air, reaching down every so often to tap at her paws with his own.

"Yes, yes, yes!" he said.

"Not clear enough!" he said.

He said, "Try again! Try again!"

So Leonora tried again, her foreleg quivering with the effort and oddness of the motion. And then again.

"Bigger. Bigger! Uroum Bashou has never read the dust before."

As soon as they had a symbol he could work with, the Reading Cat became thoughtful, and he seemed to forget Leonora altogether. "Mm," he said. Slowly, paw by paw, as if he were stalking a mouse, he came down off his cushions to look at it from another angle, then another. He introduced his whiskers to the air above it. He wandered off, sniffing aimlessly at the tumbled heaps of books, then pounced without warning, scraping and scratting with his forepaws until he found the volume he wanted. This he addressed in the same way until it fell open and he could turn the pages over. One cat's intellectual impatience, Leonora concluded, was sometimes as hard on a book as another's jealous rage. Many pages were already in ribbons. Dust flew up into the glaring moonlight.

"No," said Uroum Bashou. "Not here."

Then, running his paws delicately across some line of print: "Baldini's always worth a try, of course."

He said, "Not there, either. I didn't really expect it. But

wait, perhaps— Ah, no, much too late in the day. There is always—"

Once he had begun, his energy did not seem to abate. The night deepened. A stale smell came up from the dead pigeon. Leonora sneezed suddenly, and wondered if her parents missed her. She supposed they were too involved with themselves. For a while she watched the Reading Cat's efforts with a kind of detached amazement; then she went and sat on a window ledge, as far away from the dust as she could get, and stared down into the moonstruck empty street.

"Yes!" Uroum Bashou called every so often. "Yes!"

Only to add each time, "No. No."

She fell asleep.

How much of the night had passed when he woke her at last? She felt as if she had been asleep for days.

"Listen!" he said. "You must go."

She stared at him. He was trembling.

"What's the matter?" she said.

"I'll show you something and then you must go!"

"Kater Murr!" cried Leonora. "Is he back?"

"In the garden," said the Reading Cat simply. "He will come in very soon. Now look at this—"

🐾

The tide was up, to gurgle and shoosh in the pilings on the seaward side of the esplanade. Sunshine the color of cowslips struck down through the mist, failing for the moment to warm the cottages on the hill. A door opened here and there, to release smells of porridge, milk, bacon frying. You could hear the shriek of kittiwakes following the fishing fleet back into harbor.

In the Beach-O-Mat, Tag asked Leonora, "And what had he found, the Reading Cat?"

"A single book, very old, its pages made of something thick, yellow, and fragile that had been mounted on ordinary paper. He thought it came from Egypt and that it might have started life as something else, only to be made into a book later, to preserve it. There, among many others, was the symbol! It was faded and rather oddly proportioned, but I recognized it immediately."

"Ah," said Tag.

He leaned forward suddenly.

"What else?" he urged.

"He said that there was no explanatory text. He said that symbols like this appear very early in the history of men and cats, though never earlier than something he called 'the Missing Dynasty.' He said they are associated with the celebration, or 'bringing down,' of a goddess."

"And?"

"He thought for a long time and then said that he was sure he remembered the old Majicou asking him the same question."

"Nothing about the Golden Cat? Nothing about kittens?"

"No," said Leonora.

Tag sighed impatiently.

"Then we are still no farther forward," he said. He stared out of the laundry window at the mist and the sea.

"Don't you want to hear what happened next?"

When he was reading, Uroum Bashou customarily used his paw to keep his place. As soon as he removed it from the pages of the very old book, tensions in the binding caused them to turn over at random, like a deck of cards spilled upon a polished floor. When this process finished, another symbol was revealed:

Leonora touched the book. It was warm. She felt a faint, electrical sensation. The flutter and whirr of the turning pages had captivated her, like a whisper in the night, pigeon's wings in some mysterious dawn. It was as if the book itself had showed her something.

"And this?" she asked Uroum Bashou. "What does this symbol mean?"

The Reading Cat shrugged.

"Oh, that is a lot less interesting," he said carelessly.

He gazed at the door to the stairs.

"You will have to go!" he urged. "He is almost upon us!"

The moonlight was spectral, green-tinged, bright. It slid

off the Reading Cat's dust-runny eyes. His little black velvet body only needed a red velour collar to qualify him as some human toy. He was quivering with nerves. Who was the master here? Nothing he had said on their last visit made any sense. "I am quite tranquil about the whole thing," he had said; but Leonora thought to herself, Rubbish! He is afraid of that awful animal and who wouldn't be?

Aloud she said suddenly, "Come away with me, Uroum Bashou. Come and be looked after in Tintagel by the sea."

He blinked at her uncertainly for a moment.

Just as she thought he would agree, he said, "What you have found here is only the symbol for gold. We see it in many texts of this kind—often, of course, associated with the Alchemist. Now that he is no more, it is of little interest."

"What if he wasn't defeated?"

The Reading Cat stared at her. This momentary confounding of his assumptions made him look so vulnerable she could only try to persuade him again: "Uroum Bashou, please come to Tintagel."

"You are a sweet and thoughtful kitten," he said, recovering himself. "A kitten like you might after all heal the world. But go now, quickly, before *he* finds you here. Tell the Majicou I still do his work among the books! Hurry! Hurry! Go!"

And suddenly she was running from the room in the slick light, full of the Reading Cat's fear. Out on the stairwell, she stopped, sniffed. Nothing. She slipped down a flight, raised her nose again. There was a soft thud from somewhere out of sight. Was it the cat flap? Perhaps it was nothing. Down she went. Where was she going to hide? There was nowhere he couldn't find her. She would end up like an air-dried pigeon in the base of a cupboard. It was light for a little way, then dark to the second landing. She could hear her own breath so loud she never heard his. And anyway, how could it have been him? Without any warning at all there was something huge and made of metal, hurling itself up the stairs toward her with hallucinatory speed, in a rage at being so confined, its broad brassy chops full of teeth promising her death every time the stairwell brushed its ribs on either side. Its bared red tongue was bigger than her head! Its *face* was a foot and a half wide and its claws were taking chunks out of the fibrous old wooden risers as it came. Suddenly it was on the landing with her, pacing up and down, giving a great coughing snarl, weaving to and fro in the slippery light. Up close, the metal appeared to give way to fur, coarse and orange. With every bunch and pull of its huge muscles, violent markings of a slightly lighter color roiled down its sides like painted flames. It stank of ammonia, pheromones, death. It lifted its head and roared.

Leonora backed away.

The open landing window banged to and fro above her. She jumped out of it.

For a while she seemed to float. The night air pressed up against her. She turned over and over as she fell, so that first the sky then the street passed slowly through her field of vision. Below her was a basement area with its pointed railings. Farther out, parked cars. She thought she saw three or four shadows milling about down there between the wheels; but by the time she could look again, the street was empty, lunar silent. Suddenly, everything speeded up. She looked down. The railings! she thought. The railings! Then they were past, and she had landed heavily on a pile of wet cardboard boxes and plastic garbage bags liberally spattered with the produce of the pigeons that lived on the window ledges above. The breath went out of her, along with everything else.

When she woke up, she felt light-headed with her own luck. Her first thought was: Still alive! Her first instinct was to look up. She would not have been surprised to see her pursuer burst out into the air after her in an explosion of glass, the window frame a few sticks of wood clinging around its massive shoulders. Nothing, not even a head thrust out. It was silent up there. Limping and sore, she made her way out of the basement area and into an alley, where she took the first highway entrance she could find.

🐾

"So here I am," she said, "safe if not entirely sound."

No trace of mist remained on the bay. There was a great keening and crying of gulls, where the fishing fleet was tying up in a gauze of daffodil light. The new day was starting, and she was glad to be home for a change. She felt a great uplift of her heart.

"Well then," she said. "Has the apprentice done well?"

Tag sighed.

"I would like to know how much of this we are ever going to be able to tell your parents," he said. "Were you tired again on the return journey?"

"A little. Something tried to follow me home. But I got so upset by that I lost my way again, forgot how to dance, and it took me all night to get home."

She gazed at Tag for a moment.

"There's one thing I didn't tell you."

"What's that?"

"Uroum Bashou couldn't place any value on the symbol the old book showed me. But I could. Remember that day you led me such a dance along the Old Changing Way? Well, I saw the symbol on one of the places we passed through!" And she added cheekily, "How do you like that? Better than follow your nose!"

"Well," said Tag, "perhaps we were following your nose all along, not mine."

Then he said, "You had better take us there now."

🐾

They found the sign quite easily—

⊙ LABORATORIES
Winfield Farm Site

—and walked up past it, along a tidy gated road between cow pastures the broad gentle slopes of which were sprinkled with buttercups and dotted here and there with clumps of dark green thistle. Though the sky was blue and tranquil, it already had a metallic sheen, a promise of heat at noon. A few crows circled lazily in the shimmering air somewhere up ahead.

"Such a beautiful day," said Leonora.

She said, "Here we are!"

The road made its way into a little intimate fold of land, stopped. At first, Tag couldn't make anything of what he saw.

The building had been split as if by a single clean stroke from some vast cleaver, its two halves then settling slightly, still joined at the base but leaning away from each other.

"Stay here, Leonora."

Cautiously, Tag approached one of the shattered windows. He sniffed, jumped up, peered inside. Loops of black cable hung down where the ceiling had buckled and split. Everything inside had been smashed beyond identification. The floor was thick with bits of wood, bent metal, warped plastic panels, stinking of char, coated with plaster dust that days of rain had turned into a kind of cement. He identified a table that seemed to have been thrown bodily against the wall, a white human garment with one sleeve torn off. Among the disordered objects, silent cats lay in windrows. The air over them was infused with the sour simple smell of death.

"Leonora, don't—" Tag began.

Too late. She had jumped up beside him and was staring in.

"Who would do this?" she whispered.

She stared at him.

"Who is doing this to us? The wild roads are spoiled. Cats are dying everywhere. Tag, I was so happy to be home this morning. But nothing is what it promised to be!"

Before he could answer, she had jumped down and begun to sniff her way between the bodies. He knew what she was looking for, but he hadn't the heart to help her. After a little while, he heard her say, as if to herself, "I don't want to be a kitten anymore. It isn't worth it."

At last she came back and looked up at him.

"My brother was here," she said. "But he isn't here now."

"Then he may not be dead."

"Tag, what can we do?"

"We must talk again to Uroum Bashou," said Tag. "I begin to see a shape to all this. But with Loves a Dustbin gone, only the Reading Cat can confirm my understanding."

He stared into the ruined laboratory.

"Leonora," he said. "I'm afraid."

Chapter Twelve

MAMMY LAFEET

*F*or five thousand years the great Mississippi, Ouachita, and Red Rivers have wound their way through the broad plains of the South, shifting their courses, meandering lazily across the low ground like sidewinders snaking across desert sands, in no hurry at all to reach their eventual destination in the Gulf of Mexico; for like Sealink they are aware, in some primeval consciousness beyond thought, that the journey is the life, babe. The journey is the life.

Late, very late, in this geological span, when men came to Louisiana across the sea from the Old World, they discovered a fine natural port and the potential for a great settlement, could the swampland be drained and controlled. And so they built flood walls and levees to channel the course of the Mississippi, and there founded, according to a plan scratched by swordpoint in the ground, a perfect rectangular grid of a city: New Orleans—a most remarkable testament to human ingenuity and determination, to the power they had to change and rule the natural world.

So one might think even now, looking down upon the modern city, with its glittering towers, freight liners and docks, the elegant houses of the Garden District, the vast mesh of automobile highways and oak-lined avenues, the fantastic causeway across Lake Pontchartrain. But when they trapped the main channel of the mighty river, the backwaters had their revenge.

For thirty or forty miles around the city of New Orleans, as far north and west as Baton Rouge and Lafayette, and south, down to Thibodaux and the delta coast, lies a fluctuating, fragile, secretive, and duplicitous landscape entirely inimical to man. There, the parishes of Iberville, Terrebonne, Lafourche, and Ascension eke out a tenuous existence among a maze of channels and quagmires, abandoned river channels, or bayous—dead-end cricks and sloughs, marshes, abandoned ponds, and oxbow lakes—an impossible place to map; an easy place to be lost in; a breeding ground for a billion insects, for fish with teeth as sharp as rats', and for creatures seeking larger prey . . .

And all throughout this five-thousand-year period, and well beyond that meaningless man-made time scheme, the wild roads of the animals of the South have wound their way across and through this area, oblivious of the temporary changes inflicted upon it by humankind. The territory into which the wild roads debouch is still the treacherous, mystical landscape recognized—and avoided—by most humans; but the wild roads have traditionally offered safe passage through this quaggy labyrinth for those cats and other creatures willing to use them for their journeys. Until now.

When Sealink entered, in a state of blind panic and horror, the wild road whose entrance lay between Iberville and Bienville streets in the old French Quarter of the city of New Orleans, she sensed that something fundamental in the nature of the roads had changed since last she had set foot upon them. For a start, all was dark, and the compass winds that all cats know to be not only themselves but a gale of souls were silent.

Where were the ghost cats?

It was too quiet.

She raised her great head. The air inside this highway was sluggish and stale, as if the swamps were extending their domain into the very heart of the city. Perhaps, then, it was this road alone that was affected and, as Téophine had said, no one used it anymore, perhaps not even the shades of earlier cats. But if the road was long abandoned by living and dead alike, it would soon cease to exist. And if that happened, she would have a long and dangerous journey through the bayous. Better run, then, and make use of it while she could. Great paws striking and flexing with every footfall, Sealink let the powerful chemicals of her primal self absorb and dissipate her doubts and fears.

❦

So it was that some time later an observer might have seen a rare sight: a great, striped cat emerging as if from nowhere into the fronded shade of a flooded forest. Luckily, there were no observers here, at least no humans sighting down their hunting rifles for prey—for if there had been at that precise moment they might have bagged the trophy of a lifetime and started a fervor of debate about the natural life of the Louisiana swamplands.

Now, just a second or two later, all anyone would have seen was a much smaller member of the Felidae family: albeit a large and well-furred calico cat, its patches of orange and black and white now a far more random and less terrifying camouflage arrangement in that strange twilight than her wild road pelt.

If there were no humans here, of other life there was no lack. Where the highway had been eerily silent, the bayou was bursting with sound. An extraordinary din of life filled the heavy air—chirrups and peeps, buzzing and rasping and whining—heralding the presence of cigarriens and chiggers, crickets and gnats and ticks, and a thousand bird-voiced tree frogs.

Sealink stared at this unfamiliar new environment. Channels, viscous and bubbling with gas, were punctuated by islands of floating water hyacinth and edged by natural levees bound together by mud and mangrove roots like claws. Beyond, a tangle of willow and hickory, dog oak and sweet gum and myrtle, all swathed in trailing beards of gray Spanish moss. Webs inhabited by spiders as large as her head spanned the branches of a nearby cypress.

Sealink shuddered. Where the hell was she to find Mammy Lafeet among all this chaos? She turned a tight circle. In particular, how was she to find the Mammy without getting her feet wet?

At that moment there was a loud whirring and a flash of neon green and blue, and suddenly a pair of large, prismatic eyes were hovering just in front of the calico's nose, borne up by a rotor of sparkling, translucent wings. Sealink took a surprised step backward and found herself hock deep in water the color of tea, water that left a shower of tiny black particles plastered over her fur. Then, just as quickly as it had appeared, the dragonfly banked away steeply and vanished between the dark trees.

Sealink shook her soaked back legs with an expression of disgust. What sort of place was this that the Mammy had chosen? What the hell kind of cat was she? You'd only retire to this place for pleasure if you were a *fish*. She rotated her ears back and forth, listened intently; but all she could hear were the tree frogs, gearing up for their evening chorus. The light was fading now, taking with it any semblance of normality.

Cats have remarkable vision, an ability adapted over millennia for efficient hunting. In bright light, the pupil needs only to form the narrowest vertical aperture; in full dark, it will dilate to a full circle to detect and absorb the faintest glow of light, channeling it down thousands of rod-shaped cells into the retina and the mirrorlike *tapetus lucidum*, the bright tapestry of feline legend, to give back an extraordinarily clear image of the visual field.

Sealink could feel her eyes adapting to the changing light; but being able to see quite clearly the tangles of vegetation and the wilderness of the bayou made her no happier with her situation. She was, she had to admit, an urban cat—by birth and choice. She *liked* streetlights. She liked the bright neon of restaurant signs. Even the glare of a pair of car headlights would have been welcome here.

Instead she was faced with the gathering, unrelieved, fetid darkness of unreconstructed swampland.

She was just about to reenter the wild road and try a different exit, when a whirring and a disturbance of the air behind her ears alerted her to the return of the dragonfly.

"Hello, little guy." Her voice sounded unnaturally loud. She looked around, feeling more than a little foolish.

Instead of disappearing again on its erratic flight course, the dragonfly circled her head. It buzzed at her, the lenses of its eyes twinkling furiously; and Sealink almost thought she heard it say something. Then it veered off into a stand of willows; and even as the calico turned to watch it, it was back, its whirring and buzzing even more insistent. This time, it clipped her nose with a wing tip, a featherlight brush, and a minute, tinny voice sounded in the back of her ear, *"Follow."*

Sealink shook her head as if to dislodge a flea. She must be going crazy. Still, why not? She'd fit right in here. Feeling dislocated from her species and her own experience, the calico made a leap from the floating island on which she stood to the more substantial ground where the willows grew. Ahead of her, the dragonfly dipped and darted; and Sealink followed.

🐾

A short while later, led far into the swampland, Sealink was distracted by an interesting smell. It was quick and sharp and warm-blooded, and not far away. The calico had never been the most skilled of hunters: when traveling with the Queen of Cats across the desolate moors of Cornwall they might well have starved had it not been for Pertelot's unexpected talent. Give Sealink a trash can, however, and she would rip the life out of it in seconds. There weren't too many of those great symbols of civilized life around here, and, not having eaten for hours she was, she realized suddenly, ravenous. Let the dragonfly hover for a moment: she'd inspect the food source.

Some yards to the left, beneath a stand of mallows, there sat a fat rat. Sealink had never seen one quite like it before, but right now its precise taxonomy seemed unimportant. It sat there, apparently petrified by her presence, the moonlight glinting off its beady black eyes, exuding a fine, strong reek of well-salted food. The calico, delighted with her luck, squatted into stalking mode, waggled her ample bottom until she had the beast properly sighted, and launched herself into the mallows. From its lair, the nutria watched her with alarm; then, as soon as she leapt—a great, ungainly mass of fur and claws—shot neatly into the water.

Sealink paced up and down the bank, hoping that it might have a very short memory, as some more stupid rodents do, and return to its lair, but the water remained smooth and silent in its wake and after some minutes she had to concede that the rat really had vanished.

When she turned around and retraced her steps, so had the dragonfly.

Sealink cursed her stupidity. She was lost, lost, lost. The wild road lay far behind her and would be impossible to locate until morning . . . perhaps not even then. All she could see in any direction were the dim shapes of trees, the glimmer of water through vegetation. All she could hear were a thousand cicadas serenading one another as if the night was their world alone.

All she could smell was rot.

She suddenly recalled something she'd once heard down on the boardwalk from one of the older toms about the disappearance of a cat who lived out on a shrimp boat.

"Fell in the water, mama," the old white cat had said. "Fell into the bayou and his body got et by crawfish."

And Sealink, with the sublime wit and cheek of youth had retorted, "Ain't you got that the wrong way 'round, Chalky?"

Now, with the wisdom of age, the calico recognized the eternal truth in this reversal of nature. Everything got recycled, from the greatest tree to the largest beast. It fell, it rotted, it was eaten by the shrimp and the mud bugs and the scavengers; and they fell and died and were eaten in their turn. Just as cats lived and died to fuel the wild roads, so the rest of the natural world made its own simple, elegant economy. But Sealink knew with sudden force that she was not yet ready to submit to that process. She grimaced defiantly into the dark and, all of her senses on the *qui vive*, walked determinedly on.

♣

Some time later she had walked a fair distance and had begun to feel more confident. The starlight clarified the definition of objects whenever there was a gap in the canopy, allowing her to identify a stationary owl upon a branch, the tall white flowers of an arrowroot, a cricket frozen against the bark of a live oak. But when something shifted in her peripheral vision, it seemed to come from the dark hollow between two logs, and even with her night sight working overtime, she couldn't quite make out the originator of the movement. She stepped closer, her paws making no sound on the soft leaf mold underfoot.

Then, suddenly, something shone out of the gloom.

An eye!

She sprang back, swallowing a cry. It was a big, golden eye, glowing in the darkness. With a sigh of relief she recognized the vertical black slit of another cat's pupil.

"Mammy Lafeet!"

The relief was immense. It washed through her like hot milk.

"You sure take some findin', Momma. Can't imagine why anyone should want to hide themselves away from civilization to such an extent—not that it's all that civilized back there at the moment. Which is why I need to talk to you. But first things first, eh, podna? After that trek I sure could do with some nourishment, y'know, honey. You don't happen to have a little something I could chew on while we talk, do you?"

The eye regarded Sealink steadily.

Then, even as she was congratulating herself on locating the Mammy at the dead of night in the midst of this fearsome wilderness, the eye blinked, and the relief curdled in her stomach.

The eye had blinked sideways.

Sealink's mind scrambled to make sense of this. Perhaps the Mammy was suffering from some kind of optical disorder. Perhaps she was lying with her head on one side. Perhaps—

Then another detail insinuated itself neatly into this rickety structure of rationalizations. The pupil that split the golden eye was the narrowest of lines, yet she knew her own pupils must be distended to full, black circles in this darkness.

Not the Mammy, then.

Not even a cat.

Her paws started to go numb with shock.

Then whatever it was moved, and a second golden eye came into view. The eyes were some distance apart and did not look straight ahead. They twinkled at her. There was a subtle movement, and the starlight picked out rows of crooked ivory gleaming beneath the eyes. They looked like *teeth*.

Sealink stared. They *were* teeth. More teeth than she had ever seen on any creature in the world. In a strange empathy of panic, the calico cat suddenly found herself baring her own teeth.

Then it spoke. Its voice was loud and cultured, deep and French and definitely male.

"Eating is good."

It paused. Sealink could feel its cold stare assessing her snack value.

"I like to eat, as do all the beasts of the earth, for the sin of our existence."

Its lower jaw dropped down. Sealink stared into the depths of a vast, glistening maw. The stench was overwhelming. Perversely, she found herself examining its dental array. Some of the teeth were sharp and pointed. But others, many others, were broad and inturned, and little scraps of something indefinable were wedged between them. The word "alligator" slowly permeated the calico's brain, and she felt her joints turn to water. Then the jaws snapped shut with an echoing thud an inch or two away from her nose. The alligator grinned.

"Dead things have the most subtle bouquet, I find. Especially dead things I have stored away in the bayou for a week or two, down beneath the roots of the mangrove. When they have marinated in the tannin of these fine brackish waters they have—" the alligator considered "—a certain piquancy. A certain *je ne sais quoi*. Would you like to visit my secret store, little cat?"

One eye blinked for a second, then focused sharply on her again. Sealink realized, with a sudden twinge of hope, that it had *winked* at her. She struggled to find her voice.

"Er, not right now, babe. Maybe some other time?"

The grin widened a crack.

"That's a shame, *cher*. I have a nook down there that's just your size. Unfortunately, I visited my store only a short while ago and gorged myself on the most succulent little white-tailed deer you could ever imagine. *Ciel!*" It smacked its chops together appreciatively. "Sheer bliss." It pushed itself up on its stubby arms so that Sealink could observe the great swell of its scaly belly. "Indeed, I am so full it hurts. I couldn't fit in another morsel. *Vraiment, c'est dommage,* it is a profound pity, *mon ange:* it has been such a long time since I had the pleasure of partaking of the subtle flesh of a feline friend."

Sealink decided to push her luck.

"You wouldn't happen to know where I might find a very old, and I'm sure extremely stringy, feline known as the Mammy Lafeet, would you?"

The alligator laughed, a strange creaking sound like a dead branch sawing in the wind. "Even creatures of the greatest age and gristle become tender when subjected to my fine Louisiana marinade, *cher.*"

"Oh."

"Although I pride myself on being a true *gourmand*—" he leered "—even *I* must draw the line somewhere. And the Mammy has, how you say, 'laid the bones upon me.' I eat her: I die of the bellyache. This is what she promises me. Not a friendly gesture in this cruel and hostile world. Not the sort of hospitality one would expect from a neighbor. *Alors,* I think she is not to my taste *pour le déjeuner* or as company! You, however . . ." He paused.

The calico watched him distrustfully, flight plans formulating swiftly in her head.

". . . may keep on walking. She's somewhere out there." He waved a tiny, clawed hand airily. "*Eh bien*, it is time now for my swim. Life on the levee is hard and lonely. Do visit with me again, *bébé*, when you are passing in this direction." He finished with a toothy grin. "I will be sure to make you welcome, *cher.*"

Then, with a slither and a great splash, the alligator launched himself into the bayou. He lay there in the murky water, his eyes just above the surface. After a few moments he winked again—a wink of vast and deliberate irony—and was gone with a flick of the tail.

The calico watched the water for some time to make sure he was not suddenly going to erupt out of the bayou in a thunder of spray and down her in a single gulp, then, affecting nonchalance, strolled with stiff-legged anxiety through the alligator's reeking domain and into the dark vegetation on the other side of the logs.

A narrow escape, that.

She shook her head irritably.

The damned dragonfly was back. She heard it well before she saw it, descending from above the canopy as if homing in on a target. A few seconds later she realized that target was her. Then she thought: What the hell is a dragonfly doing out and about at *night*? Like other bugs, they liked the sunlight, used its warm rays to stir to life their cold insectile blood.

She stared up into the darkness. "Come near me, fishbait, and you're history!" The whirring continued, grew louder. She snapped at the air. "I ain't kiddin'. You led me right into that set of jaws on legs, so get too close and I'll have me a little bitty crunchy snack."

"Follow!"

This time the voice was unmistakable; and beneath the high-pitched buzzing there was even inflection and cadence.

But how could it speak, let alone intonate? No bug *she'd* ever ate even had vocal cords . . .

Sealink shivered. Perhaps it was all in her head. Certainly, something weird was going on here.

The dragonfly was visible now, its magnificent wings iridescent in the starlight, hovering about a foot above her head.

"Come at once. Want to drown, foolish cat? I lead you and what you do? Take eye off me. You chase rat. You miss it! Then you get lost!" It tutted. Sealink could almost see it shake its tiny head in vexation. When it continued its tone was severe. *"Walk into Monsignor Gutbag. Greed meets greed. And you blame me! Ingrate."* A pause. Then, so softly that Sealink could barely catch it: *"Not called fishbait."*

That was it. She was definitely losing it. She was lost in the most horrible wilderness she could ever have imagined, an alligator had nearly had her as a postprandial treat, and now she was getting lectured by a dragonfly!

"Mammy close. Follow now. Pay attention this time."

Sealink sighed and followed as instructed.

The dead time between day and night, those two or three hours that precede the rising of the sun, when humans lie in the deepest trenches of their sleep and diurnal beings take to their burrows, is the time when the Felidae and other creatures of the night tend to be at their most active and acute.

Sealink, however, preferred to sleep at this time, particularly when there was no food to be had. It took her mind off things. She would also have been the first to concede that full dark could make her a little edgy. She was not, therefore, in the best frame of mind for her next discovery.

On the barely discernible track along which the dragonfly led her there had been at intervals a number of partially rotted and foul-smelling objects that might once have been small rodents or reptiles. A few yards further and there was a small turtle shell, minus its occupant. Then cat and dragonfly rounded a bend and emerged out into a small clearing, in the middle of which lay two large identically round stones like garden ornaments, and something else . . .

This object stood higher than her head and seemed to soak up all the available starlight, which it gave back in a great albescent glow, illuminating its component parts: an intricate, obsessive jigsaw of skulls and rib cages, spinal columns and hipbones, fish bones and rigid claws, open beaks and empty orbital sockets—the ghastly remains of a thousand soulless bodies.

Sealink stared, for a moment trapped motionless in her native curiosity. She sniffed at the bone mountain. Then she tapped it cautiously with a paw. At once, the entire heap collapsed, sending tiny skulls and skeletons skittering down upon her, as cold and smooth and light as a shower of dead beetles.

The calico recoiled as if shot, fetching up against one of the large round stones; but as soon as she bumped into it, the stone also started to move.

Not sure which way to run next, Sealink stared wildly

around her. What sort of place was this where nothing was as it seemed?

Overhead, the dragonfly zigzagged furiously, buzzing like a creature possessed, then made itself scarce in the dark canopy beyond the clearing.

The stone continued to uncurl itself—as rock should not—revealing a number of stout armor plates, which now expanded and flexed; and it suddenly produced some feet, followed by a long, delicate-looking snout and a pair of eyes that blinked in bewilderment. Whatever it was smelled quite strongly of earth and swamp; and when it finally saw the calico cat, all four of its little clawed feet left the ground at the same time, and it leapt high in the air in a parody of terror, all the time wailing, "I wasn't asleep! I wasn't!"

It came to rest in front of Sealink. It blinked myopically at her.

"You ain't the Mammy."

"I know that."

"I wasn't asleep. Honest." It looked sly.

"Honey, I don't give a damn—"

At this point the second "stone" began to move. Sealink watched it with suspicion in case it revealed some other strange ability apart from imitating rocks and jumping.

Unfurling itself with greater dignity than its partner, alerted perhaps to the presence of a stranger by the recent kerfuffle, the second "stone" came to its feet smartly and declared, "Reporting for duty, ma'am."

"What?"

It gave her a hard, evaluating squint. "Thought you might be official."

"What?"

"From the Mammy—checking up on us."

Sealink felt a strange wash of emotions: relief that Mammy Lafeet must finally be close, rapidly followed by disorientation and self-doubt.

"Who the hell are you and what are you talking about?"

"How do we know this isn't a test?" It sidled closer, snuffling. Sealink put a paw out defensively. Her claws popped from their sheaths and gleamed in the cold light.

"Back off, buddy." Definitely not as fearsome as the alligator. She decided to take a stern tone with it. "Look, I'm here to see the Mammy. I ain't here to play games. Please go find her and tell her she has a visitor."

"You knocked over our pile."

The first guard now had its back to Sealink and its companion and was trundling disconsolately around the debris, gathering skulls into one heap, fish bones into another.

"Er, yes. Sorry."

"Took us ages, that did."

It started to stack bones haphazardly. The new foundation reached a height of perhaps five inches, tottered, and collapsed. At once the second guard waddled over, muttering disapprovingly, "Not like that. Don't you ever learn? Start with *these* . . ."

She'd get no sense out of these guys. Shaking her head, Sealink left them to it.

🐾

Some yards beyond the clearing, the calico found herself at the water's edge again and out in clear, if stifling, air. A dull glow in the eastern sky announced that dawn might not be far off, for which she found she was truly grateful. She sat down to await the new day, staring out over the spreading ripples of rising fish. Eventually, new light lent color to her strange surroundings. It infused the pink of the mallow flowers and the lilac of the water hyacinths. It delineated the leaves of the dog oak and the fronds of the buckler fern and crept into the duckweed on the surface of the bayou to light it to a phosphorescent, neon green. It marked out a snapping turtle on a rotting log, long neck stretched out to catch the first of the rays, his mouth as leathery and puckered and downturned as that of a toothless old man.

Sealink was just about to address the turtle when a voice above and behind her made her jump.

"*Que veux-tu*—what you at?"

The speaker was positioned with care upon the boughs of a moss-shrouded tree, the angularity of her posture enhancing the dry dustiness of her sparse fur. Her claws, buried in the deeply fissured bark, were as yellowed and gnarled and horny as old tortoiseshell, and her coat was fiercely brindled—a dull orange that must once have been tiger bright, overlain with a complex patchwork of black. Her eyes were hidden in shadow, and Sealink found herself suddenly and unexpectedly as unsure as a kitten.

"Que veux-tu?" the cat in the tree rasped again.

"I—I came to seek the Mammy Lafeet."

"What your bidness?"

"The cats of the French Quarter need help—they're dying. It's all gone crazy . . ."

The old cat cackled. "We all crazy, honey; and we's all dyin', too. You had a long and wasted journey, chile."

"Are you the Mammy?"

"The Six-Toed Cat. Kadiska. The Watcher at the Threshold. Madame Lafeet. The Mammy. T'ey call me many names." She leapt down from the branch with an agility surprising in one so aged. The rising sun revealed eyes veiled in milky cataracts, but she fixed the calico squarely with her gaze and pronounced, "Maybe I let you call me Eponine."

"Merci bien, madame." She bowed her head. Even Sealink knew enough to remember her manners in the presence of a Guardian, however fallen. But to refer to her as Eponine, an ordinary, if antiquated, Cajun name, seemed faintly sacrilegious, or even dangerous. Was this some sort of test? Then she realized that an anticipatory silence had fallen and that the Mammy was regarding her sharply. "They call me many things, too. I was known as Rocket when I lived in Houston, and Amibelle in Missouri. In Alaska a guy called me Trouble. And in Europe—hell, I forget. Down on the Moon Walk I had the name of the Delta Queen. My friends—" She paused. What friends? Who was she kidding? She cleared her throat, started again. "Folks mostly call me Sealink. After a boat I once came in on."

"Sealink." The old cat savored the word in her soft Creole. "It is good that we trade names with each other, chile. It is a matter of trust, *hein?* Cats' names are important: they are words of power. So, Sealink. A traveler. One who bridges many worlds. *Une voyageuse.* A cat bearing news and a gift of gold who crosses oceans—an ocean of salt, and of fire."

"Fire?" Sealink was alarmed.

"I have myself passed through fire. I have smelled the smell of fire," pronounced Eponine in a singsong voice. She turned a serene face to her visitor. *"Viens."*

Without checking to make sure the calico was following she disappeared abruptly into the dense undergrowth and, stepping neatly between aerial roots and knots of vegetation, made her way unerringly to another, hidden shore of the bayou and the upturned hull of a small wooden boat, its timbers weathered to silver by the passing seasons.

All around the skiff lay an assortment of tiny bones and feathers, some arranged in curious patterns, others scattered as if at random, all making a stark contrast against the peaty ground. The Mammy sat down and began to pat some loose bones into a small pile. She looked up at the calico and her mouth parted to reveal a few sharp, white teeth in what might have been a smile, or maybe it was just senility. Sealink found it hard to tell.

"Eh bien, cher; you made a long journey down old roads to get here. You take your life like a mouse in your mouth—*une souris dans ta bouche*—and held it tight but gentle through fear and peril. You been through hazard to reach me, *alors, je pense que t'as bonne raison.* I figure you got just cause. And even though you ain't brung the Mammy no *cadeau*, because I sense you got troubles, I'm gonna allow you to ax me three silver questions, and in exchange I give you three silver answers."

The calico looked bewildered.

"Honeychile, you gets to ax three questions. Don't you ever listen to no stories?"

"I'm sorry I don't have a gift for you. But only three questions? I got hundreds." Sealink was appalled.

"Got plenty to choose from then, *cher.*"

Sealink thought about this for a minute. Her stomach growled. If she were to ask the Mammy for some food, would that count as one of her three questions? It seemed rather harsh. Perhaps she could phrase it in a different fashion . . .

Eponine cackled, a short, staccato sound like an old cat dislodging hair balls. "You don't need to waste no questions, honey: your belly is most eloquent. First we eat—t'en we consult the bones."

❧

They ate. The Mammy appeared to have an enormous and secret cache of food. She had vanished into the undergrowth and reemerged a few moments later dragging the best part of a dead catfish, its eyes white with glaze and a querulous bottom lip protruding, as if out of disappointment with its fate. And while they ate, they talked—or rather, the Mammy, who had an appetite like a bird, talked while Sealink tore at the catfish and listened, making sure to ask no inopportune questions. It seemed there were still creatures who wished to seek advice from an old, wise cat. And when they came, they brought gifts and tributes—little offerings of food and dead things to add to the old cat's bone pile—not just as payment for the favor they asked but to appease the bad spirits that might surround so powerful a seer. They came from out of the swamps, where they shared a house—or at least a garbage can—with humans of the fragile fishing communities, who made a small living from the brackish waters of the bayous where freshwater met salt, netting shrimp and crawfish, sheepsheads and drumfish, redfish and bass that they sold to the restaurants and markets of the city. Some even hunted and skinned alligator.

"I encountered an alligator on my way here."

"I know *dat*, honey. You met wit' Monsignor Gutbag." Despite the fish scales around her mouth, the Mammy looked supremely serene, in control of a whole world of knowledge to which the calico had no hope of access.

Monsignor Gutbag: the very name the dragonfly had applied to the beast. A deep furrow scored Sealink's forehead, but she kept her lip buttoned.

Eponine regarded her through slitted eyes. A tiny buzzing sound rose from her throat, followed by a tiny voice barely more than a reverberation.

A tiny sound of amazement escaped from the calico. It was an uncanny piece of mimicry. But how could a cat use an insect thus? Sealink had the sense of being teased.

"I have my ways. Proxies can be very useful to a cat wit'

bones as old as mine, but I got to take what I can—flies, armadillos . . . T'ey ain't too smart, but when you stuck out here you don't got much choice. Even so—" she fixed Sealink with a gimlet stare "—it takes two to work: one to guide and one to follow; and if the one who follows don't pay attention—*bouff*!" She expelled a great cheekful of air that bespoke irritation and waste. "You take my meanin'? So when you ax your t'ree questions, *cher,* you listen real good, 'cos when da bones talk t'ey can be real obscure."

So saying, the Mammy retrieved a collection of bones from beneath the timbers of the boat. They lay in morning light, pale against the dark ground.

"Touch da bones, chile."

Sealink sniffed at them, but they gave back no clue of their origin. They looked smooth and polished with wear, their ends yellowing with age.

"Touch da bones." The Mammy's voice was suddenly fierce. "Touch dem and t'ink about your questions. Concentrate wit' the wildest part of yourself. Make dem a part of you. Believe in da bones."

Sealink tried to clear her mind of all but those questions that demanded answers, but her thoughts milled about subversively—thoughts of times long gone, pointless memories of meals she had eaten, places she had been. She remembered eating noodles with Tom Yang outside a Bangkok temple, sharing fried chicken with the cats on the boardwalk. She remembered mates she had taken and friends she had made. She remembered Cy and Pertelot and an old seacat by the name of Pengelly and how he had been good to her when she had been less than kind to him; she remembered Loves a Dustbin and Francine—and cut the thought off before the guilt came. Then there came through the melee of images a pair of mismatched eyes, one cool blue and one lively orange—eyes that gleamed at her with love and pride and amazed delight out of a brindled face. Suddenly she could think of nothing but an old scarred tomcat with frilled ears and a taciturn manner—a cat called Mousebreath—of his taste and his smell and how they had lain together under the arches at Coldheath, and how after that first mating he had stolen for her two cooked sausages off the plate of a surprised man in a café behind the market, and, legs pumping, had raced all the way back so out of breath and full of adrenaline that he couldn't say a word but only dropped them, steaming with flavor, at her feet, with saliva dripping off his chin and a wicked look in his orange eye . . . And all at once her heart contracted in a single pulse of agony as the memory of her loss tore through her for the first time since that terrible meeting at Tintagel, when Tag had told her how he died; and she opened her mouth and wailed as if her heart would burst.

The sound ripped out into the quiet, sticky air of the bayou, and was gone, absorbed by the moss and the waters; and suddenly Sealink felt a profound calm settle over her. It was not acceptance but something more, something that would bear examination at a later time, perhaps. Then another face swam into her mind. Silver and barred with a darker shade, eyes of lambent green; eyes filled with anxiety and a vast responsibility. It was Tag; but why she should think of him at such a time, she could not imagine.

Tintagel and the King and Queen lay far behind her now. The journeys they had made, the battle they had fought, like stories from another age. She was in the New World now, or so humans termed it—but what did they know? All the world was old, as ancient as the Great Cat from which it sprang. And something was very wrong with it, something that made her bones sing out to the bones on the ground beneath her paws; and all at once some of the responsibility she had seen shining in a silver cat's eyes had found a home inside her, and she knew what her first question must be. She opened her eyes and stared at the Mammy.

"Eponine. Tell me: What has gone so wrong in the world that the cats of the city are sick and persecuted?"

The Mammy closed her eyes and fell among the bones. She rubbed her cheek glands upon them. She rolled onto her back and twisted her spine against them. She leapt to her feet and danced upon them, and Sealink had a fleeting memory of the jig that she and Baron Raticide had shared down on the Moon Walk only a few days before. Then the Mammy scooped up the bones and juggled them with clever paws. Balanced between momentum and gravity for a moment they hung, freighted with magic; then they fell in a series of dry clicks to the ground, where they made a curious, disjointed creature, a creature with three legs and a single round of vertebra for a head.

Eponine looked at the pattern the fall of bones had made, then jumped away from the symbol as if scalded. She started to murmur to herself, agitated little grunts and grimaces; but the calico could make out not a word.

At last, Sealink could bear it no longer. "What do the bones say?"

The Mammy stared right through her. Then in the strange singsong voice she had adopted earlier, she announced, *"Dans le coeur . . . Isaac le noir et le chat noir . . . la danse macabre. Bon 'ti ange et gros 'ti ange, ils dansent toujours. Ils mangent le monde jusqu'à la mort . . . Les rues sauvages se meurent . . . Ça ne fini pas . . . Tempora mutantur . . . Et les rêves—"*

"Speak English!" Sealink was beside herself with frustration. But the Mammy was oblivious.

"Les trois. Les trois sont perdus. Ils doivent être retrouvés. Pyramid, *cassé. C'est tout ou rien.* All or nothing."

Now the Mammy fell silent. Sealink stared at her. "What? I don't understand—I don't speak that stuff. C'mon, be fair. I got the 'all or nothing' bit, and I can kinda see it's a desperate situation out there, but that sure don't help me *understand* things."

The brindled cat said nothing. Sealink felt a wave of despair. After everything, was this all she would leave with—a few words of broken French she didn't understand? Suddenly she was furious. Running across the bones, she grabbed Mammy Lafeet by the scruff of the neck and shook her like a rat.

"I ain't got time for all this voodoo shit, Granma. Make it plain English or I'll eat your heart out."

The Mammy gurgled something. Sealink set her down, sides heaving with spent fury. Then she realized the old cat was laughing.

"Eating the heart out. Yes, yes, very good. *C'est le même*

chose. It's all the same. You understand without knowing it. Ha ha ha!"

Sealink sat down in confusion.

"*Eh bien, cher.* Your second question?"

"What the hell's the point of my asking anything if the answers come back in gibberish?"

The old cat considered. "You know, honey: you locked into somet'ing here and you don't even know it." She mused, eyes half shut. "I once met a cat, chile, a cat who read and he tole me some oddities. Gibberish—ah, t'at's an interestin' one. Dat word come from a human man called Geber, an ancient alchemist who hid his knowledge in a secret language no other human could make sense of." She fell silent for a moment, then her eyes opened wide.

"I feel the hand of an alchemist in this. I feel the hand of a human who cannot leave the secrets of the world untouched."

"But the Alchemist is dead. I saw him die. Him and the Majicou together."

"What your eyes see is not always the beginning and end of truth."

This was enough of metaphysics for Sealink. She was a cat who trusted the evidence of her eyes. "Can't believe nothin' else," she'd always said, and there was still a part of herself that felt this whole journey was no more than a foolish charade, the casting of the bones a ridiculous, superstitious game. Another question was hovering. It seemed inconsequential in comparison to the first, but even so—

"What was in the *cadeau* I brought to Kiki la Doucette?"

The Mammy regarded the calico with suspicion.

"You a friend of Kiki's?"

"Er, no . . . not exactly."

"Because if you are, *ça fini ici*—it ends here."

"I'm not, truly."

Eponine dealt the bones again. This time she cast them high in the air, and when they came down they had formed a rough circle with a single dot of a bone in its center.

"Gold. It is the symbol for gold."

"Oh."

So there it was. She had dragged a lump of gold through

the streets of the French Quarter. But what cat would have a use for inert metal? Her brain struggled with metaphors, then gave up. She'd had an answer in plain English, and she was still no closer. So much for her attempt to seek wisdom, to find the knowledge that would free the cats of New Orleans from the strange affliction that had them in its grasp, so much for understanding why the humans of the city had started to hate them so. Téophine would be disappointed. Téophine, and Red.

A twist of the stomach, a flush of shame. After the Pestmen had done with them, there would *be* no Téophine and Red to explain all this to . . .

Her last question. Giving up all pretence at selflessness, Sealink decided on this: "I had five kittens once upon a time. I believe I know about four of 'em. But if the last is still alive, where can I find it?"

For the final time, Mammy Lafeet cast the bones. They landed all over the place. She shuffled around them, putting her head on one side, then the other. She screwed her face up as if trying to focus on something very small. At last she pronounced, "Two are with the Great Cat. Two are with la Mère. The fifth lies between."

"Look. I know you can only tell me what the bones tell you, but at least try to give me some help here," Sealink pleaded. "This is my kittens we're talking about. I traveled half the world to find my family."

The Mammy sighed. "Chile, I tole you the bones could be obscure. But kittens are special. I know that, for my pain." She brushed her paw over the bones again. When it reached a particular outlier she groaned. She passed the paw back and forth across it, gazed at it till her eyes crossed. Then she said, "Seek for a sun of fire in the Fields of the Blessed."

Sealink stared hopelessly at her. Then she shrugged. "What the hell? I ain't never believed in any of this stuff in my life. It probably don't work for disbelievers, huh?"

Eponine shook her head. "I'm sorry, chile. I tried."

She leaned across the space between them, the sacred space of the bones, and touched the calico lightly on the muzzle.

"I see somet'ing else, too."

She looked the younger cat in the eye, and it seemed to Sealink that for a second the Mammy's milky cataracts appeared to clear, like clouds moving slowly across a moon.

"Sometimes da bones offer a gift, chile. *La Verte te benisse*. The Great One must be watchin' over you. She says you will be healed, *cher*. Oh yes, your heart will be healed."

"It ain't broke." At once the calico was all defense, fur bristling.

The Mammy smiled knowingly. "Da bones never lie."

"Yeah, well, they can be damned obscure with the so-called truth. Anyway," Sealink deflected hurriedly, "what did you mean about it finishing here if I was a friend of Kiki's?"

The Mammy rubbed a paw across her face. She looked old and very weary.

"You stay away from Kiki la Doucette. You have a good heart, *cher,* for all your impatience. And Kiki is—how shall I say?—*traitresse*. She is poison, honey; a traitor—to all cats and especially to me."

"How do you know that, way out here? Did you read it in the bones?"

"How do I know? Didn't she usurp my position and drive me out of my city? Why you t'ink I'm out here and she's queening around callin' herself la Mère? I know her poison better than most. I should; for I bore her. *Elle est la mienne*. I'm her mother."

Chapter Thirteen

BETWEEN FIRE AND WATER

*T*hat day he had green flames inside him from the moment he woke. They flickered out of the soft place in his head to dance like pale candles on objects in the real world.

The weather had turned brassy and close. Animal X and his friends followed the river into mixed woodland, where it abandoned them quietly and went off somewhere on its own. The woods were oppressive and full of insects; they were crisscrossed by sandy ridges arranged in parallel lines. For much of the day the sense of order these lines gave him kept Animal X from giving in—not just to the dancing flames but to the voices and echoes and half memories that filled his head and that he supposed must be his own. Even so, he left everything to the other two. The kitten was always a hundred yards ahead, looking back impatiently, its restless golden limbs barred with sun; while Stilton, much improved, ambled along behind in the soft sand, talking to himself cheerfully as he went.

Thunder rolled in the distance all morning. By afternoon it had caught up with them. The woodland rides, full of an oozing, sappy heat, closed up like green tunnels. Animal X could barely breathe. The air thickened and browned; then lightning cracked it apart and suddenly the rain was falling as if someone had turned a switch.

It was shockingly cold. It fell not as individual drops but as silvery sheets and cataracts, forcing its way down through the trees with an intense rushing sound. Leaves and twigs danced under the force of it; branches bowed low then sprang up again in slow motion. The world vanished behind the blurry curtains, the shifting gray lenses of the rain. Animal X, filled with a terror he cold not name, ran about at random, blundering through the tangled undergrowth and calling, "Stilton! Stilton!" The voices in his head made it impossible to tell if Stilton had answered. More by luck than judgment he got back on the nearest ride and ran until he burst out of the woods. There was the river again, and water meadows, and a village. Black birds flew up from the yews around the village church and began to circle through the gray sheets of rain. The whole sky seemed to be running and melting into liquid around them. They knew he was there . . .

The crows! thought Animal X. The crows!

He saw Stilton and the kitten come out of the woods and look at him as if he were mad.

"Run!" he called.

He saw the light come out of the woods after them and flicker about their heads. It glittered and crackled. Animal X winced. He flattened his ears and ran toward the river. All around him it was water. Behind him he could hear the green fuse burning. Above him the great black birds swung and banked, shrieking and cawing. He shook his head to clear it. He could hear too many shrieks for the number of crows.

Run! he thought. Run!

Halfway across, the fuse burned out, and there was a great soft silent explosion in the woods. Flames sprang up in the meadow around him, turning immediately into little fires that seemed to burn without any fuel. Animal X ran harder. Then he saw the river in front of him. Caught like that between the fire and the water, he was branded with awe and fear. The birds seemed to gather above him. Their cries redoubled. They were ready to swoop down. He knew he couldn't cross water, even on a bridge; to enter it was beyond him. He was trapped. The little fires were everywhere, like green animals. Suddenly they came together in his head and he was engulfed. All he could hear was the crackle of the flames and the sound of the birds wheeling in the sky above the trees. Animal X felt himself falling. As he fell, something green and glorious inside his head pounced on him and began shaking him and filled him with pain and wonder. It was the same thing that had destroyed the laboratory. He wondered if it had always been inside his head.

❧

He woke groggily, to hear Stilton explaining, "He's afraid of water. This time it was the rain." And then "He won't cross the river, yet he grumbles if we are away from it for any length of time."

A second voice answered, "We must be very practical about this. Is he awake yet, do you think? He needs to be able to walk if we're to help. Can he see? Some of them can't see very well."

The cat who had spoken was a blue-cream longhair. Her dense, silky coat made a kind of nimbus around her in the twilight, so that Animal X wasn't quite sure where she ended and the soft smoky air began. Her eyes, a startling coppery orange color, gave her an occult look—an impression of not quite seeing the known world—which to counter she exuded energy, purpose, a sense of identity. She was out of her first youth. But it was her aim in life, as she put it later, to be "uncompromisingly present" to herself; and in this she seemed to have succeeded.

"I think he can see," Stilton hazarded.

"You know quite well I can see," Animal X said. "Stop talking about me as if I'm not here. I'm all right now."

In fact he had rather a headache. He shook his head to clear it and looked around. The rain had stopped. It was evening. Crossing the pastureland from the direction of the village was a long line of cats. Every shape and size and breed, they pooled around him, rubbing their heads against him, purring in the twilight, eyes like oval mirrors to the greenish afterglow. The warmth of all those cats around him made him feel secure. The golden kitten regarded them with caution, and withdrew into the shadows of the trees. Stilton introduced himself to everyone. "Hello," he kept saying. "I'm Stilton, and I'm—" Animal X never seemed to catch the rest. He was glad to see Stilton so happy. His headache receded, and he felt emptied out, washed clean by whatever had happened to him, rather lighthearted.

"I can see perfectly well," he repeated.

"Good," said the longhair. "Now, can you walk? Or will you need help with that?"

Animal X stared at her.

What followed was a series of strange and disjointed episodes. How he got from one to the next he was never entirely sure. If the fit had left him calm, it had also left him prone to sleep on his feet, with the result that as soon as he got used to being in one place, he found himself somewhere else. As soon as he became comfortable with one conversation, he seemed to be taking part in another.

🐾

The long procession, having barely reached its objective, reformed, and, with the newcomers at its head, made its way back to the village, where individual cats evaporated steadily away into their own houses and gardens until none were left. It was like seeing steam drawn back into the spout of a kettle. Animal X stopped to watch the last of them go. Night had fallen as they came up from the water meadows; the village lay white-and-thatch under a fattening moon. There was an oak; a cenotaph; a tiny shop from which, senses sharpened by *petit mal*, he could smell oranges, licorice, yesterday's bread. He thought he would remember it all his life—the sweet smell of bread, the cats' eyes like candles in the night, the blue-cream walking at his side like a beautiful ghost.

"Why did they come out to me?" he asked her.

"Because you are a cat. And because many of them have had experiences like yours."

"I don't—"

"Look!" she interrupted.

Before him stood the church he had seen from the river: small, old, set amid yew-shaded graves, with a tower of soft-edged gray stone. Waiting for them in its shadowy wooden porch sat a white cat with bright blue eyes, who said, "Well now, Amelie. What have you found for us this time?"

She was old, but her voice was firm and true. Her gaze went from Stilton to the golden kitten—on whom it rested for some time in a kind of amused maternal delight—and then to Animal X, who felt that he was being assessed by an intelligence rather greater than his own. "How interesting," she said. And then, as soon as he opened his mouth to speak: "Oh, no, no, it's not a bit of use introducing yourselves. No use your saying anything at all, in fact: I'm as deaf as a board. Deaf as a board." After she had enjoyed Animal X's reaction to this, she went on. "I'm the post office cat. Although in another life they called me Cottonreel." She laughed. "The names they give you!" she said. "Such a burden. Mind you, I can't say I never answered when they called. Come on. We're going to put you up in the vestry. No one will bother you there."

And without further explanation she led them inside.

The church was silent, full of a filmy gray moonlight. It smelled of cut flowers and polish. The kitten, raw-nerved and skittish, glared up into the ceiling. It was driven to investigate everything—a hassock that lay in its own reflection on the shiny floor, the brass-bound lectern, the stained glass of the great east window—and would not move on.

"Can't you hurry him?" suggested the post office cat.

"He becomes angry if you say the wrong thing," Animal X was forced to admit.

"Do come along, dear!" urged Cottonreel.

The kitten gave her a look, then followed grudgingly.

"Now. Here we are," she said.

The vestry, a bleak, white-wainscoted room barely larger than a cupboard, contained a heavy wooden armoire black with time; one bentwood chair, across the seat of which someone had bundled two or three items of human clothing; and a cheval glass in a mahogany frame. On an iron rack on one wall hung more clothes, mostly white, their shadowed volutes like sculpture in the moonlight.

Animal X looked around.

He thought, What a strange place to end up.

The post office cat twinkled at him, as if she could read his thoughts. "You'll be safe here until morning," she promised. "We're quite expert at this. The humans seemed interested at first; we get less help from them now, and keep to ourselves. I daresay they wouldn't care that we housed you here; but what they don't know doesn't hurt them."

"Thank you," he said.

"No good thanking me. Can't hear a word."

He was swaying on his feet from tiredness again. He heard her voice go away from him as she explained something to Amelie; and then Stilton saying, "I'm Stilton, and I'm hungry."

Then he simply fell asleep where he stood.

🐾

He woke alone, an hour or two later. Moonlight fell in a thin bar across the floor from the single window. The vestry was deserted, a little chilly. He found that he had made himself a kind of nest out of the clothes on the chair, which smelled not unpleasantly of dust and human perspiration. He felt quite hungry, though disoriented. He was getting up to go and look for his friends, and see what was happening in the village, when Amelie the blue-cream came quietly around the door, sat down beside him, and began to groom herself in a self-possessed but companionable fashion. Animal X watched her for a moment or two, hypnotized by the long, soft strokes of her tongue in the cloud of bicolor fur and rather wishing he could offer to groom her himself. Then he said, "Why are you helping us?"

"Because you are cats."

She seemed to consider this—as if she might qualify it some way—but then started off in quite another direction.

"We haven't been here long ourselves," she said. "When we came, it was snow." She shivered. "It was snow everywhere. We had been taken by furriers. They stuff you in cages and drive you about for hours in a filthy vehicle, until you're sick from oil fumes and being shaken about. Horrible! It was Cottonreel who got us out of that—though she had help from a cat we never saw again—and Cottonreel who kept us together afterward. To start with we were ordinary cats, rather out for ourselves, unable to relinquish the sheltered self-centered lives we had lost. But Cottonreel wouldn't have any of it. She is simply the most sensible animal in the world! She made sure we found homes, with humans or without them. And as soon as we were settled we began looking after the others."

"The others?"

"Cats are always escaping the place you were in," said Amelie. "One here, a couple there. They find the river if they are lucky, and, if they survive, this is where they end up. We try to help them back to being themselves. The welcome you had this evening—" She paused. "I'm not sure how to say this. They—"

"What?" said Animal X.

"They *feel* so much more, the ones who recover. They are so grateful to have their lives. They remember just how bad it was."

There was another silence.

Eventually Animal X broke it by saying, "I'm all right, but Stilton has been quite ill."

"Your friend will be fine," she reassured him. "You looked after one another as best you could in that place. You looked after one another beautifully. Now: come here and see yourself." And she led him over to the cheval glass in its corner. "Do you know what they have done to you?"

"Is that me in there?"

"That is you. And next to you, me. Do you see? You're not frightened by this? Some of them are frightened."

"I'm not frightened," said Animal X.

"Then what do you see?" she asked him.

"Something in my head," he said. "Something metal in my head."

"They all have that," she said.

Animal X contemplated this in silence. Then he said, "They put something metal in my head." He said, as much to her as to himself, "They put something metal in my head, but I feel it less these days. The gap it made is not so big." He said, "I like standing next to you like this."

"And what else do you see," asked Amelie, "when you look at yourself?"

"I see a cat like any other."

"No cat is like any other," she said.

She said, "You have some way to go yet, Animal X."

"The river will bring me somewhere in the end."

"I did not mean it in a geographical sense." She thought for a moment. "Though if you keep following the river it will take you to the sea. That may be no bad thing."

"What is 'the sea'?"

"Well, I will tell you, because I was once there. I caught a glimpse of it from a carrying basket, somewhere between a cat show and a car park. It was late afternoon. The air was so different! Behind me was a hall full of cats—the least of them had been judged and found acceptable. In front, a sky so bright it seemed to go on forever!" She closed her eyes, opened them again. "You can see farther there," she said. "But the sea, the sea— For one thing, it smells of salt and cooked fish and items that have been dead for quite a long time. For another, there are huge white birds there—birds as big as a cat—that make the loneliest noise you have ever heard. They hover for a moment, then swing away on the wind and disappear among the rooftops. The sea—The main thing to remember about the sea is that it is more water than you can ever imagine. It is so big that it heaves up and down, gray and blue, with a kind of cotton wool floating on it." She thought for a moment. "What else? There is always an old man leading two dogs. Oh, and at the sea, human beings walk around waving their arms and pointing things out to one another." She cast about for one last thing to add. "All that day I smelled fried onions," she said. "I was first in my class, best in show."

When he heard about the sea, Animal X felt himself fill up like a clear glass with excitement. I was always going there, he thought. He had no idea why. Whatever I was, I was going there. Suddenly he thought, Even though I am frightened of so much water.

To Amelie he said, "That is where I am bound to go," he said, "that 'sea.' "

"Well then," said Amelie, "how lucky I am to have hit on it so soon. Sleep well."

And she left him to the mirror.

🐾

He woke perhaps an hour later to find her looking down at him from the back of the chair, where she was balanced with the unconcern of a performer. He had the feeling that she had been there for some time. The moon was down, but an odd backlight or afterglow, filtered through the yews in the churchyard outside, gave her face with its metallic orange eyes a disturbing look—at once unworldly and fiercely honest. Her ears, he noted, were small, round tipped. When she saw that he was awake, she continued to study him for a moment, then jumped quietly off the chair, so that he was compelled to look down at her. Her tail was up. She seemed expectant. He looked away from her, yawned suddenly, and washed one paw.

"Your friend ate so much he was sick," she said. "He is overexcited, and talks constantly about some kind of cheese no one here has heard of."

"He isn't used to other cats."

"Clearly."

"What about the kitten?"

"It is the biggest kitten anyone has ever seen. Only Cottonreel dares approach it. Even Cottonreel cannot get it to speak. It seems rather attached to you. At the moment it is lying across the church doorway in case we hurt you; or, I suspect, in case you think of leaving without it."

"Ah."

"No human being has plugged anything into that animal's brain."

"Its anger is all its own," agreed Animal X.

There was a pause, during which Amelie walked up and down in front of him, waving her tail to and fro as if she couldn't make up her mind about something. Animal X watched her uneasily, wondering why she had woken him up in the middle of the night. Suddenly she said, with an impatience less directed at him, perhaps, than herself, "Am I attractive to you?"

And then quickly, before he could answer, "Because I am beginning to be in heat. Tomorrow I will be calling and calling, and any half-decent tom will be able to come to me and welcome. But tonight I should like it to be you."

"Ah," said Animal X, who had suspected something like it. "Are you sure?" he said. "To tell you the truth, I am not certain I remember all that. I have not had the opportunity to do it for some time."

She looked back down the length of her body at him.

"I will begin to think you are stupid," she said softly.

🐾

Later, they stood side by side again, looking into the mirror, and she told him, "A great change is coming about in the world. I have felt that since I was a kitten. I work here now to help it happen—or perhaps just to be ready for it. I forget which."

"What was it like to be a kitten?"

"I was all success in those days," she said.

She examined her image, next to Animal X's in the mirror.

"But nothing lasts. We Persians find it hard to give up our youth, especially after a career on the show bench. If we aren't careful we become sulky, narcissistic, demanding."

"You look beautiful to me," said Animal X.

She rubbed her face against his.

"Oh, this body is a little too cobby now, and the fur goes in need of a groom longer than it should—" She saw that he was no longer listening and laughed to show she didn't mind. "What are you thinking?"

"There's something I have to tell you," he said. "We will be the last cats who come down the river."

"Why do you say that?"

"Something destroyed that place for good," he said. "Broke it to pieces. Many of them died. We were the last to leave."

"I don't understand."

He said, "Something broke it open one morning, right in front of me, some green fire, I wasn't sure if it was there or not. Have you ever seen anything like that?" After a moment, when she didn't answer, he added, "I'm sorry it took us so long to get here. We didn't know much about being outside."

He said, looking in front of him, "We'll be the last of them now. You will need to tell the white cat that."

Amelie stretched.

"I'll tell her in the morning," she said.

Later, she slept curled in her beautiful fur, while Animal X, suddenly feeling as if their roles were reversed, watched over her or, staring out of the vestry window into the warm night, thought puzzledly, I am a cat who fears water and yet is drawn to the sea.

❀

The Dog had observed all these comings and goings, right from the moment the woods first filled with rain. Rain held no terrors for the Dog. It had been rained on many times in a long life, four legs and three. It preferred a doorway if it could find one, but generally rain was nothing to a dog like itself. The cat, though, had rushed about in circles in the water meadow. Its friends called to it. Foam was coming out of its mouth; other cats came and fetched it. The things cats did were always inexplicable. Why they made this fuss, the Dog had been unable to understand. It is only a cat falling down, it had thought—but, being a dog, followed them all into the village.

The Dog watched. No one knew it was there. Things it saw: trees, shadows. Shadows of trees. A tree is a good thing—you can always use a tree. It saw the golden kitten, guarding the door of the church all night. It saw the blue-cream cat go in and out. Various noises came from the vestry. When the Dog had looked in through the vestry window, an hour or two before, it had not understood what it saw. Who knew what cats did to each other anyway? You would never want to be a cat. The difference between dogs and cats was simple. A dog had a coat; it had a smell. Being a dog was something you could rely on. When you're a dog you have a very strong face, which you can push under things, or you can rag them about with your mouth. A dog never need let go. A dog's teeth will hang on.

And another thing— it thought. But it had forgotten what that was.

Later, it thought, No one ever gives me any food.

And later still, How did I come to be the Dog? It thought, I have been the Dog for too long now to remember. It had been the Dog for a long time. Too long to remember how, it concluded, far too long.

Then it thought, Still only one golden kitten.

It would keep watching until dawn. It would keep watching all the next day if that proved necessary. A dog can watch forever, it thought.

It thought, What else is there to do?

Chapter Fourteen

OLD FRIENDS

The wild roads were tangled and elusive: they withheld themselves. The endless rush of cat souls seemed diminished. A mournful light crawled down the long perspectives. It was cold, but not, Tag saw now, the cold of winter, the kind of cold he remembered from those early journeys in the service of the old Majicou. Rather, the tear-stricken, blurry light sucked at your heat and energy as you ran. At each successive turning of the ways Tag found himself more exhausted, asked himself, "What is happening here?" and received no answer. The wild roads are no longer giving, he thought. Instead they are taking away. It's very sudden. It was nothing he had been warned about. It was nothing in his experience. "We're lost, Leo," he told her, as they stood shivering in damp mist somewhere he did not recognize, with a sound like sad human singing in his ears. But then Leonora danced for them; and suddenly everything seemed to unglue again, and they felt a little stronger; and soon they stood in the sunshine before the house of Uroum Bashou. There, it was Leo who faltered.

"I'm afraid to go in," she said.

She shivered.

"It looks so wrong inside," she said.

She said, "Something has happened here. The great brass animal I met on the stairs: Was it Kater Murr?"

"I'm rather afraid it was," Tag said.

She looked depressed.

"Adult life is more complex than I imagined."

"You often find that."

"In the kitchen of this house, then," she said, "that was the two of you. You fought over me."

228

"It didn't come to fighting," said Tag.

"But you were the other cat."

"I suppose I was," Tag said. He admitted, "I haven't been altogether fair to you, Leonora." He had intended to explain further, but she seemed so disheartened it made him shy. He looked away from her, and in the end all he could think of to say was "You don't have to be right all the time, you know. Life isn't a test."

"Even so," she said. "I feel a fool."

"You will never be a fool, Leonora," he said as severely as he could. "That side of things—how we are when the wild roads change us—well, it's sometimes hard for a kitten to accept. I'm the one to tell you about that: I hated those roads when I was young! They seemed so pitiless to me. You haven't quite found yourself yet, out there on the Old Changing Way. When you do, you will be something to reckon with. You have all your father in you, and much of your mother. You should see them when they are over there, Leo! They are the two most beautiful and terrifying animals in the world!"

She purred suddenly.

"You're my favorite animal," she said.

"I am only Tag."

"Tag is a lot. Tag is a very great deal."

After this exchange both of them became thoughtful and, in the absence of anything to say, studied the house of Uroum Bashou, the back door of which had been shoved outward off its hinges and now leaned cheerfully awry into the garden, encouraging the sunshine to stream inside. From where he sat, Tag had an oblique view down the passageway to the bottom of the stairs. Everything in there seemed broken. The light fell on scratched paintwork, torn-up linoleum. Objects lay as if they had been thrown about—a broom handle, a shoe ripped almost in half, a broken picture frame. I warned him, I warned him, Tag thought. Nothing good has gone on here. Even the passage wainscoting had been bruised, as if something heavy had blundered into it, cracking the tongue-and-groove boards as easily as matchsticks as it passed out of the house.

Paper fluttered loose in the drafts, moving by fits and starts toward the doorway. Here and there, a sheet had already floated down into the garden from the broken windows at the very top of the house. Tag looked up, blinked in the light, thought again, There is nothing good in this.

Leo startled him by saying suddenly, "We have to go in."

He considered this. "You wouldn't prefer it if I went alone?" he suggested.

"No," said Leo decisively. "I am worried about the Reading Cat, and I want to see what has happened."

🐾

Sunshine lay callous and bland across the wreckage of the library, which reeked not just of one tomcat but of two or three. Not an object was unbroken. Not a book remained whole. Their pages wrenched and torn, their spines cracked and split, they were littered across the blackened floorboards like wastepaper in an empty street. Tag stared at them. He remembered the Reading Cat claiming with pride, *"In those days I read everything that came to me. I read 'weasels.' I read 'smoke.' I read 'meringue,' 'mystery!' "* He wondered if those things lay somewhere in front of him among the pages, if they had an existence of their own there; he wondered what they were.

Heaped in the middle of it all were the maroon plush cushions from which Uroum Bashou used to hold audience. They had been slashed open with a kind of insane care. The Reading Cat lay quietly on his side among rolls of grayish stuffing, his head stretched forward a little so that his throat seemed to be bared to whatever might happen, his body relaxed, as if he had been caught rolling in the morning sun. The fur on his belly was thus revealed to be more brown than black, in places so thinned out by age that the flesh beneath lent it a pinkish tone. There wasn't a mark on him, but his eyes bulged out of his head in an expression of fear and determination. Even as he died, he had been scrabbling in the dust with his forepaws. Tag and Leo stared helplessly at the marks he had made—

green world

It was an effort even to look at them.

"Is it a message, Leo? Are they words?"

Leonora shook her head. "I don't know," she said.

"This was bound to happen," said Tag sadly. Then, thinking of Kater Murr, "As for that poor, deranged animal, where will he go now? Who will look after him?"

Leo shuddered. "No one, I hope!" she said.

There was no point in staying. Tag let her mourn for a moment, then led her away from the Reading Cat's stiffening form. At the door she turned for one last look, as if by that she could fix the old cat in her mind forever.

"His tail!" she cried. "Look at his tail!"

"What?"

"The knot is gone out of it. The World has got its memory back." She gave the wreckage a bitter look. "I hate the way things are," she said. "Oh, Tag, he was so happy to be able to help me. When I last saw him here his shadow looked like ink thrown by the moonlight on his scattered books."

🐾

The journey to the oceanarium was silent, fraught. Since no news had arrived there of the missing tabby, Tag left Leo with her parents and took to the wild roads on his own. The news from Egypt, along with the accidental discoveries of Uroum Bashou and Leonora Whitstand Merril, had enabled him to understand several pieces of the puzzle. But they were of such strange, nightmarish shapes that they made no recognizable whole. The harder he tried to join them up, the more they resisted. How was the disease of the wild roads linked to the thing Ragnar and Pertelot had fled from in Egypt? He had a growing—and appalled suspicion—that he knew who had taken the kittens; but he had no idea how that could be or how it fitted with the rest! Something was missing: he couldn't find it, but he couldn't stop himself from trying to fit things together without it. His worst fear was for Isis and Odin: if he was right, they were in fearful danger. Yet he could do nothing! Frustrated and driven, fueled by anger, impatience with his own intellect—which did not seem to be up to the task his mentor had bequeathed him—and a sense of imminent disaster, he flickered briefly into existence at a dozen points along the coast, a lonely silver cat standing square into the wind, gazing out to sea from a beach, a cove, an outcrop of rock high above the waves. He visited St. Madryn's Church and the caves beneath.

Nothing.

Local pathways, he discovered, were the easiest to travel. They seemed to tire him less. Based on the traditional comings and goings of cats—benign pursuit of love or mice—they remained the sunny trickles of history they had always been. " 'Powerless little roads,' " he remembered his old mentor saying. "But I preferred them from the start: there was more power in them than Majicou ever saw." He stitched them together to make the longer journeys. Even here, though, cunning failed and exhaustion set in; and he could not dance like Leonora Whitstand Merril. Instead, he came to depend on the fierce certainties—the steady heats and angers—within. When the worst came to the worst, head down into the sucking cold, he could push on through. He was the new Majicou! His great striped mask swung from side to side as he stalked along. He lashed his tail, an echoing snarl came up out of his chest, and the drizzle turned to steam where it touched him.

Thus, tacking to and fro into the psychic weather, he forced the ghost roads, and came to the old pet shop on Cutting Lane. There, stripping his claws impatiently, he waited an hour or two in case any of his proxies brought news. But the pieces of the puzzle remained scattered. Out he went again, and—hoping he might relax enough to give his thoughts a chance to think themselves unencumbered—took himself to familiar city gardens at twilight, where lupins plumed in the warm air and the night insects were just beginning to blunder across the recently mown lawns. From there he could watch the common human goings-on. Suppers were being served. Televisions were flickering in corners. Here and there a cat slept on a sofa. And from one lighted window a kitten gazed out owl eyed and curious into the evening. He took to it for no reason he could see. It was such a nondescript little thing, saved like them all by the gawky elegance of extreme youth. Square lines, fluffy sparse fur a pale ginger color, the tiniest paws Tag had ever seen. When he jumped onto the outside windowsill, it blinked, held its ground; then with a jerky, determined motion reared up and beat its front paws softly on the glass. In the wake of this announcement they stared at each other.

"Don't be afraid," said Tag.

The kitten fluffed itself up.

"Why would I be?" it said. "I'm bigger than you."

"I didn't notice that at first."

"This light is poor," the kitten acknowledged comfortably.

After a moment, he wasn't sure why, Tag said, "When I was about your age I was taken away on a great adventure. I lost my home and my life was changed forever. Was it a good thing or a bad thing? I still don't know."

"I would like to go on an adventure," said the kitten wistfully. "Have you come to fetch me?"

"Certainly not!" said Tag. He was horrified. "Stay at home," he advised. "What are your owners like?"

"Dull. Nice, but dull."

"Ah."

There was a pause.

"I expect they give you pretty good stuff to eat, though," Tag said. "Game casserole, meat-and-liver dinner, fishes in tins—all that sort of thing?"

The kitten examined him. "Anyone can get that," it said.

Tag, who had experienced such confidence himself, felt there was a further argument to be made. Somehow, though, it escaped him. "Well, anyway," he said, "you want to stay in, where it's safe." He jumped down off the windowsill. "Another thing, never pay any attention to what a bird says." Suddenly unsure of what he had achieved here, and looking for some final expression of a position fatally unthought out, he added, "Eat as much as you can."

The kitten stared down at him. "Oh, I do," it said. "Still. An adventure—"

Hands appeared from nowhere and carried it off before it could say more. Tag yawned. He sat on a corner of the lawn thinking, Why did I do that? Night fell. Cars passed in the street on the other side of the house. A thrush continued to sing. Tag heard snuffling and rootling noises, as of forced passage, in the tangle of woody rose briar, rotten old trellis, sycamore saplings, and Russian vine that separated the garden from the one next door. Hedgehog, he thought automatically—they were such determined noises—and wrote them off. But a moment or two later the undergrowth shook and a large dog fox shouldered its way out onto the lawn, where it stood panting with effort just outside the parallelogram of diffuse yellow light cast by the window. It was a gnarly, experienced-seeming animal with yellow teeth, a long pink tongue, and on one haunch a pure white patch. Every time it looked toward the house, its amber eyes gleamed, restless and cunning, in the darkness. Tag's heart began to pound so hard it rocked him to and fro where he sat. After a moment of astonished silence, he said, "Loves a Dustbin? Is it you?"

The fox limped over, set itself down next to him as if nothing much had happened since they last met, and stared out over the garden. It scratched thoughtfully beneath its chin.

"I wondered if I might find you here," it said.

Then it said, "The past is the past, Tag. You can't bring any of this back, you know. None of us can."

🐾

They talked and talked, two old comrades silhouetted bluish black against the house light, now facing each other, now sitting up side by side again. The fox snapped at a passing moth; the cat licked its tail suddenly. To begin with there was a kind of shyness between them. It was a shyness born of events, of separation, but also the shyness of creatures who are so close they don't know how to express it. In the end the fox told his story first: how, after the battle at Tintagel, he had traveled across country with the vixen Francine, and, for a while, Sealink. How Sealink and Francine had bickered and fought. The discovery of the dead badger. Francine's tumble into the rabbit trap and the consequences of that. It was a long story and finally a sad one, a story of hard travel, mismatched companions, happiness fading to puzzlement.

"When we set out," he said, "we were so hopeful. The Alchemist was defeated. We had our lives to live. He stared across the lawn. "Then Sealink and Francine began scratching away at each other like that. I knew they didn't get on, of course. I knew that from the start. But I thought—" He shook his head sadly. "I don't know what I thought. My life had been given back to me in more ways than one. If I was free of the Alchemist, I was free of Majicou, too. I was changed, and I expected everyone else to be. There was such a spirit of generosity on that headland after we won the battle. And yet within days those two had frittered it away! I couldn't blame either of them. That calico cat, she's in full sail the moment she wakes up—she never gives an inch. She'd lost her mate, and she isn't good at loss. She was full of guilt—even as she left us, she was transferring it to some obsession with kittens she had abandoned long ago. I wonder where she is now? She's a tough old thing, but she can't bring back the past any more than you can." There was a silence. Then he shrugged. "As for Francine, well, Francine had her faults. I'd be the first to admit it. Her world was narrow; she never understood the events that caught her up. She was just a fox. But, Tag, I never saw a fox as beautiful as her!"

He fell silent and stared at the ground.

"What happened?" Tag asked him.

No answer.

"We can't help who we love," said Tag. This made him think suddenly of Cy, off somewhere in the deep world without him. He surprised himself further by adding, "Love lies in wait and forces us to care."

The fox gave Tag an anguished look, then stared hard into the dark as if the past still lay there, just out of sight.

"What happened?" Tag repeated gently.

"When Sealink left, Francine seemed to perk up a little. We decided to go on. But the highways were unreliable and we were forced to walk again. It was hard going, hour after hour of clay soils, deep woodland, steady drizzling rain. We had no idea where we might be. All this time her leg was swollen, hot to the touch. The wound leaked an ugly fluid. It smelled of nothing good." He laughed bitterly. "I know that smell!" he said. "That night she was full of fever, by morning she was raving. I got her to the edge of a stream and sat by her for three days and nights. She wouldn't drink. She thought she had cubs. She kept saying, 'I want to go home. Please take me home.' The rabbit trap killed her after all."

There was a silence.

"She was just a fox from the suburbs. She came because I called her, and died in a place she hated. We can't help who we love—you're right. But Francine's death was my responsibility. Since then my head has been on fire, and I am wounded worse than I was by the gun."

He stared at Tag.

"I looked up from her agony, and the world was full of green flames. What was that, Tag?"

"I don't know."

"Green flames were on every tree, like leaves. The fire sprang from branch to branch until everything roared with it. It filled my head, and I couldn't hear my own voice. Do you want to know what I think—?"

He stopped.

"I'm sorry," he said wearily. "I haven't had anyone to talk to."

"No," said Tag. "Tell me. I—"

"I think the world has seen enough deaths like hers," the fox said.

They were silent after this. A sense of separateness returned to them, less comfortable than before. At length, Loves a Dustbin shook himself and went over to the gray-stone bird-bath raised two or three feet high on a plinth at the center of the lawn. There he got up awkwardly on his hind legs, and, with his front paws resting either side of the water, drank from it, lapping noisily for what seemed like some minutes. When he had finished he dropped onto all fours again and walked stiffly to the far edge of the lawn.

"Are you going?" said Tag. "Don't you want to hear what happened to me?"

The fox looked back at him. "I am trying to work the arthritis out of my leg," it said.

"Ah."

"So then tell me."

Tag began by describing the oceanarium, and how he had

lived there with Cy and been happier than at any other time in his life. He touched briefly on the domestic arrangements of the King and Queen. How they, too, had prospered. From there he moved on to the inexplicable loss of Odin and Isis. He drew the fox's attention to the mysteries attendant on this— the signs and symbols he could not interpret, the journeys that seemed to fold into themselves and reveal nothing, the proxies who brought back no answers. He spoke of the hard death of Uroum Bashou. "Something is wrong in the world," he said, "and I am followed everywhere I go. I fear the worst. Who does the Great Ray serve, and why did it take the Mau to Egypt? Where is Cy? What is happening along the wild roads?" He sighed exasperatedly. "The clues mean nothing to me, and I am in a fog," he concluded. Then he sat back and waited for the fox's opinion.

But Loves a Dustbin only said, "It was clever to take the third kitten as your apprentice. The old Majicou would have appreciated that."

"I feel the weight of these responsibilities," Tag prompted. "I don't know what to do."

The fox greeted this admission in silence, its eyes yellow with some emotion Tag couldn't interpret. Then it ordered, "Come with me," and, plunging immediately through the overgrown hedge, set off across the gardens at a pace Tag soon found difficult to maintain. They squeezed between the loose boards of fences. They trotted down the passageways at the sides of houses. There was a road—"Come on, come on!" urged the fox—and then more gardens. Eventually Tag found himself sitting in an arbor or summerhouse of old gray wooden trellis, twined inside and out with clematis and climbing rose. Moonlight poured into this frail structure, giving a curious depthless shine to its inner rear wall, which had been made from a single large mirror.

"But—" he said.

"Yes," said the fox. "You've been here before."

"This is where you showed me who I was."

"You were a kitten. You had only just poked your nose outside a house, and you were already half dead of starvation. Now look at you!" said the fox with satisfaction.

Tag looked. The animal in the mirror was long bodied and elegant, having a silver mask striped in charcoal gray, in which were set eyes of a pale green color darkening toward their enlarged pupils. It was self-possessed if wary, muscular and durable without being heavy, and carried its head high. It was alert to night sounds. Some half-forgotten adventure had robbed it of part of one ear.

"Did I do you a service, back then?" asked the fox.

"Of course you did. You showed me myself. Everything changed after that."

"Good," said the fox grimly. "Because everything is going to have to change again. You have been sheltered from the worst of it, down there on the coast. Your own power protects you. As if that isn't enough, the glamour of the King and Queen surrounds you. Even the *name* Tintagel is a kind of shelter; while the place itself is a magic made to last a thousand years. But the news along the wild roads is this: animals not so fortunate are dying. They are dying, and no one is helping them."

"You're angry with me," said Tag.

"I am not," said the fox. "I am trying to make you understand something. Look! Look in the mirror. Who do you see?"

"Tag."

"Well, I don't. I see the new Majicou. *That* is the cat who must act now!"

"I would act if I knew how."

" 'If I knew how'!" mimicked the fox. "You hoped Uroum Bashou would tell you what to do. You hoped I would." He stared contemptuously up at the lighted house. "And what can you learn here, sniffing around after your kittenhood?" He sighed. "You are the new Majicou," he said heavily, "like it or not. I can serve you as well as I served the old one, but you must make yourself worth the effort. Everyone depends on you." There was a long pause, in which the two animals stood looking defiantly at each other. In the end, Tag blurted out the thing that worried him most, the thing he had been trying to keep from himself: "The Alchemist is still alive."

It was a relief to have it in the open.

"We didn't save the world back then," he said. "We only thought we did."

The fox stared at him.

"Then what are you going to do?" he demanded. "Francine and One for Sorrow and all the others—are they going to have died for nothing?"

"I would not allow that," said Tag, holding the fox's eyes with his own. "Did you imagine I would?"

The fox looked away. "Of course not," he said.

"Then let's not quarrel anymore. I must speak with Ragnar Gustaffson. We may not be too late if we act now. One avenue remains, and I will need his support, as well as yours, if I am to explore it."

"That's more like it!" applauded Loves a Dustbin. "Good!"

Tag laughed. His spirits lifted. Friendship had returned to him the energy leached out by frustration. He felt like a giant. He remembered the fox, long ago, dancing around a lamppost in winter light and sleet. He remembered a black-and-white bird, so full of itself it fell off a post.

"Creatures of Majicou!" he whispered to himself.

"Pardon?"

"I said, 'We must be quick.' "

"Then it's the mirror for us!" cried the fox, and sprang toward the back of the arbor. With a feral grin and a tongue lolling like a yard of pink ribbon, his own image leapt to meet him in the glass. At the last moment, when collision seemed inevitable, there was a sound of fabric tearing. The mirror was breached. Great prismatic rings of light rippled the length of the fox's body. Everything slowed down, speeded up again. Then he was gone, and Tag had jumped in behind him. The summerhouse vibrated softly for some minutes after they had vanished; one or two rose petals drifted down on a sudden breeze.

🐾

The wild road is a dream. It began as part of the long, subtle species dream of the cat; but by now it is a dream of its own. If you travel the wild road too often the dream touches everything. Every time you disembark, a little of the dream flows out into the world around you. The world soaks up the dream and seems none the worse for it. You soak it up, and seem none the worse for that. Yet something is changed.

When Tag returned to the oceanarium, he thought he was dreaming. The light had modulated to a hot greenish gold. The air was suffocating. Ragnar and Pertelot, composed in formal stances facing away from the great tank, stood as if painted on a background, shoals of silver fishes suspended behind them like glittering regalia in a museum. Between them, their remaining daughter, her coat gilded by the strong illumination, sat in the ancient pose of the Felidae—front paws together, head held high, eyes narrowed, tail wrapped around—judgmental, ironic, proud. The fox was kneeling awkwardly before her, his neck stretched out, his eyes glittering feverishly. It is this hard for one species to honor another. The silence was palpable.

Tag swallowed. Though he shook his head to clear it, his friends remained stubbornly heraldic. Then there was a commotion in the tank. The mackerel turned and fled as one; the water swirled with thick white pelagic mud and began to slop down the outside of the glass, as if displaced by something monstrous.

At the same time he heard a joyful voice call, "Hey, Ace! I'm home!"

Chapter Fifteen

A MESSAGE

"Well, that got me a whole load of nowhere," the calico grumbled bitterly.

The Mammy's pronouncements had left her feeling quite defeated. Tough-spirited and enterprising, Sealink would never normally have given herself up to self-pity, but now, surrounded by hostile swamp, in a country she no longer recognized as home, having traveled perilously to seek the answer to a problem not of her own making—and that "answer" having proved utterly impenetrable—she found her usual optimism slipping like a spider down a drain. Everything was so much larger and more complicated than she had ever expected. She saw herself suddenly, with unprecedented objectivity, as a tiny mote of life spinning, lonely and desolate, in a void.

"You lost, ma'am?"

Alerted as much by a strange, musky scent as by the question, Sealink's head shot up. Staring inquisitively at her was the second of the guards she had encountered earlier at the bone pile. She recovered her composure with impressive speed.

"I guess so. Lost in all senses of the word."

The guard made a kind of hoarse snuffle. "The Mammy has that kind of effect on folks. Bet you're no nearer knowing what to do than you were when you came here, huh?"

Sealink shook her head. "Whole loada stuff she sang out. Can't recall more'n a few words here an' there, and they're not all that *indicative*, y'know? Don't help none that a lot of it was foreign."

241

The guard made a stiff little bow. "Allow me, ma'am, to introduce myself more politely than when we first met." He extended a cool, clawed hand. The calico sniffed at it uncertainly. "My name is Cletus. I believe I may be able to cast some light on the Wise One's auguries. I've had some experience with the poor, befuddled souls who come away from her ladyship. Try me." The creature sat back on its shell and crossed its little arms on its plated chest. It looked ridiculous in this posture, but Sealink was in no mood to poke fun.

"You've got to be kidding."

It squinted at her. "That's not entirely charitable, if you don't mind my saying, ma'am. When you need help you maybe shouldn't look a gift, ah—armadillo in the mouth."

Armadillo.

Comprehension came with infuriating ease, along with a vivid picture of armor-plated roadkill adhering to the tarmacadam of human highways.

She laughed. "Hell, what have I got to lose? Seems my sanity's already gone tail up over the hill. Okay: see what you make of this—" She dredged through her recent memories. *"Danse macabre . . . chat noir . . . er . . . mangent le monde."*

The armadillo looked thoughtful. "That sure is peculiar. What the hell did you ask her?" Without pausing for Sealink to reply, it continued, *"La danse macabre.* Hmm. 'The dance of death.' Often seen as an ancient symbolic representation of the Dark Lord leading folk to the boneyard that derives from medieval times. Allegorical. The dance is often seen as a way to formalize life, or the passage out of life—everyone moving in their own ritualistic patterns, steps ordained by destiny, that sort of thing."

He paused to make sure Sealink was listening. She looked thoroughly distrustful. Annoyed, he carried on. "Or maybe a dance *to* the death, a kind of duel . . . *Le chat noir.* Well, that's easy. Don't you speak any French at all?"

"The black cat." Sealink surprised herself.

"See: it just takes a little thought." The armadillo smiled patronizingly. "So who's the black cat? Think about it. The bones can be a mite arcane, but they're usually darned accurate."

She'd known a few black cats in her life. Cyrus and William, Earwax and Amphetamine . . . All these were at once obliterated by the vision of a black cat's head, flayed and displayed in a voodoo shop window . . .

"The Baron," she breathed.

The armadillo considered Sealink neutrally. "If that means something to you, sister, then that's fine by me. He likely to eat the world?"

Sealink stared at him.

"*Mange le monde.* Or maybe even *mangent le monde.* Might be more than one of 'em."

The calico shrugged. "He had a good life in his time, the Baron, but he weren't ever ill-intentioned. Loved life. I guess you could say he wanted to 'eat the world.' But he was alone when last I saw him." She shivered. "Beyond that I don't got the least idea." She wrinkled her brow and thought about the rest of the Mammy's divinations. "*Rues sauvages,* moo— something, and a pyramid, *cassé,* and—" she concentrated hard "*—les trois sont perdus.*"

"Wild roads. Moo—. MOO!" A bellow that made Sealink jump. "Ain't too many cattle round here!" He cackled, Mammy-like. The calico fixed him with such a fierce glare that he felt compelled to drop his gaze and scratch nervously at his neck. He dug around for a moment in the vulnerable area where two armored plates met, then examined his nails and sucked out the fruits of their labor. Head on one side, he considered the possibilities. "Moo—moolah: money. No. Can't be. *Mourir*—'to die,' maybe. The wild roads are dying."

Sealink nodded slowly.

"Sounds ominous. Onward, onward. Pyramid *cassé* . . . *trois sont perdus* . . . hmm . . . Broken pyramid and three are lost. Three. Prime number, very powerful: lots of magical things come in threes. Three wishes; three questions. Three wise men. The three holy threads of the ancient Brahmin. The Three Graces. The Three Fates. The Holy Trinity. According to Pythagoras the perfect number. But the three are lost? You got me there."

Sealink sighed. She had spent the greatest part of her life avoiding introspection—or indeed any sort of hard, slow thought—but clearly if anything was to be salvaged from her visit to the Mammy, it now lay largely within her own efforts. She closed her eyes and tried to think about the words with, as Eponine had instructed her, the wildest part of herself.

The Mammy's words circled in her head like flies above a carcass.

Three are lost. That much was certainly true. Two of her kittens lay long ago dead on the Mississippi shoreline, and of the third she knew nothing at all. Pyramids? Well, she had once visited Egypt, Pertelot's ancestral home, where the cat had been sacred to humans, and there were pyramids there; broken ones, too. Was her last missing kitten in Egypt? That made no sense at all. She racked her memory. The Mammy had said something about a sun of fire. *Seek for a sun of fire in the Fields of the Blessed.* Sure, the desert was hot: the sun as fiery as hell. But there had been no fields at all—just sand as far as the eye could see.

The harder she thought, the more tangled the images became. Giving that part up as inextricable, she moved on.

The wild roads dying? Well, that made a kind of sense, but it still got her no nearer the cause or a cure.

Black cats and strange dances. In her mind's eye she saw herself and the Baron stepping out together on the boardwalk; but try as she might, she could find no greater significance in the scene. And yet the Baron was dead. Perhaps it had been a *danse macabre*. Perhaps the dance had heralded his death. Perhaps it was her fault . . .

This grim thought was interrupted by the arrival of the second armadillo, whuffling with the effort of running.

"Come and see, Cletus, see what I done! You won't believe it—"

Sealink and the two armadillos made their way back to the clearing, Cletus in the lead, the second guard trundling breathlessly behind him, explaining, "It's the best . . . it's ever been, Clete . . . Taller'n we ever . . . managed before . . . Y'all said . . . the triangle was the strongest . . . engineering . . . structure in the world . . . and I know I ain't always . . . too bright, but I guess it . . . filtered through in the end . . . kinda came to me . . . in a flash—"

This exposition came to an unceremonious halt as Cletus stopped in his tracks and his companion cannoned into him.

In the middle of the glade the bone pile towered, its lines cleanly and improbably geometrical, the harsh noon light transforming the white of the skeletal remains to a gold so bright it hurt the eyes.

Sealink stared at it and felt distant echoes stir inside her head.

A tall triangle—a pyramid—and balanced impossibly upon its apex, making all perspectives unreliable, the Louisiana sun, blazing like a message from the entire natural world.

🐾

That night, far from the Mammy and her armadillos, far from alligators and dragonflies that talked, far from the vision of a bone pile gleaming like a neon message the calico cat slept, exhausted by her long trek.

And as she slept, she was visited by a dream.

As dreams go, it was neither particularly horrifying, nor did it hold the sweet sensuality of the golden reveries she had experienced in her youth. Despite this, when she awoke, she found that she was shaking; but whether this reaction sprang from fear or a sudden and inexplicable optimism or maybe from some adrenalizing combination of the two, she could not say.

As the sun rose over the distant horizon, so did Sealink. Tail up, chin high, the calico strode purposefully down the dirt road which she knew, as cats do from their deep internal navigations, would eventually lead back to the city of her birth.

She was Sealink, and she had a job to do.

Chapter Sixteen

ALCHEMIES

*T*hey slipped out of the oceanarium together, leaving the fox to tell his story to the King and Queen, and took the steep little cobbled streets down to the harbor, where they sat on a wall to watch for the returning fishermen.

It was just before dawn. A scent of mud came up from the rising tide. "Smell that!" said Cy. "Mm!" But her own smell was compounded by crackling citrine odors Tag couldn't identify; and as she struggled to tell him about her adventures, it seemed as if they had made her strange to herself as well as to him.

It was curiosity, she was quick to admit, that had caused her to fall in the fish tank. In the middle of a conversation with the Great Ray, she had decided to see how he looked from above. "I ran up the stairs, but when I got to the top I couldn't see him." The viewing platform seemed to be suspended in emptiness. Disoriented by the hot blaze of electric light, she tottered on the edge. "I saw five hundred mackerel turn as one. But my fish wasn't there!" Moments later, though, he had saved her from drowning—and saved Ragnar and Pertelot, too, when they fell in looking for her. "Which naturally led," Cy explained, "to him taking all of us on this totally real trip to Egypt! As you already know."

"I don't understand why," said Tag.

"He had a mission, that fish. He was operating on orders from below. I believe that."

"But why? What does a fish have in common with us?"

Cy didn't know. "They live in murky waters, those guys," she suggested. She sighed impatiently. "Anyway, you listen," she ordered. "Whose story is this?"

246

What had followed, she claimed, wasn't so easy to understand.

As soon as the King and Queen were safely disembarked, the Great Ray had furled and folded himself and whirled down into the tank again, back onto the fish road. "There was no time for me to get off! I was stuck! Tag, I was so excited! He was saying things to me. We were going on the journey of a lifetime, me and that fish. That was what he promised, and it was true. Soon we're down in the deeps of the sea, which is like some electric church where the inhabitants got their own light. Tag, these are guys that glow in the dark!"

South went the great fish, then east and west. Each time he surfaced it was to show her something new about the world. Humid green jungles that came down to the water, releasing flocks of birds like colored laundry. An island no more than a smoking cone, hot cinders in the air ten miles out to sea, smells that made her nose run. "I seen the bows of broken ships, ghostly in pale sea-bottom mud, all them long-ago captains fish bait now! And a beach where striped cats came down to swim in the huge waves. I would've liked to join them, but of course," she said with a certain regret, "they were bigger than me." Shores like deserts, shores like jewels, shores blackened with oil and scattered with towers and huge machines. "Oh, I felt sad, Tag—some of those things I seen!"

At last the ray turned north; and from the deepest journey of all they surfaced in a strip of benighted water like black glass. There was snow and ice as far as the eye could see. Huge pieces of this frozen landscape toppled into the sea around her while she watched. "It was hurling itself in, that stuff. It was the biggest *sugar* I ever saw. I say to Ray, 'This stuff is whiter than you!' He says nothing. I thought he was nervous, you know? But it wasn't that. He was just getting ready." Plumes of water rose in slow motion as the ice cliffs fell, only to subside in total silence as if she were watching through a sheet of glass. "Tag, even my eyes were cold. *Brr!*" All the while, her friend lay on the water, slowly revolving, like a compass needle, until, in the sky, she saw the aurora, unfolded in great unnerving wings of silent, rippling green flame.

Light poured down.

Then, very slowly, Ray began to float up.

"Tag, you got to imagine this . . ."

The tall cathedral shadows of the road, where it left the Earth between the drawn curtains of the northern lights. The mighty fishes that could sometimes be glimpsed, rendered tiny by distance, beating steadily against some invisible current on journeys of their own. And one small, rather frightened cat clinging on for dear life in the emptiness. It was amazing: but it was dark out there, and it was cold, and it was sometimes rather lonely on the great ray's back. Their oceanarium conversations hadn't prepared her for any of this—any more than she had been prepared for his size, his power, his almost stifling sense of age, the feeling she had that he knew things kept from ordinary animals.

"He's not a big talker," she admitted to Tag. Then she sighed again and said, "Still, it was like, you know, the breath of stars. We're out of the water and far up in the air. So far up— Tag, I looked back and seen the place we live!"

She thought for a moment.

"You know," she said, "however bad things are for us right now, I think it will come out okay. Want to know why? Because when I looked back, I saw these green flames. Tag, it looked like the whole world was cupped in a safe green hand!"

Tag greeted this vision with a silence grounded in frustration—while he thought, We aren't safe, any of us. I wish we were.

She seemed not to sense this. She asked, "Tag, have you ever been to the moon?"

"Of course I haven't," said Tag rather crossly.

"Well, the moon is like white gardens," she said, "only nothing grows there. You can see to the end of everything, but there's nothing to see. We floated about there a bit, but there was nothing to do. Nothing's alive on the moon, Tag, no cats nor human beings nor nothing."

She shivered.

"So we came back, as quick as we could. Oh, Ray wanted to go on somewhere else, but I said, 'Take me home.' I'm keen on Ray, but sometimes it's hard to get him to stop. That fish has got a real urge to see things. I asked him how this road of his goes so many places, even the moon, which he had to admit he didn't like either. He told me, 'Little Warm Sister'—because he calls me that, his Little Warm Sister—'the fishes were here before anyone else. We grew restless and swam down to Earth before anyone else arrived.' "

She was silent for a moment.

"Does that make any sense to you?" she said.

Tag said nothing. He couldn't think.

Then she jumped to her feet. "Look! Tag! The boats. The boats!" And there they were—the fishing boats returning safe home, a line of lights bobbing at the harbor mouth. And behind them, the first green flare of the dawn. Cy broke into a great, clattering purr.

Tag felt himself fill with love.

"I'm glad you're back," he said. "I missed you."

On the way back up to the oceanarium, she tried to explain how she had felt when she fell in the tank. "At first," she said, "I thought I'd had it. I thought I was going dancing with Davy Jones." But even as she touched the water, she had felt supported, in a way she couldn't now explain. "Ray wasn't there then," she said. "It was as if something else held me up. Tag, it was like warm green hands in the water!"

Then she asked, "Why does a fish make friends with a cat?"

"I think that's what I was asking you," said Tag.

Cy looked up at him uncertainly. "I wonder what the end of all this will be," she said.

Tag looked down at the harbor and the gulls wheeling around the fishing boats; then up at the oceanarium, where they would be waiting for the new Majicou to make decisions.

"I don't know," he admitted. "I only know that we are coming to it."

❦

An hour later he was hunting the ghost roads again, his breath like smoke in the sucking cold. He had opened a small highway down by the old lifeboat station, and from there made—jump by jump—the arterial connection. Beside him went his two old friends, calling to each other as they ran. The muscles of Ragnar Gustaffson, King of Cats, bunched and flexed beneath his thick black coat. The eyes of the fox Loves a Dustbin glittered with cunning. "Run!" they told one another, remembering old fights, bitter seasons, journeys, and losses from a time before. Their voices echoed along the Old Changing Way, and the echoes shed echoes of their own. "Run!" they called. Those three were used to life. They had seen a lot of it one way or another. They loved it, and they knew how to spend its iron heat. Cold and fear meant nothing to them. They ran. But far out in front of them ran Leonora Whitstand Merril. She was their pathfinder all that long day—a princess among kittens and a dancer to her bones.

"Come on!" she called back. "Run now! We must run!"

🐾

"I will not let you take her," the Mau had said when she heard Tag's plan.

"Yet I have to go there. I can't command the wild roads in their present state. But I have seen Leonora do it."

For this he received a look of contempt. "Because she can, she must. Is that it?" said Pertelot.

"Yes."

"It isn't much of an argument."

"No."

"She is my daughter." Pertelot laughed bitterly. "In fact, at present she is my only child. Males love to run the wild roads day and night, they love to run and fight; but they can't find two lost kittens."

"That is not fair," said Tag. "We are doing our best."

Leonora herself broke this deadlock. "Where is it you want to go?" she asked Tag.

"Be quiet, Leonora!" ordered the Mau.

"This is my life, too, you know," said Leonora.

"Leonora!"

"What if Odin and Isis are there?"

"What if they aren't?" said the Mau tiredly. "Am I to lose you, too?"

"If we falter now—" Tag began.

"We may lose everything," finished the Queen. "I have heard that argument before."

But Leonora said, "I am not a kitten anymore. I want my brother and sister back, and I want to play my part."

"Then play it," said Pertelot. And she turned her back.

"Where do you want to go?" Leonora asked Tag.

"For hundreds of years the Alchemist had a house outside the city. I found it after I became the Majicou. I go there now and then—"

"In case he comes back!"

"I don't know. Perhaps. I go there as I go to the pet shop in Cutting Lane. The Majicou is a caretaker, but to an extent he must intuit his own duties. I followed my nose, and the wild roads showed me that house. Ever since, though I hate the place, it has seemed to me to be part of my domain. I was there the day your brother vanished."

Tag shook his head.

"We might find answers there," he went on, "but the danger is obvious."

Leonora absorbed this in a kind of awed silence.

Then she said, "Wow! The Alchemist! What do you want me to do?"

The Mau laughed angrily. "Oh, you learned plenty from your predecessor," she congratulated Tag. "That one-eyed cat always knew the right thing to say."

※

The gardens had deteriorated since Tag's last visit. The wooden boathouse, leaning in on itself in a tall growth of fireweed and sycamore saplings, gaped emptily. The willows were rotted to the heart. The rain poured down from a thick gray sky to shred the mottled surface of the river.

It had been a difficult journey, despite Leonora's efforts. The cats felt weary and nervous. Across the lawn, the Alchemist's house, with its verdigris dome, its derelict iron-framed conservatories, and tall uncurtained windows seemed to be leaching the light out of the late evening air. They were reluctant to look at it. Instead, they sheltered just inside the boathouse, watching the fox—who didn't care about getting wet—quarter the sloping lawns, his nose to the leaf mold, the white patch on his hind leg the only bright item in the landscape. He came back and scratched vigorously behind one ear, showering the cats with coarse red hairs. Outdoors, he always seemed bigger than himself, energetic even when he sat down. "I remember this place," he said, "from the days of the old Majicou. We kept an eye on the comings and goings."

They waited for him to say more, but he only wandered off into the boathouse, sniffing and raising his leg like any dog.

"This rain isn't going to stop," said Leo.

"We are only putting things off," agreed her father comfortably. He stared up at the house. "We're a bit cautious about going in there," he explained, "but otherwise we're some damned determined animals."

She gave him a puzzled look.

"Come on." Tag sighed.

They fled across the lawns, over the wet flagstones of the terrace, and up the steps.

The entrance hall lay open to the weather, which had stripped and grayed the polished wood, blistered the gilt mirrors, and flecked the ornamental banister rails with rust. Double doors banged sadly in the wind. The usual detritus had blown across the floor and piled up in corners, ready to be of use to mice and rats. But a new layer of litter had been added since the day of Odin's disappearance. Someone had built a fire in the middle of the marble floor, using broken furniture from the adjoining rooms. Around its ashes were scattered empty gas cylinders, fast-food containers, the rags of blankets. "Human beings have been living here," decided Tag, wrinkling his nose at the sad odors of charred wood, stale food, urine.

The fox looked up.

"If you had a sense of smell," he said, "you would know more than that."

He had been sniffing intently about at the bottom of the stairs. Now he trotted across the room and gazed out across the lawns. "And yet I didn't notice it out there," he told himself thoughtfully.

"Didn't notice what?" said Tag.

"That's the thing," said Loves a Dustbin. "I don't know. Something else has been here recently. It wasn't human, but it certainly wasn't a cat."

"Where is Leonora?" said Ragnar.

🐾

Growing bored with their investigations, his daughter had taken to the stairs; by the time they thought to look for her, she was already two or three floors up.

There, gilt and marble gave way to fumed oak paneling. The landings were narrower, the windows smaller and less well proportioned. Cobwebs stretched in tight curves, dusty muslin set across every corner as if to trap the twilight. Underfoot was a gritty locss compounded of house dust, fallen plaster, and ash and soot expelled from ancient hearths. Small cold drafts crept forth to brush away Leonora's footprints as she passed. The stairwell closed in above her. She stopped in a ray of light from the last west-facing window—looked up, one paw raised—ran on. It was almost dark when she reached the room below the copper dome and found its door jammed open.

"I didn't feel frightened," she would insist later. "Not frightened, not at first."

It was a tall room with a ceiling shaped like an inverted tulip, braced by a tangle of old wooden beams. The walls had once been distempered white. Along them ran scarred workbenches topped with planished zinc, above which were mounted long glass-fronted cabinets, bookshelves, and sample cases. The cabinets were crowded with strangely shaped glassware—retorts and alembics glinting in the last of the light. There were rows of containers on shelves; medical tools on hooks; liquids, cloudy or clear, plain or colored, in which objects seemed to float. Crumpled in a corner—as if it had been thrown down yesterday in a fit of elation or disappointment or just at the end of long day's work—lay a worn leather apron covered in burns and cuts.

"The Alchemist!" she whispered. Tangled up in that castoff garment she might discover the mystery of her own birth, find herself at the heart of it all. "The Alchemist!"

The cold air, heavy with an odor at once visceral and corrosive, made her eyes water. Up under the ceiling, night gathered. Leonora could hear the faint, distant sussuration of the rain on the copper dome; but the room itself was so quiet, she thought, that silence itself would bring an echo there. She went about cautiously, sniffing one item, patting another in case it was alive, standing up on her hind legs to examine a third and instead catching sight of her own distorted reflection in the shiny retorts and beakers set out on a table. Papers. Hundreds of open books, their pages curled and blanched. Something unpleasant in a jar—she quickly looked away. She was reminded of the Reading Cat's domain, of a life so intensely focused it seemed to open on a vast illusory inner freedom. "No wonder he was defeated in the end," she whispered.

Then she realized there was no dust on the books.

The sound of the rain diminished. The silence was like an object, there in the room with her. Leonora began to back carefully toward the door.

Someone had been here before her. It was easy to see now which cabinets had been closed for years and which had been opened yesterday. It was easy to see which books had been flung down in impatience, which glassware knocked over, barely an hour ago, in clumsiness or rage. It was easy to see how the dust had been disturbed, but less easy to interpret the fresh scuff marks on the tiled floor.

Leonora had almost reached the door when the air in the center of the room began to fluoresce faintly. A few whitish sparks formed about a foot above the floor and drifted to and fro, first attracted to then repulsed by a strange smoky twist of light. The light was breathing. Leonora could hear it. Sparks went in and out. Then after a moment or two, a small convulsion like a sneeze took place, and a current of warm air was expelled into the room. Sparks whirled up now as if from a bonfire. She heard faint music. There was a popping sound, an apologetic cough. Leonora could not move. There was a flaw in the solid world, a discontinuity that grew and grew, then parted like rubbery human lips in the fabric of that nightmare place onto a darkness that curdled and took shape before her . . .

❧

Ragnar Gustaffson and Loves a Dustbin reached the top of the house just in time to hear Leonora's shriek of anger. When they burst into the room beneath the dome, it was full of brown shadows, disconnected movements, something that looked like smoke. Ragnar Gustaffson stood there confusedly for a moment, his eyes watering in the chemical reek, convinced the house was on fire.

"Leonora!" he called.

"I can't see her!" yelped the fox. "I can't see her!"

"Leonora!" they called together: "Leonora!"

But the new Majicou, arriving a little later, and entering the room with a curious mixture of calm and reluctance, narrowed his eyes and said nothing at all.

Leonora had backed deep into the gap between two wooden cupboards, and now—wedged fast, bubbling and spitting as much with loss of dignity as fear—faced the danger with bared claws. Above her, pacing angrily to and fro like a tiger in a cage, loomed a thing half cat, half man, the two halves shifting and roiling one into the other—one moment joined, the next separate, never quite properly connected, like shapes in a dream. It was bigger than any real human being. It was there, but it wasn't there. It was like a drawing made of smoke; yet under its onslaught the cupboards splintered and shook, and a single cumbersome sweep of one upper limb—neither arm nor leg, hand nor paw—was enough to clear cabinets and glassware off the wall and onto the floor. All the while it was groaning and roaring; and in its queer, grunting voice there was as much pain as rage.

The new Majicou watched it for a moment.

Then, "Be quiet," he told Ragnar and the fox. "This is for me to deal with."

"But—" began the fox.

"Do nothing unless I ask it of you."

With that, the new Majicou stepped into the center of the room. What happened next was unclear.

"Look away from me!" he ordered.

There was a ripping sound, like the one that sometimes precedes a peal of thunder, and an extraordinary flare of light that died quickly down through the spectrum to black. A cold, invigorating wind seemed to fill the space below the dome. There was a smell of snow. For an instant, Ragnar and Loves a Dustbin were confused enough to hallucinate a second huge figure in the room, a white tiger of the ice, cold green eyes in a charcoal-striped mask, teeth bared in a roar that shook the air in their lungs. Leonora's assailant, seeing it, too, turned and ran straight into the nearest wall. There was a quick flicker or ripple, and it was gone. Immediately, the cold wind died, and Tag was only Tag again, a silver-gray domestic cat standing rather tiredly in the center of the room under the appalled gaze of his friends. "You're safe now," he said, and went to sit by himself near the door. He seemed preoccupied, as if the encounter itself had been less interesting than the possibilities it suggested.

Ragnar Gustaffson stared up at the wall into which the apparition had vanished. "That is a trick," he said. "If you can do it." Then he set about coaxing his errant daughter out from between the cupboards. Loves a Dustbin, meanwhile, approached Tag and stared intently into his eyes. What he saw there didn't seem to reassure him.

"Take care," he advised.

"I can only do what I can do."

"Yet you mustn't exhaust yourself."

"What do you expect from me?" said the new Majicou impatiently.

The fox looked away.

"I saw your mentor burn himself to nothing, doing too often what you have just done," he warned. It seemed as if he would say more, then he seemed to shrug and went on instead, with a kind of morose satisfaction, "I knew something was wrong as soon as we arrived. I could smell it." He looked around disgustedly. "Any smell up here has been masked by these chemicals."

"I'm trying to think, actually," said Tag. "Would you mind leaving me alone?"

🐾

A little later, when he seemed in a better temper, Leonora went to thank him.

"I'm sorry," she said.

"So you should be, Leo. It would have killed you."

Leonora shivered.

"What was it?" she said. "The Alchemist?"

"No," said Tag. "It wasn't."

But she could see that something about the question had made him think.

" 'No cat has ever wanted to walk like a man,' " he whispered to himself. "Majicou used to say that. No cat has ever wanted to walk like a man. Unless—"

"What?" said Leo.

"I don't know," Tag said.

But he was on his feet now and quartering the room as if by willpower alone he could force things to give up their secrets. "Come on, Leo!" he urged. Ragnar and the fox, who had been sitting in a corner talking to each other in low voices, raised their heads to watch him. He studied the contents of splintered cabinets, eyed drifts of broken glass as if they might speak. He sniffed and coughed over the bitter spilled liquids of the alchemical trade. He took a moment to look up into the roof. Everywhere he went, books were piled in disarray, their covers stripped, their pages like broken white wings in the gathering darkness. It was the books that brought him to a halt.

"Look at this, Leo," he said.

He said, "My pride is to blame for this."

He laughed.

"What we have just seen here was a sideshow," he told himself, "not the main event. I saw that plainly, yet—"

His tail lashed from side to side.

"I have been a complete fool!" he cried.

"Ragnar! Loves a Dustbin! Think back," he asked them, "to the battle with the Alchemist. We were scattered in disarray across Tintagel Head. He loomed above us like death. Everything was lost, until the birth of the kittens! The Alchemist stared down at them, cried out in something like dismay, and faltered. In that moment, we had him. But we never asked ourselves why! We never asked what he had seen, what he had guessed, or why he lost his nerve so completely.

"Once I had recognized and accepted what happened in that moment," he told them, "so much of what has been hidden was made clear to me! There was no Golden Cat in the Mau's litter—only three odd but delightful kittens, each with a clear and recognizable quality of its own. We have asked ourselves again and again which of them might wear the mantle—Leo the dancer, full of subtlety and life; Isis the singer, whose voice speaks to the unseen, the way between the worlds; Odin, the hunter, closer of the circle. None of them has yet turned out to be what the Alchemist was seeking—the magic animal whose creation he had worked toward for three hundred years . . .

"Yet the Golden Cat has been with us since the moment Pertelot gave birth.

"Oh, it is a paradox, I admit, but I should have resolved it sooner. It is a tangled skein, but that is no excuse. Still—" here he stared grimly around "—I am the Majicou, and I believe we are still in time to retrieve the situation. Leo, stay close: without you they can do nothing. Hurry! We must get back to the oceanarium!"

Racing to keep up, his friends followed him back down the stairs, across the sodden lawn, and into the highway by the boathouse.

Part Three

The Bright Tapestry

Chapter Seventeen

THE FIELDS OF THE BLESSED

So it was with all the brazen opportunism of her earlier life that much later that day Sealink strolled up to a busy bait shop in the middle of a small fishing town and listened intently to a group of men leaning against a dusty pickup, drinking beer as the sun went down. When the group split and two of them climbed into the truck and pulled away, bound with their haul of crawfish for the Friday market, they left with an extra load on board: a thirteen-pound calico cat, already intent on making herself at least a fourteen-pound cat by the time they arrived at their mutual destination, by availing herself of their abundant hospitality.

In the dream it had seemed both extraordinary and perfectly normal that the Majicou, that mystical guardian of the roads, should appear to her and speak warmly as to a lifelong friend. When first he had shown her his face it was in his guise as the old black tomcat, a little grayed and ragged, his single pale eye stern yet gleaming with vitality. Yet it was in this embodiment that she found him most awesome, for she could sense that this manifestation was in some way a display, most likely not directed at her, of his burning will and self-determination—a measure of his true power.

"I apologize," the Majicou said. "My experiment with the Mammy and her bones was not entirely successful. I must, it seems, try something more straightforward. I can only pray I am granted the time . . .

"Come with me, Sealink, trust me—"

The next moment, the black cat was gone, and Sealink

261

found herself slipping deeper in the dream into a more profound and wilder place by far.

A creature four or five feet tall—with shoulder blades as sharp as knives, its fur of a savage, shiny black, dappled like woodland shade with faint tobacco-brown rosettes—sat nose to nose with a glorious tigress with paws as big as plates and teeth like scythes, the orange, black, and white harlequin patches of her calico coat strained by packed muscle to a network of vibrant bars and stripes. The scent that rose between them was rank and untamed, and their great, stony eyes rested unblinking upon each other.

Equal to equal now, Majicou opened his mind to the tigress. At once, a succession of images passed before her like beads on an abacus, shuttling past one after another as if propelled by an unseen hand.

At first there was darkness. Then, as if from a great distance, she perceived a great blur of movement, whirling and dancing like a dervish. She felt wind in her fur, a cold subterranean wind, and with it came a profound rumbling that vibrated inside the chambers of her skull. Mesmerized, she found she could not look away. She felt its pull upon her, deep inside the marrow of her bones. It was a feeling at once unpleasant and addictive.

For a moment she gave herself up to it, allowed it to draw upon her, like a tick upon a sheep. Then, revolted, she pulled free.

She heard the Mammy's voice and behind it the deeper roar of the Majicou, *"The wild roads are dying . . ."*

She saw the badger, untouched but with its life sapped away. She saw the white tomcat at the Farmer's Market, how his skin had slipped between her teeth, her own exhaustion on the roads . . .

And then she saw, spinning out of the vortex, something small and golden. It eddied before her in the darkness—a tiny golden triangle. She stared at it. She had seen it somewhere before. She remembered an earlier dream. Yes, she had seen it there. She remembered how the sunlight had struck off the armadillos' bone pile. Yes. But there was somewhere before that, somewhere important . . .

Concentrating hard on anything other than food was not something Sealink was used to. It made her head hurt. And the more her head ached, the more elusive the symbol became.

All at once there was a roar in the darkness, and the golden triangle broke apart into its component lines, shivering in the air. One aspect of it spiraled deliberately in front of her for a moment, then it was gone only to be replaced a second later by a small shape, a tiny golden creature who stared helplessly upward as if beset by something dark and formless, something that leaned over it in predatory rapture.

Sealink felt her heart thump painfully.

It was a kitten . . .

At once a great wave of empathy and love flowed out from her toward this helpless creature. Something in her recognized it not only as a kitten in distress but as a kitten she *knew*. Somehow—she could not imagine how or why—one of Pertelot's beloved kittens was in danger. She felt its presence, reaching out for her, and she felt, like a red blast in her head, its fury and its pain. The vision dissolved into night. This was followed by a flash, almost subliminal, of a city skyline, a city she knew well—then all was dark again.

Oblivious of fear in the heart of the dream, Sealink embraced her fate.

"Majicou, help me to find this kitten!"

Silence. Silence and darkness. A rush of air.

Then she was back in the presence of the great cat. The tobacco-brown rosettes shifted and flowed beneath the oily sheen of his fur. He opened his mouth and roared.

"There are miracles in this life, as there are in all lives. Take on this task and save the Golden Cat. Wish for the most impossible thing in the world with the wildest part of yourself and it shall be yours." He cocked his head. The one eye shone like a lamp. "Go now, Sealink, I—"

Suddenly he began to dwindle, his mouth opening and closing silently; then he started to spin away as if caught in the vortex of terrible power.

A wild thought struck the tigress as if from another life.

"The Fields of the Blessed!" she called after his receding form. "Where can I find them?"

The Majicou made one last, desperate effort. Twisting for a moment out of the gravity that drew him down, he opened his mouth and roared. The howl of the wind carried his first words away. All that remained was this, "Be yourself. Never give up hope. I have great faith in you, Sealink!"

🐾

The truck drove through the night and Sealink dozed in the back, sated with crawfish. The stars shone down upon her unchanged. It was hard to imagine that the world could be such a terrible place when its skies looked so serene. But in the dark places of the earth, hidden from view? That was a different matter.

Sealink shivered.

She was alone in the world. Her friends and allies were either dead or thousands of miles away, caught in their own spirals of destiny. The task that lay before her was at once enormous and, in parts, obscure. The odds, of course, were weighted against her.

Some might regard her circumstances as hopeless, she conceded. But Majicou's message to her, words like a precious cargo rescued from a shipwreck, had stiffened her resolve: *"Be yourself. Never give up hope. I have great faith in you, Sealink."*

With the reckless abandon she had come to cherish as a true mark of her independent spirit, Sealink cast away her despair. She imagined it flying over the side, whirled off like a sacrifice to the winds of motion, to join the dust devils the truck left in its wake. Face into the wind, the calico cat smiled. The light of the dying moon struck off her teeth so that they gleamed with red, and the colors of her coat streamed like the war pennants of an invading army.

🐾

It was almost dawn when the truck rattled down Highway 90, along the West Bank Expressway, and over the Crescent City Connection to deliver Sealink back into New Orleans. In the east, the towers of the Central Business District lay black against the lightening sky.

She watched the buildings glide past and felt her spirits rise. *"Move, and the world moves with you."* So she had advised the Queen of Cats on the deck of a bobbing boat that was bearing them away from a city filled with horrors, a city on another continent entirely. *"That's what traveling's for— putting distance between yourself and your past."*

And yet here she was: traveling straight back into the arms of her own.

Strangely enough, it felt right. Straightforward to the point of bluntness, Sealink was inclined to tackle matters head-on. She greatly preferred to administer a sharp cuff to the use of tact. And she was looking forward to applying a bit of that to an old friend.

She had already marked Kiki la Doucette down as her first objective.

Sealink stored up her grudges with fastidious care, keeping them safely parceled away in a quiet place in her head, only taken out and dealt with when the right opportunity presented itself. And some grudges were more significant than others.

She could understand why Kiki might want to surround herself with sycophantic hangers-on who brought her so much food she had become gargantuan. Hell, yes, she could understand that.

Old insults and scratches traded on the boardwalk when the Delta Queen had been coming into her sexual maturity, lovers lost and lovers stolen—nothing so terrible there.

But Kiki was a stealer of *kittens.*

She had stolen the kittens of the cemetery cats.

And she had stolen Sealink's own. The calico considered for a brief moment how Kiki had, in fact, rescued the survivors, then dismissed the thought entirely. What remained was that she had left two to gasp out their last breaths on the river's cold shoreline. She had raised another two in her own vile image. And she knew the whereabouts of the fifth.

Find her, then, and settle the score. If anyone knew the whereabouts of kittens, it was Kiki la Doucette.

🐾

When the pickup came to a halt at the top of North Peters Street, Sealink was up and off before the doors were opened. Through the smoky half light she trotted, purposeful and resolute, with one thought in her head: catch la Mère while she's dozing and savage the truth out of her—get a hold on her throat that will have her wheezing for mercy. She imagined the sensation of thick, fat flesh in her mouth, a feeble pulse beating against her teeth, her claws sunk to their roots in the body of her enemy.

But when she arrived in the courtyard behind the tourist shops of the French Market, there was no sign of Kiki or any of her miserable retinue. The area was deserted. At the Café du Monde, there was not even a sparrow to be found. She crossed a Decatur Street empty of traffic and entered the park through its ornate iron gate. An air of dereliction had settled upon the guano-spattered benches, the silent statues, and summer-dusty trees; and the cathedral presided over the scene like a grim sentinel over a long-abandoned battlefield. Sealink quartered the square. She sniffed beneath the myrtles and banana palms. Old traces of cat: faint scents and urine markings. Nothing fresh. It was as if every French Quarter cat had vanished.

She nosed around the waste bins. No cats had called here, either. Humans had, though. She leapt onto the edge and, balancing precariously, helped herself to the day-old remains of a sausage po'boy. The mustard made her eyes sting, but cheerfully sustained by its greasy calories she trotted out into the spacious sidewalk, where during the day caricaturists and mime artists entertained passing trade, and was suddenly assailed by a terrible stench.

Even through the aftertaste of mustard and ketchup the power of the smell was phenomenal. It hung in the air like a solid presence. Sealink's eyes started to water so that she saw the source of the stink through bleary vision. Someone had fastened a large and rusty grate to the railings beside the park entrance. It stood at a forty-five-degree angle to the ground, and beneath it lay a heap of cooling, blackened ashes. Little wisps of smoke still rose from the embers, and it was this smoke that hurt her eyes. But it was less the ashes than their provenance that held Sealink in thrall; for, bound to the gate with wire, its whole body twisted up and away from where the flames must have leapt, was a skeletal shape, clumped and charred like ancient, flaky wrought iron, the tragic remnants of its head a rictus of silent agony and outrage. In the midst of so much soot, its teeth shone white as pearls, weaponry terribly outclassed by that of its opponents.

Sealink felt her legs go from under her. She sat down on the cold, hard stone and felt shocked reaction shudder through her in waves.

Someone had burned a cat. Deliberately, and in a very public place.

Without any conscious thought, she found her feet and put them to good use. She ran and ran through the dawn-lit streets until she was stopped by the four-lane highway of North Rampart Street. On the other side of the road, the crumbling walls of the old boneyard rose up; above them, still white angels and a woman with a cross, her hand raised in greeting, or warning. Early-morning traffic rumbled past, expelling noxious fumes. Sealink breathed deeply. Even diesel oil was preferable to the stench that followed her, so she sat by the side of the road and let the exhaust smoke infuse her coat.

She sat there, motionless, in a sort of daze.

The next thing she knew, there was a screech of brakes and a shrill voice shrieking out of a car window: "Look—a great big one—we could get us at least ten dollars for it!"

There was a din of doors opening and slamming and a clamor of voices, and Sealink ran for her life. A big ten-wheeler missed her by inches, its air horn blaring wildly. A station wagon swerved around her. In the other direction, a truck jammed on its brakes, and its tires screeched against the tarmac. The last car came straight at her. She just had time to see a pair of hands clutching the steering wheel with white knuckles, a manic face leaning forward, mouth open in fury or triumph, and then there was darkness. Hot metal seared the fur on her back. A fiery pain and burning fur. Vile fumes engulfed her. Sealink had time to feel a terrible, sad irony at this useless loss of life, when suddenly there was light and air again and she realized that the car had passed right over her.

She stared wildly around, barely able to believe her luck, then scrambled for the sidewalk and fled through the gates of the St. Louis Cemetery.

Inside the boneyard all was quiet.

Around the back of one of the tombs she sat down and inspected the damage. It really wasn't too bad, considering. A patch of fur in the middle of her back was dark and sticky, the hairs fused together by heat. It tasted nasty when she licked it. But the worst casualty was her tail. Sealink had always been vain about this attribute. Her tail had been the subject of a thousand compliments and admiring glances. It was a barometer of her inner climate: held high and tip curled when she was happy; thin and lowered when rarely she felt depressed; and when it fizzed and dilated, a wise cat took to its heels. But now a strip of skin and fur had been torn right off the end of her great and gorgeous plume so that it ended in raw pink on one side and ragged hair on the other.

Sealink gave a little wail of despair.

"Where y'at, sister?"

She looked up, startled. It was Hog, the big stripy neuter.

"Hell, honey, forget me: all I lost's my tail. Should be grateful for small mercies, huh?"

Hog dropped silently off the mausoleum to land in front of her. He inspected the wound solemnly. "Say, you had a narrow escape there, lady. Unlike the rest of us."

"Hog, where is everyone?"

"They's mainly gone. We lost Téo, y'know."

Sealink nodded dumbly.

"Heard the Pestmen took her." He regarded the calico askance. After a pause, which Sealink failed to fill, he continued. "Some kids took old Tulane, put him in a bag. We never seen him again. An' Azelle, she wandered off, said she was goin' to search for her babies." His eyes went blank with memory. "Others, they just lay down an' died . . . of the sickness, y'know. They was glad to go by then. Kiki's band stole two of our remainin' kitties—slipped through the gates when there was no moon and carried 'em off. They laughed at us— too sick, too tired and slow to stop 'em." He sighed.

"We've had a few new arrivals since then. Owners kicked

'em out, decided they didn't like cats after all. Now we all starvin' together—"

He stopped abruptly, for he had lost the calico's attention. She was staring above his head, eyes round with surprise. Her whiskers trembled. Then her coral lips stretched into the most beatific of smiles.

"My, my—fallen on hard times, have you, my angels? Seems there may be a little justice in the world after all."

Crouched on top of the tomb above Hog, under the protective hands of a praying plaster child, were two large tabby cats, their coats a little thinner, their expressions a little less assured, a little less arrogant than the last time Sealink had seen them in the dusty storeroom of the Golden Scarab bookshop.

Kiki's helpers.

Venus and Sappho.

Sealink's daughters.

And even as she recognized them she remembered something else. Something that had evaded her all this time.

❦

Life had recently dealt the erstwhile bookshop cats a number of setbacks; but the revelation of one half of their parentage left them speechless with disbelief. Sealink watched with slow, grim satisfaction as the information settled and was absorbed.

"Well, I guess you never could accuse Kiki of behaving toward us in a motherly way," Sappho said eventually. "She'd upped and gone by the time we were thrown out. Didn't leave any forwarding address."

"She can't have gone far, not being so fat n'all," said Hog. "But no one's seen her around in a day or so."

"Not since the burning." Venus hung her head.

Sealink turned upon her. "What do you know about that?"

"I heard it was a cat who crossed her was burned."

The calico shook her head slowly. "None of this makes sense to me. Whole world's gone crazy. Sure wasn't Kiki who raised that grill and tied that poor creature up; nor who struck the match, neither."

"But she bin there, in the square. I bin seeing her, *cher*."

A new voice had joined the group. It belonged to a color-point with a squashed-in face that Sealink recognized vaguely from her last visit to the old cemetery.

"Hey, there, Celeste. Where you been?" asked Hog. "We been worried for you, thought you was a goner."

The colorpoint gave him a gummy grin, revealing three ivory teeth and a furred tongue. "Don't y'all worry about me, *bébé*. I too skinny and too wily for those humans. Sides, how could I stay away from my *cher*?" She rubbed her dry old cheek against his head until he purred. Sealink watched in surprise. Hog might have lost his balls, but he didn't seem to have lost his touch.

"*Oui*, I seen Kiki, sure enough. It was after the crowds had moved on, and the light was fadin'. She was sittin' there, watchin' that poor dead crittur, and she was smilin'. And as I watched, a little gust came out of nowhere like a little whirl-wind, y'know?—and there's *des mouches*, big blue flies, comin' out of it like the fellas you get around trash and they's hummin' and buzzin' fit to bust. Made my head itch to hear 'em. Then all the dust and bits of garbage and the ashes from *le mort* gets caught up in this wind, and it's all whirlin' and spinnin', and the buzzin' gets louder and louder; and Kiki, she's still just sittin' there smilin' and smilin' with her big yellow teeth, *comme ça*—" Celeste gave a hideous parody of a contented cat's grin "—and her coat's all ruffled, and her eyes go all lazy like someone's strokin' her; and then she starts to talk to it. Made me shiver up my spine to see her." She shuddered theatrically. "World ain't right when a cat talks to the wind. *C'est crack*." She lowered her voice. "But when the wind talks back . . ."

The boneyard cats stared at her. "The wind spoke?"

The colorpoint's skin twitched as if reliving an earlier repulsion.

Her audience stared expectantly.

"I heard it sigh—" She stopped suddenly.

"What?" cried Venus impatiently. "What then?"

Celeste scratched her ear. "I ain't sure if I should tell you this next bit or not. Y'all t'ink I gone nuts."

"We won't, I promise," Hog said gently. He held the color-point's amber gaze for a moment or two till she carried on.

"*Eh bien*— Now of all my faculties, it's my hearin' bin least affected, so y'all got no cause to t'ink I gone deaf or crazy, y'hear? On all that's sacred, I heard it sigh, and then all those flies they spoke wit' a man's voice."

Sealink frowned. "Honey, run that past me again."

"I know flies don't usually talk—"

Sealink squinted at her.

"—but I know what I heard. The wind, it sighed and it buzzed, and then it spoke with a human's voice. And it said, quite clearly, *'Come here, my dear. I need your soul, too.'* And then there's this other voice, deep and dark, like it's tryin' to drown out the first one. A cat's voice. So *then* I lissen real good. And it sayin', over and over, *'Save the kittens. For the sake of all cats, save the kittens . . .'* And then there's a great roar from inside the wind, and then, well then, *chers*, then I took off as fast as my old legs'd carry me, and even so, I swear I could hear the buzzin' of those flies and Madame Kiki laughin' at me all the way.

"There's witchery abroad, *mes chers,* witchery and mayhem."

Later that night the boneyard cats sat huddled together inside one of the larger tombs. There was nothing left to eat. Sealink had searched the garbage cans in the nearby projects and come away empty pawed. She had, in fact, discovered the remains of some spicy chicken in one plastic bag and without a second's pause had wolfed it down and only then found herself trembling with embarrassment at her own greed; but the shame barely outlasted the taste of the spices.

In order to assuage her conscience she went out to look for more and discovered her luck had not, after all, deserted her. Some kids, returning with takeout from a local Chinese place, were fooling around on their bikes. Remembering the hunting cry from the car window, she skittered between the wheels, causing quite a stir. Shouting and pedaling furiously they had given chase; but the calico, slimmer and fitter after these lean weeks, was quicker. She nipped up and over the wall and, doubling back to where they'd dropped the food, seized a fragrant carton between her substantial jaws and legged it back to the cemetery.

The noodles were messy, and eating them fast resulted in a certain amount of nose bumping, but everyone agreed it was the best food they'd ever tasted.

Afterward, as they groomed one another's fur, Sealink regaled them with stories of food she had stolen on her travels; and as she did so the eyes of her daughters grew round and admiring. She reminisced about oysters in Detroit, lasagne in Los Angeles, and alligator sausage here in N'Awlins. She had eaten beef enchiladas in Guadalajara, prawn soup with lily buds in Phuket, pork and pumpkin curry in Rangoon, *galbi jim* in South Korea, and cullen skink in South Shields.

"Food like that," she concluded, as if completing an old mantra, "makes you proud in your flesh."

She looked around. The cats who gazed back at her were still proud, even if their flesh hung a little loose, and some of them were drooling. They were the last free cats of the French Quarter, and she needed their help.

"Bad things been happening for some time," she said abruptly. Her voice echoed around the tomb. "And now we're seeing bad things go to worse. We don't do something to stop all this, there won't be nothing good left.

"I came back here from another country, an old country across the sea. While I was there I seen some *real* scary stuff . . ."

And she told them about the Alchemist and his pursuit of the Queen of Cats, how he had subverted the wild roads and used cats to do his bidding; how he had determined to steal her kittens, believing one of them to be the famed Golden Cat.

"And now one of those three kittens is here, in New Orleans. And I think I had a part in delivering that very kitten to its fate." She regarded her two daughters steadily. "You might remember a certain package—?"

There was a sharp intake of breath. Venus stared at her mother, aghast.

"Kiki's *cadeau*." It was less a question than a statement of fact.

"Kiki's *cadeau*. The package you two offered up to me. The one I dragged, through the streets of the Quarter. The one Red tried to persuade me to open. And I, stupid and uncomprehending, refused to do so; gave him a darned good bite for his pains and hurried off to present it to Madame Kiki, nice and intact. And when I laid it down on the ground at her feet, it squirmed, right there in front of me! And what did I do?" She laughed bitterly. "I ran away. It's something I've become damn good at lately."

"We didn't know it was a kitten." Even Sappho, the snootier of the two, looked shocked. She stared at her sister. "We wouldn't have given her a *kitten*. Let alone a *golden* kitten . . ."

"A golden kitten is sacred to the Great Cat . . ."

"It is a powerful being . . ."

"Enough of the metaphysics," Sealink said briskly. "All I know is I got a job to do, and it starts with Kiki la Doucette. I met up with her mother in the bayous—"

"Eponine Lafeet!" Celeste's tail twitched rapidly.

Hog looked surprised.

"Kiki's the Mammy's *daughter*?"

"*Cher*, you just too young to remember," admonished the colorpoint.

"Honey—" Sealink addressed herself to the big stripy cat "—don't you go strainin' your brain none." She raised her voice. "Yep. The Mammy. She said to me, among a load of nonsense I can't understand, something about seeking a sun of fire in the Fields of the Blessed. Now I don't know what the hell that means, but it seems to me that if Kiki ain't in any of her normal haunts, these fields is where I might find her."

Sappho laughed. "Paradise? Kiki la Doucette in the Happy Land?"

Sealink looked puzzled. "Ain't that a bar down on Bourbon—"

Venus giggled.

The calico turned on her. "What's so funny?"

Sappho sniffed in a superior sort of way. "It's from Greek

poetry. A translation of *Elysian Fields*, where the blessed souls gather. I think it's in Homer."

Sealink stared at her daughter, unsure whether or not she was being mocked. She wondered how she ever came to have daughters who knew about Greek poetry. The nearest she had come to it herself was a sultry night on the beach at Kos . . .

"I heard that somewhere before. Elysian Fields." She screwed her face up. Then her eyes brightened. "Shine. Shine the mule. Ain't it where the mules go when they retire?"

Sappho curled her lip. "I wouldn't know about that. I've never spoken to a *mule*."

🐾

Decatur Street was quiet that night. Five cats of various colors crouched under the wheels of a dented dark blue Plymouth and watched the road. Ahead of them, stretching up toward Jackson Square, the mule carts were lined up, waiting their turn for the passing tourist trade.

"Stay here," hissed Sealink. "I'll go find Shine."

Easier said than done. She dodged in and out of the parked cars, slipped silent and apprehensive between slow feet, in and out of the colorful chassis and spoked wheels. The first two mules she checked out sniffed cautiously at her, then blew air noisily out of their nostrils. Sealink ran on. The third mule skittered sideways. The next one tried to kick her. On down the line she passed, but none of them was Shine. At the head of the queue she stopped and stared around. No further cover. She crouched beneath the mule cart with her heart pounding.

A curious head peered between its legs at her, failed to get a proper view, and tried to twist around.

"Who are you, cat? What you want?"

Sealink shuffled closer to its head, keeping a wary eye on the human feet passing on the sidewalk.

"I'm looking for a mule called Shine."

The mule snorted.

"What you want with *dat* old bag of bones?"

The calico persisted. "Do you know where I might find her?"

"Sure, if you wants a ride in a cart that overturns. Maybe

get kicked in the stomach if you're real lucky. Besides, what's a cat doin' out on the streets of this city, as bold as a mutt?"

Sealink didn't feel all that bold at the moment.

"Don't you know there's a price on your head?" The mule continued mercilessly, "If Shine don't get you then the Pestmen will!" It whinnied its amusement. "Humans, they don't like cats none at the present time. Burned one down near the Cabildo yesterday. Boy, did that smell *bad*."

"Look. I'm risking my neck here. Do you know where Shine is or not?"

No reply.

"Or the Elysian Fields?"

The mule bent its head around and gave her a hard look.

"I ain't speaking to *you* of such things. You's a *cat*." In case Sealink hadn't noticed. "But if you want Shine you might go right the way back down Decatur by the market, where you'll find a café servin' Creole food. Can't recall the name, but you'll have no problem findin' it. Its window gets all steamed up. That's where Joey goes when trade's bad, parks the cart right outside. Old Shine, she give us all a bad name, so we don't make room for her in the queue. I hear old Joey's going to retire her soon. Won't be before time. No, ma'am."

Scalink didn't even hear this last remark: she was already haring up the street to her companions.

In the shadow of the parked car, they stared out at her, round eyed.

"Did you find her?" Hog asked.

"Follow me."

❦

Past the Margaritaville and on toward the crossroad with Barracks, the north end of Decatur Street was a quiet and seedy place at this time of night. Which suited Sealink's purpose fine since, where it was darker, there were generally fewer people. And indeed, pulled up at the side of the road was a familiar sight: a black-and-red cart and a mule with its ears poking through an old felt hat.

Shine the mule stood outside Enrico's café, listening to the dull humor of the men inside. Her breath steamed in the air. It wasn't a cold evening, but Shine had found a way of super-heating her breath so that it came out as a satisfying white vapor. If she kept her mouth shut tight and drew the air up out of her lungs very, very slowly it worked best. She blew another jet. After a while she grew bored with that and started to paw the ground, tracing patterns in the dirt with her hooves. The gaudy neon of the café lights struck off the brasses on her harness.

As the five cats approached she looked up in surprise.

"Remember me?" Sealink touched noses with the mule.

Shine sniffed at her, velvet muzzle twitching with sudden interest.

"Sure I do. You were nice to me once."

"I came here to ask you a question," Sealink said without further preamble. "I was told by a friend of mine that you spoke of one day going to the Elysian Fields . . ."

The mule's long pink lips stretched into some approximation of a smile. "Fields of the Blessed. Oh my. Ah, yes. Green grass there, long green grass and the shade of sweet-smelling trees." She blinked, long-lashed lids covering eyes of liquid night. "The Elysian Fields."

"Do you know where they are?"

The mule regarded her obliquely. "Honey, if I knew where they were, why do you think I'd be standin' here, watchin' my life ebb into the night outside Enrico's café?"

There was no answer to that. The calico's disappointment must have showed in her face, for after a moment or two the mule said, " 'Don't be so downcast.' Ain't that what you advised me? Life can't be that bad, honey, can it?"

"I've kinda hit a dead end," Sealink said softly. She looked back over her shoulder at the four cats watching this exchange. "Thought I had an answer to a mystery, but it didn't lead nowhere. That's what you get for following your hunches."

The mule dipped its head conspiratorially. "Want to go for a ride?"

"What?"

"Come for a ride—you and your friends. I ain't tied up."

Sealink hesitated, then she grinned. "Hell, why not? We got nothing to lose."

Some minutes later a small black gig with a fringed canopy and wheels gaily painted red might have been seen disappearing smartly up Esplanade Avenue, heading lakeward with five cats. As they went, the calico sat on the mule's back, her claws buried anxiously in the leather harness, and explained their situation to Shine: how a cat called Kiki la Doucette had betrayed her own kind, how people were paying for cats to be caught and killed, how they had burned a cat at Jackson Square, and how a very special kitten—and a great deal more—was at risk.

Shine was philosophical. "Man is a fierce wild animal at heart," she opined. "We usually see it only in that tamed condition of restraint known as civilization, and so—" she turned her head in order to make eye contact with the cat on her shoulder "—the occasional outbreaks of its true nature terrify us."

🐾

Some time later they crossed a turning bounded by clapboard houses with peeling blue shutters and came upon a yellow dog sitting by the side of the road. It had no collar, and its tongue lolled cheerfully out of its mouth. As they approached, it looked up and did a double take. Its lower jaw hung suddenly slack.

"Hi there, honey!" Sealink declared cheerfully.

The dog gazed at her. "Oh, my Lord," it said. "Do I truly see a mule cart full of cats driving up Esplanade?"

"You sure do, son." Sealink was enjoying herself.

The dog started to trot alongside. "May I be so bold," it said, keeping pace with Shine, claws tapping on the sidewalk, "as to enquire why that might be?"

The calico laughed a little bitterly. "Honey, it's a nice night."

The dog cocked its head at her. The moonlight glinted off his full black eye. "That's not what I'd heard."

"Now what can you mean, honey?"

The dog looked shifty. During the silence that followed, Sealink noticed that he was quite an old animal—that his coat was rather unkempt and that his claws were blunt with road travel.

"You ain't from around here, are you?" she asked softly.

"No, ma'am. I'm something of a traveler, myself. I've taken a truck ride here, a bus ride there. I've crossed the country from east to west and back again. I've been to New York and New Mexico, Old Forge and Ocean City—"

Sealink found herself grinning. "Ah, the journey is the life, hon. You and me must be soul mates beneath the skin!"

"But I've never been to New Orleans before," he continued, ignoring the calico's interruption, "and I don't think I'll be coming back for a while."

Sealink gave him a hard stare.

"What I mean—what I *heard*," he said, returning the look, "is that it may not be such a nice night for some. Some cats, anyhow."

"Go on."

"I heard there was something going on—some kind of gathering to do with cats up on the Elysian Fields. Didn't sound too pleasant."

A sharp electrical current ran the length of the calico's spine. The raw tip of her tail twitched involuntarily.

"The Elysian Fields. Do you know where they are?"

The dog opened his mouth to answer, and as he did so, a car came around the corner, blaring its horn as if it were a weapon.

Shine bucked, one lashing hoof catching the back bumper as the vehicle sped past. Then she started to run. Shine had never in her life run while pulling her cart; even at Joey's insistence she had barely even broken into a trot, but now she took the corner at such speed that two wheels of the gig came clear off the ground. Sealink, slung sideways by the momentum, found herself flying suddenly and spectacularly through the air, legs pinwheeling. She tumbled over a broken picket fence, through an untidy privet hedge, and at last came to rest in a heap among a clutter of terra-cotta and pelargoniums.

With the adrenaline of outrage combating any immediate sense of physical injury, she sat up and looked around. It would be hard to pretend that plowing through a hedge had been deliberate. Had anyone seen her ignominious descent?

The yellow dog was still at the junction, his sharp muzzle turned in her direction. Sealink ducked away from his steady gaze and started to groom furiously, noticing as she did so that her head hurt and one eye was already beginning to close.

"Hell of a day," she muttered.

Satisfied with the cursory licking, she shook out each leg in turn and a shower of privet twigs, dirt, and petals scattered from the long quasi–Maine Coon coat. Everything appeared to be in working order. Sealink nodded grimly, then clenched her teeth and leapt the fence to follow the disappearing buggy.

The yellow dog watched all this with a quizzical expression on his face. This was a crazy place. Still, that big old calico cat sure had some grit. Grinning lopsidedly, he followed the strange cavalcade as it rounded the bend into the long, wide, nondescript boulevard known as Elysian Fields.

🐾

WORK: THE GREAT LIBERATOR read the proclamation in rusted wrought iron on either side of the black-barred gates. Raised after the fire that swept the city in 1794, on the Feast of the Immaculate Conception, the building behind these gates had been in its time a mill and cotton warehouse, stuffed with bales for export to the Old World; a slave market; a poorhouse; and latterly the place where the broken-down workhorses and mules of the city were sent to be dispatched into the great, blue beyond—or, more likely, into a thousand cans of dog food. Down the generations, borrowing from the road on which it resided some of the sense of the original Greek, it had passed into mythology as a place of well-earned peace: the fields of the blessed.

It had not operated as a knacker's yard for many years now.

But it still smelled of old blood.

🐾

As Shine and the buggy, containing four cats clinging to the cracked leather seat with their claws buried up to the hilt, emerged at the junction with Hope, the calico cat and the yellow dog caught up with them.

The mule hung her head. "I got spooked," she explained to Sealink. "Sorry. Climb aboard again, chile, and I'll continue my tour." She scanned the lifeless avenue. "Though it ain't exactly the scenic route."

Sealink turned to bid farewell to the dog, but it had wandered off to nose around the base of a rusted iron gatepost farther up the street. Venus shook her head. "Canines," she enunciated with disdain. "They just can't resist making their own scent mark wherever another dog has pissed."

But the yellow dog, having completed his study of the iron post, left it unblemished and slipped through the open gates. He walked cautiously up to the flaking wooden doors of the building and started to sniff around. The hackles rose down his back like the crests of a small dinosaur. Then he recoiled as if his nose had been assaulted, and, as Sealink was wondering what could smell so awful that a *dog* would be repulsed, he turned and fled back to the buggy.

"Welcome to the Fields of the Blessed," he announced, panting. "I think we found that gathering. There are humans in there. And cats. A lot of cats—"

Hog and Celeste leapt down from the cart.

"—not all of them alive."

Venus and Sappho stayed rooted to the seat.

"Get back on the buggy," Shine ordered. "We're going in!"

The renegade mule with a spitting calico cat on her shoulder and a buggy full of ferals cannoned through the main doors of the old knacker's yard on the Elysian Fields, straight into a scene out of a nightmare.

The last time Sealink had witnessed anything similar, it had been in a decommissioned warehouse in another country, a warehouse lying between Carib Dock and Pageant Stairs, a warehouse that stank of terror and human sweat, smoke and friar's balsam; where a defiant Queen and her brave King had faced off the Alchemist and an army of cats with eyes as empty as glass.

Sealink stared. There was smoke here, too, a lot of smoke. Some came from exotic incense and vast candles burning in brass dishes on the floor; but the stuff that stung her eyes came from the pyre that dominated the center of the great stone floor. As the smoke eddied and whirled, Sealink could make out a pile of bones, higher and more newly rendered than the last she had seen, a great heap of skeletal remains spitting out flame and reeking vapor.

A bonfire.

A sun of fire.

A bone fire.

On the top its latest victim, unrecognizable in its death throes, rested on a dozen others whose fur still smoldered and whose glazed eyes reflected ever more dimly the leaping flames. All around moved humans in dark robes.

As the mule cart gate-crashed into their gathering, these humans stared at the intruders, mouths open, almost comic in their surprise. Some held cats by the scruff of the neck, bodies drooping, all the fight gone out of them. Others dragged crates closer to the pyre, fiddled with hinges, clumsy in their big leather gloves. Others still poked at the fire, feeding it with a fuel that sent up unnatural-looking flames of green and blue. A smaller group knelt at the back, oblivious of the ruckus, eyes closed, chanting in a language Sealink did not understand. From somewhere in the cavernous room, echoing among the iron girders, came the sound of perverse, arrhythmic music: bells, a reed flute, small drums. A disembodied human voice, that said, slowly and indistinctly, as if with much effort from a great distance, "Bring me the kitten now. Bring her to the fire."

Sealink had heard *that* voice before.

She looked wildly around the room, but the Alchemist was nowhere to be seen. How could he be? She had seen him die on the cliff tops at Tintagel. There was nothing to betray any supernatural presence except a column of milky light, illuminated from within with dark reds and blues like the arteries and veins of a whole new life-form, pulsing and straining with some horrid birth. Where the column spun close to the pyre, fragments of bone and fur were sucked into its path to join the *danse macabre*, and with each new arrival the light grew stronger, the voice more demanding.

"Bring it to me *now*!"

For a moment the smoke cleared; and Sealink saw on the other side of the flames a sight that made her heart stop, then beat like hammer blows in her chest.

A huge ginger cat haloed with fire.

A cat whose tabby markings swirled like a magnetic field in storms of ocher and orange and cream. A cat with an irregular patch of black that spread from ear to eye, lending him a distinctly untrustworthy air.

It was Red.

And by his side a smaller black-and-white cat: Téophine, bristling with fighting chemicals, her lips drawn back from gapped teeth.

Between them, a small golden shape, curled into itself like a dead insect.

Sealink's heart felt as though it would burst.

Isis. Oh, Isis. Pertelot's smallest kitten, lying as though dead.

The calico's mouth opened in a wail.

"Isis!"

At the sound of her name, the kitten's ears twitched, once, twice. As though awoken from a long, slow dream of Egypt, she stirred.

The column seemed to become agitated. It flexed, bending from the middle to lower over the kitten. Lights went out within the milky haze.

Dapples of violet ran like fingers over the golden coat. The kitten stretched her supple backbone. Her tail flicked from side to side. Crouching on her haunches, she extended her front paws, a miniature sphinx. Then she lifted her head and opened her mouth.

An unearthly sound ripped through the air. It was not discordant. It was not harmonious. It was a sound neither natural nor synthetic; it was a sound that defied interpretation.

All at once there was pandemonium.

The mule skittered, and the occupants of her cart shot out into the room with their fur on end. Humans clamped hands over ears and their eyes began to water. As if from nowhere, ruptured highways flickered into life on the edges of the room. A dozen cats burst out of these, followed by a dozen more, stolen away from whatever journeys they were making on the wilds roads of Louisiana. Drawn toward the nexus in the knacker's yard they came, fur streaming in the highway winds, dwindling second by second from their great cat forms—a leopard here, a lion there, a rosette-coated jaguar, a puma, a lynx . . .

As if the advent of these highways had released a new energy into the room, the column of light flared up suddenly, then flew apart into two separate streams. Joined only at the base, they danced like two cobras—high in the air, looming up the walls and the tall, barred windows, sending grotesque shadows flying across the floor. Voices could be heard from within, echoing vaguely as if from the depths of a well, indistinct through the kitten's song; then there came a determined suspension of sound as the two streams fled back together in a sudden rush of air, to twine in a violent struggle.

Isis opened her mouth wider still and the sound swelled. It wavered through a succession of eerie musical registers, finally resolving itself into a single powerful note.

The bone fire collapsed as if it had imploded. Smoke and ash swelled into the air in billowing clouds. The dual streams of light went out, as though someone had thrown a switch. There was a great, dark roar; then a despairing voice could be heard fading to a vibration, like a ghost of itself, in the recesses of their skulls. In the sudden darkness humans wailed and ran out into the street, pursued by the larger cats.

Somehow in all this, Shine had lost her cart. It lay now on one side, wheels spinning. The mule herself, unnerved by the scene she had interrupted, stood motionless at the edge of the pyre, staring into the pile of smoldering corpses.

"Oh, my. Were they alive when they came to this?" she said softly.

"Some of them."

Shine swiveled around to face the speaker. A grossly fat cat had appeared behind her. "But some of them died of fear before they made it that far!" It laughed so hard that spittle shot out through yellowed teeth. Jowls wobbled over a shiny collar. Behind this monstrosity stood a collection of well-muscled cats, their coats gleaming with ill-gotten health and vitality.

"I've come for my *cadeau*," said Kiki la Doucette, her eyes focusing past Shine to the pitiful gathering of cats on the other side of the bone fire. "Now that my master has no further use for it." But between her and her goal stood a large calico cat and her friends from the St. Louis Cemetery. Kiki curled her lip. Her followers' whiskers bristled in anticipation.

"My, my." La Mère trembled with delight. She raised her voice. "Why, I do believe it's the Delta Queen."

Sealink glared at her.

"And look: she has located her own dear daughters. How very . . . touching. Kill them all." She waved a bored paw in their general direction.

At once a number of Kiki's band surged forward.

The calico cat flexed her claws. She looked about her with devastating calm, assessing the odds, gave a little satisfied smile. "Here's something I understand, at last," she said to the little group behind her. "I been spoiling for a fight for some time now."

"Can't wait," grunted Hog. He squared his wasted shoulders.

Two of the collared cats came bounding toward them.

"Come on, then," Sealink growled. "Come and play with Momma."

The two males—a short-haired tabby and a long-haired gray—charged at her, backs arched and fur on end. As thick as kapok, the calico's coat confounded tooth and claw. She hit the first one hard on the side of his ear and bowled him over. At once, Hog leapt upon him. The second, and smaller of the two, Sealink simply fell on. He went down with a soughing sigh as the air rushed out of his lungs, then lay there dazed.

The next two came, and Celeste hurled herself at one, burying the few teeth she had left in its throat while Hog and Sealink dealt with the other. Fur and howls of rage flew into the air.

They came in waves after that. Sealink fought savagely. Like the feral queen she was, she bit and tore—a whirlwind of fury.

"That's for Mousebreath!" she muttered grimly, raking the back of a lithe black tomcat now fleeing for its life. "And that's for my lost kitten." A patchwork cat was bowled over.

"You been destroying your own—" she mumbled through a mouthful of gray fur "—so that's for Azelle." A tortie female flew through the air. "And that's for Candy." A big black-and-white cat was trampled underfoot.

Kiki had a large retinue. The promise of food and comfort in a city of starving ferals had brought her new recruits daily, cats whose morals, like their bodies, had been eroded by their hunger; cats who thought little of stealing kittens and betraying the presence of other cats to gain the favor of their queen. What did they care that the humans wished death upon others of their kind, so long as that enmity did not fall upon them? They had eaten well, these last few months: too well.

One by one Kiki's courtiers fell to the teeth and claws of the last free cats of New Orleans, cats carried forward only by the power of their will for revenge. Many lay still, gasping on the stone floor. Many more ran away through the open doors. Shine chased them on their way, getting in a kick here, a nip there. It was still not enough.

Celeste went down at last under the weight of three of the collared cats. Hog stood over her, teeth red with his opponents' blood; but it was impossible to withstand the tide. Before long, an exhausted Sealink found herself shoulder to shoulder with Red. Behind them, Hog and Téophine joined forces, Isis a tiny spitting bundle between them. Of Venus and Sappho there was no sign. It didn't surprise the calico: they just hadn't been raised right.

Some time later the waves parted and there was the yellow queen, the size of three cats, with candle flames flickering off her pale eyes.

"Might have known you'd still be alive in the midst of this carnage," the calico hissed.

"Why, *cher*, no need to be so unfriendly—"

Kiki rolled forward: an unnatural motion like some great hovercraft fashioned of flesh and fur. Her eyes grew round and greedy at the sight of the golden kitten. A scorched reek of grease and decay wafted in her vanguard. Sealink recoiled at the stench.

"I only came for what's mine—"

Red confronted the monstrous queen. "Come any closer," he said grimly, "and you'll be crapping teeth for a week."

She roared with laughter.

"You ain't takin' *this* kitten, not without you take me first." And without hesitation he lunged at her.

Kiki la Doucette raised a languid paw and raked it down his face. The ginger cat rolled in agony at her feet, blood spurting. Immediately, Sealink hurled herself to his defense.

La Mère cackled. "Very maternal, *ma cher*, very moving. Still you got a lot to make up for, leavin' your only son to the mercies of the Pestmen!" She started to laugh so hard that waves of fat rolled across her body and collided with one another like crosscurrents in a sea. Sealink, for once in her life, was dumbstruck. Red, her son. A son. Not a sun. A *son* of fire. And here he was, her fifth kitten, neither in life, nor yet out of it. Kiki inched forward so that she was within a foot of the calico and lowered her voice to a conspiratorial whisper. "For, *bébé,* this fine creature here, whose beauty I just so unfortunately marred—" she examined a broken claw, stripped it carefully between ivory teeth "—this here's the lad I dragged up from the Mississippi shoreline on that cold and misty day and fed on my own milk for you—didn't you *re-a-lize* when you was hanging together? What you got for a brain, honey? An ant?" She guffawed, then clapped a paw to her mouth. She winked at the calico. "I hope you two didn't—you know—get too *friendly*, down there on the boardwalk . . ."

A movement from the floor. A sudden flash of bright fur; a determined, bloodstained face. With a roar of defiance, Red launched himself at la Mère's throat. Sealink leapt for the yellow queen's back. Mother and son struck together.

That oily fur gave no purchase: Kiki shook them off like fleas, laughing all the while. As powerful as a tank, she shouldered past a helpless Téo and Hog and loomed over the golden kitten.

"Good to see you awake at last, *cher*." She leered. "Come to mother."

Isis faced her resolutely, the lines of her head as accurate as an ax. With all the courage of her parentage, she lifted her chin and spat neatly into the yellow queen's eye.

"I am not for you," she said clearly. "Not in this or any other life."

She opened her mouth, and out came the song. It soared into the iron rafters, drew to its singer the power of the deaths suffered in that room. Many, so many—too many over the years. She felt their pain and the power of their will to live. She drew it in, harnessing, shaping. The note swelled.

Sealink fell over, with Red beneath her. Other cats fled for the doors. Téophine dropped like a stone. Hog, with a groan, closed his eyes and slid to the floor. Shine kicked up her heels and bolted out into the street. Kiki, suddenly, clutched her head.

A highway pulsed in the air above them. There was a flash of light, and, without further warning, a cat appeared twenty feet above their heads. Plummeting groundward, it twisted in midair, righted itself, and struck the stone floor on all fours.

It was the Mammy.

Isis sat back, panting. The song died.

Eponine Lafeet looked around her. She gazed at Isis with her milky eyes. She smiled. *"Bonsoir, mon ange.* It is a pleasure to be back in my own town. And—" she bobbed her head "—it is a pleasure and a privilege to meet you."

She walked past the golden kitten and stared with disgust at the heap of greasy fur in front of her. She extended a claw. *"Vas t'en!"*

Against all the laws of nature, the yellow queen began to levitate. Up she went, up into the mouth of broken highway from which the Mammy had issued. There was a sudden flurry of activity as Kiki returned to consciousness and realized where she was; then the highway took her into its maw and vanished.

Eponine smiled. "See how she likes de bayous. Hah!"

Isis stared at the Mammy, round eyed.

"Well!" she said. "That was a good trick. Can you teach it to me?"

❧

Two days later the survivors had gathered in the early morning sun down on the Moon Walk. Behind them, the Mississippi River rolled past as if nothing in the world had changed.

"We're going back to the old country," the calico explained to all present.

The golden kitten, restored to itself, blinked shyly. A Nile-green fire sparked from those elongated, oriental eyes. "Sealink's taking me on a *plane*!"

Suddenly overcome by this idea, she hopped excitedly from foot to foot.

Sealink placed a restraining paw on Isis's neck. "Take it easy, babe," she advised, "or you'll be traveling in the hold." It was ironic really, she thought: she'd come to her hometown to find her own kittens and had instead found some grown cats and was leaving with one of Pertelot's. With a purr like a pneumatic drill, she rubbed her head against Red's unscarred cheek. "Take care of Téophine, won't you?"

She felt very grown up, bestowing her approval like this.

The pair of them, ragged and unsightly from a dozen healing wounds, grinned from ear to ear. Téo touched noses with the calico. "Don't you worry none, *cher*. I'll make sure he gives me plenty kittens." Red looked embarrassed. He wasn't used to having a mother, let alone one in cahoots with his mate.

"*Eh bien,* Rumby-Pumby, better start now, eh?" Celeste, leaning on Hog for support, smiled lazily.

From the fence post behind them, the Mammy surveyed the scene with satisfaction. It was good to be back in her hometown, good to have some of her own to look after again. A couple dozen ferals and a few homeless domestic cats had made their way across the city to the boardwalk. She recognized some as former members of her daughter's retinue; but the malice had gone out of their eyes, just as the worst of the madness had gone out of the city. Two large-furred tabbies had arrived just that morning, bearing, respectively, a shrimp and a crab claw, heads bowed, rather shamefaced. And later that day she had watched, from a safe place, as a large, dark-haired woman came down to the Moon Walk, followed cautiously by a yellow dog, to empty cans of strong-smelling tuna fish in the old place by the steps.

Eponine Lafeet smiled. It was a start. A good start.

She waved the calico cat and her golden charge on their way.

Chapter Eighteen

THAT WAS THE RIVER, THIS IS THE SEA

*A*nimal X enjoyed his time in the village. Life there suited him. He ate a lot, though not as much as Stilton. By day he shared the church doorway with the golden kitten, or wandered through the graveyard as far as the lych-gate and curled up on the low gray wall to watch the world go by. "The thing is," he told himself, "to do no more than you have to. That's the thing." He felt that if he took care of himself he would get better. To an extent that was true. His weight increased. The soft place inside his head seemed to retreat until it was like a remote pool he had once visited in a wood somewhere. But his memory did not improve, and he was still troubled by dreams from which he woke in fear. He was too embarrassed to admit this to Amelie, whose beauty and determination sometimes left him feeling shy.

As he improved, the old cat Cottonreel sought him out, and they began to walk together in the afternoons. They made an odd couple. Despite her age, Cottonreel still loved male cats and would look up at him with undisguised delight in her eyes as they strolled along, her admiration mixed with a kind of teasing gallantry. Nevertheless, it was some days before she made clear what it was she wanted from him.

"How I envy you great brutes!" she said. "You traipse about from place to place, taking your lives as they come, never a care in the world. I was always such a stay-at-home, little velvet collar and all!"

It was hot. The village street being all dazzle and bake, they had taken the narrow staircase to the top of the old church tower instead. There, while they sat on the wide parapet and waited for a breeze, they could gaze out across the neglected rear section of the churchyard—where the graves were tossed like little boats on a sea of the tangled grass, like no other grass in the world, that mats all churchyards—and over the wall into a rather neat garden with clumps of yellow poppies.

"Oh, I know very well what you think," she chided him before he could answer. "You think, 'This fragile spinster.' You think, 'This pet cat who came from nowhere in a furrier's van.' You think, 'However did she make herself the village queen?' Well, I wonder that myself sometimes!"

"I think you are all steel underneath, and always were" was Animal X's quiet reply.

"It's not a bit of use you speaking," she said irritably.

At that moment, two houseflies, borne up on some ecstatic updraft of which they were only partly aware, blundered onto the warm stone in front of her and began immediately to copulate. Locked together in that way, they looked like an iridescent enamel brooch in the sunlight. Every so often they buzzed groggily and lurched into a new position. Cottonreel stood up, stretched, and examined them lazily.

"I don't think I could eat them while they were doing that," she said. "Do you? It seems unfair."

She dabbed at them until they flew away.

Suddenly she said, "You'll leave us soon, Animal X. Oh, no, don't protest. You pretend to be calm, but you are the most driven cat I ever met." She stared out over the treetops. "Though perhaps not the angriest," she continued in a softer voice. And then, "Will you do me a favor as you go about the world? Will you look out for a black cat?"

She ran her eyes over Animal X.

"He is rather bigger than you, if that's possible. Longhaired, and with a great tangled mane. I only met him the once. He was very dirty, rather fine and gentle yet quick to act on behalf of weaker animals. If you ever see a cat like that on your journeys," she said, "remind him of me, will you? Tell him that Cottonreel sends her love."

Later she said, "Is it me, or is it a little cooler? Shall we go down?" And then, on the stairs, "You will be careful with Amelie's feelings, won't you?"

Amelie was never very far away. When he saw her by day, he remembered her in the night; when he watched her in the night he thought, Nothing like this will ever happen to me again. Moonlight barred the vestry floor, glissed her eyes, hung like mist in her fur. She sat staring into the mirror, identifying tranquilly the signs that she was no longer young: a fleck in the copper-colored iris, a squaring of the muzzle.

"Are you happy here?" she asked.

She visited him less often, and looked so directly at him when she did. The days stretched out. Did she know, too?

She said, "You seem restless now."

When he didn't answer she said lightly, "At least your friend is well again."

Indeed, Stilton grew daily less frantic. He stopped trembling. He had found temporary accommodation with two or three other cats from the laboratory, in a gas-tarred chicken hutch belonging to the old woman who ran the village shop. He fed all over the village—on back doorsteps and in custom-built kitchens—ruthlessly exploiting the sympathies of human beings until his spine lost its nervous curve, his ribs vanished one by one, and his flanks filled out. Food and rest completed the job begun by the golden kitten's tongue. Stilton's burns healed, and a thin but determined growth of fur appeared in their place. It seemed quite gray, at first, but soon an engaging tabby pattern showed through. When Animal X went to congratulate him on this, he said, "You should come down and join us. We've got quite a good thing going in that shed!" And he began to talk as tirelessly about his new companions as he had about his made-up life and favorite cheese. Everything they did struck him as amusing or apt.

"Old Runcer!" he said. "Don't talk to me about him!"

"I can't say I know him very well," said Animal X, who didn't know Runcer at all, though he thought he had seen him in the village—a small black-and-white with sticky fur and a disconnected gait, who scuttled from one safe spot to the next, staying close to the walls. "He seems nice."

"Oh, he's an entertainment in his own right, that cat!"

But if he had exchanged cheese for friends, food was still

the axis of Stilton's life. He had eaten so many new things! He described them to Animal X, one by one. "Bread and milk, now." He sighed. "That's quite something the first time you have it. Then somehow you can have enough of it."

He looked thoughtful for a minute. Then he brightened up. "And as for seafood cocktail with cold-water shrimp! Have you ever had that? As Runcer always says, 'Seafood cocktail. That'll make your bowels come up.' It slips down well, a bit of the old seafood cocktail. It really hits the spot—"

"So you're happy here," interrupted Animal X.

Stilton looked puzzled.

"I suppose I am," he acknowledged, as if Animal X had shown him something new about himself. Then he laughed. "But do you know, there are nights I wake up and miss the cabinet?"

Animal X said he found this hard to believe.

"That wasn't a good place for cats," he pointed out.

"Oh, I don't know," said Stilton. "There was some real companionship. And the stories we told one another! Those weren't such bad days."

"Perhaps not," said Animal X. "Perhaps they weren't. Think how bad the food was, though." While to himself he said, "Stilton is beginning to forget: that is how I know he is cured."

He said, "I was thinking of leaving soon."

Stilton stood blinking at him in the sunlight.

🐾

At night Animal X watched the chains of laboratory cats, still a little bemused by the change in their lives, wandering through the moonlight. Their eyes were like small oval lights in the fields down near the water. Sometimes they were like a living carpet, wheeling down from the woods to silently fill the village street. They had been released, he thought, but not released. They were waiting for something more. He was like that. He saw and heard with absolute clarity—he could see dew form on a leaf—but everything was at one remove. Ever since his talk with Cottonreel, he had felt it stealing over him. He had had a life before this one . . . He wanted this one to lead him to it. He wanted to be following the river to the sea. Green dreams plagued him.

The kitten, too, chafed. It could be found grooming itself ferociously in the morning, pacing to and fro in the middle afternoon when the sun beat straight into the church doorway. It rarely left this position. When it did, it seemed to have no real objective, and only ranged with a kind of awkward dignity down the village street, occasionally shaking its head as if it had received some errant signal from its stitched-up eye-socket. The other young males promptly tried to draw it into squabbles over status and precedence, being rewarded first by regal incomprehension then by levels of violence they could hardly credit. "Be fair," they temporized, backing away. "It was only a joke." But the one-eyed kitten's understanding of the world was too remorseless for jokes; it roamed the surrounding woods and fields incommunicado, ambushing any cat it found. Animal X, watching it return from these expeditions, felt helpless.

"I don't know what to say to you," he told it one evening. "You're not a force for good at the moment."

Then he went on into the church, where he found Amelie waiting for him under the east window. The air pooled cold and still, strong with the odors of metal polish, dust, beeswax, and white lilies. The tall window glowed above her, its deep reds and blues slashed here and there by sudden sharp yellows and greens. When she moved, lozenges of colored light fell upon her coat, confusing and softening her outline. He tried to make sure that he would remember her. He tried to take her in, forever. In that moment his awareness of her was so great it only seemed to sharpen his senses further, so that he could smell the faint balsam of the yew trees outside and hear from up among the ceiling beams the feathery echo of his own footsteps on the floor of the nave. He found that, rather than hindering, all those other sensations helped.

"I am leaving soon," he said.

"You would be bound to go. To find the sea."

"Will you come with me?"

"No," she said, as if it was a decision she had made some time ago. "Part of me would like to. But something is happening in the world. Is it good or bad? Who knows what it will mean to all these half-healed cats." She turned to face him. "I want to be here when it happens."

She said, "They will still need my help."

"I knew you wouldn't come," said Animal X.

"Part of me would like to," repeated Amelie. She said, "I hope you find what you want, and that your life is a good one."

"Perhaps I'll come back and see you."

She laughed.

"Perhaps you will," she said.

He left with the kitten a few days later, in the undecided light of early morning. A few birds sang. Later, the air would glitter: now it was dove gray and so damp as to be palpable, an air on the edge of being mist, through which had recently fallen a steady drenching rain. Stilton came out of his chicken hutch to say good-bye to them, and they all three stood looking awkwardly at one another for a moment. The kitten lurched unhappily about, bumping into the others, licking Stilton's head one minute, hissing at him the next, in the confusion of whatever it was feeling. Then Animal X, with too many things to say and no way of saying any of them, rubbed his cheek against his old friend's and told him, "I'll miss you."

"I'll miss you, too," said Stilton.

"It's best you stay, though."

"It's best I stay. I never had a life before."

"You'll be happy here."

They stared at each other for a moment longer, then Animal X turned resolutely away.

He said, "I have to go now."

He said, "The kitten is very disturbed now."

"Good-bye," called Stilton. "Good-bye!"

He followed them along the street, still calling, "Good-bye!" At the river he seemed to lose his impetus, and stopped and watched them go. The river was looping and slow here, a deep green snake in the pale dewy water meadows. On the other bank, the trees lay motionless. The sun, a fainting yellow behind translucent white clouds, was trying to break through and make this the hottest, most humid day of the year. All the way out of the village, Animal X looked for Amelie and Cottonreel. They didn't come. I suppose they have already said good-bye, he thought to himself. Still, I should like to have talked to them once more. But later, when he looked back at the church tower, he saw two cats up on the parapet. Distance made them tiny but he was sure they were cats. At that moment the cloud thinned, sunshine struck the top of the tower, and he imagined them up there, dazzled but warmed, already feeling better about the day, wishing him the best.

I wonder how things will go for them, he thought.

To the kitten he said, "Come on."

🐾

Hills approached, fell back; the river valley expanded and contracted like a slowly beating heart. Conifer plantations gave way to lighter stands of oak and hornbeam. At first, the pastures were spangled with flowers and scented with meadowsweet; but then the landscape began to change subtly, unfolding into sandy heath above which larks sang from dawn to dusk in the hot bowl of the sky. Here and there, two or three wind-eaten pines kept watch over the bracken from the top of a steep little hill. Awed by the openness of it all, they slept by day and traveled at night.

But it was handy country for cats. Animal X cornered a mouse in a hollow in the turf and showed the kitten how to deal with it. "Look here," he ordered. He caught the mouse and let it go again. "See?" The kitten blundered about behind Animal X's back, making angry bubbling noises and trying to dodge in and take the mouse off him. "You'll have to get up earlier in the morning than that," said Animal X.

Nothing happened for a day or two. He wondered if the lesson had taken. Then he woke out of his hot mid-morning sleep to find a half-grown rabbit staring him straight in the face, one agitated blowfly crawling over its glazed eye. After that, despite its obvious limitations, the kitten became an efficient, indeed merciless, hunter. Its movements retained an adolescent touch of exaggeration. But there was killing torsion pent up in the flex and spring of its body. Rage, unalloyed and barely diverted, informed the freeze into immobility, the sudden hyperbolic leap above the tangled bracken. Animal X winced at its violence, yet found himself recipient of an embarrassment of riches. One evening a pile of voles; an entire family of mice wiped out the next. The kitten never touched anything it brought him, so he had no idea what it was eating; but he had already seen it bring down a full-grown pigeon that was five feet from the ground and flying hard when the golden jaws closed on its neck.

Mile flowed seamlessly into mile. They rarely strayed from the river. But the surrounding land rose steadily until no riverbank remained worth speaking of; they were forced to walk far above the water where dwarf oak and broken walls clung to steep ground and a system of green lanes ushered them out onto spacious upland lawn—sheep-cropped, studded with tormentil, drenched in light.

Outcrops of rose-pink rock stood up out of the rolling turf, quartz veined, surrounded by dense, wind-sculpted stands of gorse. The air was different up there: it went lively, unfixed, free. There was such a sudden sense of space. Animal X stared around. We're very high up, he thought. But that's not it. The turf stretched away; the sky was so bright it seemed to go on forever; at the junction of the two lay a broad, supple, glittering band of silver. Then, racing toward him out of the dazzle and haze, a huge bird! It hovered for a moment and swung away on the wind and disappeared; and all he had left was an image of its cruciform shape, its snowy body and strong yellow beak, its forlorn cry. "You can see farther there," he remembered Amelie saying. "And there are birds that make the loneliest noise you have ever heard."

We're at the sea, thought Animal X.

The kitten came and stood beside him.

"We're at the sea!" Animal X told it.

But the kitten wasn't listening. It stood foursquare—head high, coat turned to live gold by the liquid glitter of the ocean—and raised its nose to the laminated, vivid streams of air, as if it, too, might plane away on the wind.

Its entire body was trembling with excitement.

🐾

They slept in the salt winds that day, huddled up under leggy, bitten-looking gorse, half awake much of the time, listening to the lonely shrieks of seabirds. Those cries led Animal X to dream. In the dream he was still young enough to need his mother. He tottered up to her and sat down suddenly in astonishment. She was so big and safe! He sprang contemptuously upon his runny-nosed brothers and sisters. What did he need them for? Yet he loved them more than anything. When he woke up it was night, and the kitten was gone.

Animal X poked his head out of the gorse. He felt lonely. The night had broken everything into shapes and planes. Bulky outcrops of granite leaned away from one another at odd angles. The gorse, though quite still, seemed to stream in the wind. Clouds raced across a moon-rinsed sky, their filmy, turbulent shadows agitating the land beneath; the shadows of the rocks, darker and more formal, came and went. After a moment, Animal X thought he saw the kitten, perhaps forty yards away, a brassy color under the moon, stalking something at the base of the nearest rocks.

"Hello?" he called.

No answer.

Stretching and yawning, he left the gorse and looked around. "Hello?"

There was a muffled thud. The soft place in his head burst open like a door, and the world was filled with hot green light. It was in the rocks and stones, in the gorse, in the air, it was in Animal X himself; all these different kinds of things fizzed with light, as if a fuse had been ignited within them. Expectancy glittered and crackled down the edge of every blade of grass. For a heartbeat everything paused . . .

"Hello?" said Animal X.

Birds flew up, carking and cawing from their hidden roosts in the granite, their wings like black rags on a hot wind. They circled above his head. Like the light, they had been nestled down inside things all along, waiting for him to arrive in this place. The crows! thought Animal X. The crows!

He felt the light try its strength, and leap out of the stones and flicker around his head. He flattened his ears and ran for it. Where could he go? Halfway to nowhere the fuse burned out. Green fire laced the gorse without consuming it. Flames roared silently across the turf, gathering into shapes he didn't want to acknowledge. The crows wheeled and sideslipped above him, dipping down to strike at his head; their cries redoubled—plangent, coarse, full of some hateful irony. Fear drove him toward the place where the land finished, where the huge ocean awaited him, gray and lavender, touched with silver. Then he was right on the lip of it all in the reek of salt and iodine, staring down a hundred feet at rocks, foam, booming and turmoil far below. The land shook with every wave. Spray shot up in rainbow arcs. It was more water than he could ever have imagined. Animal X didn't care.

I've seen enough now, he thought. I've seen too much.

And with a quiet sense of relief he threw himself over the edge. He would fall now. He would give himself up to it. He would escape the crows and whatever they were trying to make him understand. As he fell he had a brief, puzzling glimpse of something glorious and golden. Its jaws closed firmly on his neck, and he went quickly away from himself and everything else—

—to dream of a cat that lay beside a cold river.

It was morning, early. Winter grayed the air between the elder saplings. The tangled willows put up the undersides of their leaves in the breeze; dead bramble suckers and ground ivy thickened the riverbanks. The water was gelid—clear yet colored at the same time, as very cold water often is, a kind of light green-gray. Its surface was dimpled with eddies. Hidden currents tugged, strong and amiable, at a stem of nightshade berries that curved into the water like an arc of bright red beads, fumed away from partly submerged objects—the root bole of some long-dead elm, a worn tractor tire—to sculpt hollows in the smooth gray mud below the fringe of vegetation.

One bank was heavily undercut. Back eddies had made a sloping wet beach of the other, and that was where the cat lay, a sodden bundle of tortoiseshell fur among all the other rubbish that had washed up. Its lips were drawn back off its yellowed teeth in a snarl of pain. It had been quite a large, powerful animal before the river had taken charge of it and cast it up here with its back legs entangled in a cheerily printed supermarket bag. Recent injuries about the head and neck had left its fur sticky with blood that the water had failed to lave away.

It was clearly dead, but the crows were still cautious. They had spotted it at first light while they were still squabbling— *"Craa! Craa! Craa!"*—in the tops of some beech trees two fields away on the other side of the river. Since then they had been swaggering about in a heavy-shouldered way in the mud, every so often working themselves up to a floundering run, circling their way in as their confidence rose. Fights broke out among them. When they settled down again, they were always a little closer.

Mid-morning, the cat opened its eyes suddenly. It blinked and coughed. At this, the crows boiled up into the air and circled in disappointment above the sodden fields. A single black feather drifted down.

"Cark-cark! Craaa!"

That was how the cat woke from death: to the sound of crows, to the darting black shapes, the beaks, the wings buffeting the air above. It raised the front part of its body and looked at the world—mud, bushes, somewhere it had never been before. "Tag?" it said, in a thick, surprised voice, and fell back. "There's something on my legs." Where was this place? A question which soon dissolved into unconsciousness.

The sky opened, and rain poured down for the rest of the morning, smearing the air, trickling through the cat's sodden fur. It was cold, large rain; the riverbanks were like sponges with it. The crows returned, and—inch by inch, less quarrelsome now, more focused—moved upon their meal. Toward noon, when a faint yellow sun began to be visible behind the clouds, two or three of them became too hungry to wait any longer. They darted forward, ready to hammer at the cat with their big black beaks. Crows will hammer all day long to get what they want, work forever over a bit of bone, the rag of a lamb in a bare field. Sensing something of this, the cat dragged itself awake again. Its eyes were mismatched, one blue, one a strange sodium orange more fitted to city streets than country lanes. Through them the cat saw painful flashes and arcs of sunlight, mixed up with sleek, jostling, intelligent heads. A crow can hammer all the way to the heart of things if necessary—get the good bits before they go cold. The cat gathered the last of its strength. It dragged itself partway out of the encumbering plastic bag and went for its tormentors, teeth and claws bared. *"Cark! Aaargh!"* they sneered, from the safety of the air. A crow always has the last word. The cat looked up in anger and fear. Then, the remains of the supermarket bag still trailing from one rear leg, it made off at a kind of lumbering trot along the muddy bank and up onto the nearest road where, after walking for about a mile, it was brought down again by its wounds.

Half an hour passed. The sun had broken through. The cat lay in the gutter near some trees, not thinking much. The supermarket bag fluttered idly. A vehicle came into view. It was a white panel van with rust marks around the door sills. It passed the cat at high speed, then stopped suddenly. Two men dressed in light blue overalls got out and, talking in low voices, walked back to where the cat lay in the gutter. They looked down thoughtfully, and one of them began to pull on a pair of thick, worn leather gloves.

"Any good?"

"Nah. It's well stuffed, this one."

"It's alive."

"That's about all you can say. What are they going to do with it in this condition?"

"You never know."

"Well, you can pick it up. I'm not touching it. They'll never want this."

"I wonder how it got tangled in that bag."

Throughout this exchange, the cat remained conscious but too tired to think. They picked it up and put it in the back of the van, where it passed out from the pain of being handled. That was the last time it remembered its own name. When it next woke, it would be a different animal altogether. The van pulled away quickly and disappeared down the road. On its side, if you could read, you might have read:

⊙ LABORATORIES
Winfield Farm Site

When he woke from this dream, Animal X was surprised to find himself still alive, and in the lee of some rocks a little way back from the cliff top. It was a fine day with a few clouds high up; he felt tired but lighthearted and hungry, as if the fit had finally washed something out of him. He considered things. Clearly, the grip he had felt on his neck as he hurled himself over had not after all been the jaws of death but those of the golden kitten, which now sat a little way off, regarding Animal X with a wary respect. Its eyes followed every movement he made—in case, perhaps, he tried to jump again.

"That got your attention, then," said Animal X.

"Pardon?" said the kitten.

It was Animal X's turn to stare.

"Well, well," he told himself softly. "Here's a turn up for the book and no mistake. Surprises all 'round, today."

"Why did you do it? Jump off like that?"

"I'm not sure I know," said Animal X. "It seemed like a good idea at the time."

"You would have been killed."

"I thought of that."

The kitten said, "I don't want you to die. For one thing, I need your help."

"Well, that's heartening," said Animal X. There was a silence. "Could you speak all along, then?" he said. "I wondered if you could speak, all along."

"After what happened to me," the kitten said, "after the indignity of what they did to me in that place . . ." It seemed to lose its thread, and for some seconds stared out to sea. Then it began again. "Human beings snatched me from my sisters. I was dragged under the earth and stuffed in a sack. They took me away in a boat, and then some filthy vehicle brought me to that place. They took my eye!" it cried bitterly. "They took my eye, they took Stilton's wits, they took your memory! After what they did to us all in that place, my throat would not speak." And then, in wonder, "It would not speak, however hard I tried, until I was home again."

"They took nothing from me," said Animal X gently. "I took my own memory away because I wasn't ready to face it."

As he spoke, he was studying the cliff top with new interest. There were pools of ruffled water among the rocks, tufts of salty grass—not much else. "I can't see how a cat lives in this wind," he said. "How does a cat get a living here? You live here?"

"Near here. My name is Odin, and I am a prince. I believe we are all in terrible danger. Will you help me find my mother, the Queen? I promise she is near."

He sniffed the air.

"Home is so close," he said quietly, "over that headland, or the next."

As soon as he heard the word *Queen*, the healing of Animal X was complete. He laughed softly to himself. I remember *that* one, he thought. I remember the tongue on her! He knew who he was now. He knew the meaning of the crow dream stitched like a loop into the middle of his life. He understood the irony of his journey to this cliff top; he remembered his friends; he wondered what had become of the world he knew. He was filled with energy when he thought about it. "It must have worked out, one way or another," he told himself. "All that. It must be gone like a dream now. Something new will be going on now." He would find out about everything. I want to be in on it, he thought; then he said out loud, "I want to be in on it!" The sound of his own voice, now that he recognized it, made him laugh out loud. Then he had another thought. He passed one of his front paws over his head as if to groom it. The thing they had put in his skull was gone! Green fire had gently eased and melted it away while he slept, like warm winds melting an icicle in spring. There was already a bridge joining past to present across the undependable ground inside him.

I can think again, he thought.

He looked at the kitten, first out of his blue eye, and then out of the orange one. A huge sense of warmth spread through him.

"I knew your mother before you were born," he said. "You're already bigger than she is. But you'll never be as good-looking."

Odin was so busy talking he barely heard a word. "I

wanted to tell you how fine you were," he was saying. "I wanted to tell Stilton how brave and decent he was. I wanted to tell all those cats how well they had done in that place. But I couldn't speak!"

"Well," said Animal X, "it's the thought that counts."

"I didn't want you to die," Odin said. "You looked after me. You looked after everyone. My anger went away when I thought you would die."

"We all looked after each other," said Animal X. "We did the best we could." That made him think of Stilton. It made him think of Amelie.

"Let's get you home," he said.

☙

The Dog hid among the rocks. The damp had got into its bones during the night. Its eyes were sore from the salt wind. It watched the two cats walk away along the cliff top, the old hunter and the new one chattering excitedly away to each other. It thought, They talk about the best way of killing a bank vole. But a bank vole isn't much.

It thought, Still only one golden kitten.

After a moment or so it followed them.

Chapter Nineteen

THE BEAUTIFUL FRIEND

*T*he return journey was difficult and slow.

Well-known roads proved impassable or were simply no longer there; those that still worked had turned into a maze of seeping corridors through nothing, opening suddenly on to bleak woods under gray, mucous airs in country no one ever visited. Leonora, compelled by each impasse to invent ever-more-complex dances, grew tired and muddled. The new Majicou, goaded by anxieties he would not explain, chafed at each delay, lost his patience with her, and tried to force passage where none existed. As a result, they lost their way. Later, at some point of decision so subtle they were past it before either of them guessed, they lost Loves a Dustbin and the New Black King, too. Back by the sea at last, still alone, they found the night old, the moon down, squalls of cold rain racing landward across the bay.

Leo said they were lucky to have arrived home at all. That was her opinion, anyway.

She stuck her head into the familiar hole at the base of the oceanarium doors. Then she backed out again very suddenly without saying anything.

This is what she had seen inside: A dozen verminous tom-cats thrown into silhouette by the fish tank's brilliant glare, which, pouring between them, threw their elongated black shadows across the concrete floor and up the peeling walls. They sat in a half circle idly stripping their claws—already as sharp as straight razors—scratching their foul ears or staring with greedy puzzlement into the aquarium at the silent, mysterious, unreachable world within. Between them and the tank they had trapped Pertelot Fitzwilliam of Hi-Fashion,

Queen of Cats. Her head was held high, and if she acknowledged her captors at all it was only to look down her nose at them. Next to her crouched Cy the tabby, her tail lashing, her voice rising in a bubbling, angry wail.

They were all large, but one of them was rather larger than the rest. It never sat down. Some inner compulsion sent it restlessly to and fro across the seeping concrete outside the half circle—sometimes shouldering one of the other cats aside to enter and pass close to the two females—who hissed and spat, though it rarely so much as glanced at them—sometimes disappearing entirely as it ranged around behind the bulk of the tank, unable to rest or stop talking to itself. It was a sore and mangy animal, marmalade in color, with marks like dull flames roiling down its sides. Its tail lashed constantly, its eyes were inturned, its gait was lurching and painful. It suffered, too, an occasional blurriness or shifting of its outline unlikely under such a clarity of light, a sense of undeveloped potential, as though its boundaries were uncertain—as if it might be even larger than it seemed.

It stank.

Leonora was appalled.

"It's—"

"Kater Murr," said Tag.

"How do you know? You haven't even looked."

"I knew he would come here when I drove him out of the Alchemist's house. That was an overconfidence I regret! I thought we would arrive first."

Leo stared at him.

"That *thing* was Kater Murr?"

"Kater Murr was always at the heart of the puzzle," said Tag.

"Oh, why did you let him come here!" Leo cried.

He shook his head. "I've been at fault, Leo," he acknowledged. "This could have been prevented long ago—and Uroum Bashou's life saved, too—if I had asked myself a simple question."

"I don't understand," Leo said. "What question?"

"I should have asked: Is there a highway entrance inside the house of Uroum Bashou?"

"And is there?"

"No."

"So?"

"Cats are larger than life when they leave the Old Changing Way, but they always return to normal size in a minute or two. So how does Kater Murr maintain himself as the great brass animal you encountered first in the Reading Cat's kitchen and later on his stairs? If I had thought about that, instead of showing off to you—" He sighed.

"Kater Murr has a line of power," he was forced to admit, "the other end of which leads to the Alchemist."

"What are we going to do?" demanded Leonora.

"Think for a moment."

"No! No! My mother is in there! Pertelot and Cy are in there!"

"Yet if we rush in now, all will be lost. Kater Murr has achieved less than he imagines. The Alchemist has not so much empowered him as prepared him like any other proxy for some undisclosed purpose. Without his master, he could not stand against me for long—"

"Then go in and deal with him!" interrupted Leonora. "You're the Majicou."

"Yet if I challenge him directly he will kill your mother before I can kill him," he went on gently. "Do you want that? I only know I would not like to lose Cy that way."

Even as he spoke, Leonora was darting past him to squirm through the hole at the base of the doors. From inside he heard her mutter, "Leave it to Leonora, as usual."

And then, "Tag?"

"Oh, Leonora, Leonora," he said.

🐾

It was hard to hide in the oceanarium. Since the only object in it was the giant glass tank, and since the lamp was positioned directly above that, there weren't even many fixed shadows to be found and they were all associated with the spiral staircase. Tag and Leo kept in among them, as far back as they could under the bottom tread. From that viewpoint, much was obscured by the curve of the tank. About half of Kater Murr's tomcats were visible as anonymous black backs or as faces bleached of any but the cruellest expressions by the harsh light. Of Pertelot and Cy, Tag could make out only a pair of rose-colored ears, a sullen tabby muzzle resting on the dirty floor. Generally he could see more fish than cats. Kater Murr, though, was always in view. Up and down he ranged—his image as unsteady as a reflection in water, his gait disconnected and uneven, his rank odor coming and going like the reek of harbor mud on a humid summer day—rehearsing his endless monologue as he went.

"His bowels itch but he welcomes that. His brain hurts but he welcomes that. Kater Murr is something to see!"

So it went on, until Pertelot Fitzwilliam interrupted in a quiet but penetrating voice, "Kater Murr has a filthy smell."

There was a sudden silence.

"Hello," said Kater Murr, "what's this? Royalty?" He approached the Queen. "Are you royal?" he asked her quietly. "Are you *very* royal, I wonder?"

Pertelot backed away.

Kater Murr watched this operation with interest, his head on one side. "Because I've heard you are," he said thoughtfully. "I've heard you're very royal indeed." Then he said, "What you might ask yourself next is this: Does he care? Does Kater Murr *care* how royal I am?"

He sat down suddenly and scratched at one of his scabs until it bled. He seemed tired, as if it was an effort to keep control of his own boundaries. He looked around vaguely. "Kater Murr wonders where he is," he said to himself in quite a different voice. Then he leapt to his feet again—agile and energetic, hard as a bunch of rusty springs—and, pushing his great orange mask within an inch of Pertelot's nose, pinned her gently but firmly against the fish tank. Though she tried hard to turn her head away, she had no room to move. The aquarium octopus pulsed and flexed above her, shifting its suckers carefully upon the glass.

Kater Murr purred. His outline flickered.

"Come to Kater Murr, my dear. You're enough to make anyone feel brand-new."

At this, Tag told Leonora, "Stay here if you want to live!" and stepped out of the shadows.

"Empty speech, Kater Murr," he said.

Kater Murr became very still.

"Is there someone else in here with me?" he asked his companions. "I thought I heard someone speak."

The tomcats stared at him, then at one another, anxious to please but too full of testosterone to know what was happening.

"Was it," Kater Murr wondered, "a fish?"

"You know me, Kater Murr," said Tag. "I am the Majicou."

Kater Murr stared hard at a shoal of mackerel. They moved uneasily behind the glass. "I think it was that one there," he said. "That was the speaking fish."

"You know me, Kater Murr."

Slowly, slowly, Kater Murr turned his head until he was able to look at Tag out of one amber eye. Then he said, "I don't need to know anyone now."

He said, "Oh, I saw you at the library—your head was in a book, but you can't read—listening to his endless boring stories, day after day. It was always 'the Reading Cat knows this, the Reading Cat knows that,' but what is reading anyway? Reading is not so difficult. *Kater Murr* learned to read. Oh, yes he did! But Kater Murr learned *what* to read. Kater Murr is a successful cat. Kater Murr has important friends—"

"Kater Murr is nothing," said Tag. "You killed the Reading Cat out of jealousy. Had you already found your way to the room beneath the copper dome? I think you had. I think that was where you were taught to read. Kater Murr is a pet cat, who dabbled where he had no understanding. Kater Murr is still a doorkeeper."

He paused.

"Though now he keeps the Alchemist's door," he said.

He left a long silence, then mused, "What did he offer you, Kater Murr? *The chance to be a human being?*" Tag laughed. "Well, that's a poor enough ambition, but you won't achieve it, any more than your master could make himself a cat. He will finish with you soon, Kater Murr. He will use you up. Look at you! You can barely hold yourself together."

Throughout this exchange they had been moving toward each other in the mannered, stealthy way of male cats. Now

Tag found his face so close to Kater Murr's that their foreheads were almost touching. Despite the oceanarium glare, Kater Murr's pupils were fully dilated while the surfaces of the eyes themselves had a swimmy, iridescent sheen. What could he be seeing? Only light, Tag supposed. Only shapes moving through a painful light. *He's far gone in some direction a cat isn't meant to go. I've got his attention away from the Queen. But what am I going to do now?* All along his scabby back, the gatekeeper's fur was up like a scrubbing brush. In response, Tag could only sink his weight back onto his haunches and, rocked back and forth by the beat of his own heart, open his throat on the low and angry bubbling noises that had somehow taken up residence there. Behind him he could feel Kater Murr's tomcats shifting slyly about as they prepared to flank him. The smell of Kater Murr's breath was as thick as tar. Tag could see the mites in his ears.

It was bound to come to this, Tag thought.

They were about to embrace when several things happened at once.

Cy cried, "Behind you, Ace! Look out!"

Leonora Whitstand Merril, unused to obeying anyone and half-blind with her own impatience, jumped out of the shadows shouting, "Do you call this fair? You bullies!"

And Ragnar Gustaffson Coeur de Lion, Egyptian silver symbol tangled proudly in his unkempt mane, burst upon the oceanarium like the seventh wave. He was followed by the dustbin fox, full of sheer bad temper at recently being lost on the Old Changing Way. Black lips wrinkled off a yellow snarl. Foam flew from his lolling tongue, and his limp had quite vanished. Sizing up the situation in an instant, these two drove straight toward the Queen. Tag stared at them. *How had the situation deteriorated so fast?* He shrugged and sprang at Kater Murr. The astonished doorkeeper, bowled over in a reeking heap, squirmed and paddled himself away, then returned and took a good hold of Tag's cheek below the left eye. Their heads went back briefly, and they spat in each other's faces—and with that everything came apart for good. It was like a signal. Cy jumped up and began worrying the haunch of Kater Murr. Pertelot and her daughter, their eyes glittering with malice, addressed themselves to his astonished lieu-tenants. Soon the oceanarium was a melee of screeching cats and flying fur, at the center of which pounced and darted a single large dog fox, giving much better than he got. Left to itself, despite the uneven numbers, this situation could only have developed in one way; several of the tomcats were al-ready thinking about leaving. But Kater Murr was no ordi-nary cat.

Some blow of Tag's had sent him reeling. Trying to escape another, he ran full tilt into the fish tank and slid down it with his cheek pressed to the glass. When he came to rest, the eye on that side had closed for good. The other had a glazed look.

He groaned.

"Kater Murr knows a thing or two," he said.

His outline wavered. The air around him crackled and spat. Every cat present felt its hair stand on end. They stopped fighting and regarded one another warily, while large slow bluish sparks, wandering aimlessly about at head height, dis-charged themselves in perfect silence against the spiral stairs. Kater Murr tried to get up. He convulsed. He seemed to shoot out from himself in all directions at once, and the assembled cats felt him *pass through* them like a ripple in the air. Then he was gone, and in his place appeared the dream cat, the avatar, the gatekeeper's savage icon of himself. It was the size of a small horse. Its fur was coarse and orange. Black mark-ings chased each other down its sides like drawings of flames. Every bunch and pull of its muscles brought forth a reek of ammonia, pheromones, and death. It lifted its blunt muzzle and gave a coughing snarl. Cats ran about in panicky circles, friend and foe alike: there was nowhere to hide. The new Ma-jicou's voice rang out.

"Look away!" he advised them.

At that, the air temperature fell steeply. There was an in-tense flash of light, a smell of snow. The oceanarium walls drew back like sliding doors and vanished, leaving the ani-mals to huddle together under a vertiginous gray sky. Hoar frost formed instantly in their whiskers, and they could barely hear themselves think for the howl of the wind. Snow filled the air like fog. The spiral staircase, bearded with ice, remained visible for a moment. Then it, too, vanished.

"This is absurd," said Loves a Dustbin to Ragnar Gustaffson.

The King looked down. His medal had frozen into his ruff. "It is some bad weather even for a professional like me," he was forced to agree.

Only Cy, huddled up between Leonora and Pertelot, seemed unconcerned. "Woo!" she said. "It's raw-John blind here. It's white-eyed Jack!" She craned her neck to stare up into the rushing snow, her eyes gleaming with excitement. "No one's identifying themselves out there tonight. But look!"

Out of the icy air he came—out of the moil and rime of it all, out of the bitter, driving wind—the new Majicou, white tiger of the postglacial snows. His eyes were a fierce and freezing green. His long legs flexed and stretched, flexed and stretched. His huge paws thudded soft and rhythmic on the ice. He might run forever, his old friends thought, the light spilling off his fur like that, and each movement would be full of the same force and clarity. He was a picture. He was a million miles away and yet more present than the ground beneath them. He seemed always to be arriving, expanding, rushing forward to the encounter Kater Murr had made inevitable; at the same time, somehow, he was always already there . . .

They stepped around each other warily. Light flickered off the edge of an eye, the point of a bared tooth. A front paw was spread and displayed, an attitude struck then folded. There was a sudden, coughing snarl, then a flurry of violence. It was hard to see what was happening through the shifting veils of snow. Two huge bodies collided with a groan like cars in a fog, disengaged immediately, began to pace around each other once more, turning this way and that in anticipation of some advantage lost even as it was gained. Suddenly they embraced again, less briefly. They writhed and fell. Hind claws raked and ripped, fur flew like raw and rusty wire. Then they were up and pacing restlessly again, panting for breath, trembling with blood chemicals, looking for an opening. But now Kater Murr seemed quite blind.

"Go home, Kater Murr. Be a cat."

"Did I hear someone speak?"

To the watchers, everything seemed confused—too quick, too real. It was finished in an instant. Saber teeth flashed across a bared orange throat. Blood heat warmed the air. Kater Murr looked surprised. "Kater Murr is a cat among cats," he said, his life streaming away into the ice. "His body hurts, but what does he care?"

His rank smell overpowered everything for a moment, then another smell—of musk and winter, powder snow on an icy wind—washed it away. There was a distant, fading roar.

The watching animals shivered.

"I didn't want him to die," whispered Leonora Whitstand Merril. "He was a cat like us."

The next time they looked, the oceanarium had reassembled itself around them. It was warm and dry. The fish circled endlessly in the heat of the electric lamp. The only sign that anything had changed was the corpse of Kater Murr, which lay sodden and used looking, like a doormat in the rain, a little distance from the foot of the spiral stairs. His lieutenants had seized the day and were gone.

"Wow," breathed Cy. "Home again!"

The fox looked around, shook himself suddenly, and went to the doors to keep an eye on the night. Cats! he was thinking. What can you say?

One by one, they relaxed. The new Majicou had transported them briefly to some country of his own. It had been a country without consequences for them, but he looked exhausted. He licked gingerly at his wounds, while his friends gathered around him, all trying to talk at once. For his own part, he seemed to be waiting for something, and every so often cocked his head as if he were trying to listen to a voice in the distance.

❧

"Well then, Mercury," said Pertelot, when things had settled down again. "It's harder to be the Majicou than you thought."

"I always thought it was hard," said Tag.

"Other than the defeat of that wretched animal, what have we gained from this?"

"Nothing." He shrugged. "Everything. Whose answer would

you like—mine or the new Majicou's? Two worlds are crossing in front of me, Pertelot, and I can no longer reconcile them."

But Pertelot would not be put off like that. She was the Mau. Love and demand were never separate in her. Her tantrums, her fits of melancholy or prophecy or overwhelming love, were a way of navigating the world. She smelled of cinnamon and almonds. Her eyes were still full of Egypt, which he imagined as a landscape of the senses rather than the heart, a palette of harsh colors and exciting speech, a place where the very dust was infused with bravura tastes and smells. He thought, She is the thread that links our past to our future. Her needs drive us all. Sensing this, she was able to persist.

"Will I ever see my missing children again?"

"I believe you will, and soon."

The fox had followed this exchange intently, his yellow eyes glittering. Now he got to his feet, shook himself, and, blunt nails clicking arrhythmically on the concrete floor, limped across to warn, "The night isn't over yet, Majicou."

Tag cocked his head again, as if he could hear something more than the thrum and mumble of the onshore wind across the oceanarium roof.

"Did I say it was?" he asked.

After a moment he added, "I wish you'd call me Tag."

🐾

The cats slept in a heap: two bodies here curled yin and yang, two heads there resting on the same flank—more paws than you could imagine. The fox watched over them for a while, grinning his feral grin as he tried to work out who was connected to what, then, giving up, went off to doze on his own by the door, thinking, I rather like them. But I'd prefer cubs. While behind the glass, exalted by the light pouring down, the fishes turned and danced. All was calm in the oceanarium until, perhaps two hours before dawn, Kater Murr's bedraggled remains began to stir.

It was some internal rearrangement, the fox thought, some contraction of the ligaments: the faint paradoxical gestures of rigor. A paw twitched. The stuffed-looking head, with its glassy eyes and snaggle teeth, seemed to settle minutely. That would have been that for an ordinary cat—but not for Kater Murr. His outline seemed to shift. The air around him flexed and creaked. Suddenly, the fox's mouth was filled with a bad taste. Head low and hackles stiff, he approached the corpse. Warm drafts curled around it briefly, lifting dust into his eyes.

"What's this?" he asked himself.

He thought he had better alert the new Majicou; but as soon as he turned away from the corpse, a polite cough came from behind him, then another noise which, once it had begun, went on and on.

The cats woke up to find him darting around them in desperation, nipping at their ears, their noses, their tails, yelping, "Wake up! Wake up!" They jumped to their feet, fur on end, blinking in sleepy alarm. The electric light pulsed slowly and nauseatingly; while inside the tank itself, lightning seemed to flicker as the panicked fish twisted to and fro. "Wake up!" All they could tell was that the half dark was full of the drone of some faulty machine. A strong, insistent wind, rattling and banging at the oceanarium doors until it tore them open, deafened the cats and made them stagger. A stinging litter of plastic straws, cigarette butts, grit, sheets of newspaper, and discarded fast-food cartons blew into their faces, to whirl past and be sucked up into the great spinning inverted funnel of shadow that had issued from Kater Murr's body and now tottered over them like a humming top about to run down—a smoky, uneven vortex twice as tall as the fish tank, bulging and bending and losing its definition but growing denser second by second as it sucked the rubbish up into itself.

Rags and Pertelot stared up in horror.

"I smell heartbreak, Ace," said Cy, prudently backing away.

Leo, ambushed by memory, stood stock-still and whispered to herself in a kind of hushed delight, "I knew. They were down there under the earth. I knew they were down there, all the time!"

The fox stared at her as if she were mad.

"What's happening?" he demanded.

Tag said, "The doorkeeper has become the door."

Then he said, "Run! We must all get out of here! Out of here and up the hill! Run!"

Even as he spoke, the vortex hummed and darkened, drawing in a gale that smelled of rain and the sea and carried with it larger objects from outside—an orange life belt, billows of nylon fishing net, some slats from a wooden bench. The oceanarium seemed to wince under this onslaught. Its doors flapped wildly for an instant, were wrenched off their hinges, and toppled end over end toward the vortex, disintegrating as they went. Splinters filled the air.

"Run as hard as you can!"

But running of any kind was out of the question. Instead, they assembled themselves in single file behind the King's reassuring bulk and, step by step, head down, his great mane rippling back in the gale, he led them toward the door. The entire structure creaked and flexed around them as they dragged themselves along.

At the door Pertelot Fitzwilliam stopped. "Mercury," she cried. "What is happening?"

He laughed suddenly. "Wait and see," he said.

When she had gone, he looked up at the vortex once more. It bellied toward him briefly, breaking up into the loose whirl of litter you might see at any street corner on a windy day. Then a note or two of music was played, on reeds and finger drums, and a human figure became visible. "Bring me your kittens," the figure said. "Bring me all the kittens." Mutilated in some way and wearing a mask, it held its arms in stiff, hieratic positions.

There was a deep, hollow groan of pain, and a different voice said clearly, "Tag, we can still defeat him if we keep our heads."

Tag withdrew hastily. The last thing he saw was Kater Murr, who could still be made out at the toe of the vortex, where it tapered down to a single point gliding here and there at random an inch or so above the dead cat's fur. Tag expected to see him sucked up like everything else, but he simply lay there while it buzzed and groaned above him, his teeth drawn back in a terrible grin.

This was what he wanted, that grin seemed to say. *Kater Murr was no ordinary thing.*

🐾

Five cats and a fox stood above a seaside town in the hour before dawn, waiting to see what would come next. The sky above the bay was full of rushing cobalt blue cloud, a layer of gray impasto obscuring its junction with the sea. There were no lights in the cottages that tumbled away down the windy hill to the harbor.

"Cold here," said Cy to Tag. She looked up at him. "Get closer," she ordered. When he didn't reply, she purred anyway. "Hey, don't worry, Ace," she advised him. "It'll all come out in the wash. Get it?"

He stared at her. "I'll never understand you," he said.

She wriggled with pleasure.

"What's to understand?" she said. "Girls just want to have fun." She looked down at the oceanarium. "It's a roary old night," she said grimly.

"It is," said Tag.

He left her for a moment and went to talk to Ragnar and the fox. "There isn't much cover here," he said, staring across the hilltop. It was desolate and exposed: tourist-worn grass, one or two concrete benches, a litter bin, some small gorse bushes, and outcrops of rock.

"We'd be better off in the streets," the fox suggested.

Ragnar Gustaffson agreed. "It would be harder for that thing to follow us there." He shivered. "In the tombs, it was not good at corners."

"There are human beings down there," said Tag.

"Why should we care?" said the fox. "None of them knows what is happening up here."

"It is not their part to know," said the King.

No, thought Tag, with an unkindness that rather surprised him. *Their part is to sleep, while the secret world revolves around them. They will never know what happened here.* Aloud, he said, "Ragnar is right. We must try to make sure their houses don't fall on top of them."

This gave Loves a Dustbin some amusement.

"After all," he said, "they have always done the same for us foxes."

"Even so, my friend," said the King, "even so."

Tag looked down the hill. Shortly after their escape, the oceanarium had begun to make the sound of a chord played on a church organ. They could feel it vibrating in the deep cavities of their bodies. Powerful currents of air rushed into the gaping doorway from every direction; the walls shook and juddered and shifted on their foundations. It seemed as if the building itself were alive, drawing down the wind the way a sea creature filters the water for food. All the wastepaper in the town came flapping and dancing up the hill. The telephone wires tautened and bowed. Even the beach sand had begun to move upward in little trickles and drifts.

"I hate this!" said Leonora Whitstand Merril suddenly. "Why is that thing taking so long? Why is it waiting down there?"

"Look!" called Pertelot Fitzwilliam. "Oh, look!"

Out of the corner of her eye, she had glimpsed something in the maze of roofs below the oceanarium. Uninterpretable at first, it was less an object than an event—a tantalizing flicker of movement between two chimney pots in the night and the rain, a sense that *something* had quickly descended a slate roof and was already out of sight. But it was coming toward them, whatever it was . . .

"Look now!" urged Pertelot. "See? Rags, Mercury, can you see?"

And as it came closer, its movements resolved into the distinctive body language of a hurrying cat: the steep leap up onto the wall, the quick deft padding run extended into a graceful arc, the scuttle across rain-blackened granite setts. Even so, at that distance nothing was certain except that these actions had been performed. No one—they were all watching expectantly now—had yet seen the cat that performed them. Then the fox said, "There, by the base of that wall. Two of them!" After a moment he added, "They know what they're doing."

There they were, moving fast and agile through the gale and the flying wrack, giving a wide berth to the oceanarium, keeping to the lee of things when they could. They were out-door cats, lean and muscular, hard as nails. They were clearly a team, but one was always a little ahead of the other, stop-ping and waiting briefly before running on, as if it alone knew the way.

Larger but more lightly built, with long and rangy legs, it had a short thick pelt which shone a kind of dull gold in the dirty light. Catching sight of the cats on the hill, and sud-denly unable to contain itself any longer, it left its companion behind at last and came bounding up toward them, calling out their names. For their part, they observed with sadness its missing eye but marked the power of its limbs, the joy and en-ergy in every stride.

Then Pertelot was turning in excited circles, calling, "Odin! It's Odin! Oh, Rags, oh, everyone, look. Do look!"

The first of the lost kittens had come home.

🐾

Some years before, an autumn storm had torn two score Welsh slates from the seaward side of the oceanarium roof. The panels of corrugated iron that had replaced them—painted first black and then a curious cheap aquamarine color soon streaked with rust—were now trying to take flight in their turn, screeching and rattling and tearing grimly at the nails that held them. Suddenly they had got loose! One by one they flapped dizzily into the air on some countercurrent or eddy, only to be sucked savagely down into the humming pit beneath. After a moment, the three-cornered symbol ap-peared, larger than it had ever been, floating just above the apex of the roof. It was large and bright, but something was wrong with it. Two lines were there—the base and one side—but the third, which would have completed the apex, was only implied. Closure was withheld; something more, perhaps, was necessary. In response to its appearance, however, the hum of the vortex dropped to a throbbing rumble, and the whole hill began to shake. The cats felt it through the pads of their feet, but they were too happy to notice.

🐾

The Mau, who was now about half her kitten's size, boxed his ears until he rolled on his back in front of her, his whole body wriggling with laughter. "That will teach you to worry your mother!" she said. "You brute of a thing." And she began to laugh, too.

"Be careful with that son," warned Ragnar. "I might never have another."

"What do males know?" said Pertelot Fitzwilliam. She gave him a direct look. "You'll have another one sooner than you think," she promised.

"It has been mostly daughters so far."

"This one is not a daughter," said the Queen softly. And overcome with tenderness, she licked and licked at Odin's empty socket, as if she could bring back the missing eye.

Growing impatient with this after a minute or two, the kitten shook his head and jumped to his feet, to chase first his mother and then Leonora Whitstand Merril in a circle around the concrete waste bin, while Ragnar and the fox egged them on with vulgar yelps and yowls. The Queen was soon out of breath. She had quite lost her dignity. But brother and sister ran on, around and around like a clockwork toy. They ran with their eyes popping and their tails curled into question marks. They ran with such vigor that earth and grass flew up from their feet. In the right place, you felt, their efforts would have rolled the world along beneath them, and their joy reclaimed the bleak little nighttime hilltop and made it a park.

It was such a reunion! But the new Majicou stood apart from it all, looking puzzledly down the hill. Just outside the reach of the last good streetlamp, where the cottages petered out and the grass began, Odin's companion waited alone, a shadowy figure blinking uncertainly in the dim light.

"Won't you come up?" Tag invited.

No answer.

He felt a sudden dread.

"It was good of you to bring the kitten home," he said.

Still no answer.

"He says you know us. He says you once knew Pertelot Fitzwilliam."

Silence.

"Won't you come up and let us thank you?"

Only silence.

"Then I'll come down," said Tag.

"Nah, nah," said a quiet voice. "No need for that. I was a bit shy, that's all. I'm all right now. No need for you to come down."

Out of the shadows stepped a cat the color of a shellac comb. His coat was so heavily mottled and patterned, so dark in places as to be almost black. The fur itself was very short and coarse, with a suspicion of a curl. One of his eyes was a frank and open speedwell blue, the other was the color of sodium light. Both were framed by the gray, ridged scar tissue of the compulsive street fighter, and despite his numerous old wounds he still moved with a heavy, rolling grace.

Tag stared. "You're dead," he whispered.

Mousebreath looked down at himself. "Nah, mate," he said. "I'm not."

He said, "It was touch an' go for bit, though. I'll say that."

He studied Tag out of his blue eye.

"You don't look a day older," he said. "Catching any mice?"

"Oh, Mousebreath, *Mousebreath*!"

"That's me name."

The old fighter looked around. "Nice here," he said noncommittally. "Seaside an' all." He indicated the Queen and said, "*She's* here then, I see. Kittens turned out nice. Good little hunter that One-Eye, got a good style on him, keen as mustard, plenty of energy." He was silent suddenly. "Yes," he said, "you all made it through. I'm glad. I'm glad to see that." This admission seemed to make him thoughtful, but he soon brightened up. "Where's that old calico cat, then? Where's that old Sealink? I bet she's got a thing or two to tell!"

Then he whispered, in a lost and broken way, "How did it all work out, Tag? How did it all work out?"

"Oh, Mousebreath. I don't know where to start."

Mousebreath looked away. "I lost so much of my life," he said hoarsely, "one way and another." He shook his head. "Start anywhere," he said, "so long as I *know*." Then he sighed. He gave the oceanarium the benefit of his orange eye. "Start with that," he said. "You can tell me about that. I might be able to help." He held one paw up in front of his face. Suddenly it was full of razors. "Well, would you look at that," he said. He winked. "I got two names now," he said, "but I'm the same old cat."

"Well—" Tag began.

As he spoke, the oceanarium began to disintegrate.

Electricity pulsed and sang in the stonework, crackled down over the outer walls like torn lace. The vortex collapsed briefly into silence. A dead calm set in immediately all over town. Garbage fell into the gardens. Bin lids rolled down the street, toppled over, and were still. Then it wound itself up again. A long pulse of bitter white light poured out of the doorway and at the same time the whole building seemed to lift a fraction and become very slightly larger than itself. Every stone was outlined in light as it separated gently from the stones around it. The noise ran rapidly up to a whine so high-pitched you could barely detect it. At the instant it snapped into inaudibility, there was a soft contemptuous *"Pah!"* as of expelled breath, and the building blew apart. The cats were bowled over by the force of it. Stone blocks, broken slates, and bits of timber the size of railway ties rained down, thudding deep into the earth around them. They took shelter under a concrete bench, and found the fox already in possession.

"Look at that," he said disgustedly.

There was just enough light left to see the fish tank, standing complete and undamaged on its circular concrete base. A flicker of motion here and there inside suggested that its inhabitants, though surprised, remained mobile and in their proper element.

"How does that happen?" said the fox. "How does a thing like that happen?"

"Ask yourself what has happened to the whirlwind," advised the new Majicou irritably. "We will never be safe if all this is not brought to an end!"

No more objects fell. One by one the animals pulled themselves out from under the bench and looked around cautiously. They looked inland. Nothing. They looked out to sea. Nothing there, either. Out in the bay a light breeze had got up and was blowing toward them. It smelled of dawn, though the eastern sky remained dark.

"We are okay now, I think," declared Ragnar.

The earth in front of him shook and rumbled. Out of it, with a grinding noise like ancient machinery, rose two figures.

Vast and silent, as posed and hieratic as the stone giants in an Egyptian temple, they loomed up motionless against the sky, Majicou and the Alchemist, the wise black cat and his erstwhile master. The cat's tail lashed. The Alchemist's rags fluttered a little in the wind. They seemed uncertain. They had been a long time in their own domain, bound one to the other. They had been much under the earth, in the darkness, unwilling to give up. They were unfamiliar with the world. They stared down at the animals on the little hill in a kind of puzzlement: life, they seemed to be thinking, but so small. Did they remember the battle for Tintagel, in the days when they had been small life, too?

Who knew?

The Alchemist said, in a voice that echoed over the bay and out to sea, "The kittens! I'll have them, Hobbe. They're mine now."

And the Majicou replied, "Not while I live."

And they lunged at each other as if for the first time, tit for tat, blow for blow, faster and faster, until, humming and groaning with all their rage and pain, they became a single entity again. The vortex roared off across the hill, ripping up the earth and throwing it about. In the attempt to escape its own duality, it flung itself into the sky and stormed across it, glowing like a meteor. It plunged into the sea in a welter of steam and rose again unquenched. Then it arrowed inland again, toward the hill and the waiting animals.

What could they do? The winds raged around them. There was no sign of dawn. They had made up their minds not to hide in the town, and there was nowhere else to go. They stood up bravely, into a rain of dirt and stones, waiting for whatever would happen. Then Mercurius Realtime DeNeuve, the new Majicou, began to laugh.

"I believe we've won," he said.

His friends looked at him as if he were mad.

"Look! In the sky!"

And there, glowing and pulsing in the air above the oceanarium, was the triangular symbol. As they watched, its third side shimmered into existence, winked out, returned . . . held. The figure had completed itself. At its apex, a tremulous globe of light could be seen, so faint it was like an unremembered word on the tip of the tongue.

"Behind me!" cried Tag. "If you want to survive, get behind me, all of you!"

The look he gave them was so intense they could only obey. They tucked in one by one—Rags and Pertelot, Odin and Leonora—as if they were entering a building, as if some real shelter might be had from him; and indeed the wind did seem to abate a little in the lee of his warm body. The dustbin fox gave him a strange, long, yellow-eyed look—"Take care, my friend!" he warned. "You have done this too often already!"—and tucked in behind with Mousebreath. The last to come was Cy the tabby. She rubbed her head against him and purred so loud he could hear her above the gathering storm.

"I always had faith in you, Ace," she said. "Don't let me down now."

Tag laughed.

"Tuck in!" he cried. "And look away!"

There was a crash of thunder and a smell of distant snow.

❧

Arriving disoriented and irritable after her recent hometown travails, Sealink the calico regarded the scene on the hilltop with disbelief.

She had enjoyed the flight—when had she not enjoyed a flight?—but not the grim and tiring journey from the airport, struggling like an insect in the shredded web of the Old Changing Way. Isis, preoccupied and driven and sometimes not what you would call good company, had sung them through the difficulties—an act in itself less than comforting. Her music often engaged something eerie in the world. To be frank, it set your teeth on edge. Despite all that, though, and despite the kitten's disappointment when she found her Tintagel home abandoned, they had made it. Where they had made it to was another matter.

"It looked like hell," she would say later. "And, to tell the truth, so did you guys."

The symbol that—from Egyptian tomb to Louisiana swamp to Tintagel cave—had presided over every turn of these events, now pulsed on and off in the predawn sky like neon outside a fish-and-chip shop. Dimly and intermittently revealed by this eerie half light, the top of the hill, with its half-buried lumps of fallen masonry, seemed like the surface of the moon; while the remains of the oceanarium resembled some recent, disputed archaeological find.

If the sign illuminated this desolation, the whirlwind commanded it. Eighty feet high by then, a tight and graceful twist of darkness, it came and went as it pleased. Not a blade of grass or a tuft of bilberry remained on the hilltop. The topsoil itself was being whipped up in a furious ground blizzard, even as the astonished calico watched, to form a kind of veil or caul for the lower third of the vortex. Concrete benches groaned and strained: they were plucked free of their bolts in the bedrock and sucked in. The litter bin lasted a moment longer, then went spinning up to join them.

Nothing, Sealink remarked to herself, could be left alive in the face of that nightmare. It was simply a bad place for small animals. And yet there they were, flattened to ground, half blind, a handful of cats and one bruised-looking fox, giving the world anxious glances as it broke up around them. And, interposed between them and the oncoming storm, a white snow tiger. Iron-striped, one huge paw raised emblematically, he was fifteen feet long from nose to tail. The light now spilling off his fur had shone in arctic summers long ago. "Be careful," the fox had warned him. Yet when you reach inside yourself there is always more. He denied the passing of things. His mouth was open on the roar of his own life—as if breath, blood, and bone were in the end all you needed to prevail ten thousand years. From saber tooth to domestic cat, the fields of ice to the Battle of Tintagel, and now this bald, bleak little hilltop: in the face of disaster, Mercurius Realtime DeNeuve, the new Majicou, had held his ground.

Sealink couldn't take it in.

"That's *Tag*," she said.

She said, "I've seen that triangle in the sky before. It was real recent, too."

She scanned the hilltop carefully again.

"I was hoping we would get some answers here," she told Isis. She narrowed her eyes. "But I can't seem to take any of this in. Is that a fish tank, hon?"

Chapter Twenty

GREEN WORLD

*B*ut Isis wasn't listening. She had run off to join Odin and Leo.

"Honey," Sealink began, "I don't think—"

Too late.

Everything hung for an instant on the edge of disaster, then toppled over.

Isis called out to her brother and sister. Hearing her voice but unable to see her, Odin and Leo abandoned the lee of the white tiger and ran about aimlessly through the wrack.

"I'll have them all now," the vortex told itself.

Isis froze, one forepaw lifted. She glanced desperately this way and that.

At the last minute, as the whirlwind bent toward her, Mercurius Realtime DeNeuve reared up between them, offering his iron claws . . .

Deprived of shelter by this maneuver, the remaining cats scattered and went to ground in shallow scoops and pockets in the exposed pink granite bedrock. There, they hung on grimly. They would have to endure, they supposed. They tried, as cats do when things have gone too far, to hunch down inside themselves and persist.

Sealink, watching in a kind of paralysis, unable to think of anything at all to do to help her old friends, imagined for a moment she could see a tortoiseshell tom among them. Her heart leapt: but it was only the dustbin fox after all, his coat mottled with dirt. Who else might be there was hard to tell, though she thought she saw Ragnar Gustaffson, trying with some success to shelter his Queen.

"Steady, girl," she warned herself. "No use folding now. This is an extreme situation . . ."

Locked in a strange uneven struggle, the air around them distorted and full of mirages, tiger and whirlwind staggered together around the remains of the oceanarium. Their groans and roars went twenty miles out to sea, like some experimental warning to sailors—a hint of risks less easy to comprehend than the rocks, shoals, and lee shore fogs of ordinary nautical life. At the same time, bizarre odors enveloped the hilltop—hot brass, chemicals, and incense tars—dispersed by the smell of a wind that had passed recently over a thousand miles of ice.

The kittens called out to one another as they ran, in voices plaintive yet somehow harsh and penetrating, as if designed for just this eventuality. Each time Sealink caught a glimpse of them, through curtains of suspended earth, their cries had brought them closer together. They seemed larger than before. They moved purposefully, bringing to the brutalized hilltop a whiff of the burnt sand and dry savannah that lie in the history of every cat. Above them in the sky, the triangular symbol pulsed and brightened ecstatically as if to welcome them, then faded forever; and it was as three points of a triangle that they finally converged. What began then, no one could be sure.

At first they greeted one another like kittens, bounding around, rubbing heads, exchanging playful cuffs, rolling on the scoured rock. At length this behavior was replaced by something more measured and formal. They sat straight and tall, perfectly motionless, and regarded one another in silence.

Then Odin's head went up. He began to stalk the wind.

He sniffed. He crouched. He waggled his haunches, then sprang. After that, he leapt straight up into the air from a standing start, turning and elongating his body as he went, and snapped his jaws together like a trap. Landing with careless precision, he made one of those intent, scuffling runs you are sometimes forced into if the prey is lucky enough to take off before you have arrived. He shrugged. "It is ugly but it is a technique," he seemed to be saying, "like any other. The cat never gives up, or how will it eat?" He stopped and stared at his sisters until he was sure they were watching. "And this is how I do it when they hide in the long grass. See? More height in the jump, and bring your weight down behind your front paws. Like this!"

They observed this demonstration gravely.

They exchanged a long confidential glance, as if to say: Yes, that is how to hunt. But now this. Look! Listen!

Then Leonora Whitstand Merril began to dance, and Isis began to sing, and the hunt and the dance and the song wove a kind of pattern into the air around them. It was long and intricate, and the threads in it were made of gold and blood and all the things cats have ever done. And this is some of the meaning of it—because it is still being sung:

Eat, bear kittens, sing the song of the cat in the night. This is a grasshopper, this is a mouse, but this only a bit of grass in a dry wind. These are the leaves of the trees and the birds among them—which also sing. This is how to change direction at full speed—you may need that trick sooner than you think. Hush! That is a kitten, lost in the dark; and this is the sound the lark makes as she rises through the morning— never eat her feet. This is how we were in Nubia, and then in Egypt. Men welcomed us. The Nile comforted us. Her pigeons were in our mouths . . .

It was less a song, or a dance, or practice for the hunt, than a tapestry, the *tapetus lucidum* of the Felidae. The task of weaving it brought the kittens closer and closer together until they were facing one another from the points of a triangle again. A ripple seemed to pass through them. A shaft of light struck down from above. Their images were progressively overlaid, shimmering like cats seen through heat haze on a summer morning. Suddenly, they had slipped into one another, and a single animal stood where three had been. It looked back at its parents, then turned and loped away into its own dance and vanished.

Only the *tapetus lucidum* remained, intricating itself across the hilltop, febrile and tenuous, as if the very air were gilded with the life of cats.

Sealink looked up.

Ragnar and Pertelot looked up from their shallow refuge in the granite.

Cy the tabby blinked and looked up.

"Wow!" she told the fox, and he looked up, too.

A hush spread over the hilltop and down to the waiting town and its harbor beneath.

The sky began to brighten in the east.

"I ain't never seen anything like this," said Sealink.

🐾

Still himself and yet half Mousebreath—or was he still Mousebreath and yet half himself? he was too excited to be certain—Animal X watched the day infuse the horizontal clouds with color, layer by layer. At first it was a gold on the edge of green, transparent as a thin wash on alabaster, deepening as it spread until it was the color of light falling through hot foliage in some country no cat has ever seen but which all cats remember. I always loved the dawn, he thought. He held his breath. *He knew what was going to happen!* Slowly, very slowly, the tapestry the Golden Cat had made reached up. Slowly, the dawn reached down. They touched. There was a sound that was no sound at all. Suddenly, green light was everywhere, running over every surface—the sea, the harbor mole, the palms and bus shelters, the deserted Beach-O-Mat! It quivered in the shop windows—which, in response, boomed faintly, as if they had been touched—it ran up the cobbled hill, it fizzed and crackled across the roofs of the cottages and leapt the gap to the oceanarium steps!

Animal X shivered.

Light was on every barren inch of that hill like flames, a green dream like a lighted fuse, like soft laughter. It *was* laughter. It gathered and sparked. It held back for a moment, and he felt his own heart beat in the heart of it. Then the dawn broke, and the birds were singing. Every bird in the world was singing, and there was nothing left but light, and the thing that came out of the light, and everything was changed forever.

🐾

Who can see the Great Cat as She is?

We know how Animal X saw her. Since his experience in

the laboratory, She had rushed in upon him day by day as a green fire and taken him in the jaws of love.

But the dustbin fox said he saw this: shapes, perhaps not even animal but moving with the fluid violence of leopards, glorious unassuaged green forms like archangels, flowing through the world determined to change it. Was it the Great Cat herself or only her servants? "Who knows?" he asked himself. "She is the world." It made him remember why he had thrown in his lot with the old Majicou, so many years ago. "In that moment I remembered," he was to say later, "what we were trying to accomplish. But I still wept for Francine, wasted in someone else's war."

As for Cy the tabby: no one ever knew what she saw.

"I mean," she tried to explain later, "now you see it, now you don't. You know? It's couched in the shapes of things. It's crouched in the bus shelter. It lies in wait in the curve of the bay. What's familiar, you see it new. Over and out, Ace: Is that enough for you? Anything you look at's true!"

And what Ragnar and Pertelot saw was this.

A great triangle of light—the signature of their children, made to bring forth something even stranger than themselves—and, dawning at its apex, a light the color of peach and amber. Inside that light, curled in the vast sleep of time yet wakeful as the day, the Great Cat herself, the Mother of everything, the green dream that beats like a heart at the heart of the world. They knew her by her body, which is hill and bleak mountain, jungle and forest, and at the same time home and hearth. They knew her by that endless rumbling purr that is the sound of the world, the deep engines of the weather, the wind and the wave and the ocean the wave plays upon, and everything under the ocean, even to the deep halls of the fish. They knew her by her fur, which is a transforming fire, green on the edge of gold. They knew her by her seasons, which come and go. They knew her by her delight in every kitten, every scuttling mouse, every fallen leaf—and She knew them.

She opened her silver eye.
She opened her golden eye.
She woke to Herself.

She woke to the Little Mother and Father.

"I waited so long for you," She said.

Her voice sang in the very atoms of things. It sang inside Ragnar and Pertelot. When She stepped into the world, She emerged from inside them, She emerged from the light that surrounded them, She emerged from every grain of dust beneath their paws. She emerged from everything at once.

"Don't be afraid," She said.

Why should they be? Weren't they cats, too?

They sat straight and tall and threw out their chests and purred and purred and purred.

"When we were kittens," they heard themselves say, "you calmed us in the dark. Later we saw you in the noon heat, when life had us by the nape."

And Ragnar added, "I saw you in a picture, not so long ago."

She was the world. At the same time She was a cat like them, if very much larger. She had brought Egypt with her as a kind of backdrop, because She thought it might reassure them; also because She had once woken there for what seemed to her a brief instant—though to the humans of the Missing Dynasty who had worshipped her, it had been a thousand years—and had fallen in love with it. Palm and lemon flourished, and insects hummed across walled gardens barred with dull gold sunshine, and the ancestors played in the damp soft evening airs, the gray-feathered airs of every dawn. She had brought the trickle of irrigation, the lift of the egret's wing, the hidden pulse of the Nile. Behind her you could see the groves of trees like receding columns; music spooled between them. While all about her paws the ancestors were dancing, too! Queens and kittens, grave old toms with graying ears, they tumbled and purred, perhaps for her, but more likely for themselves. But when She saw that they needed none of this, She let the music die away. With a sound like a single drop of water falling into a pool, everything was subsumed under the great argument of time, the millennial dream.

Only the Great Cat remained. Green as jade, gold as the sun, She left the King and Queen and flickered like flames across the hilltop and wove her way into the heart of the storm, where She sat down suddenly and began to clean her paws. The air boomed and pulsed around her. Long streamers of cobalt-colored detritus were pulled out between earth and sky, twisting and interleaving themselves. Blue lightning flared and banged, and out to sea the wind ripped the gray waves to spray. The ground shook. The whirlwind loomed up . . .

"Be still now," She commanded.

She said, "Come to me now, both of you, and be still."

But the whirlwind would not obey. The two beings inside it raged across the hilltop, out to sea, and back again. They would not even answer. They wanted nothing she could offer. They were the Opposites, the sibling rivals, the dynamo of a vanishing age. They only wanted the struggle. After three hundred years, they had forgotten almost everything else.

The Great Cat laughed.

"The wild and the tame are only names for the same thing," She chided them.

"Will you come to me?" She said gently.

They would not. Why should they humble themselves in that way? Though each would like to humble the other. They tore up the bedrock and threw it about.

"It has been a long time, I know," She said.

She said, "Aren't you tired?"

At this, the winds died so suddenly that the world ached with silence. They *were* tired. They were old. As they wavered, so did the vortex. Its rate of spin decreased, a shudder passed through it. It toppled and lost coherence. There was a long pause. Then the air breathed a sigh of relief and began to clarify itself, like liquid in a glass. Everything which had been suspended—from mica dust to roofing slates, from cigarette packs to old car tires—was released. The sky filled with objects caught in a reluctant, dreamy, slow-motion fall.

"I absolve you," said the Great Cat.

She said, "I resolve you."

For a second, they reared up, separate and huge. But She was the Mother, always larger, always patient and determined; and that was the last time they were ever Majicou the one-eyed pet shop cat and the Alchemist, his erstwhile enemy. The cat's tail lashed. The old man's rags fluttered in the onshore wind. Then the Great Cat sprang upon them both without mercy or favor and stripped them bare in the jaws of love; and they cried out in their pain.

At last She released them.

The boy's name was Isaac. He was tall for his age and rather awkward in his movements; he wore sailcloth knee breeches and a full white linen shirt somewhat scruffy about the neck. His face was alive with curiosity, and he had a high opinion of himself. The cat had a high opinion of itself, too. It was a black barn cat the size, as the boy would often boast, of a horse. He had called it Hobbe because it was the very devil with a rat. It was still in possession of both its eyes, the unearthly green *tapetus lucidum* of which had already given him an interesting idea or two about light. They were an intelligent pair, inseparable and full of trouble.

"There!" The Great Cat laughed.

"At the foot of this hill," She said, "you will find a harbor and a new day dawning." She said, "Go and see what you can find. Boats for one and fish for the other!"

Hobbe ran out ahead with his tail up.

"And now, Little Father and Mother," said the Great Cat, "you have been patient long enough." She had drawn Egypt about her again like a mantle. They could hear white doves flutter in her voice. "Like your ancestors before you, you accepted a hard task. You accepted it out of faith and goodwill, not even knowing that it was a task. It was a life, and you lived it, and much will come of that."

Despite the spell of the Mother's voice, Pertelot stared around wildly. Where had her children gone?

"Did you think," the Great Cat went on, "that, having asked this of you, I would steal your kittens, too?" She laughed. "Well, perhaps I would," She said. "They're perfect enough—"

"I have always thought so," agreed the King of Cats complacently.

"Rags!" his wife admonished him.

"But watch!" finished the Great Cat.

There was a curious twist of light in the air beside her. Out of it to stand by her side, deep-chested and lithe, its legs impossibly thin and elegant, its strange long back curving away from high-pointed shoulder to rangy haunch, came the Golden Cat. Its eyes were unearthly.

"Here they are," She said. "I give them back to you, three kittens in one. Odin the hunter, with his dance of death. Isis, who stands for resurrection, protection, reincarnation, and song enough to wake the dead. Impetuous Leonora, whose joy is in the moment: she dances the dance of life. This is your child and mine," She told the King and Queen. "It is the child of the time to come. The birth of this cat was planned long before the white ship landed your forebears at Tintagel. See how it will run, through all the next age of the world. Look!" She said. "Oh, look!" A highway was opened before them, and the Golden Cat ran away down it with long, graceful, tireless strides. At the same time, it was somehow running toward them, shifting and changing into Odin and Isis and Leonora Whitstand Merril as it came.

"Mother!" cried Leonora. "Tell Odin I was right! *They were down there all the time!*"

"This is the problem with daughters," said Ragnar Gustaffson. "They always have to quibble."

"I have no answer to that," the Great Cat told him. "I was a daughter myself." And She began to fade away into her own dream. "Your lives were broken, but now they are mended," She told them. "Run!" She said. "I will always be with you now. Run and eat!" She said, "You are *all* Golden Cats."

And then, when only her voice was left in the jasmine-scented air, barely distinguishable from the soft sound of water in the hidden gardens of the Nile, She advised them gravely, "Go to your beautiful friend. He looked after you well, and now you must look after him."

🐾

They found him a little way away, half in and half out of a puddle of rainwater in a hollow in the bedrock. He was stretched out less like a cat than the long white pelt of one, unmarked but for a little blood around each nostril and a tarry deposit at the corner of each eye, for all the world as if he had been crying. His mouth was open on a tired snarl—or perhaps it was only a sigh of regret. Mercurius Realtime DeNeuve, an accidental prince from a pet shop in the city, had fought the whirlwind once too often and burned out his great Burmilla heart. The dustbin fox sat by him, looking angrily out to sea, and would not speak when the King and Queen approached; while the distraught Cy walked up and down, up and down, repeating, "This is no good, Jack. It's just no good."

Then Ragnar Gustaffson Coeur de Leon stepped forward. The New Black King had fought a storm or two in his life, and though his reputation rested elsewhere, he knew how it felt. But more: he never allowed another cat to be sickly for long. It was a point of honor with him.

"Dear me," he said, "what's this?"

And with the rough care of a mother with kittens, he began to clean Tag's face. He cleaned the nose. He cleaned the tear streaks below the eyes. Then he began to pass his tongue in long, powerful sweeps across the whole head and down the silver fur. A drowsy calm filled the watching animals. That tongue had eased away every kind of injury, spread warmth into young pains and old bones. The New Black King had halted sepsis and brought forth hale kittens from breech births. He could feel along the most elusive line of life, and follow it as he followed the wildest of roads. He was the King! He could find the most benighted of souls and lead it home. Ragnar could heal the sick.

But though he licked and licked he could not wake the dead.

He raised his head exhaustedly.

"I cannot understand you," he told his old friend. "I don't know where you've gone."

The tabby pushed her way between them.

"You let me down!" she cried. "You let me down!" It wasn't clear which one of them she meant. She touched the side of Tag's face gently with one paw. "Come back!" she said. "You come back now!" For the twentieth time since she had found him, she shut her eyes, put her mouth close to his nose, and exhaled sharply into his nostrils.

Nothing.

"This stuff is broke," she said, looking up at Ragnar and Pertelot as if it was their fault. "I was woke by it myself enough times before. Now it just don't work, when I know it should!"

"Nothing works," the fox said.

Without turning around, he added, "Life can be very remote. It can hide somewhere very deep inside. But a fox can always smell it."

"We know this," said the Queen.

"I cannot smell any life in him. I'm sorry."

"You should be ashamed to say that," the Queen told him. "You shouldn't give up. He is your friend."

"I've lost other friends," the fox responded darkly.

Pertelot didn't know how to argue against this. "The world is new!" was all she could think to say. "Why is this happening, when the world is new?" She looked around rather desperately, as if she expected the Great Cat to come back and help them.

"I think the world is us," said her husband gently.

"Oh, Ragnar, Ragnar!"

During this exchange, Cy the tabby had been prowling restlessly up and down, stopping every so often to knead the bleak ground by Tag's head, while she purred in a confused way.

Now she whispered, "Don't die, Ace. I got something so good to tell you. Don't be dead."

The fox got up and tried to comfort her, and all four of them stood looking down at Tag for a long time. "I remember when he was a kitten," Loves a Dustbin said. "He was in trouble the moment he left the house. But he never stopped loving the world." At last, they became uncomfortable and embarrassed, as animals often do in the presence of death, and began to walk away. Even the tabby appeared to forget why she had come.

"Don't you want to know what happened?" said a familiar voice from behind them.

They turned back in astonishment.

For an instant, they seemed to see a kind of fluttering transparency in the air around him, like very fine gold leaf applied to a window, so that the light shines through it. Here and there, as it wrapped him around, the shapes of cats seemed to coalesce for a split second—a tail, a muzzle, the tilt of a long tufted ear—only to vanish again. If they were cats, they were moving too fast to see; and it was clear that only a moment ago they had been moving even faster. The Golden Cat! As they watched it faded and vanished—with a flicker of laughter which might have been Leonora's—and suddenly three large gold-furred kittens had appeared, separating moment by moment from one another; and between them was Tag, yawning and shaking himself, examining in surprise his sodden underfur. No cat likes to wake up in a puddle. If he seemed a little frail—well, he had faced the storm, and reached inside for the last ounce of himself and given it away; and a cat is going to be tested by that. If he seemed a little vague, it sat well with his new demeanor. For, as his friends were quick to see, something more had happened to him while he was the White Tiger, the cat within the cat: Tag the kitten, still lost, still yearning for his old home, had quietly slipped away forever. In his place stood the Majicou: forceful, dignified, full of hope and authority.

"Don't you want to know what it all meant?"

They gathered around him on the hilltop, and this is how he explained the things that happened to them.

"It began with the defeat of the Alchemist," he said. "Something ended there: yet nothing was resolved. The Majicou and his enemy sank beneath Tintagel Head, where their struggles spun them like a huge dynamo in the darkness of the earth and the deep sea. There they remained. The weeks went by. The kittens thrived. Leonora Whitstand Merril insisted, 'I hear them down there at night.' If we had listened to her then, and asked ourselves what to do, would things have been any different? Who can tell? What is certain is that neither of them could get the upper hand. Neither of them dared relinquish the struggle for more than a second or two. Yet both were preoccupied by their own thoughts. The Alchemist, who in the instant of his downfall, had at last understood the meaning of what he had done, began to wonder how he might locate and destroy the Golden Cat. Majicou, while he had known all along that, for his old enemy, the moment of success would be the moment of defeat, had not expected to share it. Now, both of them realized that while the kittens remained alive, the Alchemist was not safe.

"In that moment, it all began again.

"Within the vortex, they began to use the wild roads, each in his way. They sent out proxies to do their work for them.

"The Alchemist worked through human beings and animals—Kater Murr was one of his proxies, and there will have been others in every city in the world. Majicou was less successful at this, though, as he and his opponent spun and boiled along the bottom of the sea, he was able to enlist the services of Ray the fish, who subsequently befriended Cy. Hoping in his impatience and despair to speak more directly to us, he began to send us a message: the Triangular Sign . . .

"Could they keep their thoughts and intentions from each other, those implacable enemies, as they struggled within the vortex? We can't know. Item by item, they renewed their connection with the world above. It was a connection tenuous, intermittent, hard to control. Their plans could be blown awry by a strong wind. Only one thing remained hard and certain: where one went, the other must inevitably follow. What one tried to make, the other tried to undo. That was how things stood the day the first of the kittens disappeared."

Tag was silent for a time, ordering his thoughts.

"Even then," he went on, "I knew that something was wrong with the wild roads. That was how I put it, and how my proxies put it to me: 'something wrong.' "

He laughed softly.

"The scale of the disaster had already proved beyond me," he admitted. "In their effort to maintain themselves, Majicou and the Alchemist had begun to destroy the object of their original dispute. Day by day, the Old Changing Way was leached of its power. Soon, instead of giving, it began to take. Cats were dying. Roads led nowhere. The world shrank. At the same time, the Alchemist's message—'Find and kill three golden kittens!'—was blurring fatally along the chain of proxies. Chaos and anger spread out like ripples. Men killed any cat they found; soon *cats* were killing cats. It was in this climate of terror that human proxies took Odin, returning a few weeks later for his sister.

"The rest we know."

There was a silence among the animals.

Then Ragnar Gustaffson spoke up.

"We may know what happened," he said, "but we do not know the meaning of it. The Sign, for instance. And as for the animal called Kater Murr—"

"Ah," said Tag, "the unfortunate Kater Murr! Driven by his hatred of Uroum Bashou, he taught himself to read, and reading entrapped him. Long before Leonora and I first visited Uroum Bashou's domain, Kater Murr had been lured to the room beneath the copper dome. There he became the Alchemist's proxy. All his powers came from that direction, and in the end they burned him up. That cat was never more than misled. In a way I am indebted to him. My eyes were opened by our encounter in the Alchemist's house. But Kater Murr was never more than a doorkeeper."

"Twice he could have killed Leonora," objected the King.

"The first time he was too busy boasting to her," said Tag. "Just as, later, he was too busy killing his old master out of spite." His voice turned cold and hard. "Kater Murr was only a cat that tried to walk like a man."

There was silence.

"And the Triangular Sign?" Tag prompted himself softly. "You should be proud to wear that, Ragnar. It is the Sign of Three." He considered this for a time. Then he went on, "Imagine yourself in the dark—beneath the earth or under the sea. You cannot speak. You dare not stop struggling. You are locked forever in the coils of your own duality. Your enemy is you. You are your enemy. Your sole means of speech is through a fisherman or a fish. The Majicou could only try to tell us what he had always known. None of Pertelot's kittens was the one the Alchemist sought. This wasn't some small piece of magic: to change the world forever, *all three* would be needed. That is what the Sign meant: three sides for three kittens and the three different qualities, the three inter-woven dances, which would bring down the Great Cat—that great rising sun at the apex of the pyramid. What seems so obvious to us as we stand here now, he was trying to tell us all along. The fish took you to Egypt so that you could read the old story—how Atum-Ra and Isis were beloved of the Great Cat. Majicou hoped that, of all of us, you two had the best chance of understanding. He may have tried to be there to talk to you himself: if so, he brought the whirlwind down on you instead. He was yoked to it—so how could he not?"

He was silent for a moment. Then he said, "I shall miss the Majicou. He taught me as well as he could in the time he had left to him. He fought a long hard fight for cats, and I don't believe he foresaw—though he foresaw a great deal—how he would suffer before She released him from his task."

Pertelot Fitzwilliam shivered.

"The Great Cat was behind it all," she said.

Tag replied, "The Great Cat is always behind it all."

"It is over now, though."

"It is."

"Things are made anew."

"They are."

"You looked after us well, Mercury."

"We looked after each other, Pertelot Fitzwilliam."

🐾

Even as this exchange took place, the green dream was settling into the world. Sometimes it was visible, sometimes it was not. One moment, the hilltop was bare. The next it had been clothed with soil, and the soil put forth shoots like flames, and the shoots put forth flowers as you looked. The coats of the cats shone with health. The fox looked like a beacon in the morning. He was so full of his own foxy life that sailors could smell him out to sea.

The dream coiled down through the waking village. Pelargoniums ran riot in their pots as it passed, and the steep little lanes were full of the smells of sea lavender and thyme. It glittered in the fish scales on the harbor wall, and laughed to find the tubby colored boats. It flowed in and out of the chip shop, and across the seafront to the sand. It gathered at the tide line, then hurled itself across the sea!

Everything it touched was changed, even the air. Everything it touched was healed. In New Orleans, Eponine Lafeet felt the green dream in the air and smiled. It had come at last, as she had foreseen. *Green world.* Ripples went out, out, out, and touched it all. They touched the last free cats of the French Quarter, who were delighted to find human hands outstretched to them once more in alley and restaurant, and crawfish back on the menu. Red and Téophine rolled in the sunlight and in that moment *knew* the kittens of their future. They touched Shine the mule—fragrant grass sprang up in the Elysian Fields around her. They shyly touched the body of Uroum Bashou—the old hero was plush and velvet among his books in green dawn light! They touched the Winfield Farm laboratory, where a riot of jungle vegetation had already grown over the examination table and choked the rusting cages, and dangerous new feline shadows stood guard motionlessly in the arboreal gloom to make sure human beings never took it back. The same ripples touched Cottonreel and the beautiful Amelie, looking out hopefully across the water meadows for what would come. They touched the gas-tarred chicken hutch where a fat tabby called Stilton turned comfortably in his sleep and whispered, "You get a lot if you're a cat."

The green dream touched all these things, and passed on around the world.

🐾

Now the King and Queen—followed in stately, measured procession by Cy and Tag, while the dustbin fox brought up the rear, his pink tongue flapping like a yard of ribbon as he stared about in amazement at the new morning—made their way down to the ruins of the oceanarium. The fish tank had survived against all odds and was now laced with grape ivy and convulvulus. Down through the water struck shafts of sunshine so massy and palpable that the fishes seemed to turn like dancers between the columns of a temple. Honeysuckle and clematis wound the treads of the spiral stair. Ragnar and

Pertelot trod and purred and kneaded. They felt that they had survived against the odds, too. To mark this event, and give it its proper weight, they circled the fish tank three times; and the Golden Cat twined itself between them as they went. Now it had three selves, now it had one. Isis, Odin, and Leonora Whitstand Merril merged and flickered into a single tall lean unfocused shape that wound back and forth between the King and Queen like living gilded ribbon.

❦

All this time, Sealink and Mousebreath had been rather shyly standing to one side, each eyeing the other but making no overtures. They were both so changed by their experiences they hardly recognized each other. He could not believe how tired she looked, or how different she smelled. She couldn't quite come to grips with the Animal X in him. It had been long hard roads for both of them, and there were many stories left to be told; and neither of them understood just yet the things that had happened. So they stood around on opposite edges of the celebration, full of awkwardness, separated by death and adventure and perhaps pride; and she was a little angry with him for not coming forward and making things easy, and he was a little angry with her for the same reason; and both of them were a little afraid.

"Won't you come and talk to him?" suggested Tag to the calico.

"Tell you the truth, honey, I can't quite believe he's there," said Sealink, in rather too loud a voice. "Last time I hear anything, he's dead. Now he comes back with a split personality."

She washed her tail energetically.

"These tomcats. They can't never make up their minds."

"At least come and talk to him."

❦

"Won't you come and talk to her?" the Queen begged Mousebreath. "She's missed you so."

"I'm a bit shy, to tell the truth," said Mousebreath. "Thing is," he added, after some thought, "I bin someone else for so long. It changes you."

"At least come and talk to her."

❧

In the event, the calico boxed his ears.

"You had no call to die on me like that!" she said. "No call at all."

Mousebreath studied her speculatively, a glint of amusement in his blue eye.

"I didn't have no option," he said, "at the time."

And rather to the surprise of everyone, he stood up on his hind legs and gave her a couple of good cuffs in return. She hissed and narrowed her eyes and backed away an inch or two.

"You were never any good for anything but the two *F*s anyway," she accused him.

"I never heard you complain about that."

She thought it over.

"But honey, how *could* you? I mean just die on me?" she said.

"Well," he conceded, "it was a bit sudden, I suppose."

"But you won't do it again?"

"Come here," suggested Mousebreath. "No, come here close an' listen."

"What?"

"This might come as a surprise, but I feel I got to tell you. I always loved you when you was angry."

Sealink gave him an oblique look.

"Why, you ain't changed a bit, you ol' bastard." She laughed. "Oh, hon, I missed you so!" She looked out over the sea, remembering Louisiana and the old life—with all its disappointments and splendors—she had closed the doors on back there. "I got a thousand things to tell you," she sighed.

Mousebreath winked his unreliable eye.

"I got one or two things to tell you, too," he admitted, thinking of Amelie.

And they fell to rubbing heads, and rolling about like kittens in the sun and the smell of the sea. After that, they walked off together for a while, talking ten to the dozen, down through the village toward the harbor. Their tails were straight up and tip curled. Her great furry haunches rolled like a ship at sea; he gave them an appreciative look. The sidelong glances she cast him when she thought he wasn't looking would change your views on love. His mismatched eyes caught every one of them; and you could hear him say, "It's nice ter come back from the dead. I might do it more often."

"You'll get the chance, if you ain't true."

🐾

The Dog had watched all these events with puzzlement. There had been some bad weather in the night. You couldn't deny that. Cats had made a lot of fuss about the weather and run about shouting at one another: you couldn't deny that, either. There is never any sense in courting trouble; the Dog had done the sensible thing and waited it all out in a doorway in the village. Even so, it had got wet. Now it waited again until Sealink and Mousebreath were safely out of sight, then set itself to limp slowly to the top of the hill. There it cast about. If its eyes were no longer good, its nose was still reliable.

A dog can take its time about things, it thought as it went. That is another thing about a dog.

After several false casts it found Tag, and stood there panting a little in front of him, the smell of its coarse damp coat overpowering the odors of honeysuckle and convulvulus. Its body rocked backward and forward.

"You are the new Majicou," it said.

"I am."

"I do not know the names of all these other cats."

"No."

"They look like cats to me, whatever you want to call them. One cat looks very much like another."

"Cats are cats and dogs are dogs."

"True," acknowledged the Dog. It sighed. "At Cutting Lane you asked for news of two golden kittens," it said.

"That was a long time ago."

The Dog ignored him.

"Well, there are two golden kittens here," it said. "In fact there are three."

Tag stared.

"I knew that already," he said.

"Nevertheless I found them," the Dog pointed out. "For a

long time," it added for the sake of accuracy, "there was only one."

"You might say," said Tag, also for the sake of accuracy, "that there was only one here now."

The Dog stood for a long moment, shifting its weight about between its three tired old legs. Then it said, "A dog is an animal you can rely on. I was asked to find two golden kittens, and I did. You said I would have a reward." It had borne the events of a long life with stoicism, asking itself at every turn, What can you do about the weather? and answering, You can't do anything about the weather. Now it told itself, "A dog is an animal that can grow old and still present a plausible face to things. A dog endures, rain or shine—that is one thing about a dog. A dog deserves its reward. That is one of the other things."

"You promised me," it said.

Tag had no idea what to say. He looked at the Dog. The Dog looked back.

"I don't know what to give you," said Tag.

"The old Majicou fulfilled *his* promises," commented the Dog.

At that moment, there was a disturbance in the oceanarium tank. Between the skeins of ivy and masses of white convulvulus flowers, shoals of mackerel and herring could be seen darting this way and that in unsynchronized panic. Suddenly the water had turned the color of ocean-floor mud, through the grayish swirls and coils of which could be discerned an eye as big as an orange and as expressionless as a black bead, a white wingtip upcurved, and gill slits—as Sealink might have put it—the size of intakes on a jumbo jet. Something large had arrived.

"It's Ray!" cried Cy the tabby. "He's back!"

To the bemused Dog she confided, "When Ray gets here, that's when the party really begins." She added, "He's a fish, but he's, like, also my friend." And she ran up the spiral stairs to welcome him.

Below, a curious silence prevailed. The Dog continued to stare expectantly at Tag. The King and Queen stared puzzledly at the Dog. Then the Dog seemed to become aware of the fox. It studied him as closely as it could. It said, "This is not a cat. But it is not a dog, either."

Loves a Dustbin hung his tongue out amusedly.

"Don't get trapped in simple oppositions," he advised, "if you intend to enjoy life's rewards."

Hearing only the word *reward*, the Dog forgot him instantly and turned its attention back to Tag. Just then, Cy came down the stairs. In five minutes, all the joy had gone out of her.

"What is it?" said Tag.

"Oh, I love that Ray guy, but sometimes he's just so *irritating*. I ask him to the wedding, but no, he wants to go on somewhere else. I say, 'Where's that?' He says, 'Just down the road.' I say, 'Oh yes?' And he says, 'It's the stars, Little Warm Sister. It's out among the stars!' I go, 'What? What's out there?' Tag, he can't even say what! So I go, 'No way, Ray, I never liked it much the first time.' There's nothing out there but cold and like that."

She shook her head.

"These fish!" she said.

"I would have stayed here anyway," she told Tag, "even without the special reasons I got now." Nevertheless, she seemed bereft. "I'll miss that Ray, when he goes swimming back to the stars for kicks. I never had a fish for a friend before. I just ate them."

"He'll come back," Tag reassured her.

"Oh yes, in another thousand years."

Suddenly Tag had an idea.

"Ask him not to leave for a moment," he told her.

To the Dog, he said, "I am the Majicou."

"You are the *new* Majicou," the Dog corrected him. "I liked the old one better."

Tag heard Loves a Dustbin laughing quietly.

"I promised you a reward," he went on, "and this is it. You can go to the stars with the big fish."

"I would like something to eat, too."

There was a silence.

"Ah," said Tag.

Pertelot Fitzwilliam stepped forward. "Mercury," she said,

"I'm not sure you should be sending this animal to the stars at all. You certainly cannot send it unfed. Remember that the world is made anew."

Tag stared at her. "I don't think we've got anything to give him," he said.

"Wait, Ace!" said Cy the tabby, "I got this *idea*!" And she began to burrow through the dense vegetation at the base of the oceanarium, wriggling into the space between the tank and the concrete floor until only her bottom showed. After some excited scrabbling about, she carefully backed out of the convulvulus, dragging a single bicycle spoke.

The Dog studied this item without much hope.

"Look at *that*!" encouraged Cy.

But the Dog concluded, "A dog does not eat bicycle spokes."

"More fool you," said the tabby; and she was back under the tank like a shot. In quick succession, she brought out: one condensed milk can—empty—one plastic clothes pin, and two small fragile white shells. After some thought she added an empty crisp packet from the floor of an arcade, ancient breadcrusts she had won off a herring gull. She pulled out a square of disintegrating linoleum, part of a broken picture frame glimmering with gold and cinnabar paint. She brought out a deflated tennis ball, one white piano key, and bunch of plastic anemones. The Dog examined each of these items as it appeared, giving them full and proper attention. But in all honesty it could only shake its head, and say, "Dogs don't eat that."

"Neither do cats," said Tag in a heartfelt way that made everyone look at him.

"I don't know what people have got against my food," said Cy angrily. "Well, there's one more thing, *Ace*—" here she gave Tag a significant look. "—then the cupboard's closed." And she drew forth her *chef d'oeuvre*: two squares of milk chocolate still in their blue-foil wrapper.

"This is all we have," said the Queen to the Dog, with the generosity of the very royal.

The Dog sniffed the chocolate.

"Mm," it said. "That's nice."

With its great blunt claws and yellow teeth, it stripped off the foil, its muzzle creasing up, its lips wrinkling. Then it ate the chocolate with its mouth. It ate very slowly and carefully, so as to prolong the sensation as long as it could, looking up at the cats every so often and chewing with its mouth open. Then, with equal care, it licked the ground where the chocolate had been, relishing every crumb. Its energetic tongue propelled the foil into the air, where, caught by a breeze from the sea, it seemed to turn into a small butterfly with blue wingtips. Cy chased off after it, clapping her paws in the air. She looked like a kitten again. The Dog watched her with something like appreciation on its face.

"Well?" asked Tag. "Was that good?"

The Dog considered.

"It was. It was good. One thing about a dog—a dog knows about chocolate. Now," it said, "for the stars."

It got itself turned about in an almost lively way on its three legs, and stared up the spiral steps. Its gaze carried on past the rusty viewing platform and into the sky.

"This is a good reward," it said to Tag. "Anything could be out there." It lowered its voice. "I would never admit this to any cat but you: but it can get boring, being so dependable."

With great effort, blunt claws clicking and scraping, it made its way up the spiral staircase to the viewing platform. There it stood panting for a moment, looking around as if it might change its mind. Then it seemed to shrug. There was a flash brighter than the sun. The oceanarium water thickened to pearl. When it cleared again, fish and dog had gone.

🐾

After that, things were quiet. Later there would be stories to compare, boasts to be made, tales to be told. Everyone would catch up. Everything would be put in perspective, so that it could be narrated to kittens as the story of the Golden Cat. For now, though, they all seemed quite tired.

Sealink and Mousebreath, returning from the harbor, argued desultorily about the places they would visit when they started traveling again. The fox scratched himself in the warm sun, thinking that if he found the right vixen he could still settle down and have cubs . . .

I'm not too old, he thought. I would have a lot to pass on, especially about Chinese food—what to eat and what not to eat, and so on.

And the King and Queen of Cats, about whom the whole world had pivoted for a while, had simply curled up together and gone to sleep.

Their children never slept. It was their delight to weave the bright tapestry. But that is another story.

As for Tag, he was tired, too. He looked at his friends with love. We're all just cats in the sun now, he thought. He remembered himself as a kitten. All the way from a cloth mouse under the Welsh dresser, he thought, to this. He sat with Cy, washing her ears companionably, and after a while he said, "What was it you wanted to tell me?"

She purred and rubbed her cheek against his. "You got to guess, Ace," she said.

A white gull swept over the harbor and sped away inland.

Join us online to find out
even more about

THE
GOLDEN CAT
by GABRIEL KING

Visit us at

www.randomhouse.com/delrey/promo/king

for a special look at the
wild road with Gabriel King and his cats,
and much more.

DEL REY® ONLINE!

The Del Rey Internet Newsletter...

A monthly electronic publication e-mailed to subscribers and posted on the rec.arts.sf.written Usenet newsgroup and on our Del Rey Books Web site (www.randomhouse.com/delrey/). It features hype-free descriptions of books that are new in the stores, a list of our upcoming books, special promotional programs and offers, announcements and news, a signing/reading/convention-attendance calendar for Del Rey authors and editors, "In Depth" essays in which professionals in the field (authors, artists, cover designers, salespeople, etc.) talk about their jobs in science fiction, a question-and-answer section, and more!

Subscribe to the DRIN: send a blank message to
join-drin-dist@list.randomhouse.com

The Del Rey Books Web Site!

We make a lot of information available on our Web site at
www.randomhouse.com/delrey/

- all back issues and the current issue of the Del Rey Internet Newsletter
- sample chapters of almost every new book
- detailed interactive features for some of our books
- special features on various authors and SF/F worlds
- reader reviews of some upcoming books
- news and announcements
- our Works in Progress report, detailing the doings of our most popular authors
- and more!

If You're Not on the Web...

You can subscribe to the DRIN via e-mail (send a blank message to join-drin-dist@list.randomhouse.com) or read it on the rec.arts.sf.written Usenet newsgroup the first few days of every month. We also have editors and other representatives who participate in America Online and CompuServe SF/F forums and rec.arts.sf.written, making contact and sharing information with SF/F readers.

Questions? E-mail us...

at delrey@randomhouse.com (though it sometimes takes us a little while to answer).